AND GRANT YOU PEACE

A JOE BURGESS MYSTERY

AND GRANT YOU PEACE

KATE FLORA

FIVE STAR

A part of Gale, Cengage Learning

GALE
CENGAGE Learning·

Farmington Hills, Mich • San Francisco • New York • Waterville, Maine
Meriden, Conn • Mason, Ohio • Chicago

GALE
CENGAGE Learning

LIBRARY OF CONGRESS CATALOGING-IN-PUBLICATION DATA

Flora, Kate, 1949–
    And grant you peace : a Joe Burgess mystery / Kate Flora—
First edition.
        pages cm
    ISBN 978-1-4328-2939-1 (hardcover) — ISBN 1-4328-2939-4 (hardcover) — ISBN 978-1-4328-2941-4 (ebook)—ISBN 1-4328-2941-6 (ebook)
    1. Police—Maine—Portland—Fiction. 2. Muslims—Crimes against—Fiction. 3. Threats—Fiction. I. Title. II. Title: Joe Burgess mystery.
PS3556.L5838A53 2014
813'.54—dc23   2014020035

First Edition. First Printing: October 2014
Find us on Facebook– https://www.facebook.com/FiveStarCengage
Visit our website– http://www.gale.cengage.com/fivestar/
Contact Five Star™ Publishing at FiveStar@cengage.com

Printed in the United States of America
1 2 3 4 5 6 7 18 17 16 15 14

To my family

ACKNOWLEDGMENTS

Gratitude, as always, to those who have tried to make my police procedure realistic: Deputy Chief Joseph K. Loughlin and Sergeant Bruce Coffin of the Portland, Maine, police department; Deputy Chief Brian Cummings of the Miramichi, New Brunswick, police department; and Lieutenant Pat Dorian and Roger Guay of the Maine Warden Service. Thanks also to the many Maine librarians who support my writing and answer my questions, including Lisa Joyce and John Clark, and Charlene Clemmons, who is my greatest fan. No writer gets far without the help of librarians. I am grateful to Nancy Ross McJennett for her careful reading, to Gordon Aalborg and Deni Dietz for continuing to believe in the Joe Burgess series, and to Tiffany Schofield and Nivette Jackaway at Five Star, who remind me of what a joy it is to have a responsive publisher. I also owe a deep debt of thanks to the Virginia Center for the Creative Arts for granting me a writing fellowship so I could finish this book. VCCA is a magical place. I have been well-advised. I have also taken liberties with geography and allowed my fictional cops to deviate from Standard Operating Procedure.

CHAPTER ONE

Most people run away from fires; firemen and cops run toward them, especially when someone inside is screaming.

Joe Burgess was sitting in his car, window down to catch the soft spring air, not ready to face the chaos at home, when a kid he knew from the street came running up. He got a gasped "Fire at the mosque and someone's in there," and a frantic gesture toward the battered old commercial building that now served the religious needs of part of Portland's growing Somali community.

The kid's name was Jason, a spindly towhead with a bad haircut and shabby clothes. A few years earlier, he would have been a likely candidate for setting the fire, but a good social worker and a decent foster family were gradually turning him around. Now his eyes were wide with alarm and there was an audible asthmatic wheeze in his chest. "You gotta come right now, Sergeant Burgess," he said, "there's someone in there screaming."

Burgess was out of the truck, flashlight in his pocket and phone to his ear, before the boy had finished saying "screaming," making the calls to get the fire department on the way and for more officers to help manage the scene. It was a dense neighborhood, both in terms of the number of residents and their average IQs. He couldn't count on anyone having reported the fire, and crowd control would be necessary to let the firemen do their jobs. Despite three decades on the job, he'd never understood people's avid desire to gawk at tragedy.

Jason at his heels like a puppy, he sprinted past some shabby older houses and across the ragged, muddy space that passed for lawn. The cheaply built one-story had been thrown up for some small business, long defunct. Set back from the street behind a parking lot and that lawn, it had a double entry door, a couple of picture windows now covered with heavy fabric, and a cement walkway leading to cement steps. To the right of the door, someone had spray-painted "Go Back to Africa" and "Ragheads Suck Pig Dick" across the dirty white siding.

So much for "Give me your tired, your poor, your huddled masses yearning to breathe free."

He paused at the walkway and turned to Jason. He knew the boy would follow him right into the building, and an undersized, undernourished, asthmatic kid as a sidekick going into a smoky building would be a very bad idea. "See if you can flag down some cars, Jase, will you? Maybe get us some more help here?"

Happy to have a task, the boy trotted off.

As he headed up the walkway, Burgess could hear a desperate female voice, pleading for help, and see billowing smoke and flames licking the north end of the building. Behind him, he heard a vehicle screech to the curb, a door opening, and running footsteps. By the time he reached the building, the runner was right beside him.

He had a fleeting impression of youngish, and large, but he didn't turn to look. His focus was on the building.

He tried the knob. Hot. And locked.

"Let's kick it in." The voice had just a faint trace of Ireland.

Together, he and the runner backed off and then attacked the door with their feet, the flimsy lock giving way and the hollow-core doors splintering. They shouldered them open and stepped inside. The wide hallway was dark and smoky.

"Hold on," the runner said. "You got a handkerchief?" He

held out a bottle of water. "You might wanna wet it, hold it over your face."

They soaked their handkerchiefs and headed inside. The building was bigger than it had seemed from outside. A long, dark corridor with many closed doors stretched ahead of them.

"You take the right side, I'll take the left," Burgess said. "If the knob feels too hot, don't open it." He snapped on his flashlight. The other man had a little LED light on his keychain.

Wet handkerchief pressed to his face, Burgess started trying doors, opening and closing one after another, flashing his light around dark, empty rooms. Calling out, "Police. Here to help you. Let us know where you are?" then pausing to close his eyes and listen.

But the screaming woman had fallen silent.

"Hello? Hello? Please. Let us know where you are?" he called. There was only the opening and closing of doors, and the crackle of flames. No smoke detectors or alarms were going off. So far, all he'd found were small offices. Nothing that looked like a sanctuary, or whatever the Muslims called their actual place of worship. The runner had disappeared, so maybe it was on that side and he was searching some large room.

The deeper he went into the building, the denser the smoke got. He was having trouble breathing. From outside, he could hear the deep roar of distant fire trucks, their sirens echoing through the streets, and he thought about the times over the years when cops and firemen had clashed at scenes like this. Could already hear the ration of shit he was going to get when they arrived, about going into a burning building without proper equipment. Not his job. Overstepping.

"Hello?" he called. "Hello? Please, if you can hear me, let me know where you are? Hello?" His lungs hurt. He was having trouble getting enough air to yell.

He thought he heard a muffled response. Closing his eyes, he listened hard, trying to shut out all other sounds. He heard it again and hurried toward the door it seemed to be coming from. He grabbed the knob and turned. After so many unlocked doors, this one was locked.

"We're right here," he called, "we're going to get you out."

He slammed his shoulder into the door. Unlike the others, this door was solid, the lock strong. He called to the stranger working the other side of the hall. "This door's locked. Help me."

"I got it." The man's work-booted foot slammed into the door just below the lock. The door splintered, but didn't give.

There was a whoosh as flames shot down from the ceiling above them.

The man backed off and hit it again, then Burgess put his shoulder to the door. It gave, finally, and he catapulted into a small, dark space that felt like he was flying into an oven. He'd expected a room, maybe even one with something of value in it because of the lock, but he was standing in a closet.

He flashed his light around shelves crowded with boxes. There was so much smoke his light barely picked out a figure in a long skirt and headscarf curled on the floor in the corner. As he shoved his arms under her to lift her up, the wall behind her burst into flame, setting her clothes on fire. He grabbed her, turned, and ran, holding her with one arm while he beat at the flames with the other.

Behind him, he heard the other man. "Oh my God. There's another. It's a . . . there's a baby here."

Then they were pounding down the hallway toward the door, flames leaping toward a fresh oxygen supply and chasing them like something from a horror movie.

Outside, they handed the limp woman and her bundled child over to the waiting firemen. Then, as though they'd been doing this together all their lives, Burgess and the man he didn't know dropped to their knees together on the muddy grass, trying to cough up the smoke from their lungs. Some senior firefighter, his voice only a harsh drone behind their racking coughs, stood over them like Sister Mary Peter and castigated them for taking foolish chances.

When he could breathe again, Burgess got up, wiped his muddy hands on his muddy pants, and then thrust one toward his fellow rescuer. "Joe Burgess," he said.

"Connor O'Day." O'Day was a big man with unruly reddish hair and surprisingly blue eyes. "Do you think they're going to make it? That baby wasn't breathing. And who the fuck locks a woman and a baby in a closet? What do you suppose that's about?"

Burgess wondered about that, too, but cops didn't share their wondering with the public. He was already making lists and taking notes. Trying to file away what he'd seen.

He looked toward the curb, where O'Day's truck sat, the driver's door still open. It was a surprisingly quick and heroic response, one not too many people would have had. Parked, maybe, and thought about helping, but most men would have waited for the firemen or instructions Burgess had not had time to give.

It was a well-worn truck, one of thousands of silver trucks in a state where trucks probably outnumbered cars. A medium-sized Ford with some dings. A silver toolbox mounted in the rear. A rack for carrying equipment or supplies, loaded with cardboard boxes and lengths of white PVC pipe. A plumber, maybe.

"Let's go and see how they're doing."

On his way over to where EMTs were working on the victims, he spotted Jason, hanging at the edge of the crowd, bouncing in his agitated way. Burgess went to him and put a hand on his shoulder. "You did good today, Jase. Probably saved a couple of lives." The boy's pinched face lit up. "You'll get a letter from the chief for this. Maybe get your picture in the paper."

Jason shook his head vigorously. "Don't do that, Sergeant Burgess, please. I don't want my picture in the paper."

The boy's reaction surprised him. But then he thought about it. Something else for his follow-up list. Maybe Jason had seen something and didn't want anyone to know he had. A kid like that, always around the neighborhood, became invisible. Maybe it was better to keep it that way.

"Just so you know that we're grateful," Burgess said. "You're a hero today." He tousled the spiky blond hair. "At least let me take you out to breakfast sometime?"

"Pancakes?" Jason said. "Blueberry pancakes and lots of bacon?"

"You bet. Whatever you want."

The boy was wheezing badly. "You have an inhaler?" A faint nod, like the boy really didn't like to have to admit that. "Well, use it, okay? All that smoke is bad for your lungs."

"Yes, sir." The boy ducked his head, pulled his inhaler from his pocket, and melted away into the crowd.

Burgess and O'Day continued toward the EMTs. One of them looked up and recognized him. Her face was tense, her steady hands continuing to work on the infant. "Hey, Joe," she said. "Not looking good for this baby."

Beside him, he heard a groan from O'Day. He shot a glance at the man, saw big fists curled at the ends of weight-lifter's arms.

He nodded. "I'm going to keep hoping for good news."

"Me, too," she said, shaking her head. She rose, already moving toward the ambo, the tiny body on the gurney looking like a lifeless doll. A dark, alien doll, given the mask and the tubing. "We'll see you over there?"

He nodded, watching the tiny body disappearing into the

brightly lit vehicle. They all wanted good news. He wasn't an optimist, though. Burgess had lived in the sewer of other people's lives for too long.

He hadn't caught his breath yet and he smelled like a fireplace. Now the weight of this was settling on him like a heavy black cape. He wanted to go home, sit down with his new, crazy family, and hold them all, reassuring himself that everyone was okay. Instead, he would be making a series of phone calls back to the higher-ups at 109. Then he'd be heading over to the hospital to learn the condition—and identity—of the two victims.

A young woman and a baby locked in a closet at an empty mosque? A fire that instinct already told him was not accidental? Serious personal injury and possibly a death? The violent crimes detectives were going to be involved. The arson unit would be involved. The fire department's investigators would be involved. Most likely the state fire marshal's office, too. A bureaucratic cluster fuck where everyone would be arguing about who owned what, too many people would be holding too many cards close to their chests, and getting answers and justice would be as easy as swimming in a tar pit.

He sighed and turned to O'Day. "Thanks," he said.

His fellow rescuer sketched a salute, turned, and headed back to his truck. In a moment, he was gone. As he hurried toward the ambo, Burgess realized he'd just let a prime witness walk away, and he'd never gotten anything more than the man's name.

CHAPTER TWO

It looked like they were being pretty successful at knocking the fire down, but Burgess knew fires were deceptive. They liked to hide and lurk, waiting for someone's inattention, then springing out to finish devouring their prey. So just in case the PFD didn't win this one, he took out his phone and snapped some pictures of the writing on the wall. Adding the possibility that this was a hate crime would bring even more people into the mix. By morning, the reflexive bleeding hearts who hated anything that felt like an unfriendly gesture toward their new African citizens—never mind what the facts were—would be out with posters and flags, interfering with fire investigation and getting them all kinds of press attention they didn't need. No one ever believed that when the cops came into these things, their bias was against bad guys and bad acts, not people's racial or ethnic makeup.

He hated fire scenes. All the cops did. In addition to the necessary disruption and destruction that came with firefighting, too often the fire department's own looky-loos had to stomp through the scene after the fact, staring at things and further destroying their ability to collect evidence or get a sense of what might have taken place. At least there were no bodies at this scene. Get a body so crisp it didn't take an ME to declare death, and someone was still likely to tromp right up to it, just to get a closer look.

Okay. His prejudices were showing. He was just as territorial as anyone else. At least he tried not to make other people's jobs harder. He wished people would do the same for him.

His call back to 109 had brought Stan Perry and Terry Kyle, the two detectives he thought of as his team, out to the fire scene. They'd brought Rudy Carr along, with his video camera, to take pictures of the crowd. With fire-setters, more than any other type of criminal, there was a significant likelihood that the bad guy would show up at the scene. Sometimes they performed heroics, getting into it to rescue victims. Other times, they'd just stand in the crowd and watch. This was a big crowd, plenty of gawkers to record. And Rudy was a master at getting the pictures without people being aware of what he was doing.

Burgess's plan was to hand the scene off to Kyle and Perry, and get over to the hospital to check on his victims. Hoping he might even have a chance to interview the woman who'd been locked in the closet, if she was well enough to talk and the dragons over at Maine Med didn't lock him out to "protect" their patient. As always, with a major crime, the first hours and days were critical, before memories failed or witnesses were influenced by their friends or what they read in the paper.

But getting away wasn't so easy. First, as a matter of interdepartmental courtesy, he had to let the fire guy finish his lecture on Burgess's careless and irresponsible behavior. Then he had to bring Kyle and Perry up to speed. He let the droning finally come to a stop, then pointed toward the building. "Thing flared up right after we brought that woman and her baby out, didn't it?"

Fire guy nodded.

"So would your guys still have gone in after them?"

"Once they got their gear on."

"How long you figure that would have taken?" He didn't wait for an answer. Yes, safety mattered, but so did human life. It might have already been too late for the baby. Another few minutes and it would have been too late for the mom. Instead, he changed the subject. "You think someone set this fire?"

Fire guy gave him a look. "Too soon to tell," he said. "We'll have our people on it once we get this knocked down."

"Yeah. We'll have our guys on it, too. Probably the fire marshal's office, too. Keep us up on what you learn, okay?"

The guy nodded, but Burgess knew the only way they'd get decent information any time before the snow fell again was because the department had its own arson investigators. Territorialism was rampant among safety organizations. And too often stupid. But culture was culture, and he wasn't changing any of that. He'd put Lieutenant Melia in the loop, get brass talking to brass, and they'd get what they could.

He pulled Kyle and Perry aside. "We'll do a canvass once things calm down, but for now, work the crowd, find out what people know about this place. Who runs it. What population it serves, whether anyone saw anything before the fire broke out. The usual stuff."

"You think it was set, Joe?" Perry asked.

He nodded.

"This place is a mosque," Kyle said. "We know if it's Somali or Sudanese? Shiite or Sunni? How long it's been here?"

"Community relations will know," he said. "I'm surprised there isn't someone here, saying he's in charge, asking us about the situation."

"Community relations. FBI, DEA, Homeland Security, the gang squad," Perry said. "Lotta people around with an interest in our new refugees. You gotta wonder, did the resettlement agency have any clue what they were doing when they started inviting them here?"

It sounded uncharitable, Burgess knew, but the truth was it was an ongoing challenge for a small, financially strapped, mainly white city to integrate and understand such culturally different populations as the flood of refugees from Somalia and the Sudan who had come on the heels of Cambodian refugees. They'd taken a bunch of workshops on the subject—subjects—and the cops were trying hard, but the cultural gap was wide. Many of the refugees came with a deep fear or hatred of the police, and it made investigations a thousand times harder when one of the first things their new neighbors learned was to play the racism card early and often.

He hadn't had much more than a glimpse of her before he'd handed the mom over to the EMTs, but she hadn't looked Somali or Sudanese. The baby had been darker. Another thing that made him wonder what she'd been doing in that closet.

He looked around at the crowd, figures as merry as though they were at a block party, everyone out on this mild spring night to be entertained by destruction and tragedy. He gestured toward a small knot of people standing apart, arguing among themselves, the only watchers who didn't seem to be having a good time. Women in headscarves and long skirts, the men dark and glowering. "You might start with them. See if you can find out who's in charge of this place, and how to get in touch to set up an interview with him."

He wasn't being sexist when he used the word "him." Like the Catholic Church, the Muslim religions had no place for women leaders. "I'm heading over to the hospital. See how our victims are doing."

"Sheesh, Joe," Perry said. "You really found 'em locked in a closet in there? They didn't just lock themselves in, then panicked and couldn't find their way out?"

"Door only locked from the outside," he said. "It was a closet, Stan."

In the moment, in the dark, the heat, the smoke, he could only focus on saving lives. Little time to observe the situation, take his usual mental notes. Now the scene was probably destroyed. Certainly contaminated. He needed to be alone for a while, consolidate what he had seen, and preserve it for the record. Something he could do on the drive to Maine Med.

Perry shook his head. "Gonna take a detective to figure that one out."

Kyle patted him on the shoulder. "Well, son. That would be you."

Perry shook him off. "Wish you two old farts would stop treating me like a kid. It's not like you're so old, Terry. You just act old and think old, 'cuz you've spent so much time around Joe."

"Methuselah," Burgess agreed. "Back when I was helping Noah build the ark—" He broke off, feeling the weight of time, and all the unknowns. "Go work the crowd, my children. And bring me something."

"Yes, Dad," Perry said.

His standard joke. Until recently, the closest Burgess had come to having kids was the detectives he trained.

"You'll call me about the baby, Joe?" Terry Kyle, a father himself, always worried about the kids in their cases. Hoped for the best and feared the worst. Burgess took it one step further. He hated cases involving children. Even when you solved them, got justice or what passed for justice, they stayed with you. And babies were the worst. He desperately wanted this baby and this mom to be okay.

Stan Perry was still young, impulsive, unattached. Still into the adrenaline of the chase. Burgess was losing that. These days, the hard cases felt more like ten cords of firewood to be shifted than like facts to be chased down and bad guys to be nabbed. It made him appreciate Stan's youthful energy and ponder retirement. But this was all he knew how to do.

He left his guys to work the scene, hefted himself back into the Explorer, and headed across town. It had gotten colder, but he left the windows down. They'd had another endless Maine winter, snow piled up until there was no place left to put it. The city had had to truck it away, creating dirty gray mountains in empty parking lots. There were still stubborn snow piles in shady corners and deep drifts of the sand they'd used on slippery roads banked along the roadsides. This suddenly mild April weather felt like a gift. A gift they'd earned through suffering.

He dictated a memo of everything he'd observed, getting the detail into his phone before it was crowded out of his mind by later observations, then called Chris to say he wouldn't be home any time soon. Another night when she'd shoulder the tasks of homework police and referee alone. She said she didn't mind, and the fact that she smiled more often, and sang while she bustled around the house, were probably clues that she was telling the truth. But Burgess minded for her.

In his fifties, and after years of letting his fear that he'd inherited his father's violent nature force him into a monkish existence, Burgess had become a family man. In a matter of months, he and his live-in girlfriend, Chris, had acquired three children, two of them teenagers. The learning curve was steep and his long-held belief that he'd be bad at it was often confirmed. His once spare and quiet home now resembled a lunatic asylum. Toys, clothes, books, electronics, and people and noise everywhere.

Sometimes, before going home, he found himself driving around the neighborhood after an especially bad case while he took the visuals and the emotions of what he'd dealt with and stuffed them in the lockbox cops carried in their heads. Tonight, he'd have plenty of mental housekeeping to do.

"Hey," she said, "Neddy got one hundred on his spelling test. Nina thinks she's too fat and needs to go on a diet. And Dylan has locked himself in his room and is playing his guitar so loud

21

I'm expecting the neighbors will be calling the police soon. How's everything with you?"

"Just dragged a woman and a baby out of a locked closet in a burning building," he said. "Heading over to Maine Med to see how they're doing."

"Damn," she said. "You don't need that." A pause, then, "I was hoping you were coming home."

"So was I."

There was a crash behind her. "Oops," she said. "Got a little bit of warfare going on here." Her voice dropped into a lower register. The voice that always made his pulse quicken. That had brought them together and kept them together. Her "meet me in the bed" voice. "Catch you later."

"Count on it." What he said. And wanted. They both knew a case could sweep him up and keep him away for as long as it took.

He drove through his darkened city, the warm red of brick buildings in the West End still glowing faintly in the fading light. Elegant homes now cut up into condos and doctors' offices. He pulled into the emergency room lot and got out. Stiff and sore from a little door kicking and rescue op. Getting too old for what the job sometimes called for.

Chris said he had a bad attitude. So did his boss's boss, Captain Cote. He thought there wasn't much to be upbeat about, doing what he did. Chris had taken to calling him "Mudgy," short for curmudgeon. Like that was supposed to lighten him up.

He shoved through the doors and up to the information desk, two officers in tow that patrol had sent over. He'd station one of them in each room to note what happened, collect clothes and anything else that might be evidence. They got directed to a curtained cubicle where a team was bent over the baby, desperately trying to revive it. It was a very small infant, not

more than a month old, with fine dark hair. He could tell from
their faces that they were losing a battle they didn't want to
lose. Heard the doctor whisper, "Come on, little guy. Stay with
us."

So his baby was a boy. He left an officer named Rob Staines
in the room, Staines looking like he'd rather be any place else
on earth. Staines, he recalled, had a newborn at home.

He and Remy Aucoin moved along to another cubicle,
another set of curtains, where the faces told him they were having better luck with the baby's mother.

"Sergeant Burgess, Portland police," he said. "How's she doing?"

Without looking up, the dark-haired young woman in the
long white coat, who seemed to be at the center of the operation, said, "She'll be okay."

Peremptory. Dismissive. Words he read as "stand back and let
us do our jobs."

Remy, who'd done this before, stepped into the corner, making himself as invisible as possible, and started taking notes.

The head nurse caught his eye and stepped outside the
curtain with him. Good relations being the one plus of a job
that sent them way too often to the hospital with victims. Maryann O'Malley. A friend of Chris's. "She's just a baby herself,
Joe. And scared stiff. Hasn't said a word to us. I think she's
processing, she just won't speak."

"She have any ID? We got any idea who she is?"

"No. No tats, no scars, no piercings. No rings. No jewelry.
Nothing in her pockets. Someone should be with her, but she
won't tell us who to call." She hesitated. "You really find her
locked in a closet?"

The nurse shouldn't have even known that detail, but of
course she did. Protocol was not to answer, but it would be all
over soon enough. "Yeah."

He'd have to wait. Move on to the other questions, like "when can we talk to her?" when they had her more stable. Both sides were used to this—the cops anxious to get their information before someone died or lapsed into unconsciousness. The doctors protective of their patients and wanting to be left alone to work. A collision of objectives where everyone wanted to win. Nurses were frequently the go-betweens, trying to balance everyone's needs.

"You'll call me when she's ready to talk?"

"If she's ready to talk. She's terrified of something, Joe, and it isn't us."

"Thanks, Maryann." Someone had locked the girl in that closet. Someone who very much wanted her under control. Until he knew who, and why, he needed to keep her safe. He crossed to Remy. "Stay with her," he said, "wherever they take her."

Aucoin nodded.

He went back to where they were working on the baby, meaning only to watch and merge his hopes with theirs, as though collective will could make a difference. He came through the curtain just as everyone stepped back, heads bowed and shoulders slumped, Staines looking as drawn as the rest of them.

A tired-looking man in blue scrubs glanced up at the big clock on the wall and said, "Time of death: six twenty-three p.m."

CHAPTER THREE

His phone rang, and he stepped back into the waiting room to take the call. Stan Perry's voice, a burst of aggravation and profanity before he got to the point. "Took us all this freakin' time to get them to cough up the name of their Imam," he said. "Like it was some kind of secret. Anyway, Terry and I have got an address, thought we'd head over there and ask some questions. Terry thought you might want to be in on it."

"Terry's right." He checked his watch, an unnecessary gesture. It had only been about three minutes since the baby had been declared dead. He had told his boss, Lieutenant Melia, "No more dead kids." And this was worse. It was a baby. But he couldn't lay it at Melia's door. This one had come straight to him.

"Listen Joe, Terry's got a source here in the neighborhood he wants to track down. Says can you and I do the Imam so he can follow up with that?"

"Sure," he said.

"How are things over there?"

"The baby died," he said. "Give me the address." Stan read it off and he wrote it down.

It would be one of those long nights of driving back and forth across the city. No way around it. After he and Perry went to see the Imam and Kyle spoke with his source, they'd circle up back at 109 and share what they'd learned. By then, maybe the mom would be stable enough so he could talk to her. At least he wouldn't have to be the one to tell her that her baby had died. A scrap of silver lining in this big dark cloud.

He'd left word at the hospital that he'd need a call when the mom could be interviewed. Sometimes they called, sometimes they didn't. He'd drop back later, see how things were going. He'd had little chance to form an impression of her when he'd carried her, other than small as a child herself, and light. Too small and too young to have a child of her own. Seeing her on the gurney, surrounded by medical personnel, he'd learned little more. She was pale skinned, not simply from shock and trauma, and had long dark hair.

As he drove, he called dispatch, gave the address of the building that had burned, and asked if they could get him the name and address of the owner. He called Melia, to let him know about the baby, asked if Melia could have the department's fire investigator liaise with the fire department and the state fire marshal's office, so they could stay in the loop about the cause of the fire.

Stan Perry would have done a records check on the man they were going to meet and called for an interpreter to meet them there, just in case there were language issues. Sometimes they dealt with people who didn't speak English, sometimes with those who were just more comfortable in their own language— and, sometimes, with those who hid behind language barriers as a way of controlling the conversation. Offering an interpreter was part of their efforts to improve their relationship with the Somalis, something the department was trying to do.

Burgess understood that the refugees had come from a place where the police were feared, and he worked hard to change that image. He just sometimes wished they'd try and understand where he was coming from, too. But there he was, doing that generic "put people in a box" thing again. One-on-one, he had often been very successful in crossing barriers and establishing trust.

Burgess didn't know much about the Muslim religion. Probably, depending on what they learned tonight, he'd have to get himself some kind of a tutorial. He also knew that he came into this situation with assumptions based on experience that he'd have to guard against if he wanted to keep an open mind about what he was learning. It had not been—it still was not—easy for Portlanders to integrate this raft of foreigners into their city. The cultural differences were great.

Taxpaying Mainers, by and large, had a deep dislike for people who lived off public resources, as many of the refugees did. It wasn't just refugees; they had the same prejudices against welfare mothers, people on disability who weren't disabled, and people on unemployment who wouldn't look for work. When you work hard for meager pay, you want everyone else to do their share.

They hadn't called ahead. They wanted a purely spontaneous interview. They wanted the opportunity to observe the leader of this spiritual community as they questioned him about what they had found in his mosque.

He parked behind Perry's car and slid into Perry's front seat. "Our translator on the way?"

"Says he is. Oh lookie . . ." They both watched a gray van creep around the corner and slowly nudge its way into the curb.

"Sure doesn't look like he wants to be here, does he?" Burgess said, as the van's driver sorted through some papers on the passenger seat, adjusted his glasses, adjusted them again, and only then climbed slowly out of the vehicle.

They went to meet him. "Hussain Osman," the man said, extending his hand. He was small and neat, and in his white shirt and wire-rimmed glasses looked an engineering student.

Burgess and Perry introduced themselves. "We're going to

see a man named Muhamud Ibrahim," Burgess said. "We need to ask him some questions about his mosque."

Osman looked troubled. "Questioning an Imam? That's not a proper thing to do, Detectives."

"There was a fire at the mosque," Burgess said. "We need basics for our investigation. Whether they own or rent. Have there been threats or trouble with the neighbors. Things like that. To know how that fire might have started. It's perfectly proper." He wasn't mentioning the girl in the closet until they'd gotten the conversation well under way.

Osman nodded, looked toward the house, and waited. Burgess led their little party to the door.

The young man who opened it looked pretty Americanized, if a rapper t-shirt and baggy jeans showing a wide swath of cartoon boxers meant anything. He had a rounded, baby-faced look and round, innocent eyes. He stood blocking the doorway, and, innocent face or not, he looked as sullen as the teenagers Burgess had at home. Some things, it seemed, were universal.

"Detective Sergeant Joe Burgess, Portland police, here to see Muhamud Ibrahim." He flashed his badge. He did not add "may we come in." It was too easy for people to say no.

When the boy's face didn't change and he didn't move, Burgess added, "It's urgent police business. About the fire?"

"What fire?" The question seemed genuine.

"At the mosque."

Even in societies vastly different from America's, common facial expressions like happiness, fear, surprise, and shock are the same. What he was seeing was surprise and shock, followed by a nervous shifting of the eyes. He didn't know if the boy knew about the people who'd been locked in the closet, but something about a fire at the mosque alarmed him.

"May we come in?" Burgess asked now, moving forward quickly so the boy automatically stepped back, allowing him to

edge into the room. Perry piled in behind him, while the translator held back. There was a pile of shoes beside the door. "Would
you like us to remove our shoes?"

The boy nodded.

"Can you please tell the Imam that we're here and that we
need to speak with him." Command and control. Don't give
people time to think or resist. He'd been in thousands of places
over the years where he was unwelcome. He looked at the room.
It seemed like any other house he might go into in this neighborhood. Furniture a little tired, and all arranged to view the TV.
In this case, an impressively large, expensive TV. Usually, he saw
TVs like that in drug dealers' houses. Nothing much in the way
of furniture or décor, but always outsized TVs. Maybe it was
just to get the full benefit of Al Jazeera in English.

He reined in his thoughts. Detective's rule #1: Don't let
your assumptions get ahead of the facts. So far, he had no facts.
He looked at the boy, then at the translator. "Can you ask him
if he speaks English?"

"Of course I speak English."

"Then you can tell us your name."

"Ali Ibrahim." The boy divulged it like a miser giving up
gold, then said, "I will go now and tell him you are here." He all
but stomped out of the room.

"Do you know the Imam?" Burgess asked the translator.

Osman shook his head. "I am not in this part of the city."

"So he is not a well-known community leader?"

A shrug. "He is a leader in his community."

Another cultural thing. They were incredibly class-oriented,
clan-oriented, and sons inherited their status from their fathers.
Sometimes, immigrants who had had no status at home claimed
to be elders who spoke for the community here. When they
were done with the Imam, he would ask Osman to explain
further.

A door at the far side of the room opened, and a very old man shuffled in, followed by two men who might have been around Burgess's age, and three younger ones. The boy was not with them. The old man took a seat while the others remained standing.

"Detective Sergeant Burgess, Portland police," Burgess said. "Are you Muhamud Ibrahim?"

The translator translated, and the old man nodded. "And these other gentlemen. Their names? Their addresses?"

In a reluctant mumble, they gave up their information, and Perry wrote it down. All except one were Ibrahims. All gave their addresses as the Imam's house, though the place was too small to have housed them all, especially if they had families. Perhaps city records would help locate other addresses.

"Are you the Imam of the mosque on Ashton Street?" Another nod. "There is some writing on the walls of the building. Some hateful writing. Has it been there long?"

The old man spoke, and Osman translated. "It was not there yesterday. It was there this morning."

"Do you have any idea who might have done it?"

A shrug. A flurry of words among the men and with the translator. "Many people do not like us. They resent the fact that we want to live here. They do not understand our religion or our culture. They see much about terrorists on the television, and they think that anyone who is a Muslim is a terrorist."

"Have you received any specific threats? Do you know of anyone who might want to harm your mosque?"

This time, the men conferred among themselves before answering. Finally, one of the middle-aged men said, "There are so many. There are the Sudanese young men, who quarrel with our young men. They have moved away from their elders' civilizing influences. They do not care what they do or who they harm. They think that being gangsters makes them more American."

"Do you know of specific people? Do you have any names?"

The man shrugged. He knew but he wasn't saying. Burgess heard Perry's pen stop. Nothing more to note about this. The officer who worked with gangs might have some information about Sudanese and Somali gang issues.

"Is there anyone we might talk to who could give us names?"

Another conference. Another set of shrugs. Burgess couldn't understand their words but he was good at reading faces. He saw conflict, dislike, power plays, and the decision to lie. Their final answer was they were sorry, but they didn't know who that might be. Not a problem. There were other ways to get at information among the young people. Youth workers. Teachers. Some of the more progressive parents. Sometimes even from the young men themselves. Even, though more rarely, from the young women. At least there were other avenues to follow.

But the writing on the wall didn't seem like something a Muslim would write, unless it was someone trying to deflect suspicion from himself or to confuse a simple act of arson. It wouldn't be the first time a suspicious fire was traced back to the owner of the building. Or an aggrieved tenant.

Somewhere in the house, he heard soft women's voices, and a baby crying.

"Is there anyone else who might have written on your walls?"

There was a flurry of conversation. This was such a slow process, the translator trying to get them focused on a response, then testing the response for accuracy before he conveyed their words back to the police. Finally, Osman said, hesitantly, "Motorcycle gangs. We sometimes have trouble with them. They like to harass our women and scare our children. We have complained about it many times."

"Anyone in particular? Anyone you can identify or describe?"

They conferred, and then one of the men answered. "We don't know his name. He is a very big man with a . . ." His hands made gestures indicating a ponytail.

"Old man or young man?" Burgess asked.

"My age, perhaps," the man said, which Burgess took to mean around fifty.

"Can you tell me anything else about him? Or about his motorcycle? Did he have anything distinctive about his clothing?"

Leather jacket. Bandana. Ponytail. Something embroidered on the jacket, they couldn't say what. They might do better if he could show them pictures. The motorcycle was big, black, noisy, and had a lot of chrome. No one had recorded a license plate. In short, a generic picture of any of dozens of Portland's finest motorcycle outlaws. Maybe the department's records of their complaints would be illuminating. He wasn't optimistic.

"Okay," he said, as Perry's pen scratched behind him. "Maybe Sudanese. Maybe members of a motorcycle gang. Is there anyone else? Anyone in the neighborhood?"

"Some people in the neighborhood are kind to us. Others would like us gone. They stand and stare when we are going to our prayers and say bad things. They call us bloodsuckers and welfare cheats. They call me 'Osama.' But I know of no one in particular."

Burgess realized that everyone in the room was standing except the Imam. Cops weren't the only ones who understood the use of power and position in an interview.

One more question before he moved on to the fire. "What about members of your own community? Someone angry or disaffected? A rival mosque?"

Forgetting that he was not supposed to understand English, the old man spoke without waiting for the translator. "Always you do this," he said. "Someone attacks us and you make it that we have attacked ourselves. Why would we?"

He sat up straighter and said, almost shouting, "You shoot our young men and claim they drew their guns first. It is always what *we* did. Never what you did." He repeated his earlier question, "Why would we do this to ourselves?"

A good question. Burgess had a few answers. For sympathy. For public relations. For funds to enhance their building. Perhaps a power play in a dispute with the landlord? And often, a power play in a dispute with the city. They held many cards. The race card. Religion card. Immigrant card. For that matter, the young man he assumed the Imam was referring to had had a gun and drawn it in a confrontation with an officer. It wouldn't help this conversation to bring that up, nor to mention the rash of armed robberies of convenience stores and other small businesses.

He wondered if the Irish would have fared better when they came to America if they'd been able to knock back those old Yankees with claims of prejudice. If "you owe us because our potato crops got the blight and we had to emigrate or starve" would have brought food and shelter? Everyone in this country except Native Americans had been a refugee or an immigrant at one time. It probably meant he was a bitter old cynic, but he thought that there were more stubborn lumps in the melting pot these days. Guys he knew who worked at the federal level were even more cynical than he.

He moved on. "This building that you use for your mosque . . . are you the only ones who use it? There are many rooms in that building. Are there other groups who also have offices there or do business there?"

This time, the discussion went on for quite a while. Then the translator said, "We have offices that do community outreach and help us to administer some of our programs to serve our people, but it is only for our members. For our work."

"Do you own the building?" It should have been a straight-forward question, but that also brought a flurry of discussion.

At last the Iman said, "No."

"Do you rent?"

He got what felt like a rather reluctant, "Yes."

"And who do you rent the building from?"

"I will have to check my records." Which also seemed odd. Presumably they paid rent to someone.

"You have records of rental payments, and to whom they are made?"

Another nod.

"And you keep those records here? Not at the mosque?"

The Imam nodded, then looked like he wished he hadn't.

"Can you check those records and get back to me tonight?" Burgess offered the Imam his card, which one of the other men collected.

This time, the Imam didn't answer at all.

Perry was taking notes, but Burgess had his own notebook out, too. Now he pretended to consult it. "You know that there was a fire at the mosque earlier tonight."

"We have heard about it."

But you didn't rush over there? What did that mean about the girl in the closet? About what they knew? Was there nothing in that building they wanted to save? In those brief moments in the closet, searching with his flashlight, he'd seen that the shelves were stacked with boxes, and that the boxes were labeled as computer equipment. A lot of computer equipment. New computer equipment.

"All of you heard about the fire?" he asked. They nodded. "But none of you went over there to see what was happening? To assess the damage? To try and save your property?"

He shifted his eyes from face to face, seeking an answer from each one of them. Each man, in turn, said he had not been there.

"Do you have insurance on the building?"

The Imam inclined his head in an affirmative. About this he did not have to check his records.

The boy who had answered the door had crept into the room, hovering quietly by the door, listening. The others didn't seem aware he was there.

Burgess watched their faces closely as he asked his next question. "We found two people inside the building. A young woman and a small baby. They were locked in a closet and could not escape."

He saw visible shock on the boy's face before he slipped out of the room again. The others stirred in agitation, their voices a low murmur that began before the translator had delivered his words.

"They both suffered from severe smoke inhalation. The girl was burned." He watched their faces. Knew Perry was doing the same. "She may live. The baby, a little boy, has died."

One younger man who had stood slightly aloof, taller than the others and with a distinctive scar on his forehead, jerked suddenly, then got himself back under control, and Burgess found himself thinking about collecting DNA and questions of paternity.

"Do any of you know who this girl might have been or what she was doing there?"

The heads shook, almost as one.

"Before I go, could one of you sketch the building for me, and label the rooms and how they are used?"

Another period of shifting and murmuring. Then one of the older men, Omar Ibrahim, said, "I will do it, but it will take some time. Perhaps you could have someone pick it up tomorrow?"

"I'll have someone pick it up later tonight. Time is important. Someone has died. How long do you need?"

It should have taken a few minutes for someone familiar with the place, but they were acting like he was asking them to write their last wills and testaments. He had things to do and places to go. Finally, he interrupted, "I'll be back for it in two hours. I will find you here?"

The man nodded.

"May I have a phone number where I can contact you?"

The man gave the same number the Imam had given. Burgess expected they all had cell phones. These days, everyone had cell phones. But no one was offering those numbers.

He thanked them all for their time, gave the usual speech about getting in touch if they remembered anything else, and passed out his cards. He expected they'd find their way to a trashcan before he was back in his car.

CHAPTER FOUR

Their translator seemed in a hurry to be gone, but Burgess detained him at the curb. "How many of them do you think speak English?"

He shrugged. "I expect they all have some English. They're just more comfortable in their own language. Especially when dealing with the police."

"Can you give us any insight about their standing in the community?" When Osman didn't respond, he added, "This isn't the only mosque in Portland. Is this a prominent one? Is Muhamud Ibrahim known as a community leader?"

As part of remaking themselves in their new country, many older Somali men claimed to be tribal elders who spoke for the community. Sometimes it was true. Just as often not. Something that had been difficult for the police, and city leaders—Portland's own elders—to get a handle on. He needed to know as much as he could about this mosque, its structure, its leaders, the population it served, to effectively handle this case, and he already knew, from the way this interview had gone, that getting information would be a challenge.

A slideshow of emotions passed over the translator's face as he weighed his response. He didn't want to venture an opinion. He didn't want to betray his own prejudices. He wanted to continue to work with the police department. Finally he said, "It is a smaller group. A less well-funded one, I understand. There are rumors that—"

But he didn't want to share those rumors. Instead, he said, "You know about hawala?"

"A little bit."

Hawala was the nonbank system many Muslims used to send money back home. Mostly to their families. Sometimes, as the powers that be—FBI and Homeland Security—were discovering, to fund terrorists. As one cynical FBI type had said in a recent meeting, "They come here, they take our money, ship it overseas, and it funds the weapons and explosives they use to kill our boys in other parts of the world. Then, when we start poking around and asking questions, they wave the race card and all the public officials scurry behind their desks and tell us to stop."

It was one truth. But there were many. One of which was that these people genuinely were refugees who had come to this country to make a new life, often after horrific experiences at home. Many of them, especially the women, were enjoying the freedoms life in Maine offered. And the fact was that to be a survivor in a chaotic, often violent culture, you had to be enterprising and look out for yourself and your family. Maybe assimilation was always a slow process. And dealing with human complexity was always a challenge, whoever your witnesses, suspects, and even victims, were.

He was formulating his next question when Perry said, "Joe, there's a—"

"I know," Burgess said quickly.

Perry nodded, shifted his eyes back to Osman. "You don't like 'em much, those people in there, do you, Osman."

The translator was a small, neat man, Stan Perry a big, scary one with a shaved head that gave him a thuggish look. The man squirmed uncomfortably. "I am only a translator. It is not my place to have opinions about these things."

"Right," Perry said. "Just like us. We're only the cops. It's not our place to have opinions. Never mind that a poor helpless baby died tonight because someone locked him and his mother in a closet and left them there to try and claw their way out before the smoke and fire got 'em. That's not something you need to be worried about, is it?"

Sometimes Burgess missed the days when Perry had had longish, curly hair, and a disarmingly boyish look. It had been useful in getting some people to talk, especially women and kids. This fierce, tough look had its uses, too.

The translator shuffled his feet and glanced toward the house. "Maybe we could talk about this another time. Another place?"

So he, also, knew the boy was listening. "We could," Burgess said. "When and where would be good for you?"

Osman named a coffee shop in South Portland. "You know the place?"

"We can find it. When?"

"Tomorrow morning, perhaps eleven?"

They made the date, then drove away. All the time they'd been talking, they were being watched from behind the curtains, and by the boy crouching in the shrubbery at the edge of the lot, not as quietly as he probably imagined. He'd wanted the boy to listen, and Perry had almost blown it. He couldn't fault Perry for being observant, though.

The boy's reaction inside, and his lurking to eavesdrop, confirmed Burgess's instinct that he should find the boy away from this house and try to have a conversation. The boy clearly knew something about the situation, and Burgess never knew who might be willing to talk. Maybe he'd find the boy at the high school. He looked to be the right age.

His phone rang. Kyle, checking in. "I'm done here. Are we still meeting at 109, 'cuz if we are, I've got to give Michelle a heads-up that I won't be home."

Michelle, Kyle's live-in girlfriend, would be at home with his two girls. Kyle tried hard not to leave Michelle with too much of the childcare for kids that weren't her own, but the detective's schedule was an uncertain one. Michelle wanted marriage, and a baby of her own. Kyle loved her like crazy, but after escaping the marriage from hell, he was gun-shy.

"You learn anything?"

"Not much. But I've opened the door. You know how it is, dealing with a source, especially when you haven't got leverage. It's like dating. You gotta give 'em reasons to like you before they'll let you get to first base."

Burgess read frustration with a game-playing resource. Kyle wasn't usually crude.

"You eat?" he asked.

"Sat with the kids while they ate. I don't remember eating anything myself."

"Well, I'm starving. Chris says I missed a great dinner tonight. Woman loves to stick that needle in and wiggle it around."

"Don't be an ingrate, Joe. You're lucky to have her. And look at the alternative. You could be all on your lonesome, prying the lid off a tin of soup, or trying to make peace among the warring tribes."

"Instead of out here trying to do the same?"

"That what you think this is?"

"I know jack about what this is. Just saying that so far, everyone acts like those three monkeys—what are they called? See no evil, hear no evil, speak no evil."

" 'Fraid using the word 'monkeys' will get you labeled as a racist. It's like niggardly. Freakin' public doesn't know anything, then sees a slight behind every bush."

Niggardly. Grudging and petty in giving or spending. From an old Swedish word meaning miserly. It had nothing to do with the word nigger, which derived from the French word for black. When his drunken father was at his rampaging best, young Joe Burgess had hidden behind a dictionary, ready to swing it up to defend himself if necessary. Along the way, he'd learned a lot of words.

He turned onto Franklin and headed up the hill, blasting his horn at a kid with earbuds who had strayed out into the crosswalk against the light. "Know I say this every time, but this one is gonna be a bitch. So. What do you want to eat?"

"Anything but pizza or Chinese. I'm beginning to speak Mandarin with an Italian accent."

"Meatloaf sandwich?"

"Make it two."

"Can you pick up some coffee?"

"Roger that," Kyle said.

Burgess disconnected and called Perry. "I'm picking up some sandwiches. Meatloaf okay with you?"

"Make it two."

"Funny. That's just what Terry said."

"Great minds." Perry clicked off.

While he waited in the market, Burgess called Remy at the hospital. "She say anything yet?"

"She's conscious," Aucoin said. "But she won't say anything to anyone. When they told her about the baby, she kind of fell into this weird state, like she'd disconnected from everything. Dissociative, I think they called it. They're gonna get a psych consult. Hold on a sec."

Burgess pictured him stepping outside the door, where the girl couldn't overhear. Whatever state she was in, there was no way to be sure she wasn't hearing what people around her were saying.

"Okay, I'm back," Aucoin said. "That nurse you know, Maryann? She says they don't think this girl's a day over fifteen. Maybe even younger. Something weird going on. I did ask if the

41

baby was hers. They couldn't say for sure, but she had recently given birth, and was nursing. Poor thing. Just a kid herself. I wonder if anyone's going to come forward to claim her."

Burgess was betting that she was a throwaway kid, that homelessness or violence or vulnerability had let her get into this state. "Stay with her," he said. "If you have to leave the room, make sure someone's there to cover for you. Use security. Cote will have my head if I ask for any more personnel over there."

Oops. He wasn't supposed to talk negatively about his superiors with a junior officer. Not that everyone in the department didn't know about his antagonistic relationship with Captain Paul Cote, an antagonism that had begun when Cote had screwed up the evidence against a man who'd raped and killed a child. The killer had walked, and Burgess had never forgiven Cote for the screwup. When they were forced to interact, he and Cote circled each other like fighters in a ring, Burgess trying to watch his back, Cote trying to stab it. But protocol was protocol. "Forget I said that, Remy."

"Said what, sir?"

"Good boy. Call me if anything changes."

"Sir? I'm off in a couple hours. What should I—?"

"I'll call your sergeant. Have someone relieve you."

"Thank you, sir."

"And get security to take a photo of our girl, if they haven't already. Maybe we can find someone to ID her."

"Sergeant?" Remy's voice was hesitant. "Security's pretty busy fending off the blood maggots."

Reporters trying to get into the room. Shoot questions at that poor damaged girl. Get the story. They'd snap a photo of the dead baby if they could, sure it would increase their circulation. Even since he'd dealt with a dead kid up in Knowlton Park, and a reporter had talked her way into someone's attic with a telephoto lens to snap a picture of the body, he'd had nothing but contempt for some of the local reporters. They plastered that photo—in color—on the front page, causing people who'd loved that boy so much pain. Not that he'd ever had much use for most reporters. There were good ones. Decent people who did their homework and wrote serious stories. And then there were the blood maggots.

"I'll see about getting you some backup, Remy."

He clicked off as the man behind the counter handed over a bag of sandwiches. "Having a party tonight, Sergeant?"

Burgess nodded. "With a bonfire and everything."

The counterman handed him a second bag. "Some chocolate chip cookies. My wife made 'em. They're really good."

"Thanks," he said. "Tell her the guys will really appreciate them."

He headed back to his car. The sky over the city had turned a marvelous deep blue, the color of the midnight blue crayon in his childhood Crayola set. What a treat those big boxes of crayons had been. Hours and hours of pleasure from such a small investment. Today kids needed electrons and something jumping on a screen to hold their attention. It had been enough for him and his sisters to sit with coloring books or a block of paper.

He stood a minute, trying to smell the spring air, but all he got was smoke from his clothes. He gave up and drove to 109.

The desk officer gave him the usual greeting. "Captain Cote wanted an update as soon as you came in."

Captain Cote always wanted updates. Paid no attention when he got them. Besides, Burgess was sure he was gone for the day.

"Thanks," Burgess said. "I'll give one as soon as I have something to tell him."

He should take the stairs. He hadn't gotten much exercise today, but beating down doors and rescuing people had left him bruised and cranky, and his bad knee was already talking to him about rest. In his world, RICE wasn't something you had with Chinese food. It was rest, ice, compression, and elevation. Things a busy detective had no time for.

If he'd known what a penalty he'd pay, back when he was playing high school football, would he still have done it? Absolutely. First, because it had been such a high he couldn't have let go of it. Second, because the young are invulnerable and never believe the "just you wait" stuff that adults want to dish out. So he'd traded poetry in motion then for a gimpy lumber now. He'd do it again in a heartbeat.

Perry beat him to the conference room. Kyle was right behind him with a tray of coffees. They sank into their chairs and sat a moment, gathering themselves. Lieutenant Vince Melia, their boss, who was in charge of the Criminal Investigation Department (CID), came in as Burgess was handing out food and stared longingly at the fat sandwiches. Burgess gave him one. "Don't want anyone feeling left out, do we?"

Looking after each other. It was what they did.

Before the wrappers had finished rustling, Burgess was rolling. He asked Melia, "ME scheduled an autopsy yet?"

Melia shook his head.

That was unusual. Dr. Lee always scheduled homicide victims fast, and he liked to do them at an unholy hour of the morning. Too often, the Portland cops found themselves driving the forty-five minutes up to the medical examiner's office in Augusta without ever having gone home or gotten any sleep. Lee could take his time, Burgess thought. Unless something broke before they were done here, he was going to bed.

"Any of you guys ever work with a Somali interpreter named Osman?" he asked.

"Arrogant little SOB," Perry said.

"I think he was scared."

"I think June used him on a case recently," Melia said. "You could ask for her impressions. There a problem?"

Burgess shrugged. "Just a feeling I get. That he has some kind of antagonistic relationship with the men we interviewed tonight. Makes me wonder if I got the full story. We've got a meeting with him tomorrow to follow up. Maybe we'll learn more then."

"And you were interviewing whom?" Melia asked.

As the lieutenant, he was supposed to keep his finger on the pulse of this thing so he could report up the food chain. A suspicious fire at a mosque building that was scrawled with anti-Muslim graffiti and a dead child meant the brass would be paying attention. And that plenty of other agencies would also want a piece of it.

Cluster fucks came with the job. They also made investigation a hundred times harder.

"The Imam and some people whose roles we haven't quite figured out," Burgess said. "Not other elders, I don't think. Family members? Clan members? We didn't get much. He said he rented the building, but was silent about who he rents it from. He knew about the anti-Muslim graffiti on the building. Said it wasn't there yesterday, but was there this morning. I got some photos of that before the fire ate it."

"You get any feel for who might have written that?" Melia asked. "Anyone who's been giving them trouble?"

"The Imam said they'd been harassed by some locals on motorcycles. He gave me a description, but it would fit any of a number of men. We'll check with the gang folks, see if it rings any bells with them. Take a look at any field notes in the files."

"Press gets their hands on that, they'll have a field day."

"I expect they know about it. We'll have to wait and see what comes down the road."

Melia made a sound that was somewhere between exasperation and a sigh. "What about the girl and the baby? That locked closet? The Imam have anything to say about that?"

"Nothing helpful. He knew about the fire, but hadn't seen any reason to rush over there, which seems implausible. Agreed that they, and some social service groups they run, had sole use of the building. But he said he had no idea how someone might have come to be locked in a closet. Another man who was there, who gave his name as Ismail Ibrahim, jumped like a startled frog when I said the baby was dead, but denied having been there. We'll follow up with him. Might take a different interpreter, though, if we've got one."

He made a note and raised his eyes to Melia. "Who have we got on the fire investigation?"

"Scott Lavigne."

"Scotty gonna be able to stand up to PFD?"

"I think so. We picked the right guy to send for fire training this time. Usually we have to twist arms, but he loves to get his teeth into it. He grinned like a madman when I told him he had the job."

"Who's coming from the fire marshal's office?"

Melia smiled. "Davey Green. They're already out there, doing preliminary stuff."

Burgess smiled, too. "That's a piece of good news." Until his retirement, Davey Green had been one of them. He was a superb detective. A methodical, by-the-book man who was a genius at getting people to talk. The information flow always worked better when they worked with someone who had a police background. It helped cut down on the territorialism.

"Scotty's already out at the scene, and just to affirm our concerns, I'll put a call in to Davey," Melia said. "Ask him to keep us in the loop. And you'll have our gang coordinator at your meeting in the morning."

Burgess looked at Stan Perry. "Got anything to add, Stan?"

"Just that they're a bunch of liars, Joe, which we already know, and that it's gonna be a bitch to find a way in."

"Not the first time," Burgess said. He shifted to Kyle. "Tell us about your informant, Terry. What do you think you might get from him?"

Kyle's two sandwiches were gone, nothing but a few meatloaf crumbs on the ketchup-stained paper. Kyle ate like a starved wolf and stayed lean as one.

"Her," Kyle said, crumpling up the paper. "And I'm gonna get jack unless I can come up with an iPod. We got enough money for that in our informant's budget, Vince?"

"You're using a kid?"

"She's eighteen."

Melia made a face. "Maybe. You think what she's got is worth it?"

"Don't know," Kyle said. "You never do. She gave me this much, as a teaser. Couple days ago, she saw two men get out of a car and drag a veiled woman into that building. And it looked like the woman was holding a baby."

CHAPTER FIVE

"If that's the teaser," Burgess said, "I wonder what the main course will be?"

"I'm hoping for details. Descriptions of the men. Of the car. Time of day. Who else was around. Whether she knows who they are or has seen them there before. She claims she's holding back 'cuz she's scared, but she's a big-time game player. Knows how to pump it up so I'll think it's worth something. She could be lying. There's enough on the street already, she had something to work with. On the other hand . . ."

Kyle looked sadly down at the empty space in front of him, then at Burgess. "You don't have any more—"

Burgess shook his head. "But she has come through a few times?"

"Yeah. It just takes a lot of work."

"Sometimes you just want to grab 'em and shake 'em until their little pea brains rattle," Perry said.

"Really?" Melia said. "You do that just once and you've got shaken career syndrome."

"That's a good one, Vince."

"That's a promise, Stan. We're going to be walking on eggs on this one. There's nobody who isn't going to want a piece of it, and a piece of us if anything goes wrong. Profiling or stereotyping be damned, we are dealing with a population where some elements are anti-police and believe we're out to get them. So everyone, watch your backs on this."

Melia looked at their Dunkin' Donuts coffees, started to say something, then shook his head.

Kyle reached under his chair, brought up another coffee, and pushed it toward the lieutenant. "Looking for this, Lou?"

"More like hoping."

"Almost forgot," Burgess said, grabbing the bag the counterman had given him. "Jose's wife made all you nice boys some cookies."

"A ray of sunshine in our fucked-up lives," Perry said.

Melia shot him a look. He didn't like his detectives swearing. They all did, they just developed "us" and "them" vocabularies. Perry had a bad habit of letting it spill over.

"We got patrol doing a canvass of the neighborhood?" Burgess said.

"They're asking."

"Think it would make any difference if they knew a baby died in there?" Burgess said.

"Wish I could think so," Melia said, "but I'm doubtful. Still, it's a mixed neighborhood. Some people who've lived there a long time. One of them might still have some sense of community."

Vince sounded depressed. Burgess thought it was anticipation of the unpleasantness ahead. This kind of case, where every forward step had to be taken so carefully, and much of what they needed to know required them to rely on other agencies, was miserably hard. It was hard enough to work a case when it was just theirs. And Vince would be troubled about the baby. He got bummed whenever they had a case involving a child and he'd be feeling guilty about asking Burgess to work another dead kid.

"Oh, listen, Vince," Perry said. "These people got a sense of community. It involves picking the pockets of our community so theirs can thrive."

"So much for sending *you* to sensitivity training, Stan," Burgess said. "You sound like an rabid anti-Muslim. Ya know?"

"Just keep it in here, Stan, okay?" Melia interrupted. "You've got a right to your opinions, but I hear you've been voicing them around the city, and I'll have you on the dog poop squad."

"Hey," Kyle said. "I'm the one wants to be on the dog poop squad. I'd be so good at it. I'd have the city budget balanced in no time, the way I'd hand out tickets to people who didn't scoop the poop, violated the leash law—"

"Enough!" Melia waved his arms like an umpire calling them all out. "Low profile. Careful. By the book. Record every damned thing you do, and whenever possible, do it with another cop as a witness. Are we clear?"

"I think I got it," Kyle said. "Watch our backs, watch each other's asses, watch our mouths, venture no personal opinions outside the sacred walls of 109. And go catch a baby killer."

He reached out to snag the last cookie, but Melia beat him to it. "Pulling rank, Vince?"

"Just hungry."

Burgess was hungry, too. For information and clarity and for the case to be solved quickly. He didn't think any of his appetites were likely to be satisfied.

He tossed his last bit out on the table. "Something odd about that closet where we found that girl and her baby," he said. "The only locked room in the place? The shelves were lined with computer boxes. A whole lot of high-end stuff. I only had a few seconds . . . but I saw enough to know the seals weren't broken and the boxes were pristine. Funny that that stuff was there and the Imam didn't mention it. Funny that they didn't rush down to try and save it."

He paused. "I think there was a whole lot more going on in that place than religious services and some community service. I just don't know how to find out what."

Kyle smothered a yawn. "Follow the money?"

"Good idea," Burgess said. "Starting bright and early in the morning, that's just what we're going to do."

"What about that hawala thing that Osman suggested we look into?" Perry said.

Burgess looked at Melia. "Who knows about that? Homeland Security? Or is that FBI? Haven't we got someone working with them?"

Melia rolled his eyes. "Joe, you really think we call up the world's greatest and they're gonna tell us what they know, even if it does involve a death investigation?"

"They might be interested in working with us?" He considered. "A cop can dream, Vince. Can't he?"

"No, Joe, he can't. He just has to put his nose to the grindstone and get results." Vince looked down at the table, scratched a note, then looked back at the team. "Your interpreter really made that suggestion?"

Burgess nodded.

"I'll see what I can learn."

"You going to brief the press or is the captain doing it?" Burgess asked.

Melia's smile was a thin, cynical line. "Guess. I keep waiting for him to pop through the door, demanding reports and updates. Like we have anything to say at this point."

There was a knock at the door. They all straightened, expecting Captain Cote, then relaxed again. Cote didn't knock.

"Excuse me, sir?" An officer came in with a folder, set it in front of Burgess.

Burgess flipped it open. Copies of the pictures of the girl and the baby he'd snapped with his cell phone at the scene. He set them on the table and everyone leaned in. They were poor quality. There hadn't been time, under the circumstances, for lighting and focus. But it was just that hurried quality that gave them their power. The girl's face was visible, but she was surrounded by a blurred sea of moving hands. The baby was lost behind a mask and tubes, just a tiny head with dark skin and dark hair. More visible were the set faces of those who worked on him.

There was a long moment of silence. Then Kyle shoved back his chair. "Is that all? 'Cuz I gotta go see my kids. What time are we starting tomorrow?"

Vince stood, too. "Going to go see mine, too. Lucas hasn't been feeling well, and Gina's a little worried. I'll let you know, Joe, when the ME calls with a time."

Burgess realized that he needed to go see his kids as well. Stan was still sitting, staring at the photo. When they all rose, he looked up. "You old farts quitting already?"

"Someday, this might happen to you," Vince said.

"No way. I'm gonna be like Joe. I ever have a kid, it will be just fine if I get a phone call fifteen years down the road, like he did. Congratulations, detective. It's a boy."

Burgess had thought exactly those words when he'd learned about his son Dylan. But coming from Perry's mouth, they seemed ugly. He realized Perry had been acting ugly all day. Something was going on. Perry had a childish ability to act out when something in his private life was bothering him. He'd have to get Perry alone and figure out what was up. He'd had enough of pulling the kid's ass out of the fire.

He sank into his chair again, shoving back the urge those photos had incited to rush home and hug the ones he loved. "Let's take a moment and plan tomorrow," he said.

But Perry was staring at one of the photographs. He slid it across the table to Kyle. "Do you see what I see?"

"Isn't that a Christmas song?"

"Just take at look at it, Ter, okay?"

Reluctantly, Kyle picked it up. Burgess knew he wanted to be gone, but Kyle was a good cop. And even when Perry was being a pain in the ass, they trusted his good eye. Kyle looked at the picture, then shoved back his chair. "Be right back," he said, and walked out.

"Where is he going?" Melia said.

"To get a magnifying glass, so the rest of you blind old farts can see what Kyle and I can see," Perry said.

Burgess grabbed the photo. At first, he didn't see anything new. Then he saw it—a band of dark bruises around one of the girl's wrists.

"And what does that remind you of?" Perry said.

Burgess passed it to Melia. He watched Melia's face and saw recognition.

"Looks like when a rookie or a sadist puts on the cuffs too tight."

"Exactly."

Now Perry was back on the reservation. "Which means we've got to send some nice evidence tech over to the hospital and get us some pictures of that before the bruises fade."

Kyle came back with the magnifying glass and they all took a closer look.

"We'd better get her clothes, hers and the baby's, from Aucoin, get them back here to the lab," Burgess said.

He remembered he'd promised to send someone to relieve Aucoin. Aucoin could bring them back himself. "Vince, can you make sure patrol has someone with her at all times? Looks like there are people out there with a big interest in keeping her from talking to us."

Melia nodded. "She's not talking?"

"Not so far. Tomorrow I'll spend some time there, talk to her doctors, see what's going on. Aucoin said the nurses told him she's retreated from the world. Went into some kind of fugue state right after they told her about the baby."

There was a noise in the hall, and they all looked toward the door like misbehaving kids who expected a parent. What they expected, and wanted to avoid, was Cote. Sooner or later he would brief the press. A fire at a mosque was big news and Cote loved the limelight. Far too often, he revealed things they didn't want made public. Since he hadn't talked to anyone working the case, they had no idea what he knew, or what he would say.

When no one came in, Melia said, "What time tomorrow? Eight?"

"Unless we hear from the ME."

On his way to the door, Burgess had a thought. "I'm going to take a look at Rudy's video footage of the crowd, Stan, see who crawled out of the woodwork. You want to join me?"

"With pleasure. I wonder if any of our friends from the mosque were there?"

A few minutes later, they were watching Rudy Carr's crowd footage on one of the monitors. A sickening display of people laughing, talking, pointing, and jostling. Burgess scanned the faces. He couldn't get a good visual but back in one corner, two men sat in shadow, flashing lights bouncing off the chrome on their motorcycles. He hit pause.

"You see that, Stan? I wonder if Rocky might be able to get us some faces?"

Perry leaned in toward the screen. "Like we'd ever get that lucky. But I'll cruise around there tomorrow, see if anyone around might have a surveillance camera. Seriously, I thought the Imam was bullshitting us when he said that."

Burgess didn't know yet. At least one of their local gangs favored Nazi-style lightning bolts on the patches that celebrated a "hit." Things had been quiet lately, but they'd had plenty of motorcycle gang rivalry in the city, something that set the local merchants off, especially after a shoot-out in the Old Port in broad daylight. It was known some of their local bikers didn't take kindly to the city's new citizens. Definitely something they had to take a look at. He'd leave a note for the gang people, asking them to take a look at Rudy's tape. See if there was anything they recognized. A note for Rudy, asking if he could make stills of the men and the motorcycles.

"Let's see what else we've got." He hit play and the crowd scene began to roll again.

Suddenly, like a game show contestant hitting his buzzer first, Perry said, "There. Stop. Back it up."

They backed up and moved forward, frame by frame, until Perry said, "Right there. At the back of that group by the tree? You see him?"

Burgess saw. It was the man from the Imam's living room who had jumped when he'd told them the baby was dead. A face made memorable by a big scar on the man's forehead. The man who wasn't there.

"There's something else for tomorrow's to-do list," Burgess said.

He checked his notes for the name and address. Ismail Ibrahim. The address he'd given was the Imam's. If all the people who claimed to live there actually did, the place was crammed with cots from basement to attic.

"Why wait for tomorrow, Joe? It's not late."

Perry was right. It wasn't late. But there was the small problem of finding an interpreter.

"I'll call Osman," Perry said. "I'm sure he'll be happy to assist his local police department again. And get paid for it."

Osman didn't answer his phone. Burgess got out his notes and read through them. In their discussion out at the curb, he had asked Osman which of the men spoke English. Of this man, he had been certain. He had good English. The interpreter had said that the man worked at the mall.

"Osman said he speaks English."

Stan was bouncing from one foot to the other, eager for the chase. "So what are we waiting for?"

It was just before nine when they pulled to the curb. Lights were still on inside. And they had said they're return for the plan of the building, so they ought to be expected. Once again they climbed the steps and knocked on the door. This time, no one answered. Stan knocked again, a forceful assault of big knuckles against the wood. Burgess watched the living room light go out. Even through the door, they could hear footsteps thumping upstairs.

Perry looked at him and raised an eyebrow.

"Once more, with feeling," Burgess said. "And tell them who we are."

Perry's fist was raised to knock again when Burgess heard a noise. He put up a hand and then cupped his ear. Perry lowered his hand. In the quiet night, they could hear the scuff of shoes on the driveway that ran along the left side of the house. Silently, Burgess signaled for Perry to go that way, while he went the other, circling around the right side of the house and along the back. When he reached the driveway, he could just make out a figure disappearing between the houses facing on the next street. Tall and lean. Probably male.

Stan was moving quietly behind the figure, so Burgess slipped along the other side of the house, moving faster this time, and came out into the next street. So far, no dogs had barked and no one had flung open a window and demanded to know what they were doing there.

He and Stan hit the sidewalk together, closing in on a man who was bent over, opening a car door. A man they'd spoken with earlier in the evening and seen in the crime scene video. A man who'd said his name was Ismail.

"Excuse me, Ismail," Burgess said. "Hoping I can have a few

minutes of your time? Some follow-up questions about the fire?"

The man froze, key in the lock, body rigid, as he turned to face Burgess. "I told you earlier. I know nothing about that."

Demonstrating he both spoke, and understood, English.

"I think you do," Burgess said. "And we appreciate your willingness to assist us in our investigation."

"I don't . . . I'm not—"

"We've got your picture at the scene."

"That wasn't me. You people think all Somalis look alike."

You people. And the police were accused of stereotyping and profiling?

"You telling us you have an identical twin?" Perry said. "Who wears identical clothes? With an identical scar above his eyebrow?"

The man deflated a little, then pulled his key out of the lock. "What did you want to ask?"

Burgess noticed he hadn't said "want to know." They could ask, apparently, and then he'd decide whether he would answer. "You want to invite us inside? Talk to us there? Or would you prefer to come and sit in my car?"

"I would prefer not to speak with you at all."

"An option that isn't on the table," Burgess said. "Now, my place, or yours?"

"It would not be a good thing if it were known that I had spoken with you. I don't know anything that will help you in your investigation."

And how in hell would he know that before he heard their questions?

Perry had moved into the man's personal space so that he was backed right up against the car. The hand that held the car keys was shaking slightly and they made a metallic chatter against the side of the car.

Burgess heard a car turning the corner and heading toward

them, but when he glanced that way, there were no lights.

Then the lights came on and the car accelerated.

"Get down, Stan!" he yelled.

He grabbed the man and pulled him onto the sidewalk as the car flew toward them, its passengers firing a barrage of gunshots.

Bullets plinked off metal. There was the rustle and chatter of falling glass. Auto glass is designed not to break into sharp shards. That doesn't mean it won't break, and it has its own special sound when it does.

Keeping one hand on Ismail, Burgess got on the phone to dispatch. "Shots fired. Gray or black Honda. Maybe six or eight years old. At least three people inside and they're armed. Last seen heading toward Brighton Avenue."

When the car had disappeared down the street, they jumped up, grabbed Ismail, and raced between the buildings back toward their car.

CHAPTER SIX

They shoved Ismail into the back seat, jumped in the front, and sped away from the house, ignoring his protests that he had to stay and reassure his family about the gunshots.

"We can have an officer go by if you want. Let them know everything's okay," Burgess said. "Or you can call them. You have a phone?"

Instead of responding, Ismail clammed up.

Burgess was still trying to catch his breath. Only TV cops got into gunfights and sloughed it off with no reaction. Drive-by shootings weren't that common in Portland. He didn't like it happening in his city. Even less did he like it happening to him, though he was pretty certain the shots had been aimed at Ismail. He hoped patrol would find the car and the shooters. If he were a betting man, though, he'd bet against that.

One thing he did know—that the department would be swamped with complaints from the neighborhood, and that those complaints would be coming back down to him. It was another aspect of the challenge of integrating refugees into the community. If there were random gunshots fired in one of the public housing projects, the good citizens in other parts of the city could ignore them. But when refugees realized the American dream, and moved into a decent house in a "nice" neighborhood, the neighbors often didn't know how to deal.

Part of the problem was just another kind of cultural dissonance. While other houses on the block might contain a single family and one or two vehicles, the refugee families tended, where members of multiple generations had managed to survive the conflicts at home, to contain an extended family, often with the result that the neighbors objected both to the crowding and the noise, and to the multiple vehicles parked where there would otherwise be lawn.

Not that there weren't plenty of nice folks who'd lived in Maine for generations who parked cars on their lawns. They just weren't usually so ambitious about upward mobility and didn't do it in nice neighborhoods. As his mother—a kind woman but a realist—might have said: they knew their place. There were exceptions, though. He'd met some really appalling ones on a recent case, a family so deeply into selfishness and criminal acts they'd barely noticed when one of their children was brutally murdered.

Letting his mind wander like an old fart. He jerked his attention back to the moment. One silver lining from those predictable complaints was they might provide names and phone numbers. People he could contact who might have observations about goings on at the Imam's house. A detective never knew where good information might come from.

"You okay, Stan?" he asked, as he took the turn at the corner way too fast.

"Got a little dirt on my pants."

"Ismail?"

There was silence, then the man said, "I think that I am bleeding."

Burgess jerked the wheel, turned into a little strip mall parking lot, and slammed the Explorer into park. He snapped on the overhead and turned to the man in the back seat.

"Show me," he said, nodding at Perry to keep an eye on the man. It wouldn't be the first time they'd had someone fake an injury so they'd stop and he could jump out of the vehicle.

Ismail held out his hand. Blood oozed from his palm where it had scraped along the sidewalk. An eight-year-old kid who'd fallen off his bike wouldn't complain about something like that. Burgess passed him a handkerchief. He bought them by the dozen, and gave them out nearly as fast. Decades of binding up his city's wounds—physical and emotional—with little squares of white cotton.

"Anything else?"

The man's face was closed and sullen. Just like Burgess's son, Dylan. Burgess couldn't seem to win any popularity contests these days. Like his training officer had told him, back in the day, "You can't be a cop if you need to always be loved."

Substitute "ever" for "always" and you'd have it about right.

Ismail stared from Burgess to the door handle. Finally he said, "No."

"We get to headquarters, you can wash the gravel off in the men's room. Unless you'd rather we took you over to the hospital?" Burgess pretended to consider. "Might not be a bad idea. We could take you to see our little mystery girl. See if you recognize her. If she recognizes you."

Ismail gave Burgess one of those "if I only had a weapon, I'd kill you now" looks. "I don't need the hospital."

"Good. Then we can find ourselves an interview room at 109, and have a friendly chat."

"Fuck you."

"Nice way to talk to someone who just saved you from getting shot," Perry said.

"I don't know what you're talking about."

"The car without lights? The gunshots? The reason we grabbed you and pulled down behind your car?"

"I didn't hear any gunshots."

"Right," Perry snorted. "Thought you just said you needed to reassure your family. About what, I wonder, if it wasn't the

61

gunshots? That little scrape on your hand?"

Ismail, not entirely imperturbable, made an angry noise.

"Okay," Perry said, "Maybe in Somalia, they don't call them guns? So I'll explain it to you. Tomorrow, when you go to get in your car, you may notice there are some small round holes it? Couple windows blown out, glass all over the seats and the sidewalk? A car, by the way, that we notice you have parked on a different street from where you live?"

He shifted in his seat, a sudden, angry gesture. "See, in this country we have these things called guns. They shoot projectiles called bullets—"

"Enough, Stan."

Perry shut up, but Burgess could still feel his angry vibe in the silent car. He'd meant to use this drive to probe into what was bothering his detective, something sergeants were supposed to do for the people they supervised, but they'd gotten kind of sidetracked.

He called Melia, told him about the gunshots and that they were bringing a witness in. Asked if he wanted to sit in. Melia told him to handle it.

There was a long silence, then Melia said, "Call me when you're done. I'll fill you in on the press conference."

That sounded ominous. Burgess drove the rest of the way to 109, imagining the many ways in which Cote giving a press conference without a briefing might have screwed things up for his investigators. His first choice was the man pursing his duck's ass mouth and uttering smarmy platitudes about getting justice for their newest citizens. His worst nightmare was that Cote had spewed out everything they knew about the girl and the baby. Not that there was much to spew at this point, but he didn't want the GP to know about the locked closet. Or that the baby had died. Yet.

He felt a headache starting just thinking about it.

His phone rang. He hoped it was going to be some good news, maybe the shooters caught, but he didn't work in the good news bureau. A report from the home front. Chris was short and to the point. "You need to talk to your son. He and Nina have been yelling at each other for twenty minutes about who is hogging the computer. Twenty minutes, Joe! Here."

There was a rustle and Dylan's voice, so like his own it was eerie, came down the line. "So, Dad?"

He'd tried to be patient and understanding. The boy had lost his mother. Been shipped from the only family he'd ever known to live with the stranger who was his father. Transitions were always hard. So were losses. Fifteen was a hard age for a boy under the best circumstances. But Dylan was making this harder than it needed to be.

"So, Dylan," he echoed, "what's the problem?"

"That little bitch Nina won't let me have a turn on the computer, and I've got homework, too."

Chris would deal with Dylan's language, Burgess was brought in here only as referee. He checked his watch. Ten past nine. Just over ten minutes since they'd pulled to the curb at the Imam's house. It had been a long ten minutes.

"How long has she been on the computer?"

Dylan didn't answer.

"How much time do you need?"

"Hour, maybe."

"Let me talk to Nina."

For decades, Burgess's fears about relationships and children had been that he wouldn't be good at it. He wouldn't have the patience. It would bring out the violence he feared lived in him just as it had lived in his father. He'd never gotten to the point of imagining the actuality, the day-to-day complexities of managing the needs of different humans. Even Chris, who was steady as a rock and had really wanted this, sometimes struggled to deal with the endless squabbling.

Nina's voice was a little shaky. "Hey, Joe?"

"What's your side of this?"

"Dylan's just being an ass. He had the computer from seven to eight, spent the whole time online with his friends. Then, when I get a turn and I'm almost done with my homework, he's suddenly all, 'I didn't get a turn and I need it right now.' "

The truth, Burgess knew, lay somewhere in between.

"How long will it take you to finish?"

"Ten minutes."

Jesus. They call him in the middle of investigating a child's death, the roar of gunshots still ringing in his ears, to squabble about ten minutes? Welcome to the world of happy domesticity.

"Thanks, Nina. Ten minutes and you get off, okay? Put Dylan back on."

"Dad?" Not a name or an endearment, but a snarl.

"It's yours in ten minutes. Do we need to create a schedule? Would that make things easier?"

"What we need is another fucking computer."

"What you need is to watch your language."

His son hung up on him. Maybe if he'd been dealing with this boy since birth? Maybe the web of connection made all of this easier. But he knew better. He'd been dealing with families long enough to know none of this was easy. That at a certain point, even nice children could morph into teenage monsters.

There was a humorless laugh from the back seat. Ismail said, "Mixing business with pleasure, Detective?"

Burgess ignored him. He took his file of domestic issues, stuck it in a mental filing cabinet, and slammed it shut.

They parked in the garage at 109 and went in the side door, in case there were still reporters around. Took the elevator upstairs, waited while their witness cleaned himself up, and settled him in an interview room. Burgess was going to do the interview. Perry would watch it on a monitor in another room. While Perry escorted Ismail to the interview room, Burgess went into the restroom, put on gloves, and retrieved his bloody handkerchief from the trash. He put it in a paper bag and labeled it. Whether he liked it or not, Ismail had just given them a DNA sample.

Before he went into the room, Burgess took a few minutes with Perry. "Get someone to do a records check on this guy. His address. His family. See if we know anything about them. Also on the Imam and his family. And that kid—the one who was hanging around in the bushes, watching."

He turned away, then swung back. "And on our translator."

Perry jerked his chin toward the closed interview room door. "That asshole really pushes my buttons. What's his problem, anyway? Somebody freakin' died today."

Burgess nodded. "Maybe I'll find out."

He didn't expect they taught civics in Somali schools, to the extent there *were* Somali schools. He wasn't even sure it was still taught here. Citizens might have a moral obligation to help the police, but mostly what he heard from citizens—whether they'd had civics or not—was that they knew their rights, not their responsibilities.

He went into the room and closed the door. "Can I get you something?" he asked. "Some tea or water?"

The man shook his head. He sat like a stone in the chair, the kind of faraway look in his eyes Burgess had sometimes seen on stone-cold killers. A gaze that didn't acknowledge anything that was going on around him or even that other humans existed. Burgess started recording, identifying both of them and the matter that was the subject of the interview. He got the man's name and address again, confirmation of the man's place of employment, and that the man was an American citizen. His relationship to the Imam was grandson.

There were many ways to open an interview. Often it was friendly chat. A slow lead-in. Rapport building. Putting the witness at ease. Ismail's behavior on the ride over here had already told him there would be no rapport, so he went right to the heart of the matter.

"Earlier today, there was a fire in the building which is used as a mosque on Ashton Street. When I spoke with you a few hours later at the home of Muhamud Ibrahim, you told me that you were not present at the scene of that fire. We know that you were. Why did you lie to me?"

The man sat as if he hadn't heard. Staring straight ahead. No expression on his face.

Burgess tried a few more questions. Whether Ismail knew who might have shot at him tonight? Whether there was anyone who had a grudge. He got the same lack of response.

Finally, he pushed back his chair and went out. He went to the file on his desk and got the photographs of the girl and the baby, then went to check with Perry.

"Patrol have any luck finding those shooters?"

"Nope. Found the car, though. They tried to burn it, but the fire went out after they ran off. We ran the plate. Comes back registered to our friend the Imam. Maybe some sort of infighting, but we're checking to see if any of his cars have been reported stolen."

It would be odd if the Imam was involved. From Ismail's presence there earlier tonight, Burgess would have assumed a close relationship and the one thing he'd learned was that Ismail was the Imam's grandson. So why would the Imam want him shot? Was it shot or shot *at*? Intended for Ismail, as he'd assumed? Intended for them? Pure theater? He didn't know.

"We still need that plan from the Imam. Now we need follow-up about the car used in the shooting."

"Right. Kyle and I are heading back out there soon as I'm

done here. I expect they won't answer the door though. Like last time."

"I think we're done here. It's like talking to a stone. Anything on that records check yet?"

Perry called over to the detective they considered their computer jockey, Rocky Jordan. Jordan wasn't usually in at night. Melia must have called him in to start getting them background information for the morning. "Got anything on any of those names yet, Rocky?"

Jordan pointed to a growing pile of papers on his desk. "Plenty, but you're gonna have to make a chart to keep it all straight."

Burgess slumped down in his chair. It was wishful thinking, he knew, but he wished something about this would be easy. Witnesses sitting like stones. Drive-by shootings. A whole lot of drama tonight with no clue what it was about.

Before he went back into the interview room, he called Aucoin over at the hospital again. "How's our girl doing?"

"No change, sir. There was a bit of a ruckus a while ago, though. Man tried to get into the room. Said he was family and he'd come to take her home."

"You grabbed him, right?"

Aucoin's sigh told Burgess what the answer would be. "Sorry, sir. Security was slow to respond and you told me not to leave her."

He pictured Aucoin ducking his head. The boy was becoming a good cop. Would still beat himself up for not being everywhere and doing everything. If they weren't so short-handed, and Cote wasn't such a parsimonious asshole, they would have had two officers there, and one could have chased the man.

"Not your fault, Remy," he said. "But we could use a description. I'll swing by, talk to people, see what their security cameras got. Melia's asked patrol to send someone to relieve you. Bring those clothes back here when you come. Okay?"

"Sorry, sir," Aucoin said again. "I mean, yes, sir."

"Did he get into the room, Remy?"

Aucoin was silent.

"Did she see him?"

"Yes."

"How did she react? Did she react?"

"She reacted, sir. When she saw him in the doorway . . . the look on her face? She was as scared as I've ever seen anyone be in my life."

And they'd let him get away.

Burgess wanted to break something. "Thanks, Remy. You did the right thing staying with her. I'll be over in a few. You can fill me in more fully."

He realized there was one more question he needed to ask. "When did this happen?"

"About twenty minutes ago, sir. I would have called you, but it's been kind of hectic here."

Burgess could imagine. So it couldn't have been the man in the interview room. "Stay put 'til I get there, okay?"

He disconnected and brought Perry up to date.

CHAPTER SEVEN

He wanted to head straight out the door, get to the hospital, and see what he could do about identifying their mystery girl's visitor, but there was the small problem of Ismail. A mean part of Burgess wanted to let him cool his heels for a few hours and see if he still acted so stony. But that was against procedure, especially where the man wasn't a suspect as far as they knew, just someone with information who refused to talk. The same POS folks they dealt with every day.

Stan left to join Kyle in trying to reinterview the Imam about the shooting and whether the car had been stolen.

Burgess got his coat, checked his pockets for all the usual items—gun, cuffs, pepper spray, radio, cell phone, badge—then scooped up the photos of the girl and the baby and headed back into the room. Ismail didn't look like he'd moved an inch. He was perched on the edge of the chair, staring stonily at the wall.

Burgess tossed the two pictures down on the table. "Do you know this girl? Know anything about this baby?"

Although it was sometimes unpleasant, especially with his family and friends, Burgess had spent a lifetime reading the smallest gesture. The man tried not to look, couldn't help himself, and then, like he had at the Imam's house, he flinched at the sight of that small vulnerable girl surrounded by desperate hands. At a tiny baby smothered in medical equipment, fighting for his life.

"Who are they?" Burgess asked.

"I have no idea."

"I think you have a pretty good idea. But it's up to you whether you want to act like a citizen of these United States and actually help get justice for that little boy's lost life. Entirely up to you. You can go back to the mall and sell people electronic equipment and new computers and never give a damn about anyone but yourself."

He shook his head as he walked to the door. "Maybe, where you've come from, the death of a baby simply doesn't matter. Or a girl beaten and brutalized and locked in a closet." Ismail flinched again. "I'll get patrol to drive you home."

Just before he walked out, he added, "You'd better hope that if something ever happens to someone you care about, you don't need the police to help you sort it out. Because you know how readily people cooperate. How much they care. And next time someone decides to shoot you, the cops may not be there to save you."

He arranged for Ismail to be driven home. He was halfway downstairs before it hit him. Computers. The guy worked at the mall and sold computers. He called Kyle.

"Terry, you hear anything about any recent big thefts of computer equipment?"

"Apples," Kyle said. "Someone stole bushels and bushels of 'em. You didn't hear?"

He'd heard, but it hadn't registered, and he didn't like that. Getting careless and taking his fingers off the pulse of his city while trying to give his personal life some CPR. "I didn't."

"Out at the mall, so it's not ours. But if you drop over to property crimes, they'll fill you in. South Portland thought it was an inside job, but everyone came up clean. Why?"

"Because that's what was in that closet. And Ismail, the guy who got us shot at tonight, works at the Apple store."

"The plot thickens," Kyle said. "Don't you hate that expression?"

"I do." He told Kyle what he'd just heard from Aucoin. "I'm heading over there now. Keep an eye on young Stanley, will you? Something's eating him."

"You got that right. I'll see what I can find out." And Kyle, a model of efficiency, was gone.

Burgess humped himself down to the garage, slammed his car door too hard, and headed to the hospital. He had the window down, needing the night air to keep himself awake, and scents kept drifting in the window. Earth and damp. Cigarettes and marijuana. Wood smoke. That last might be coming off his clothes. He hadn't had a chance to shower or change. He thought it would be nice to drive out into the country, hear the high-pitched cacophony of spring peepers. Maybe take the kids along.

He had no time for larking off like that.

The nighttime security supervisor was happy to help, a little embarrassed by having let someone get so close to a vulnerable patient when they'd specifically been asked to protect her. The surveillance videos were not especially helpful, though. Dark, grainy pictures of a man rushing out the door and getting into a waiting car. The car pulling quickly away. A battered gray or black Honda. Rocky Jordan, who was good at computer enhancements, might be able to get them a plate, or a partial plate. Beyond that, about all they had was tall, dark, and bearded. The ubiquitous hoodie that made everyone look alike. This one didn't even have a distinctive pattern or design, it was just black.

The lobby video was a little better. The man had done a good job of keeping his face turned away from the camera, so good he might almost have scoped out the room in advance, but there was one clear shot—a moment when the man had had to turn to avoid running into a small child.

He had the security man pause the tape as he stared at the man's face. It was a face he knew rather well. Not Somali. African-American. A very bad actor by the name of Kimani Yates. Until he'd gone away for a particularly brutal attack on a member of a rival gang, Yates had been something of a one-man crime wave. But Yates was supposed to be in jail. They were supposed to be notified of his release. And as far as Burgess knew, he didn't have a twin.

He called dispatch, asked them to do a check on Yates's status. Then he called Rocky Jordan and asked for a more thorough version of the same. He put Melia in the loop, asked patrol for someone to sit on their mystery girl's room, and got Aucoin to come and look at the tape.

"That's the man you saw? The one who tried to get into the room?"

Aucoin's face was grim. "That's the man."

"His name is Kimani Yates. Last I heard, county had him. They were supposed to give us a heads-up when he got out. Looks like our boy might have gotten time off for good behavior. They sometimes have a peculiar notion of what constitutes good behavior over there."

Burgess was disgusted, but not surprised, by the system's failures. Bad enough when it happened to the cops. They were supposed to be on the same side as corrections. But it also happened when a victim was supposed to be notified. That was a far more serious breach.

He needed to look at Yates's record. See if there had been anything involving young girls. If their mystery girl might have been Yates's victim. If there was anyone besides the cops who was supposed to be notified if Yates was getting out. Whether he'd been out recently enough to have fathered this girl's child.

Wondered how in hell that might be connected to the mosque and to stolen computer equipment or to why their girl had been locked in a closet.

"You identify yourself as a police officer and order him to stop when he tried to enter the room, Remy?"

"You bet I did, sir."

Burgess turned to the security chief. "He get physical with any of your guys when they tried to stop him?"

"I've got a man with a broken nose."

"Get me any clothing that might have come in contact with Yates."

At least, when they found Yates, he was going back inside. Whack-a-mole. The cops kept catching them and trying to put 'em away, and the bad guys just kept popping up. Burgess called dispatch, put out a BOLO on Yates. The job like a kid's game and the jails had revolving doors.

He was putting his phone away when it rang.

Kyle sounded as disgusted as he felt. "So, Joe," Kyle said, "remember how you once said that policing is where they tie one hand behind your back, blind you in one eye, and say, 'Now, son, go serve and protect?' Well, that's how I'm feeling right now. Our friend the Imam declined to receive us, but he sent one of his grandsons down to say that as far as he knows, his car is in the driveway, and he has given no one permission to use it. When I said 'which car' the little bastard said 'none of 'em' and closed the door in my face."

In the background, Stan Perry said something. Kyle said, "Shut up." Then, "Not you, Joe." More firmly, "Stanley. I said shut up." Burgess heard a car door slam. "He's gone to go kick a tire or something. Anyway, I'm sitting here looking at five cars parked in the driveway and on the lawn, all of them registered to the Imam. But his son says that none of the Imam's cars are missing."

"How many vehicles are registered to him?"

"Eight at this address. Another two using the mosque's address."

"And you can account for five?"

"Five here. We're gonna swing by the mosque, see what's parked on the street, soon as Stanley stops kicking things."

"Check out the one on the next street. The one that got shot up tonight. Stan can show you. You get a handle on his problem?"

Kyle blew out a breath. "Damned if I know. I asked him if anything was wrong. He said 'what the fuck wasn't wrong.' You know, I used to be a pretty good interviewer, but going by today, I'd say it's time to hang it up."

Burgess knew exactly how he felt. Some days were like that. "One brick at a time, Ter."

He made a quick note about the Imam of the many cars. He had to get back to 109, start looking through the information Rocky was piling up. First, he had to check out their mystery girl. And check in at home. "Over here, we've got a confirmed sighting of Kimani Yates."

Kyle uttered an exclamation which, when the expletives were deleted, amounted to the word "that."

"My sentiments exactly."

The night was getting old and taking Burgess along with it.

"When shall we three meet again?" Kyle said.

"Morning's soon enough. We're not getting anywhere tonight."

"Think the morning sun will bring clarity?"

"And the tooth fairy and the Easter Bunny and a turducken."

"What the fuck is a turducken?"

"You really don't want to know."

"Gotta take some time off tomorrow afternoon," Kyle said. "Lexi has a soccer game. Her team's doing great and she made me promise I'd be there."

Terry Kyle really loved his girls. He'd fought hard to get custody from his ex-wife, a bitch from hell they all referred to as the PMS Queen. Now Kyle felt the heavy weigh of the court and the PMS Queen, watching to see if he could handle it.

"We'll make it work."

"Thanks, Joe."

"See you tomorrow. Meanwhile, see if you can dig anything out of Stan. He's getting as bad as he was last fall. And we both know where that led."

"Roger that," Kyle said, and was gone.

Burgess turned his attention back to Aucoin. "Let's brief your replacement, then you can ride back to 109 with me if you want."

Together, they went up to their mystery girl's room. Burgess took a moment to study the girl, who appeared to be sleeping, before motioning the watching officer out into the corridor. She was curled on her side, one hand under her cheek, looking terribly small and helpless. Her hair was long, dark, and curly. Thick eyelashes lay against her pale cheeks. Her face still had the sweet plumpness of a young adolescent, and there were the faint traces of healing bruises along one jaw. The hand that bore the marks lay outside the blanket. Seen close up, the marks were ugly and unmistakable.

A child. A child who had had, and lost, a child of her own. Where had the adults been, the people who were supposed to be looking after her? Was there anyone to support her in this terrible time? He knew nothing about her and, so far, had no way of learning much. The people who seemed to know were either bad guys or know-nothings. He didn't even know how she'd felt about that baby, only that when they'd found her in the closet, she had been curled protectively around it. A child without protection trying to save a child of her own. The pain in his chest was not a heart attack.

"Wink or Dani come by to photograph that?"

"Dani. She was pretty upset about it."

Dani Letorneau was their newest evidence tech. She was a crackerjack at a crime scene, and the guy who ran their crime lab, Wink Devlin, had made her his special pet. Wink's version of making Dani his pet wasn't to be protective or give her plum assignments, it was to ensure that Dani saw crime in all its ugly glory. Burgess wasn't sure whether Wink was trying to make her the best tech she could possibly be, or if his secret agenda was to drive her out of the business into something he thought better suited to someone with her diminutive stature and delicate beauty. Wink could be hard to read sometimes.

"I gave mystery girl's clothes, and the baby's, to Dani," Aucoin said. His hands tightened into fists. "I hate it that that poor little guy doesn't even have a name." Aucoin didn't have kids, but Burgess remembered him at an interview once, picking up a fretful baby and calming it so Burgess could concentrate on the mom. Aucoin liked kids.

"Me, too."

Burgess quietly instructed Aucoin's replacement about the situation. How the girl wasn't to be left alone at any time. To use security as backup. Not to hesitate to call for more police if the slightest thing seemed out of place. Then he headed back to 109.

His desk looked like a paper blizzard had occurred in his absence. When Rocky went to work on things, this was often the result. Rocky had left a note on top of the heap. "Sgt, I called over to the jail about Kimani Yates. They said he hadn't been released. I suggested that since he'd just been seen over at the hospital, they might want to check again. And sure enough, he's gone. They're calling it a 'paperwork mixup.' "

Rocky strolled back in, carrying a cup of coffee, as Burgess was reading the note. "Pathetic . . . right, Sarge?" His wide shoulders rose and fell in a world-weary shrug. "Those guys would lose their asses if they weren't attached. If it's okay, I'm going to head out before anything else hits the fan."

"You make it sound like a busy evening," Burgess said. "A fire that resulted in a death, a barrage of gunfire in a quiet city neighborhood, and a bad guy mistakenly released from jail? All in a day's work for Portland's finest."

"Happy to hear it," Rocky said. "I was starting to worry. But if you're going to have it all solved and locked up tight by morning, I think I'll go home and see if there's any beer in the fridge. Both my brothers are living with us right now, and . . ."

He trailed off. Didn't want to be complaining in the face of real-world problems. "See you tomorrow."

Left alone in the quiet detective's bay, Burgess dropped into his chair and started going through the papers.

His phone rang. Chris. "Are you ever coming home?" she said. She sounded tired and cranky. This wasn't what he'd anticipated when he'd longed for normal. But he knew this was what normal was like. There were ups and downs. Just like there were here at 109.

"Twenty minutes," he said. "I'm leaving in twenty minutes. Have things settled down?"

"I'm patrolling the border between two warring countries," she said. "Right now, everything's quiet."

"I'm sorry," he said. "I never meant—"

"I'm not complaining," she said. "At least, I'm trying not to. What can I say? Right now this just sucks. My optimism says this is an adjustment and later on we'll be okay."

"I love your optimistic side."

"And my grouchy side?"

"Love that, too. Keep a light on for me."

"I always do."

He stared at the papers a little longer, but his focus was gone. Unless his phone rang with something important, he was better off heading home and getting some sleep. Tomorrow, as Scarlett O'Hara said, was another day.

He shoved everything into his briefcase and headed for the truck. He'd just closed the door and was reaching for the key when his phone rang.

CHAPTER EIGHT

"Joe? We've got a problem." It was Kyle. Calm and controlled, as always, but with an undercurrent in his voice that said "real bad news."

"I'm listening."

"You're not going to believe this," Kyle hesitated. "Someone has stolen the baby's body. I was just checking. I don't know why. Some crazy instinct, and when they opened the drawer, he wasn't there."

Burgess could believe it. What he couldn't believe was that he'd been so careless he hadn't anticipated it and that the hospital had been so careless they'd allowed it to happen. Someone had been trying to control their mystery girl. It wasn't unreasonable that part of what that someone wanted was to ensure that he wasn't tied to the baby. At a minimum, when they found the baby's father, it was going to be a case of statutory rape. And kidnapping and false imprisonment for whoever had locked her—them—in that closet. He thought it was probably far worse than that. Like felony murder, even if it was a set fire and the person who set it was different from whoever had locked them in that closet.

Stealing the body at this point would not achieve what he suspected was the perpetrator's purpose—to keep from being linked to the child. They already had the baby's clothes, from which they could certainly get DNA, and the hospital would have taken blood. Unless this was some weird cultural thing that involved a need to have the body? This case was getting stranger by the minute.

"Who called you?" he asked. "And when?"

"Nobody called me. And I take it no one has called you, either. Stan and I were taking Osman to the emergency room—"

"Whoa!" Burgess said. "Slow down. You were doing what?"

"Stan was supposed to call and update you about that. He didn't?"

"He didn't."

Burgess was struggling to tolerate Stan Perry's out-of-control behavior while he got a handle on the cause, but not updating him on a major event in an ongoing death investigation? That was not acceptable.

"Where are you?" he said.

"At the hospital."

"Is Stan with you?"

There was a pause. "He seems to have temporarily disappeared."

"I'm on my way," Burgess said. "Have security cue up their surveillance video. Again."

How many times tonight was he going to have to go back to the hospital? He called Chris, briefly explained the latest development, and then called Stan. After a few rings he got a weary, "Stan Perry."

"And you were going to call me about Osman when?" he snapped. "At a time more convenient for you?"

"Oh, shit," Perry said. "I forgot."

"You forgot? This isn't an invitation to tea, Stan, it's a homicide investigation. I'm on my way over, so fill me in. What happened to Osman?"

"I don't know."

"Stan, you took him to the hospital."

"Right, Joe. Someone tried to bash his head in, but we don't know who or how or why. We couldn't get another translator to come with us to the Imam's place, so we tried to reach Osman. When he didn't answer, we went there by ourselves and you know how that went. But Terry had this feeling, so we got Osman's address and took a ride over there, found him bleeding on the lawn. We scooped him up and brought him over here, and that's when the rest of all hell broke loose."

"Do something for me, will you, Stan? Scoot up to our mystery girl's room and make sure that *she*'s still there? Way too many things are going wrong tonight. I'd really like that not to be another one."

He hesitated, about to hang up, then said, "Call me as soon as you've confirmed that she's still there, okay?"

"Okay."

Perry sounded suitably chastened, but it was past time for them to have a talk. "I forgot" was never an acceptable answer under these circumstances, and Perry wasn't the forgetful type.

Burgess pushed down hard on the accelerator, swooping back across town at an unseemly speed. He felt pressure in his chest, certain the night was going to keep bringing more and more bad news. It happened sometimes—a shitstorm that came on so fast you never had time to put up your umbrella. He wouldn't breathe easily until Perry called and confirmed that their mystery girl was still there.

Losing the baby was bad enough. It would make Portland police and hospital security look like a bunch of bozos, and give the press endless scope for snarky headlines. He had little patience for talking heads shoving their fuzzy mikes at him, especially when he couldn't tell the truth. He wasn't allowed to say that they would have had more security if Cote wasn't such a goddamned ass-wipe about overtime. He wasn't allowed to say much of anything, come to that. Cote or Melia always briefed the press. Burgess never talked to them—his reputation with the press was "grouchy and taciturn"—but they never gave up trying.

If they lost the girl, too, they might as well all resign and go live in rural Alaska, somewhere north of the Arctic Circle, where there weren't many newspapers around and a person could quietly disappear. Losing a victim's body, and a prime witness and second victim, all in a single night, would be a hard thing to live down. Especially when coupled with the drive-by shooting of a Somali related to the Imam of the mosque where the baby died. And a vicious attack on a Somali translator.

He was trying to keep the car on the road, and dial Melia, when his phone rang again.

"Jesus, Joe. Jesus," was all Stan Perry could manage.

Anxiety stabbed him with a pain so visceral it almost took his breath away. "Is she gone, Stan?"

Perry didn't answer.

"Talk to me, Stanley. Talk to me. Is she dead? Is she gone? What's happening?"

"She's not in her room, Joe. I—" He heard a crash, a commotion of voices, Stan Perry yelling, "Hey! He's getting away!"

Burgess dropped the phone and floored it, spinning around the corner and into the Emergency entrance, swinging his car so he was blocking most of it as a dark Honda came accelerating straight at him.

He jumped out, already clawing for his gun, yelling, "Stop! Police!" as he shot out one front tire. The car swerved to go around him and slammed, full tilt, into a cement post.

The two security guards who'd been chasing it dove for the car, hauling the dazed and bleeding passenger out as the driver flew out his door and took off down the street with Kyle and Perry flying after him. Burgess only had a vague impression of a dark uniform before the man disappeared around a corner.

"Pop the trunk! Pop the trunk!" Perry screamed back over

his shoulder as Kyle, who was closer to the running man, was yelling, "Stop! Police!"

"Hang onto him," he told the security guards, who were grappling with the uncooperative passenger, "until I can get these cuffs on." This one was not getting away.

Then Burgess called it in, asking for patrol to take charge of the passenger and to back up Kyle and Perry on their search for the fleeing driver.

It had all the elements of a bad TV cop show. A comedy cop show. In this case, a comedy of errors. A snafu. Fubar. Also very much like their real lives, those nights when one crazy thing after another kept happening, until trying to prioritize became like trying to catch feathers from an exploding pillow. You snatched at things as quickly as you could and they just kept coming.

Even as he hurried to the Explorer to move it so it wouldn't block the hospital entrance, and to grab a pry bar, Burgess's mind filled with a big-screen image of Captain Cote demanding an explanation for tonight's events, the man's liver-colored lips pursed in his expression of perpetual disapproval. Cote was never satisfied with "we don't know yet." He might as well have been a character on a TV show—tonight's episode was called "Black Honda Night"—he wanted it neat and clean and solved in an hour. The captain hated complexity. Anything that didn't fit on a chart or graph or couldn't be quantified was anathema to him.

Depending on how many players turned out to be involved in this mess, they'd be lucky if it was solved in a lifetime. And that was with good, diligent cops on the case.

He jammed in the pry bar and popped the trunk. Inside, along with the usual detritus of a car trunk, was the tiniest body bag he'd ever seen. If he was right, this was their missing baby, but until he was gloved, and had another officer with him, he wasn't touching it. He couldn't leave it, either. Not until patrol got here. Otherwise, the way things were going tonight, it would disappear again. Probably into the trunk of another black Honda.

He could hear the reassuring sounds of sirens in the distance. Help was on the way. But he needed Melia over here as well, someone with rank to coordinate this three-ring circus. He needed to deal with this car and what was in its trunk. He needed to get upstairs and make sure that their mystery girl was still all right. Make sure the cop who was supposed to be watching was watching, and not lying injured or dead on the floor. He needed to get to the morgue and find out what had happened.

Burgess had been a cop for longer than he'd lived before he became one. Cops like to think they've seen it all, but there's always something new. Something crazier or more unimaginable or so purely weird it went on the life list of "most crazy things I've ever seen." Today would be a contender.

He grabbed the first patrol officer who arrived, pointed to the open trunk, and said, "Stay right here. Don't move. Don't touch anything and don't let anyone near this car until I come back."

"What's—" the officer began, then remembered she was talking to Joe Burgess, the meanest cop in Portland. She lowered her eyes. "Yes, sir," she said.

Burgess grabbed the next officer and sent him to help the security guards. "Don't let that man get away. Don't take those cuffs off unless a doctor says it's absolutely necessary. Got that?" He got another nervous nod. Then Burgess headed for their mystery girl's room.

He stabbed the elevator button. Stabbed it again. Sighed for his bad knee, and sprinted for the stairs.

He found a male nurse staring at an empty bed and an overturned chair. "Where is she?" Burgess demanded.

The man turned to him, a puzzled expression on his face. "Who are you?"

"Detective Sergeant Burgess, Portland police. The girl who is supposed to be in this bed is the unidentified victim of a fire this afternoon."

He glared at the overturned chair. "There's supposed to be a police officer with her at all times."

The male nurse shrugged. "I don't know what to tell you, Detective. I just came on—"

"Joe," a woman's voice called. "Joe, we need you."

Burgess and the nurse sprinted toward the voice. A young woman in scrubs was staring into a dark room. She turned, started to say, "There's someone—" then stopped, surprised to find two men answering her call instead of one.

Burgess, being a good detective, deduced that the male nurse's name was Joe. "Where's the light switch?" he said.

The other Joe moved quickly toward it. It illuminated a sprawled figure in a police uniform crumpled on the floor in a corner. Nurse Joe and the woman moved toward him. Burgess spotted a wad of cotton on the floor. Chloroform, he wondered? Not a legal product for consumers, but then, Maine was full of creative chemists able to get their hands on prohibited substances.

He pulled a plastic Baggie from his pocket and collected the wad of cotton as they searched the fallen officer for injuries.

"What's his status?" he asked.

"Unconscious," Nurse Joe said. "But we're not seeing any signs of trauma."

Burgess felt his impatience rising as they bent back over their patient. He wanted to know where their real patient was, the girl who seemed to have disappeared. Over the murmur of their voices, as they consulted, he heard a faint rustling sound, just for a second. Then it stopped.

He stepped past them and opened the door to the bathroom.

She was huddled against the wall of the shower, clutching a blue hospital blanket around her. For the second time that day, he bent down and picked her up and carried her out of a dark room and back down a long hall.

When they were back in her room, he looked down at the girl in his arms. Her eyes were open. She was looking right at him, and he thought that she recognized him. "I'm Joe Burgess," he said. "I'm the cop who took you out of that closet. I'm trying to keep you safe."

He thought he could read understanding. "It would be easier to do that if you would talk to us. Tell us who you are and what is going on."

Her head shifted slightly, just the tiniest sign of acknowledgment, and denial. She was trembling in his arms. He had questions that desperately needed answers, but this was not the time. A nurse he knew slightly came in. "She should be getting oxygen, Joe," she said, and so, reluctantly, he put his mystery girl back on the bed.

He needed to talk to Kyle and Perry. Liaise with security and find out what the hell had gone wrong, here and in the morgue. As soon as the man was conscious, he needed to interview the officer who'd been guarding her and get the story.

It would all have to wait until he was sure he could safely leave the girl. Right now, he couldn't imagine there was any safe place in this hospital. Maybe not even in this city. Bad guys were springing up today like someone had sown the streets with dragon's teeth. He probably needed an army.

For starters, he'd take Andrea Dwyer, their "kiddie" cop. Dwyer was tough, smart, athletic, and very tuned in to the kids she dealt with in Portland. He should have had Dwyer on this case from the beginning. People who would never talk to him gladly talked to Dwyer. She had a knack. And no one was likely to get past her, whatever the failures of the day—and night—suggested about their opposition.

He dug out his phone. He needed Melia over here to co-ordinate this thing. A patrol sergeant. And Dwyer.

Melia sounded sleepy, but CID lieutenants were used to being interrupted. They needed to be adrenaline junkies, because sleep was a luxury.

"Got a few problems over here at the hospital, Vince," he said. "Our dead baby has disappeared and been found again, our translator got beaten, and someone tried to kidnap our mystery girl."

Melia uttered one of his rare expletives. "Bring me up on it." Burgess heard the thud of Melia's feet hitting the floor, Gina Melia's soft voice in the background.

Burgess shared what he knew. "Haven't had a chance to follow up on what happened with that baby, or look at the security video. We've got a car crash at the ER entrance. Stan and Terry are chasing the driver, and security's holding the passenger. They had the baby in the trunk of their car."

"I don't have to tell you this is nuts," Melia said. "I'm on my way."

"We need a patrol sergeant to coordinate security over here. And see if you can find Dwyer. I need someone to babysit this girl. Somebody who isn't going to lose her again."

"I'm on it. See you in ten."

Burgess wanted to add "and don't tell Cote," but that was not how the food chain worked. Each shiny piece of brass had to brief the shinier brass above him.

Burgess looked down at the scared dark eyes. "Just trying to keep you safe," he said.

It bothered him that she didn't have a name. He didn't want to call her sweetheart, or honey, or little girl. She was a mother. She was a victim. She was a terrified child. She was so many of the things he'd spent his life protecting, all in the same trembling bundle. He hadn't done a very good job for her so far.

As the nurse, whose had the sweetly old-fashioned name Susan, bustled around, getting the girl resettled, Burgess saw that one of the girl's hands—the one that didn't have the dark ring of bruises, lay outside the covers. He reached down and took it in his.

Her dark eyes flashed at him. She didn't move her hand away, and for moment, he thought she was going to speak. Then she closed her eyes, the dark lashes settling against her pale cheeks. In a few moments, she was asleep.

"Poor little darlin'," Susan said. "I ever get my hands on the man who made that child a mother, I'll castrate him myself."

Ten minutes later, Andrea Dwyer came in, bandbox neat and fresh as a daisy, all six feet of her. She studied the girl in the bed and then looked at him. "You've got to stop collecting these waifs, Joe."

"They just keep finding me, Andrea." This was what he got for not going straight home. The gods worked in mysterious ways.

After he filled her in, she patted his shoulder. "I've got this now, Joe. Go catch bad guys."

"You stay here, you may catch some yourself. Just don't let 'em catch you."

Dwyer grinned. "I only look like the girl next door, Joe. I'm actually armed and dangerous."

"I know that," he said. "Call me if—"

If what? If anything happened? The girl said anything? A horde of kidnappers swarmed the place? Dwyer knew all that.

Dwyer had a great smile, and she used it on him now. "I will call you, Joe. Trust me. I will."

She gave him a gentle shove. "Go on now. Lieutenant Melia's

down in the lobby tearing his hair out. Kyle's gone all quiet and
scary, giving people that cold gray stare. And Stanley has
become unusually profane. You know," she hesitated, and then
gave Burgess the answer to one of the questions that had been
bugging him all day. "That boy needs to grow up. I've never
seen anyone react so badly to his girlfriend getting pregnant."

CHAPTER NINE

Down in the lobby, Burgess spotted Melia, off in a corner, talking on the phone. He could tell by his lieutenant's body language that he was talking to Cote and didn't appreciate what he was hearing. Kyle was standing by the door, holding a Sea Dogs jacket. He waved it like a bullfighter's cape in Burgess's direction. "This is all we got, Joe. He was a slippery little bugger."

"Where's Stan?"

"He was here. Then patrol thought they'd spotted the guy and he and a couple patrol guys went out looking."

Burgess sighed. "We're not winning any of 'em tonight, are we? Why don't you go find the passenger, the guy security grabbed, see if you can learn anything. And where did you guys leave Osman?"

"Getting stitched up. We told him to stick around, but I'm not betting on it and we didn't have anyone to watch him. We're getting pulled in a whole lot of directions tonight and not a lot of people cooperating with their local constabulary."

Vince Melia put his phone away and came toward them, straightening his tie. Melia didn't go anywhere without a tie, not even in the middle of the night. He came up to them, glanced at Kyle, then at Burgess, like maybe they were hiding a bad guy somewhere. "You get the guy?"

"We got the passenger. Patrol's still looking for the driver." Kyle waved the jacket. "Got his jacket, though."

"Great. Read it its rights and arrest it," Melia said. "What about our guy who was supposed to be watching the girl?"

"Someone knocked him out. Chloroform, maybe? I left him with a couple of nurses. Left Dwyer with the girl. Nobody is getting past her."

"Let's hope not."

Melia was a dapper guy, but tonight he was looking almost as ragged as Burgess felt. Melia got paid the bigger bucks for dealing with the brass, but Burgess wouldn't have traded jobs for anything. He didn't want to explain their actions, supervise their actions, or justify their actions. He wanted to be taking the actions.

"Look, Vince. I popped the trunk on that car out there, and I've got what looks like a body bag in there. Patrol is sitting on it. I guess it's time to see if it is our missing baby, get him back into the morgue, and find out what bozo let someone walk in and walk out with him like that. Then we've got security video to view, and a couple folks to interview."

"We're gonna need more people on this," Melia said, getting out his phone again. "Who do you want?"

"Sage is good, if he can come in. What did Cote want?"

"Was it that obvious?"

"I'm a detective, Vince."

Burgess thought his city was going to hell faster than the cops could pull it back. He didn't like it when the bad guys won, and lately, it seemed like their thin blue line was getting awfully tattered. Guys off fighting a couple of wars. Retiring early. Taking sick leave like there was no tomorrow. A night like this could tie up a lot of manpower, and it wasn't like the drunks in the Old Port, or the homeless, or battling domestic partners, or the desperate who'd do anything for a fix took the night off just 'cuz the cops were busy.

"Kyle, you check out Osman and the passenger. Vince, let's

go take a look in that trunk."

Kyle was already moving toward the doors to the emergency department. Burgess called after him, "Anyone run the plate on that car?"

Kyle turned back. "While I was running through the streets, chasing after bad guys? Of course I did."

He paused a moment, and Burgess started running the possibilities, his first choice being the Imam.

Kyle, who could often read his mind, said, "Wrong. Another weary black Jap car, but this time it's stolen plates. Stolen car."

"Somebody's being awfully thorough. It's like they were prepared for this," Burgess said.

"Or prepared for something."

Kyle tore a page out of his notebook, walked back, and handed it over. "Have fun with this. I'm gonna go talk to injured bad guys and injured translators. Make their miserable days a little worse."

"Miserable nights," Burgess muttered, and led Melia out to the parking lot.

The patrol officer leaning against the car wore a face that was either "jeez, when can I get out of here?" or "I wish it was anyone but Burgess." Officer Melinda Beck didn't like him. He'd gotten two strikes in her book the first time they'd met. Strike one was that he hadn't immediately recognized her as a woman. In his defense, he'd argue that she was a sturdily built woman, and a vest under the uniform made anyone looked sexless. Strike two was when he'd read her the riot act about not adequately protecting a crime scene. Since then, their paths had rarely crossed.

Like Melia, she was looking a little worn and ragged. Probably about to go on a break when she'd gotten the call. Now she'd been here cooling her heels guarding a car trunk while he plugged some other holes in the dike.

When he'd left patrol, Burgess had thought he'd miss the adrenaline of working the streets, but there had been plenty of action in CID. Sometimes more than his aging carcass was up for. Right now it was reminding him that kicking down doors and carrying people out of burning buildings took its toll, while Beck was looking at him like he'd just come from an orgy of coffee and donuts.

"Evening, Lieutenant, Sergeant," she said. "Really hopping around here tonight."

Burgess heard regret that she had had to stand here instead of being part of what was hopping. "Anyone been snooping around the car?" he asked, as he pulled gloves out of his pocket.

"African guy came out of emergency with a bandage on his head, stopped to stare, then took off. Otherwise, no."

"Shortish guy, kind of a round head, white shirt, glasses?" Burgess said. "Walks like he's got an old knee injury?" He could have said "gimpy like me."

"That's the one."

So their translator *had* ignored Kyle's request, and taken off. Guy wants to work for the police department but he's got no loyalty or sense of responsibility, even after the cops had scooped him up and brought him here. Burgess wondered if Osman had headed back home, where he might come in for more of the same, or gone into hiding. There was a story there, for sure. Something he couldn't think about right now.

"Anyone come to pick him up?" Burgess asked.

"Woman in an old beater. Wearing a headscarf. I couldn't see her face. Got the license number, though."

"Good job," Burgess said, and wrote it down.

He looked at Vince. "How do you want to do this?"

"The easy way," Melia said. "Unzip the bag and let's see what we've got."

Inside the bag was a little girl, a toddler, by the look, with a headful of blond curls. Perfect. Beautiful. And dead. They looked at each other and swore. Even their expletives were getting a little ragged.

"Either these guys were driving around with a different dead baby already in their trunk, or they took the wrong one," Melia said.

"But Kyle said someone had taken the baby."

Melia shrugged. "Guess we'd better go look in the morgue. See if they're missing two babies. Or if they didn't check after this one was taken and they just thought it was our baby from the fire. There aren't any more bodies in this trunk, are there? And call Stan and get him back here now. We need to sit down, get up to speed on this thing. All of us."

Burgess wondered if this was just one "thing" or a maze of interconnected things. He asked Beck for her flashlight and examined the rest of the trunk. There was a lot of weird stuff in it, things he'd want their ETs to examine and inventory when they fingerprinted the car, including some small electronics in boxes that still bore price tags. But no more bodies.

He returned her light. "Gonna have to ask you to sit on this a little longer, 'til we can get it towed over to 109. You good with that?"

She stared past him into the darkness. "Just fine, Sarge."

He was sorry she was taking this personally, but policing wasn't a popularity contest at the best of times, and he was in no mood for attitude. If she wanted to end her shift and get out of here, she could call her patrol sergeant and make arrangements. If Beck had been a man, he wouldn't have thought twice about this.

They left her staring into the darkness and headed back inside as Burgess called Stan Perry and told him to come in.

"Jeez, Joe," Perry gasped over the thud of his running feet. "Not now. I think we're really close."

"We need you here, Stan. Patrol can chase the bad guys for a while."

He heard Perry draw a breath, prelude to an argument, and cut it off. "Melia says now, Stanley. He needs to talk to all of us."

Perry barely kept the whine out of his voice as he said, "Yes, sir."

Late nights and crazy cases made their normally dysfunctional family even more so.

They detoured through the emergency department to find Kyle. Found him glaring down at an African-American man in FUBU jeans and a dirty gray hoodie. The man had a bandage on his face and someone was wrapping his wrist with gauze. Kyle was watching the tender ministrations with the expression of someone contemplating dismemberment.

"Lieutenant. Joe. This is Akiba Simba Norton. Age twenty-three. Last known address Lewiston, Maine. We wouldn't even know that much if Mr. Norton hadn't been carrying a wallet. He has thus far shown a marked disinterest in speaking with us."

Kyle bent down over Norton. "According to our records, his last known arrest was last week in Lewiston for knocking down an elderly lady and taking her purse. Lady went to the hospital, Mr. Norton went to jail. Lucky for him, some kind soul posted bail. Mr. Norton is already on probation for a similar offense. He's been informed that he's under arrest for violating the conditions of his release. Never mind the conditions of his probation."

Norton seemed to be engaged in the detailed study of one of his shoes, which were new and expensive.

"Lieutenant Melia, Portland police, Mr. Norton," Melia said. "Can you confirm that you are refusing to speak with us?"

Norton shifted his head and gave Melia a look that was pure

eye-fucking attitude. The whites of his eyes were yellow and bloodshot. He looked like someone coming off a four-day high. Smelled like it, too. "That's right, motherfucker."

"Mr. Norton also has five brand new hundred dollar bills in his wallet," Kyle said. "He seems disinterested in explaining where he got them."

New bills meant fewer people handling them. Which might mean fingerprints.

The young Indian doctor who was bandaging Norton went on as though none of this was happening.

"Doctor," Burgess said, "how soon will Mr. Norton be ready to leave?"

The doctor looked up. "Going to finish this bandage and he's all yours, Officer."

"Sergeant," Burgess said. "Keep an eye on him, Terry. I'll be right back."

He went to tell the patrol sergeant in the lobby that they would need someone to transport Norton to the jail. "They can book on a probation violation and violating bail conditions. Expect there will be more coming. He and his buddy have a dead baby in the trunk of their car."

Sergeant Kenny Munroe grinned. "Never rains but it pours, Joe. I'll get Beck—"

"Beck's still sitting on the car," Burgess said. " 'Til we can deal with *that* baby."

"Oh, right. I'll take care of it." Munroe turned away, talking into his radio.

Stan Perry slouched in, looking like a man who wanted to pick a fight, and headed straight toward him. "Listen, Joe, I—"

Burgess cut him off. "In here," he said, jerking his chin toward the emergency department. "Vince wants to talk to us."

"I was gonna get that guy, Joe." His phone rang and he turned away to answer it.

Burgess went on talking. "And you're the only one who could do it? We need to talk about the dead baby. About an attack on the officer guarding our mystery girl." Every time he said "dead baby" his stomach twisted. He'd long ago learned to keep it off his face, had never been able to get his gut to go along.

They came back through the door in time to see Mr. Akiba Simba Norton grab a pair of scissors off the tray, grab the slight Indian doctor around her neck, and start dragging her backward toward another door. Mr. Norton, it seemed, was not especially grateful for the services he'd just been given. One of the problems with the welfare system, Burgess thought, people given things all their lives without working for them or paying for them didn't value what they'd had.

There he went again—making assumptions about people. He had insufficient facts about Norton on which to base that opinion. Despite the druggie affect and the smell, when he wasn't in jail or knocking down senior citizens, Norton might be a successful broker. A lay preacher. Perhaps a recently returned missionary who had snatched that purse because he had a Robin Hood complex. Steal from the old and give to the young. On the other hand, he had had a taste of Norton's record, and he'd seen this hundreds of times before.

Not doctors getting dragged by the neck around the hospital. That was rarer. But people who were bad to the core acting badly? He'd seen a lifetime of that.

Perry was no longer behind him. Burgess figured he'd slipped back through the door and would come in through another entrance, come down the corridor behind Norton.

He kept walking toward Norton, knowing Kyle was doing the same. They would keep enough distance between them so that Norton could only watch one of them at a time. They wanted him as off balance as possible.

Burgess had a lot of experience controlling his temper, but

sometimes it got away from him. Right now, they had a million important things to deal with regarding an imprisoned child-mother and her poor dead baby. This asshole who'd been paid by someone to come and swipe that baby was not important. He was just wasting their time with his "I'm a dangerous thug" act.

"So, Akiba," he said. "You sure you want to do this? You want to hurt this woman, this doctor who just spent all that time patching you up, right in front of the cops? You do, and you're going away for so long you can kiss your youth goodbye."

He moved steadily forward. "Why don't you drop those scissors, Akiba. Drop them on the floor, let the doctor go, put your hands up, and we'll pretend this never happened."

Norton had a far-away look, like he wasn't at all aware of what he was doing. He'd seemed calm before, but Burgess wondered if he'd taken something to jazz himself up for his mission and now it was bringing on some full-bore paranoia? There was so much stuff on the street from homemade labs it was hard to keep up with what it all did. They were just beginning to see some really dangerous synthetic stuff call "bath salts," crap that seemed to be coming in from China.

Druggies loved it. They didn't even know it made them crazy 'til they found themselves chewing off their mother's face or walking naked and bleeding through Walmart because they needed cheese worms.

Norton was up against the door, pushing backward through it, dragging the terrified woman with him. Suddenly, he shoved her at Burgess, turned, and darted through the door.

Burgess jumped around her as she sprawled to the floor, leaving the more courtly Melia to help her up. Fueled by anger, he dashed after the amazingly fast Norton, dodging gurneys and wheelchairs as he ran. It was like being on the football field again, except that the opposing players were mechanical.

Norton was almost through the second door when Burgess launched himself and knocked the younger man to the floor, Kyle right behind him. Stan Perry, who should have been there to back their play, was nowhere to be seen.

Together, they flipped the man and cuffed him, seeing in the man's stiff-armed resistance a lot of experience with handcuffs. They flipped him onto his back and Burgess rested his foot gently on Norton's stomach. "Next time you decide to screw around in someone's emergency room, pick another city to do it in, okay? They've got real patients here with real emergencies to deal with. Doctors don't need to be wasting their time getting dragged around by a piece of shit like you."

Norton glared up at him, teeth bared like a cornered dog, and uttered a string of filth. Then, with something that looked way too much like a smile, he said, "I'll be out in an hour, and then you had better watch your back. You have no idea who you're dealing with."

CHAPTER TEN

Burgess pressed down on the man's stomach. What he'd like to do was stomp. Break a few ribs, remind the man that threatening cops was a bad idea. Cops had an expression—make me run, you're going to end up hurting. These days, most of that was played out on TV. In the real world, it was the bad guys who had all the rights and the cops who had to walk the straight and narrow. The good old days had too often also been the bad old days, but there were times when he and many of his fellow officers longed to take someone out to a deserted parking lot and do a little shoe reeducation. Someone, occasionally, still did.

Guy like this wasn't going to stop hurting other people until someone put him down like the rogue dog that he was. Harsh? Maybe. Also true. The lapsed Catholic in him might always hope for redemption, but the realist could tell the difference between those who might learn from their mistakes and those who didn't believe they ever made them. He'd seen a quote once to the effect that you could never understand an antagonist until you understood how he was the protagonist of his own story. That was about as true as it got. He worked at understanding their psychology. But when you were faced with someone who'd misspent his entire youth preying on the weak and vulnerable, you didn't cherish much hope that that predator was going to see the light. And Burgess didn't use the word "predator" lightly.

"I had a dollar for every time some hopped-up yo tells me he's connected, I could retire," Kyle said.

He bent down close to Norton's ear. "Listen, Akiba . . . with your record . . . your pending charges, and now the attempted murder of an ER doc who's just put you back together? I don't think anyone has friends powerful enough to bail them out of this. Bail, see, part of the analysis is dangerousness. I think you just established that beyond any doubt."

He rested his foot on the man's stomach next to Burgess's and pressed just enough to make the man squirm. "Don't worry. I'm sure they'll find you a nice cellmate who will appreciate your specialness."

Burgess saw a tremble in Kyle's leg. Kyle, whose cool he could always rely on, wanted to stomp the man as much as he did.

Their last two big cases had taken so much out of them he'd labeled them "the Crips." There had been some quiet months since then. Quiet in the sense that while there had been plenty of their usual ration of ugly crime, there hadn't been any cases that kept them running on empty for days at a time. Kyle had had time to spend with Michelle and his girls. Stan Perry had seemed to be getting his restless womanizing under control. But a tough New England winter could take a lot out of you. Driving in snow and ice, standing in the cold, crawling through people's nasty apartments, cold apartments, working crime scenes in garbage-strewn alleys. Seeing how people neglected their kids to pleasure themselves. It took a toll.

Today's mild spring day had been a breath of hope, and it had ended with this. Except he thought it was probably tomorrow by now.

"Kenny Munroe's supposed to be getting someone to transport this guy. Let's hand him over and then go talk to Vince. If we're lucky, Vince will already have taken a statement from the doctor."

He looked up and down the empty hall. "I wonder what happened to Stan?"

Kyle made a show of looking, too. "He didn't exactly have our backs on this one, did he? I'm starting to worry about young Stanley again."

Stan Perry was a good instinctive detective with two persistent problems: an occasional lack of impulse control that often brought great results but equally often caused Burgess and Kyle infinite grief, and a weakness for the wrong kind of women.

Norton flopped around, trying to shake them off, and Burgess increased the pressure with his foot. "Stay still," he said.

Norton responded by attempting to flip them off.

"I said stay still," Burgess repeated.

"You guys better not have families," Norton said, "because if you do, when I get out, I am really gonna fuck them up. And if I don't get out? I got friends."

Burgess took his foot off the man, reached down, and hauled Norton to his feet, slamming him hard up against a wall. "If you, or any of your scumbag friends, ever comes near a cop's family—you, or they, can expect a body bag in their future."

He pulled Norton away from the wall and slammed him back again. "I mean it, Norton. Don't even think about it."

There was something feral about the man that made Burgess's skin crawl. Bad guys were bad. That went with the territory. But sometimes they were hollow inside. Cold, empty vessels where compassion, empathy, or any normal emotions were absent. He thought Norton was one of those. It took someone awfully cold to stomp fragile old ladies and steal dead babies.

"Let's go find Kenny, Ter. I've had enough of Mr. Norton's company."

They pulled Norton away from the wall, each took an arm, and started walking him back to the lobby.

"Joe?" Kyle said.

Something in his voice made Burgess pause. Their eyes met, and Burgess read what Kyle wouldn't say. Kyle was thinking that if this guy did get out, they were going to have to watch their backs, and their families. That threats to their families were completely unacceptable and that if it became necessary, the Norton problem would need to be resolved without the benefit of any due process. Though Burgess thought if it came to that Norton would be getting exactly the due process he was entitled to.

The bad guys seemed to be getting increasingly savage, and that savagery was having an effect on the good guys. Kyle was his conscience. It was Kyle who sometimes had to remind him that they were about catching bad guys. That the court system was about justice and Burgess shouldn't start thinking about playing God. But when it came to their families—as Burgess was learning—cops drew a line in the sand and protected it with everything they had. Cops might hurt their own families, but no one else better try it. It was the families that kept them sane and balanced, the ones who managed to hold their families together. He had always known it was hard. Now Burgess came face to face with it every day.

They passed through an emergency room that fell silent around them. There was no sign of the Indian doctor.

Melia was in the lobby with Kenny Munroe and Munroe had two big patrol officers waiting to take the prisoner to jail. Burgess briefed them quickly on the situation. "And you tell them that even if God and the governor show up wanting to post bail, this man is not to be let out."

Once they'd led Norton out to the waiting cruiser, he also made a call over to the jail and reiterated his concerns. He got them to promise they'd let him know if anyone showed up looking for Norton. They'd lost Kimani Yates without noticing, so his faith wasn't strong, but it was the best he could do.

"Where's Stan?" Melia said.

Burgess shrugged. "I thought he must be with you. He was right behind me in the ER. When he disappeared, I figured he was going to circle around to get ahead of the guy."

"Gotta get him under control, Joe. He's becoming a liability."

Another time, Burgess might have defended his detective. But Stan had gone off the reservation one time too many. At least, thanks to Andrea, he had an idea what the problem was.

"Let's go to the morgue. Figure out what that story is. Whether they've still got our baby, and if they're missing another child."

The three of them trooped to the elevator and took it down to the morgue.

Burgess needed a cup of coffee. He'd almost suggested they get some and bring it along. But while cops can eat and drink under pretty awful circumstances, higher up the food chain they were concerned with the department's public image. Walking into the morgue to talk about a dead baby clutching their take-away coffee set the wrong tone.

An hour later, they'd found their dead baby and confirmed that the one in the trunk of the car was a second child who was missing from the morgue. They'd spoken sharply with the morgue attendant who had released the baby without any paperwork or identification. They'd returned the stolen baby to the morgue and left someone guarding the baby killed by the fire until he could be transported to the medical examiner's office in the morning. Seemed like half of patrol was tied up here at the hospital tonight.

Now they did have coffee and were stuffed into the security office, watching surveillance tapes. What they were watching explained some things and pissed them all off. A man in what looked, to the uninitiated, like a Portland police uniform, walking into the hospital, consulting the information desk, and heading down to the basement. It made the morgue attendant's defensive statement, "Hey, I thought he was a cop and it was okay," more understandable. And amped up their sense that they were dealing with someone—or ones—who were both clever and devious.

But almost eight hours in, they still had no idea what this was about. They had no ID on the girl or the baby. No idea what her connection to the mosque was or who might have locked her in that closet. Not the who or the why. They had an Imam who claimed to know nothing, and a man who denied being at the scene when he had been. They had no idea why the fire had been set. Not even confirmation, as yet, that it *had* been set. Nor a reason why it had been, despite the anti-Muslim graffiti and the presence of some guys on motorcycles at the scene.

They had a translator who appeared to have an antagonistic relationship with the Imam and his people, a man who had later been attacked himself and had then run away. And they had the man who had earlier in the evening tried to snatch their mystery girl from her room who was a known criminal but who was not Muslim. What was his connection to this? And how were the two men who had tried to steal the baby involved?

Rocky Jordan had been right. They were going to have to make charts just to keep track.

His instinct said that this would be a case of overlapping circles, where some things were connected and some were not. But he was frustrated that they had so few facts to work with.

At least the surveillance video had given them a good, if grainy, look at the driver's face. A big white male in his early forties, a strong man with broad shoulders, well-trimmed facial hair that would probably disappear by morning if patrol didn't scoop him up, and a strange scoop to his walk, like his back was bad or he favored one leg. If it was his leg, it hadn't stopped him from running plenty fast when he bailed out of that car. He'd run like a man who couldn't risk getting caught. But if that was the case, why take on a job like this? Because he needed money? Because he was more scared of whoever hired him than of the police?

With luck, they'd grab his prints from the car and get an ID. Burgess wasn't optimistic that they'd get anything from Norton.

"Hold on," Kyle said. "Can we see that again?"

They reran the video.

"Those whiskers aren't real," Kyle said. "This is someone who thought it was important to get the girl and the baby, and went to a whole lot of trouble with the car, and the plates, trying not to be recognized. Careful, but not careful enough. Take a look at his watch. And his ring. Your run-of-the-mill bad guy usually doesn't have the money for accessories like that."

They all leaned in. Burgess didn't know much about fancy watches. His rule was they had to be reliable, sturdy, and easy to read. He didn't have time to learn a lot of fancy gadgets. But this one, peeping out beneath the sleeve of the faked uniform, looked like it could have been used to fly a commercial jet.

"We better take this video back to Rocky. See if he can get us some close-ups of the watch and the ring. That ring might tell us a whole lot."

Kyle's grin was wolfish. There was nothing cops appreciated more than stupid bad guys, especially when those guys were trying to be so smart.

They looked at the rest of the videos, but there wasn't anything else that was useful. "Time for everyone to get some sleep," Melia said. "Let's all meet again at eight."

"Hold on, Vince," Burgess said. "You were going to tell about Cote's press conference."

A pained look crossed the lieutenant's face. "He tried to give away the farm. Without talking to us. Said it was a set fire, anti-Muslim, and that a girl and a baby had been found locked inside, the girl survived and the baby died."

"Based on what?" Burgess said. "We don't have anything back about the fire."

They tried hard to keep facts they didn't want blabbed to the public away from Cote's eye. But the man fancied himself a keen detective and brilliant public speaker, and sometimes he got away from them. At least he didn't have any more facts he could blab to the press. But that was because all Melia and his detectives had was a growing pile of conundrums, and very few answers. Cote thought answers grew on trees.

"Sorry, Vince," Burgess said.

"Not as sorry as I am. See you in the morning."

Burgess had a couple things he still had to do before he went home. He had to stop by the fire scene and take some pictures. And if the investigators were still there, he hoped he could find out if they thought the fire *had* been set. Then he'd go to bed.

Slowly, moving like old men and not detectives in their prime, they rose from their chairs and headed out to their cars.

Stan Perry had never returned.

Chapter Eleven

Before he left the lobby, he glanced out at the parking lot. The car was being loaded onto a tow truck, Melinda Beck watching, impatience in every line of her body. He went upstairs to see how Dwyer and his mystery girl were doing. The girl was curled on her side, deeply asleep. Dwyer was in a chair doing a Sudoku puzzle. She smiled at him, stood, and stretched. "Watch her a minute, Joe?"

"Sure."

Dwyer ducked into the bathroom and he sat down in the chair. He looked at the puzzle she'd been working and shook his head. His son Dylan did Sudoku. He'd tried a few times, but he didn't get it. Dylan thought that meant he was beyond simple. Learning to get along with a kid when you didn't have a lifetime of experience was a constant challenge. Some days he wanted to throw up his hands and send the boy back. But Dylan's mother was dead. The old girlfriend who had left town rather than tell him she was pregnant. A few months ago, he'd gotten a letter telling him about Dylan, with a scrawled note on the bottom saying that the woman was dead.

He'd seen enough of how family tragedy could screw kids up. He couldn't do that to his son. It just made his own hard life harder. His girlfriend, Chris, had been extremely supportive. But her agenda included wanting kids—the two foster children they'd met through an earlier case—while his did not. What was that thing they said—life is what happens while you're making other plans? He just wished his son would try a little harder. Meet him halfway sometimes. He probably wasn't the first parent to think this.

The girl on the bed stirred. Her eyes opened. She saw him, and there was recognition there. One small hand came out from under the blanket. He crossed to the bed, and took it. She made a small sound and closed her eyes.

He watched her, wishing their hands could transmit the information she otherwise wouldn't share. If they could communicate without speaking, the way he and Kyle did. He wished he could "fix it" but there were so many things that needed to be fixed for this child, he wouldn't know where to begin. Chris, his optimist, would say "with one thing at a time." His job required patience, something he was well-schooled in, but by nature he wanted to bull his way through things, make people tell the truth, act decently, stop lying or hiding or pretending they had no responsibility for anyone but themselves. It was a constant battle.

Tonight, he had wanted so badly to pound the crap out of Norton.

He squeezed her hand gently. "We won't let anyone hurt you," he said. "We're going to keep you safe."

What he said. And what he hoped was true. But sometimes things just got so screwed up.

He looked up and saw Andrea Dwyer watching him. "It's a screwed-up world," she said. "I thought Melia wasn't going to give you any more kids?"

"No one gave me this kid. I was just sitting in my car, enjoying a quiet spring evening, when a boy banged on my car window and said there was a fire. What was I supposed to do? Just drive away because it might get complicated?"

"People do."

Dwyer arranged her gorgeous, long-limbed body in the chair

again. "If I were a betting woman, I'd bet that PFD read you the riot act for going into that building."

"You'd win that one," he said. "I guess it's a character flaw. I take an oath to serve and protect, and when someone is screaming inside a burning building, I feel like I've got to go and do that."

Her eyes shifted to the girl in the bed. "I'd like to castrate the bastard who did this to her."

"Bastards plural," he said. "This one looks very complicated. And you'll have to get in line. Lotta people already volunteering for that job."

Dwyer shook her head. "I'm the kiddie cop, Joe. That gives me first dibs. You go find 'em. I'll be sharpening my knife."

Lot of female officers might have resented being labeled "kiddie cop." Dwyer embraced it.

"You know a kid named Jason Stetson? Spindly towhead, maybe fourteen now? Lives over near the fire scene?" Burgess said. "He's the one who came and got me. After that all hell broke loose, so I didn't get a chance to get back and talk to him. But he's always around, and kids like that, they can be pretty invisible, so they see things."

"You want me to talk to him?"

"Got any kind of a relationship with him?"

"Pretty good one," she said, "and I know the foster parents. They're good people."

"If I don't find him first, I might need you to talk to him."

He needed to go. Didn't want to let go of his mystery girl's hand. Dwyer saw that. "I'll take care of her, Joe. I promise. And if I get to Jason before you do, I'll talk to him."

"Thanks," he said. "I wish—"

But he wished for so much, and wishing wouldn't make it so. Not in the cop's world. Putting your shoulder to the boulder and pushing, that got results. Instead, he asked, "I may need a window into the Somali community. You know any Somali kids? Any who might talk to you?"

"Kids?" she shrugged. "I'll have to think about that, Joe. I've got a couple concerned mothers I interact with pretty regularly. You give me some names, I can see if they know anything."

"I'll do that. Go through my notes tomorrow and give you the names." He was too tired to do it now. He needed to grab some sleep before it was time to get up again.

"I'm around tomorrow," she said. "And you've got my number."

"I think I do."

"I've got yours, too," she said. "Get some sleep."

Reluctantly, he pulled his hand away and headed for the elevator. He should have taken the stairs, but he was too out of gas for that.

The night wasn't that cold, but so many hours in and his head full of questions, the chill could get to him. He turned the heat on high and headed back to the fire scene. He hoped no one would be there and he could take his pictures, get back in the truck, and head home.

Hoping. Wishing. It only came true in love songs and Disney movies. At least the guy from the fire marshal's office was one of them. A cop. Someone who'd talk to him without playing games.

He parked and walked over to where Davey Green and Scott Lavigne stood talking, and held out his hand.

"Davey. Scott. It's good to see some friendly faces. First time tonight."

Green nodded. "This one's gonna be a ball-buster, Joe. Fast as we can develop techniques for spotting how a fire was set, the bad guys develop newer techniques to fool us."

"But the fire *was* set?"

"It was," Lavigne said. "Unusual accelerant, though. Davey's going to take it back to the lab and see what he can figure out. Done with a timer, too, so it would happen after everyone left for the day."

"Except the ones who couldn't get out," Burgess said.

"What's the story on that, Joe?" Green asked.

Burgess shared the little he knew. "So far, the girl is not talking. I mean not a word. They're getting a psych consult tomorrow. See if that helps. She's just a child."

"A child with a child," Lavigne said. "Someone out there has something to answer for." He looked over at the smoking hulk of the building. "Some things to answer for."

"I've got nothing to base this on," Burgess said. "People we've talked to so far are totally know-nothings. But I suspect whoever burned this building may be different from whoever locked that girl and her baby in that closet."

"Keep me in the loop, Joe," Green said. It was just as valuable on his side to have a good relationship with someone inside the investigation. Public safety organizations were notoriously territorial. It helped to have a personal connection.

"You know I will. And you've got Scotty." He hesitated. "And PFD."

The rivalry between police and fire was a long-standing one, with each side convinced that the other did little to nothing. They'd worked together, side by side, hundreds of times, but when the event was over and they returned to their respective stations, it seemed like memory failed.

It was years in the past now, but Burgess still remembered after 9/11, and during the anthrax scare, Portland cops having to handle dangerous situations because the firefighters wouldn't. Partly it was just culture. Firefighters liked to wait until their equipment was assembled and a game plan was designed. That was their training. Their Standard Operating Procedure. Cops often just had to go and do stuff. Get a bus and evacuate a building. Open suspicious letters. Rescue screaming people from burning buildings.

"You hear that a couple lowlifes tried to steal the baby's body from the morgue?" he said.

That got their attention.

"We stopped 'em in the hospital parking lot. One ran away, the other is sitting over at the jail, lawyered up. One of them was dressed like a cop. Well, sorta like a cop. That's how he was able to get the baby. Of course, he got the *wrong* baby. And earlier tonight, someone else tried to kidnap our mystery girl. Things been hopping over there tonight."

He looked over at what was left of the building. "I wonder if there's anything left of that closet that might give us some clues?"

The other men shrugged. "You never know, Joe."

"I was only in the room for a few seconds, but it was full of computer equipment. New computer equipment. And it was the only door that was locked." He described where the closet had been. For all he knew, there would be piles of melted plastic or boxes with Apple logos somewhere in the wreckage.

"We've got people sitting on it," Lavigne said. "No one will be messing with it overnight."

Burgess hoped that was right, but the way today had gone, he didn't feel very confident.

"Just gotta take a few photos," he said. "See you both tomorrow. And I'd appreciate hearing what you learn about that accelerant."

His living room was lined with his crime scene photos. Stark black and white pictures of the scenes after the victim had been taken away and the public safety personnel had gone home. To Burgess, they represented the questions that needed to be answered, the blanks that had to be filled in. He might need to come back in daylight, get some clearer photos. For now, he circled the smoking wreckage, taking pictures he imagined were going to look like one of the circles of hell.

When he was done, he climbed in the truck and headed home. Where he'd been heading so many hours ago, before Jason had banged on his door.

He'd like to think that if he'd gone home instead of taking a few more minutes for peace and quiet, this might have been someone else's mess. More likely, it just would have been a mess that came to him later. A mess with two deaths instead of one.

If he hadn't been there, his mystery girl wouldn't have had a chance. And what he didn't know was whether, having lost her baby, she would want that chance. Whether there was someone out there loving her and missing her and hoping she would come home, or whether she'd been in this mess because the people who were supposed to care for her and be responsible were lost in drink or drugs or mental illness, and hadn't really noticed she was missing. Or hadn't cared.

He sighed, thinking of home. At least it would be quiet there. The kids asleep. He could curl up next to Chris, and for a few hours, at least, the world would be a good place to be.

CHAPTER TWELVE

He slipped off his shoes outside the door, and crossed the dark, silent kitchen in stocking feet. There was a bottle of milk on the counter, the lid off, just waiting to go bad. That would be Dylan. It was one of his signature moves. In his former life, there had been some discipline, but the boy had also been indulged, perhaps in compensation for his rocky relationship with his stepfather. Burgess thought about his own mother, cleaning other people's houses, then coming home and caring for her own home and children. She would have been scandalized if any of her children had left the milk out to spoil. They were lucky to have milk and they all knew it. He supposed if he said that to his son, the boy would think he was just an old fart.

More than once his son had called him a dinosaur. Not, perhaps, the best way to bridge a gap of fifteen years. There was no easy way to do that. Burgess had adopted the tortoise model—slow and steady wins the race. Not that it was a race, or that there had to be a winner. It was a shared life, and there had to be two winners. It was just so easy to take refuge in work and be "too busy" to come home.

Terry Kyle was a role model for this. Kyle, whose ex-wife had dragged him over burning coals for years, while he had held onto his temper and kept his children safe and loved. None of it came without a struggle. But as his mother would have said, "Whoever told you it was supposed to be easy?"

There was a plate on the kitchen table, covered in plastic

wrap, with a note: *Nina is afraid you'll starve, so we've left you a sandwich.*

Nina could be such a little mother. Burgess found it sweet when she tried to mother him, sweet and disconcerting. Parents were supposed to look after children, not the other way around. Another one of the many crazy ways that their blended household was coming together. It was better than being afraid of him, which Nina had also been. He worried about Nina. At fourteen, she'd been through a lifetime of trauma, beginning with watching her father kill her mother. A lifetime of adults trying to blame her for their bad acts and of trying to look after her little brother, Neddy.

Miraculously, Neddy seemed to be doing all right. He had a naturally sunny disposition and genuine optimism. Even Dylan, who wore his cynicism and adolescent cool like armor, couldn't hold out for long when Neddy wanted to play catch, or play a game. Maybe it made up for some of the void created by moving away from his two younger siblings. He just wished Dylan and Nina would reach some kind of a truce. Their social worker said it was normal. They were jockeying for position and competing for love and attention. And who could argue with that?

Well, there were those in Portland who'd tell you Joe Burgess could argue with anything. If those who found themselves on the food chain below him had given him the label "meanest cop in Portland," those who were above him often claimed they wished he'd just shut up and follow orders. They might have labeled him "most obstructive cop in Portland," but he could cite decades of cases that would have gotten screwed up by following directives from above. Not the least of which was the death of his old high school friend, Reggie. His boss's boss, Captain Cote of the famously loose lips, had immediately judged Reggie's death an accidental drowning and told Burgess not to waste any resources on it.

Typically, Burgess hadn't listened—Cote's order had, after all, asked him not to follow protocol in an unattended death—and he and his team had brought that case to a successful resolution. Despite the number of times Stan Perry screwed up. Which led his thoughts back to tonight, and Perry's disappearance, ignoring Melia's direct order to come in. The kid must have a death wish, at least for his career. Melia cut Burgess and his team some slack because they got results. But he didn't look kindly on insubordination. Especially with Captain Cote looking over *his* shoulder and implying that he couldn't control his troops.

Burgess poured milk into a glass and then put the bottle away. Sat at the table and ate the sandwich. He wasn't hungry, but there were certain things he needed to do to keep the women in his household happy. One of them was eat food if they put it out for him.

He stripped off his smoke-scented clothes, showered, and climbed into bed. Chris was wearing that little blue thing that was more of an enticement than a garment. Being no fool, he let himself be enticed.

Later, when they were curled up together on the cusp of sleep, he said, "I'm sorry about today. About not being here to back you up."

"We've all got to learn how to do this, Joe. I have to learn to handle their squabbles without calling in the big guns."

"I'm the big gun?"

"What do you think, Detective?"

"I think I'm an awfully lucky man."

"We will get through this, won't we?" she said, working her head in between his neck and his shoulder. He could feel her breath on his throat.

"I think we will.

"What does Doro say?" Doro was Chris's mother. She covered the home front when he and Chris couldn't be there.

"That we're nuts, but she understands. She pretty much says exactly what you'd think she'd say. Firm discipline, a united front, and patience. She says that Nina's therapist seems to be doing her good and that maybe Dylan needs one, too."

"She might be right. I just keep hoping—"

"Give it a little more time," she said. "He likes the school. He's making friends." Her head burrowed deeper into that hollow. "It's just around here that he's a problem."

"Maybe because we're the only safe place."

"We try," she said. "Go to sleep. You've only got a few hours and we both know long before it's necessary, Cote will be on the phone complaining that he doesn't have your reports yet."

That was one of life's certainties.

"Okay," he said.

They arranged themselves like spoons, and almost immediately he could tell from her breathing that she was asleep. He wanted to sleep. His body felt beaten up and he knew he needed rest, but his mind wasn't with the program. Too many years of assessing information and triaging clues. He couldn't turn it off at will, and anyway, experience had taught him that letting the thoughts run was a great way to get insight into a case.

Not that he had enough information yet to gain many insights, but sometimes just letting his thoughts run would rearrange them in ways that would let him see a pattern, or patterns, or at least get a clearer idea of what the next set of questions to be answered should be.

By the time he finally fell asleep, with only about four hours left before it would be time to start another day, he had a list in his head for the morning meeting.

★　★　★　★　★

As Chris had predicted, the phone rang bright and early. Before he could drag himself from sleep or untangle his aching arm from the covers, someone else had answered. Through the half-open bedroom door, he heard Nina's sweet, girlish voice answering. Then, very calmly, "I'm sorry, sir, but he's sleeping. Can I take a message?"

He pictured Cote's face. The man was a natural bully, but would he use that on someone who was obviously a young girl? He got his answer pretty quickly, convincing him, once again, that Nina might have a great future in politics

"Oh, dear," she said, just as sweet as pie. "Well, I will absolutely tell him that if I'm still here when he gets up. Maybe I should write that down, in case I've left for school. Let me just get some paper."

There was a rustling, and then Nina's voice again. "Let me see if I've got this right, sir. Sergeant Burgess is to get his lazy ass out of bed and get down there ASAP, because you need to see his supports?"

Burgess could have hugged her for the "sir," an honorific the man's behavior did not deserve. And for the word "supports." Cote hounded them like a demented sheepdog for reports that he gathered in a file and rarely bothered to read. The man hoarded paperwork the way Midas had hoarded gold.

"Oh. Sorry. Reports," Nina said. "All right. I've got it. I'll leave it here on the table so he sees it first thing. What?"

Burgess listened as Nina listened, imagining that Cote would be insisting she wake him. He wondered what she would say.

"Sir." This time her voice was sharper. "My dad didn't get in until almost two a.m. I certainly am *not* going to wake him up. I'll see that he gets your message. Now, please excuse me, I've got to get ready for school." And she hung up on whatever order Cote was barking.

119

My dad. God. He was so badly qualified to be anyone's dad, yet the term felt like she'd bestowed an honor on him. The solitary man, Portland's meanest cop, now lived in a household full of children. Sometimes he had to blink and shake his head to see if it was real.

Chris came in, carrying a cup of coffee. "Morning, sleepy head," she said. "I think we've got us a new anti-Cote device."

"She was brilliant."

"Pretty proud of herself," Chris said. "I guess she hasn't missed the myriad times I've cursed the man."

"Kids, you know," he said. "They hear everything."

She clutched her blue robe with one hand, like a very proper matron. "Not everything, I hope."

"Everything," he said.

She looked surprised. "Well, damn!" she said, and sat down on the edge of the bed. "You need more sleep."

"I do," he agreed, "but I've got people to see and asses to kick."

"I don't suppose you've got time to drive Dylan to school?"

He squinted at the clock. It was a little after seven, and Melia had called their meeting for eight. "I can make time."

She gave him that smile that was like the sun suddenly appearing from behind a cloud. The smile that lit rooms. That lit him. If they hadn't had a house full of kids and he hadn't had a room full of cops waiting for him, he would have had her out of that blue robe and back in the bed in a nanosecond.

But this was their new reality.

He threw back the covers and gulped his coffee as she dropped a stack of clothes beside him. "Rise and shine," she said.

"I don't know about shine, but around you, rise is a given."

She swatted him. "Don't be vulgar."

"Honest," he said, reaching for his clothes. "Tell Dylan to be ready in ten."

"I think we need a date night," she said, and left, closing the door behind her.

Dylan was slouched against the kitchen counter, backpack slung over one shoulder, a poster boy for teenage attitude. "Hey, Dad," he said, when Burgess came in. "Can we go now?"

"You can go down to the truck," he said. "I'll be down in a minute." He tossed Dylan the keys. Gad. Soon his son would be driving.

He dropped a kiss on Nina's bright head. "Great work with Captain Cote, kid," he said. "You're a natural."

She looked up from her cereal and grinned. "At what?"

"Managing difficult people. I see a bright future ahead."

"Oh, right. I can run a call center, maybe, or . . ." The grin grew impish. "Maybe work the front desk down at 109?"

"A natural," he repeated. "Where's Neddy?"

"He doesn't have to be at school until eight thirty, remember?" Her voice rose slightly on "remember," like she mostly thought he was okay but sometimes had to wonder if Burgess was secretly an idiot. "He's still asleep."

The kids all went to different schools, which made getting out the door in the morning such a hassle. Nina and Neddy could walk, but since they left at different times, someone had to walk Neddy to school. Chris wasn't about to let him go by himself. Not when he was only eight. Not when she knew the streets were full of predators and sex offenders and creeps and careless drivers. Usually her mother, Doro, came over to do that so Chris could get to work on time.

"My bad," he said, and instantly regretted it. It was one of those expressions he hated, that the kids used all the time. It felt more like a way of blowing off responsibility than accepting it. He would have to watch himself.

"See you tonight," he said. "Hope you have a good day."

Suddenly his little Nina was all serious. "Hope you do, too." A pause. A grin. Then, "Dad."

He hurried down the Explorer, where Dylan had the keys in the ignition and the radio on. The whole car was booming.

"Trying to wake the whole neighborhood?" he said.

"They need to hear this."

Maybe his hearing was going, but Burgess found it increasingly hard to pick out the words to the songs the kids listened to. It was often just a droning blur to him.

"Translate for me," he said.

Dylan told him the words.

"What do we know about this group?"

Dylan told him that, too.

"They're awfully young to be so angry and disillusioned," Burgess said. Though he'd seen plenty of kids on the street who had much to be angry about. He thought of his mystery girl. He'd bet her story gave her a lot to be angry about. And disillusioned.

"So what is it about this music that appeals to you? Why should people listen to it?"

Dylan shifted, and Burgess expected his son was going to do his usual shut-down thing. He approached his own son with caution and an awareness of how easy it was for things to go wrong. Conversing was like crossing a rushing river on slippery, unstable rocks. One misstep could plunge him into icy coldness. But today, Dylan didn't shut down.

"Adolescence is confusing, Dad," he said. "We feel . . . I feel like this speaks to me, that's all."

Dylan reached for the dial and turned the music down. "Tell me about your case. The one that happened yesterday. The fire. And that girl."

It was the first time Dylan had shown an interest in what he did. Burgess considered what he could tell his son about a case where they were keeping most things from the press and the public. He decided to take a chance.

"A lot of what happens in our cases, for investigative reasons, we don't share with the public, so some of what I'm going to tell you has to stay just between us, okay?"

Maybe he imagined it, but he thought Dylan sat up straighter, pleased to be trusted with a confidence.

"My mom was a lawyer, and my stepdad was a judge. I'm kind of used to that."

Burgess told him about sitting in the truck. About Jason coming and banging on the door, urgently summoning him to a fire, and to help someone who was trapped inside.

"Isn't that a job for the fire department?" Dylan asked.

"It would be, if they were there," Burgess agreed, "but they hadn't gotten there yet, and there wasn't any time to waste. The fire was moving fast."

"Weren't you scared?"

There were so many answers to that question. Only a fool wasn't scared in a situation like that, but cops didn't get to sit around and assess whether they were too scared to act. They were trained to act. So that's what he told Dylan. "But I've been scared plenty of times in my life. Sometimes, when it's over, I'll start shaking and it won't stop for hours. I guess you'd say we've got these . . . we call 'em 'lockboxes' . . . in our heads, and we put the bad stuff there and shut the door. Otherwise, we couldn't do the job."

His son seemed really interested. "What's the scariest thing that ever happened to you?" he asked.

But they had arrived at school. Burgess didn't want the conversation to end, and he sensed Dylan didn't either.

"I'll tell you tonight," he said. "If work doesn't keep me away."

"Could you take me with you sometime? Just let me ride

along and watch what you do?"

They did it for citizens all the time. Mostly patrol, though, not CID. But why not? There was something about riding in the car that made talking easier. Who knew what might happen if Dylan got to actually watch what he did?

"You'd probably be bored out of your mind, you know. A lot of what we do is watching and waiting. But sure, you can come along with me some time. I'd like that."

"Me, too." Dylan reached for his backpack, then hesitated. "The mystery girl. She's about my age? And you don't know her name?"

"That's right."

"Well, if you had a picture of her, I could ask around."

It was something he ordinarily wouldn't have done. But if they didn't get an ID on her pretty soon, they'd likely be releasing her picture to the media anyway, so why not? He reached behind the seat, grabbed his briefcase, and gave the girl's photo to Dylan. "Be discreet, okay? This isn't something to pass out in the cafeteria."

"I know that." Dylan gave one of his rarer-than-rare smiles, grabbed his backpack, and walked away.

CHAPTER THIRTEEN

No one in the conference room was at his perky best, despite the DD sandwiches and coffee that Kyle had brought. It took time for coffee to work. But it was food, and they all followed the detective's rule: eat when you can. The uncertainty of their lives and schedules had taught them that. Skip an opportunity, and it might be many hours before you got another.

Melia was looking older, and pinched with worry, and Burgess figured that he'd had a call from the captain, complaining about the lack of reports and about Burgess's unresponsiveness. Burgess was sorry for his boss, but not sorry that Nina had run interference. Among other things, because it had been so good for her self-esteem.

Self-esteem. Back when he'd been in school, no one had cared about that. Humility, maybe. This was New England, after all. He'd grown up with a healthy combination of Catholic guilt and Puritan severity. Funny how that was not what he wanted for his kid. Jeez. His kids. As someone had recently remarked about him, "old Burgess was getting soft."

He shoved thoughts about his family in the lockbox and looked around the table.

Stan Perry was slumped in his chair, wearing yesterday's clothes and badly in need of a shave. On his face and on his shaven head, which was sporting blond fuzz like a baby's head. Not the look they wanted to project to the public. He hoped the captain wouldn't decide to grace their meeting with his presence.

Preston Devlin, Wink's younger brother, was there to represent the gang squad. While Wink was dark, quick-witted, and cynical, Press was a brawny redhead with a sunny disposition. No one, seeing them together, would have taken them for brothers. Until you knew their work ethic. It was hard to get either Devlin brother to stop working, leave 109, and go home. Press, whose nickname was Full Court Press because of his relentless attack on anything assigned to him, was thumbing through a stack of photographs—Rudy Carr's stills, Burgess thought—and he had a sheaf of papers in front of him. Unlike the rest of them, he looked rested and eager.

Melia hadn't said anything, which meant he wanted Burgess to run the meeting. Unless he had an agenda of his own, that was usually his way. Sit back and let his detectives have free rein, until they needed something from him or the brass had been gnawing on him in a particularly hard way.

Deciding to save Perry for last, he began to run his list. He figured he'd start with Devlin. "Press, just to bring you up to speed. When we interviewed the Imam last night, Muhamud Ibrahim, he said that they—the Muslims associated with that mosque—had been the target of harassment by what they termed 'motorcycle guys.' We don't know how serious that harassment was, but it's something to look into. Especially given that there was anti-Muslim graffiti on the building and we know that the fire was arson."

There was a murmur around the table. This was the first time they'd heard their suspicions about arson confirmed.

"The quality isn't good, but we can see two men on motorcycles in Rudy's video. Think you can do anything with that?"

"Already did, Sarge." Devlin's smile was the happy one of a

kid in a candy shop. He passed around copies of two photos. As the detectives bent over them, he explained. "I looked at the video, then checked our files. That first one is our surveillance photo of one of the motorcycles in Rudy's video. You can see that front end is customized with all that fancy chrome. It belongs to an Iron Angel named William Flaherty, known as 'Butcher' or 'Butch.' A real bad actor. Old-school knives-and-chains type. He likes to leave his victims alive, but barely. If they aren't scarred and maimed, the Butcher hasn't done his job."

He held up the second picture. "This is our boy. Not someone you'd want to bring home to mama, is he?"

Burgess was a big man, but Butcher Flaherty made him look like a midget. Flaherty was built like a human wall. Square from his shoulders to his thighs and a lot of cows had died to make a leather jacket big enough to cover him. He had Nazi swastikas tattooed on his throat and three black teardrops under one eye. The other eye was covered by a black eye patch. He looked like someone you wouldn't want to meet in a dark alley at night, or even in a supermarket aisle in broad daylight.

For a moment, they looked up from the picture, and at each other, remembering encounters with conscienceless monsters like Flaherty, the horrific damage inflicted on their victims. Burgess heard Dylan's voice. What's the scariest situation you've ever been in? It would have been with someone like this.

"He lost that eye in prison," Devlin said. "Your Imam say anything about an eye patch?"

He hadn't, and it was a pretty distinctive bit of information, as was Flaherty's impressive size. So maybe Flaherty wasn't their guy. Still, they'd have to talk to him. A conversation Burgess expected would be a whole lot like talking to Norton, or Ismail, and one to which no cop would go without significant backup. He sighed and made a note.

"Thanks, Press. You got an address for him?"

"Workin' on it, Sarge. He'd not exactly the type to stay in touch with his parole officer, keep 'em current on his address. There's a bar down on Commercial Street they like to hang out at. I'll drop in, see what I can learn."

He looked back down at his papers. "I couldn't do anything with that second bike. Just not enough information."

"Not a problem," Burgess said. "But if you've got time, you might see who has surveillance cameras in the area that might have gotten a piece of that corner. We're a little stretched right now. Could use the help."

"I'm on it, sir."

"And call me as soon as you get a line on Flaherty."

Burgess switched to Kyle. "Terry, can you follow up with your informant today, see if she has anything concrete to offer?"

"Can we meet her demands?" Kyle said.

"Demands?" Melia said.

"She wants an iPod as the price of cooperation."

"They're expensive," Melia said.

"I think we might have one or two rattling around in unclaimed property," Kyle said. "It doesn't have to be new. She just wants to feel like she's in control."

Melia nodded. They all understood about that. So much of the population they dealt with felt like they had little control over their lives. Poverty. Mental illness. Substance abuse. Dysfunctional families. Everything contributed to making people feel helpless. If an iPod could shift that a little, and they gained something in return, it was a win-win.

"Rocky, you got us an owner of that property yet?"

Rocky Jordan sat behind a stack of papers, their emperor of information. "Typical corporate bullshit, Joe," Jordan said. "Real estate trust, owned by a corporation, which is owned by another corporation. Like one of those Russian dolls, you know. I just keep opening one, finding another inside. So short answer? No, though it does look like your Imam may have a hand in there somewhere. But I'll get there."

"Anything on our stolen car? Stolen plates?" Burgess meant the car that had crashed at the hospital, not the one the shooters had dumped and burned.

"Just the obvious." Rocky passed over some pages. "Here's where the car was stolen, when, who it was stolen from. Same for the plates. Maybe Wink can pull some prints that will help us. I saw him circling the car like a hungry spider as I came in. As for that other car? The one that burned? We're not going to get any prints off that. It's one of many registered to your Imam, or members of his extended family. If living at the same address and having the same last name means they're family, they've got a whole fleet. Not just cars, but trucks."

He shoved some more papers at Burgess. "Here's the list."

Something else to look into—what types of businesses the Imam and his family, or his clan, were involved in. In particular, what kind of trucks they owned and what business they did with those trucks. What he'd like to do was have a look at their finances, but that would take a warrant. Writing warrants took hours, and he'd need to get the attorney general's office involved. The AG's office prosecuted all the homicides in Maine, and they liked to get into the investigations early. It was time to make that call.

"We'll have to pay him another visit. And find ourselves another interpreter, since Osman has proven himself both unreliable and uncooperative."

"And missing," Perry added.

Burgess turned to Melia. "Vince, have we got a list somewhere of the people we use?"

"Ask Ginny. She's good at keeping track of that stuff."

Burgess made a note. "And we've got to find our missing interpreter, see what the story is there. Who attacked him and why he thinks it happened. He's supposed to meet us this morning. One of us will go, but I doubt he'll show."

"I'll take that one," Perry said. "I'm going home to get cleaned up, then I'll see if I can find him."

"Good. On both counts," Burgess said.

"Look, I haven't been home yet, Joe," Perry said. "I was following up a hunch." He set a paper bag on the table and pulled out a handful of charred cardboard. "These are Apple product codes. From what was left of the boxes in that closet where you found the girl and baby?"

He sounded defiant and defensive, once again reminding Burgess too much of Dylan. "I figured we'd better get 'em before the scene got any more mucked up, or before someone wanting to ensure we didn't find them got there and finished the job."

"We had patrol guarding—" Melia said.

"Right," Perry interrupted, "but I was able to walk right in and no one asked me who I was or what I was doing there. Just like someone walked into the morgue last night and took that baby. I hate to say it, but we've got more screwups than successes on this one so far. So I thought," he scratched his peach-fuzzed head with slightly grimy fingers, "that I'd talk to the property guys, then liaise with South Portland and go out to the mall and talk with the manager at the Apple store."

Another pause, then another slightly defiant, "If that's all right with you, Joe?"

"Take someone from property with you."

Before Burgess could move on, Perry said, "And that's not all."

They waited while he plunged his hand into the paper bag and pulled out a smaller bag. With elaborate showmanship, he took a pair of gloves from his pocket, pulled them on, and pulled a crumpled pair of similar latex gloves out of the bag. "This is what took most of my time last night. Why I haven't been home to change." He swiveled his head around, being sure to treat them all to the full force of his glare. Too bad the peach fuzz and a grimy streak on his cheek made him look like a delinquent kid.

"I saw the driver toss them while I was chasing him, but I didn't register where he did it. I was too busy chasing him. I had to go over that whole damned neighborhood with a flashlight to find 'em."

He grinned. "Figured they might give us DNA. And if we're lucky, maybe some prints in case there aren't any in the car."

That was Stan Perry in a nutshell. Screwup upon screwup until they were ready to kick him to the curb, and then he'd pull a couple of big white rabbits out of his hat. Burgess still needed to sit the boy down and have a serious talk.

"Good job, Stan."

He shoved back his chair and went to the white board. "So, this is what we've got."

Grabbing a marker, he started listing all the people they knew of so far who had some connection to this case. The little mother and her baby. The Imam. Ismail, the man who wasn't there. The boy in the bushes, Ali Ibrahim. Their translator, Hussain Osman. Kimani Yates. Akiba Norton. The missing driver with the watch and ring. Butcher Flaherty. The as-yet unidentified owner of the mosque property. Kyle's informant. Jason Stetson.

He looked down at the list. "I'll take Jason. See if he saw anything that might be important. He should be at school today, but you never know."

He made a note and looked at Melia. "The guy from the car last night, Norton? We get anything else from him?"

"Nothing to put on paper. He lawyered up as soon as he got to the jail. Looks like he had someone just waiting for his call, that's what they reported to us. Asked to make his phone call and it was right to the lawyer. Dollars to donuts, though, he's not the one paying the bill. We've got the DA in the loop, making sure he doesn't get out."

"Speaking of people who aren't supposed to be out—"

"Kimani Yates," Melia said. He sounded as weary and frustrated as they all felt. "Captain Cote and the DA are both working on that one, trying to figure out what went wrong over there. Turns out he didn't escape. They were going to let him out early for good behavior. They just screwed up the paperwork and let him go sooner than they'd planned. Which might . . ." Melia let the "might" hang in the air a beat, "explain why they didn't notify us."

There were nods around the table. It might. It might not. "We're checking his usual hangouts. Friends. Family. We'll find him. Last night's actions definitely don't count as good behavior."

Burgess moved on. The clock was running. They needed to get back out on the street, start getting some answers. "Our mystery man. Rocky, have we got some stills from the surveillance video of that watch and that ring?"

"Not yet, Joe. By the end of the day. I promise. I've been kind of backed up."

Another part of Burgess's reputation. He was not only the meanest, he was the most impatient cop in Portland. It wasn't really true, but he had found, over the years, that a little well-placed anger and some similarly well-placed impatience meant he got results fast when he needed them. No one, it seemed, wanted to get on his bad side. Maybe he should try it at home.

"Our mystery girl. Any leads on who she might be?" No one said anything. "I'll go by the hospital when we're done, see how she's doing. If she continues to be unable . . . or unwilling . . . to talk to us, we may have to go to the media."

He looked at Melia. It would be Melia's call.

"Be better if we didn't have to, Joe," Melia said. "Let's give it a little longer. Check other jurisdictions' missing persons. It's the kind of story that goes national, and we don't want that kind of attention."

Burgess figured they'd get it anyway, because of the mosque, and the press that Maine's issues with integrating refugees had already gotten. But Melia was right, there was no sense in inviting it.

Melia's assistant came in with a pink message slip and set it down in front of her boss. He read it, then looked at Burgess. "ME's office called. They're doing the autopsy this afternoon. At one. I need you there, Joe."

Burgess nodded. He couldn't remember when he'd been to an autopsy on a baby that young. Wished he could send someone else in his place. "Lee doing it?"

Melia nodded. "Take Sage with you." He liked to have two detectives on a case, in case something happened to one of them, and they needed Kyle and Perry here in Portland, chasing down witnesses, following trails through the maze.

The autopsy was important, but it would take a minimum of three hours out of Burgess's day. The drive up to the ME's office in Augusta was forty-five minutes each way on a good day. Dr. Lee was fast, but these things took time. And without a name for the baby or the mother, any and all information became that much more important. At least he could take the handkerchief Ismail Ibrahim had used along and ask for a DNA profile, see if there was a match.

"Right, Vince," he said. "Terry, why don't you go with Stan to meet with our interpreter. If he doesn't show, see if you can track him down."

He copied the plate number Beck had given him from his notebook and gave it to Kyle. "This is the plate from the car that picked him up at the hospital last night. Then Stan, you work on the Apple angle, Ter, you see if you can learn anything more from your source. We can all touch base later and see where we are."

Everyone gathered their notes, pushed back, and headed for the door. Burgess would have followed, but Melia stopped him. "A moment, Joe," he said.

Burgess waited.

"Have you talked with Stan?" Melia asked. "Because—"

But they both knew the "because."

"Haven't had a chance yet, Vince. You know how it's been."

He sounded as defensive as Perry had, and didn't like it.

"Do it now," Melia said. "Get him under control or find someone else to work with you on this. We're going to have the media down our throats and I don't want to see pictures of that"—he waved his hands to indicate Stan Perry's disheveled appearance and bad attitude—"in the paper. I've practically got Captain Cote camped in my office, waiting for your reports."

Melia broke off. "Find him. Talk to him. And as soon as you get a chance, generate some reports for me." He squared his shoulders and straightened his tie. "Now go on. Go get me something."

Like Burgess was a magician who could conjure up facts from thin air when not one of the lowlifes they'd talked to would say word one. Like being a competent detective meant you could read minds, see through walls, leap tall buildings in a single bound. And you could always solve the case. But Melia knew all that. This was just process. The brass chews on him, he chews on Burgess, Burgess goes and chews on Stan Perry. When all any of them wanted to do was to chew on bad guys until they gave up what they knew.

"Can't do it, Vince," he said. "I'm taking a leave of absence. Going to charm school. I've got to do something different to get people to talk to me. Being big and mean just isn't working for me anymore."

"Waterboarding," Vince muttered. "A couple nights in a cell with Bubba. Or Butcher Flaherty. I think you can forget charm. It wouldn't take anyway."

"Depressed that you think so, Vince."

Melia made shooing motions with his hands. "Go find me something. And whack that kid upside the head before he screws things up for everyone. The gloves and the serial numbers are good. Very good. But he's like an idiot savant with the emphasis on idiot."

Burgess had places to go and people to see. But looking after your own people was a priority. If he didn't take care of his team, they couldn't do the job anyway.

He got another copy of their mystery girl's picture, and made arrangements with Sage Prentiss to go up to Augusta together. Then he checked the bay, but Perry had already left. He decided to swing by Perry's place and catch him there. He didn't want to hear some prepared speech about how Perry was sorry and would get it back under control. He wanted this to be spontaneous.

When Perry pulled the door open, he was still beaded with water and wearing hastily pulled on sweat pants that were inside out. He backed up to let Burgess in without a greeting or a smile. Pulled out a chair for himself and sat down at the kitchen table, leaving Burgess standing. Burgess sat down opposite him and waited.

The apartment looked great. Perfectly neat. No fast-food clutter or unwashed dishes. There was even a flowering plant on the sill above the sink. All signs of a woman's touch.

"Vince made you come, didn't he?" Perry said.

Burgess nodded. "He's concerned about you. And about appearances. But I would have come anyway. The press is going to be all over this thing. We're going to need kid gloves, Stan, and you're wearing soot and stubble."

"I'm doing detective work. Thought that was our job."

"We don't operate in a void, Stan. Appearances matter. Behavior matters. Attitude matters. And like it or not, the food chain matters. If Melia says for you to come in, I convey that order, and then you do a disappearing act, like last night, it's not just your ass that's on the line."

"So you're here to cover your own ass?"

"I'm here to tell one of my detectives—a valued member of my team with a real talent for thinking outside the box—that following orders is also part of the deal. You let us know what's happening. You show up when you're supposed to. Or you're off the case. You know Sage has been angling for your spot. Is that what you want?"

Perry's sullen expression was so much like Dylan's that Burgess had to look away.

"Stan, you've got to decide. Is following your own instincts so important that you can blow off orders, blow *me* off? Do you think that knowing that a baby's body had been taken from the morgue, but not informing me about it because 'you forgot' is ever acceptable?"

He waited for Perry to say something. Got silence. "Where did you disappear to last night?"

"I had to take a phone call. Thought it would be a minute and it goddamned wasn't."

"Personal phone call?"

Perry nodded.

Burgess rubbed his forehead, where a dull headache was forming. "We're supposed to be a team. Working together. Watching each other's backs. Sharing what we know. That doesn't work if you decide to pursue your own agenda. If we're chasing a bad guy and you don't have our backs because you're making a phone call."

Enough of the lecture. It was time to talk about what was really bothering his detective. "Something's going on, Stan. Something you're not talking about. Something that's distracting you from the job and making you chronically pissed off. So what's up?"

There was the sound of quick feet on the stairs and a key in the lock. Then the door opened and a pretty, petite brunette lugging two heavy grocery bags walked into the room.

"What's going on, Joe?" Perry said. "She is."

CHAPTER FOURTEEN

Burgess pushed back his chair and went to meet her, taking the two heavy bags and setting them on the kitchen counter. Mrs. Burgess didn't raise her boy to sit around while a woman struggled. He didn't know how Mrs. Perry had raised her boy, but it looked like sulking won out over manners or kindness. Evidently, Stan's mother hadn't whacked him upside the head often enough.

He turned back to her. "Joe Burgess," he said.

Her dark brown eyes shifted to Stan Perry and then back to him. It looked like she'd heard the name "Joe Burgess" and not always in a favorable context. But her mother had taught her manners, and she quickly held out a small hand. "Lily Leadbetter," she said.

His talk with Perry was going to have to wait for another time and place. At least he'd said what he came to say. Next time, he'd get Perry's response.

"Nice to meet you," he said.

She'd already moved past him to the counter and was taking things out of the bags.

"We'll talk this afternoon, Stan," he said. "When I get back from Augusta. Meanwhile, if anything significant turns up, text me."

"You bet, boss," Perry said.

He shoved back his chair and headed toward the bedroom. To dress, Burgess supposed, and to make sure that the conversation didn't continue. He left the two of them to their domestic affairs and headed over to the hospital.

Burgess stopped at the nurses' station on his mystery girl's floor, hoping someone he knew would be there and might be able to fill him in. He was in luck. The kindly nurse Susan must have been working a double shift, because she was still there.

"Come to check up on your girl, Joe?" she said.

"I am. How's she doing?"

"About the same as yesterday. She's not in bad shape, considering, but she won't talk to anyone. Not in bad shape from the fire, I mean. She's a child, and a mother, and someone has been beating up on her. All that has really taken a toll. She's half-starved and exhausted."

She pulled out a chart and consulted it. "Looks like someone from psych is coming down later this morning. Maybe we'll know more then. Want me to call you when that's done?"

"I'd appreciate it. You have my number?"

She smiled. "I think I do. But you can give it to me again." He dictated cell and 109, and she wrote it down.

All the time they were talking, she was moving. Checking the chart. Making a note. Sorting some other papers and putting them into other files. Hospitals, like police departments, tended to be understaffed and overwhelmed with paper. Which reminded him that he really ought to be back at 109, creating some paperwork of his own.

"Just going to stick my head in," he said.

His mystery girl was curled on her side with her eyes closed, dark hair spread out on the pillow. Remy Aucoin was sitting beside her, reading her something. He looked up, embarrassed when he saw it was Burgess. "Just reading to her, Sergeant," he said.

"What book?"

Remy ducked his head. "*The Hunger Games.* I borrowed it from my little sister. I thought she might like it."

Burgess liked that. He also liked the fact that Remy could surprise him. It looked like Remy had read quite a lot of the book. "What time did you come in?" he asked.

"Seven. Dwyer was going off shift, so they sent me. She said if I let anything happen to 'her girl' I'd be sorry." Aucoin shook his head. "She was my girl first."

He set the book down and motioned Burgess outside the door. "I know she's listening," he said in a low voice. "What I don't know is whether she can't talk or she won't talk. But she likes the book. She likes you, too. When she heard your voice, I saw her eyelids flicker." Aucoin looked toward the girl on the bed and back at Burgess. "We getting anywhere with this, Sergeant?"

"It's a maze," Burgess admitted. "But we'll sort it out. It helps to know we don't have to worry about her while we're worrying about everything else."

"I'm trying," Aucoin said.

"All any of us can do. Someone's supposed to do a psych consult with her sometime today. No matter what they say to you—about privacy or confidentiality—you don't leave her, okay. They give you any trouble, you stay put and call Lieutenant Melia."

He hesitated, unused to sharing much with patrol except on a need-to-know basis, but Aucoin was deep into this, too. "Going up to Augusta this afternoon for the autopsy on her baby. Just as soon she didn't know about that, but you should. Who knows what we may learn."

He tried to remember what Chris had said about the book Aucoin was reading. He knew Nina had read it and that Chris had worried about that. "You sure that book isn't too violent, Remy?"

"After what she's been through? I thought it might be good for her. It's about someone who's a victim taking charge. And winning. That's not such a bad idea, is it, under the circumstances?"

"I guess not. I'm going to go catch bad guys. Call me if anything happens. If anything changes, okay?"

"You bet."

Remy was moving back into the room. Then he turned, "You should come in and say hello to her. Just let her know you're there for her. Who knows what matters, right?"

Burgess followed him back into the room. She was still curled on her side, and her eyes were still closed, but the hand he'd held the night before was outside the covers. He took it in his and gave it a little squeeze. "It's Joe Burgess," he said, though he couldn't remember if he'd told her his name before. "We're still here, trying to take care of you. Hoping some time you'll open your eyes and look at me. And tell me your name. I'm not that scary."

Her hand moved in his. Just a tiny movement, but he knew she was trying. That was all he could ask.

"I'll see you later," he said. "And Remy is going to be right here to keep you safe."

Back in the truck, he checked his watch. Still time to catch up with Jason Stetson, if he could find him. He figured out which middle school was most likely, and gave the assistant principal, Lorraine Cormier, a call. He'd known her for years, and today he needed her discretion.

There was humor in her voice when she said, "Joe Burgess. So what has one of my students done this time?"

"Saved a life, for starters, Lorraine," he said. "I'm looking for

141

Jason Stetson. I need to talk to him about a fire yesterday. But I don't want to flag him to others as a potential witness."

"He's coming along nicely, Joe, I'm pleased to say. Hold on and let me see if he's here today."

He heard a murmur of voices and then she was back on the phone. "He didn't come in today."

Burgess's heart sank. He was so afraid something might happen to Jason. And while Jason was coming along, he also sometimes had more bravado than sense.

Then she said, "Hold on." There was another murmur of voices, and she said, "Joe? Sorry about that. He's here. He just came in late. So you want to talk with Jason, but you don't want the other students to know he's talking to you?"

"Right."

"We're kind of a fishbowl, here in the office. Why don't you go to the nurse's office, and I'll send Jason there. You know where that is? In that silly little trailer we've got around back, looks like a wart on the wall?"

It did look like a wart on the wall, a tinny white wart. But it was away from the rest of the school, and had a back door he could drive right up to. He knew the nurse, too. God. Dylan was right. He was such a dinosaur he knew everybody. Did that mean he'd been at this too long, or did it just mean that this is what happened when you worked the same job in the same city for years?

Jason was waiting in a little cubicle, looking puzzled about why he'd been sent to the nurse's office. He perked right up when he saw Burgess walk in.

"Sergeant," he said. "Are you taking me out to breakfast?"

"I am. Just not today. Today I am interviewing an important witness in a major case."

The boy's eyes widened. "Me?"

Burgess nodded. "That's right." He took out the tiny recorder he carried for times like this. "You mind if I record this?"

"Hell, no. That's cool."

Jason swiped at his runny nose, and Burgess gave him a handkerchief.

Sometimes, at parties, the younger people used to have the "superpowers" conversation. If you could have a superpower, what would it be? Burgess knew what his would be—what any cop would want—the ability to read minds. But when he imagined himself as a superhero, he had a vision of a bulky middle-aged man going about handing out magic handkerchiefs to a needy population. Hankies to stop tears, stop bleeding, bind broken bones and broken hearts. Not even in his imagination did Hanky Man wear a Lycra suit. The image would have been too awful.

"Tell me about yesterday, and how you happened to hear those screams."

Jason nodded and sat up straighter. "You know that we live right across the street there? In that brown house? Me and my foster family? And you know, like I really like living with them and all, it's so clean, and they're kind. I even have my own room. But we've got a baby, see, and it cries a lot, and I really can't stand to hear a baby cry. So, we've like got this other little kid, his name is Ricky, he's almost six. And like he can't stand to listen to the baby, either. And you know, there's kind of like a field in front of that building. Mosque. The one that burned? So, like sometimes I—"

He broke off and looked at Burgess. "Is this okay?"

"Is what okay?"

"That I tell it this way? My foster mom, she gets impatient with me 'cuz I'm so slow getting to things. I tell her it's just the way my brain works. But you know, she's got all us kids and so she sighs and says, 'I only wish you could hurry it up, Jase,' which I try to do, only then I get all tangled up and I forget things."

"Your way is just fine. It's your story. You tell it the way it works for you."

The clock was ticking. Soon he would have to be on his way to Augusta, but rushing a witness was never a good idea. And he was so pleased, after the way life had bounced Jason around, to have him in a good home. He liked hearing the boy say, "we," like it was a real family unit. Oh yeah. The meanest cop in Portland was really a mushy sentimentalist.

"So I took Ricky over there to kick a soccer ball around. Our foster mom, she'd rather we went over there than down to the park, 'cuz she can keep an eye on us, you know. Only some days no one seems to mind and some days, those people from the mosque, the In Man and some of the others, will come out and tell us to go away, we're bothering them."

"When was this, Jason, the last time you took Ricky over there to kick a ball around?"

"The night before the fire. Of the fire."

"Right. Okay, so yesterday you went over there to play with Ricky, is that right?"

Jason nodded.

"What time was this?"

"A little after four, maybe? After Ricky got home from school and had his snack."

"Did you see anyone there? The Imam? Ismail? Anyone else?"

"It was weird you know, Sergeant Burgess. There weren't no . . . weren't any cars or trucks there. Usually there are some of those women in headscarves and men carrying things in from trucks or out to trucks, lots of men coming in the late afternoon . . . a girl in my class told me that it's because they have to pray five times a day. But not yesterday. There was no one around."

Another pause. Another quick look at Burgess. "If they have

to pray every day, why didn't they have to pray yesterday?"

Burgess had no idea. "You notice any cars or trucks on the street?"

"Just one of those little black Hondas. They all drive these little black Hondas, you know, like it's another requirement of their religion or something. Drive white vans, or those square white trucks that look like boxes, and little black Hondas. And pray five times a day."

This kid was amazing. Burgess was willing to bet the adults in the neighborhood couldn't have told him half of this.

"Do they think praying five times a day makes them better people, Sergeant Burgess? Because those men aren't very nice to women."

"What makes you say that?"

"This girl at school. She's not supposed to talk to me, because I'm a boy, but we're friends and she tells me things about how women don't matter in their families, only men do, and how they think she should leave school soon and get married. Which she says she doesn't want to do. And my foster mom, she says she's seen things, and she also gets mad at the way those men treat her, like when she's out with the baby and stuff, you know. She says they stand around and stare and act like she's dirt or something. And like once they parked one of their trucks so it was blocking our driveway when she needed to get out so she could take the baby to the doctor and when she went over there to ask them to move it, they yelled at her that she had to get out of their building. So she came home and called you guys."

A report that might be worth looking up. Actually, it might be worth doing a general search about complaints regarding the mosque and its members from the neighborhood. See who else was watching. Good idea to talk to the officers who patrolled this sector, too. They usually had a pretty good read on their neighborhoods. See what got noted on field identification cards.

Those FID cards could be very helpful.

But he was being a dinosaur again. Now that was all computerized. No more of those handy little cards he could sort through and pick out valuable data. Now he had to figure out how it might have been recorded and filed. Practically needed a techie in his pocket just to do his job.

"Okay," he said, "so you were over there with Ricky, knocking that ball around, and no one was at the mosque and there were no cars in the lot, is that right?"

Jason nodded.

"When did you spot the fire?"

"It was Ricky," Jason said. "He had kicked the ball over on that side of the building, and when he came back he said he'd seen smoke. So I went around there and I could see it wasn't just smoke, it was flames. So I walked him back across the street and told him to go upstairs and have our foster mom call the fire department. And when I was walking him across, that's when I heard the woman screaming."

He stopped, his eyes wide. "I never heard nothin' like that, ever, Sergeant Burgess. It sounded just awful. And I looked up and down the street for someone to help her, and I saw your car parked there, and I just ran up . . . not knowing it was you 'til I got close, and then I was so glad it was you and I pounded on your door, and you know about the rest."

He had so many things to ask, but he didn't want to overwhelm the boy. "The Imam says that they've been having trouble with a motorcycle gang. Have you ever seen men on motorcycles around the mosque?"

"You mean that huge guy with the eye patch? I've seen him a couple times, maybe more. Him and this other guy, sometimes more than one guy, they'll go into that parking lot and just drive around and around, making all that noise. My foster mom has called the cops—I mean, you guys—a few times because they wake up the baby."

"That's the man," Burgess said. "You ever see him speak to the Imam or anyone else over there?"

"Sure. The In Man, he came out and yelled at the man with the eye patch, and then the eye-patch man, he drove his motorcycle right at the In Man. He's an old man, you know, Sergeant Burgess. He had to jump out of the way so quick he fell over, which is when one of his sons, or grandsons, the one that's not Ishmael, he came out and yelled at the man that if he didn't stop, they were gonna kill him. And then the eye-patch guy said . . . I mean yelled, 'unless I kill you first.' "

Jason stopped, his eyes wide. "But people say that stuff all the time, don't they? And they don't mean it, right? Anyway, they both said some things I couldn't hear and then the son helped the In Man back inside and them . . . uh . . . those motorcycle guys roared off."

"Do you remember when this happened?"

The boy considered, then shook his head. "It might have been last week, but I'm not sure. My foster mom might remember, because she came out to see what was going on. She says she's real frustrated about having them as neighbors, because they bring so much trouble to the neighborhood."

In the background, a bell rang.

Burgess had more questions, but he could see Jason was anxious to get back to class. He also thought he'd better stop in later and talk to the foster mother. She might have noticed things that Jason wouldn't have, and might remember the date of that confrontation between the Imam and his grandson and Butcher Flaherty.

He stood up. "Time to get you back to class," he said. "You've been very helpful. And yes, I know I still owe you those pancakes. Maybe this weekend, if all goes well. And Jase?"

The boy looked suddenly wary. Not surprising, given his history.

"Don't tell anyone we've talked. You're our secret witness. Like to keep it that way."

"Don't worry, Sergeant. I won't say a word. Except . . ."

Burgess wondered what the exception was. Jason's best friend? The girl he confided in?

"Would it be okay if I told my foster mom?"

"It would be fine. That's a good idea."

Burgess took out the photo of his mystery girl. "Have you ever seen her before? Around here? Or at school?"

Jason took the photo, studied it carefully, and handed it back. "Is that the girl who was locked up in the building? The one you had to break down the door so you could rescue her?"

"That's right."

Burgess felt like he was on the cusp of something important. He tried not to let it show as he waited for Jason to explain.

"I might know something," Jason said, suddenly coy. "But I'll have to ask my friend if it's okay to tell you."

He squirmed on his chair. "I'd better go now, Sergeant Burgess. It's time for class and they'll be mad if I'm late."

"Please do ask your friend. I really need this information, Jason," Burgess said. "And I might need to talk to your friend."

The squirming increased. "I'm not sure that's a good idea. She's really shy."

Now the boy was on his feet, almost vibrating with his need to get out the door.

"We'll talk again," Burgess said. "Let me know what she says." Then realized he was missing a vital piece of information. "What's her name?"

Jason looked everywhere except at him. Finally, he said, "Amina."

No last name, but that wasn't a problem. There couldn't be

too many Aminas in the school.

"Thanks, Jason. I really appreciate your information." He gave the boy his card. "And if you remember anything else I should know, you call me, okay?"

Jason tucked the card away, still looking troubled, and Burgess realized he needed to reassure Jason that he wasn't going to damage the friendship or get the girl in trouble.

"I know you understand why I might need to arrange to speak with your friend. And I know why that worries you. If I do, I will be very careful not to get her in trouble with her family. I know she will be very reluctant, so please don't say anything to her yet."

Jason put a finger to his lips. "You can trust me, Sergeant Burgess."

"I know I can. Just be careful, Jason, and like we agreed, don't say anything to anyone about this talk, except for your foster mom. Right?"

"Right."

Reluctantly, he let Jason go.

Burgess watched the boy's small, awkward figure, until the boy disappeared back into the school building and the door closed behind him. Another kid he needed to keep safe and worried that he couldn't.

CHAPTER FIFTEEN

Still, he was feeling irritated even though he had no right to be. The boy had been helpful and Burgess knew if he interviewed Jason again, he'd get more, that there were things Jason wanted to say and wasn't sure he should. But Burgess needed answers now. He was getting sick of everyone's lack of cooperation. Impatient with all the rules he had to follow, the fine line he had to walk to respect everyone's rights. Like abused girls and dead infants really didn't matter.

Burgess thought he'd need to talk to Jason's friend, but that would not be easy. Not easy at all. For him or for her, if she would even agree to speak with him. A male American cop talking to a young Somali girl was not something easy to arrange. He had an idea, though. Use the library, which was regarded as a safe place, and bring Andrea with him.

He thanked the nurse and headed out to his truck.

He called Kyle for an update on their meeting with Osman. Osman hadn't appeared. No one was answering the phone at his residence, which had the same address as the license plate of the car that had picked him up. They were going to drop by there, then split up and start working their lists. Kyle sounded frustrated, eager to get back to his informant, see if she really knew anything. If, like Jason, she lived near the mosque, she might well have something useful to add. Nosy people might be annoying if they lived next door, but they could be a policeman's best friends.

"You might drop by the Imam's place, see if he drew us that plan of the building we were supposed to pick up last night."

"We were there last night," Kyle reminded him, "trying to pick it up. He just wouldn't answer the door."

"Kid gloves," Burgess said. "And persistence. Let 'em know we aren't going to go away just because they want us to. Hang in there. We're going to get some breaks in this thing."

"Right. I'd like to break a few things."

Heads, probably. And Kyle was the calm one. Of course today he was saddled with their ill-tempered colleague Stan Perry.

"How's Stan doing?"

"Vibrating. Cursing. Veering toward the edge of the reservation."

"He sitting right beside you?"

"Got it in one."

"You didn't hear this from me, but the divine Andrea says Stan's girlfriend is pregnant. That might explain a few things. I'll catch up after the autopsy."

"Good luck with that."

Burgess thought he'd need luck. This was not going to be one of his better moments.

On his way to 109 to pick up Sage Prentiss, he called Melia and told him what he'd just learned from Jason about the inexplicable absence of people around the mosque when the fire started, and his certainty that some very important information was available if he could only tap into it. He shared his plans for follow-up.

"The captain is very anxious to see your reports," Melia said. A euphemistic way of saying that Cote was foaming at the mouth and stalking the corridors with hands opening and closing like they wanted to be around Burgess's neck.

"Sorry, Vince. You know how it's been. After the autopsy, I'll sit down and write things up."

"It's my ass, too, Joe."

"I'll keep your ass in mind."

"See that you do."

He swung into the dark cement garage at 109 and called Prentiss to say he was there. His call got a two-fer, because Prentiss arrived with Dani Letorneau, their evidence tech, in tow.

She climbed in the back, giving the lanky Prentiss the roomier front seat. "Sorry, Joe," she said. "Car broke down on the way to work this morning."

"Not a problem," he said. "I can use the company. This thing's making me grouchy as a bear coming out of hibernation."

She had the grace not to say "what's new?"

As they headed north on 295, Prentiss said, "Lieutenant Melia said you might need more bodies on this one."

"Poor choice of words, Sage," Burgess said, as he jerked the wheel and whipped around an ancient man in a battered Subaru who was going forty when the speed limit was sixty-five. "I'd rather have fewer bodies."

"I meant—"

"Dammit, Sage, I know what you meant. And yes, we can use some more help. You don't happen to speak Somali, do you?"

"A little," Prentiss said, surprising him. "I was a kiddie cop for a while. Lotta Somali kids at the school."

Finally a bit of good news. Too bad they hadn't had Prentiss with them last night when they were interviewing the Imam. He smiled, remembering Jason's very serious voice calling him the In Man.

Burgess didn't know Prentiss well. He was a lateral transfer from the Lewiston police department. But then, Lewiston had its issues with Somalis as well. Real issues of educating a population that often wasn't even literate in their own language. The mayor might have had a habit of explaining it badly, often resulting in him being depicted with his foot in his mouth in the national press, but it was hard on city systems to integrate a large new population in need of every possible service when the federal resettlement money was going to communities where the Somalis had initially settled, before their secondary migration to Maine.

"Sounds like you might be a big help. We're running up against a brick wall trying to get information about that mosque. Lotta people lying. Or just going silent on us. So far, we don't even understand the Imam's family structure."

"I'll do what I can, Sergeant. I've got some strategies. Lotta times, I've found the way in is through the next generation, the kids. Or the women."

As they whipped past the salt marsh, still fall's golden brown, not beginning to green up yet, and the marina—a field of shrink-wrapped boats looking like misshapen marshmallows—he felt Dani's small hand on his shoulder. "You gonna be okay with this, Joe?"

"Are any of us?"

"I'm dreading it," she said. "That little boy from the park, that was bad enough. But a baby? Dr. Lee doing the autopsy?"

"He is."

"At least he keeps it clinical."

She said it like that was a good thing, but Burgess remembered some of his first autopsies, with a very different ME, and the sense of reverence for the soul of the person on the table that had filled the room. Maybe she was right about today, though. Clinical might make it easier.

He wondered what they'd learn. Dr. Lee was awfully good at spotting things others might miss, sometimes things that proved essential to their investigations. And he made a great witness in court.

It was always one of the ironies—and underpinnings—of their investigations, that they had to act rapidly, in the moment, to respond to the case as it changed, yet always kept an eye on what they needed to preserve for what would come down the road. Chain of custody. Extreme caution in the collection of evidence. Detailed reports. Names and address and dates of birth. Photo and video of the scene and subsequent searches. Being alert and aware in the present and documenting that alertness and awareness for the future. It only took one heartbreaking loss because of carelessness to sear that awareness into a detective's mind forever. A good detective. Some people rolled over the screwups like they were just bumps in the road.

He'd brought the bloody handkerchief with Ismail's DNA. Was hoping for a match. Hoping for something, that was for sure.

Dani's hand left his shoulder as she shifted her conversation to Prentiss. "So is Sage really your first name?"

"It is."

"I've never met anyone named Sage before. Where did your parents come up with that?"

As Burgess had already learned, and Dani was about to, Prentiss was an extremely taciturn man.

"Mother's maiden name," he said, in a monotone that suggested the conversation was over.

Dani got the message. They drove the rest of the way in silence.

They were late. Despite Burgess's best efforts, the last part of the trip was on local roads, and the other drivers seemed to be conspiring to keep him from making any time. When he finally pulled into the lot and shoved the Explorer into park, he was ready to call it a day, when, if history was any guide, his day was barely beginning.

Dr. Lee was waiting for them impatiently, jittering slightly from foot to foot as he acknowledged Dani and then Burgess introduced Prentiss. Dani had moved immediately to the baby. They already had his clothes but she wanted to get hand and footprints and take some pictures before Lee went to work.

Burgess watched her face as she worked, bottom lip caught between her teeth, her gloved hands as gentle as though the baby were still alive. She moved him, turned him, and photographed so they'd have a complete record of the baby before Dr. Lee got out his scalpel.

He was surprised to find Lee standing beside him. "Be sure you get a good close-up of his navel," Lee said. "And of his penis. I'll put it in my report, but it helps to have a good picture as well."

"A picture of what?" Burgess asked.

"That hack job of a circumcision, for one thing. And a cord that wasn't properly cared for and probably got infected. I don't know what the circumstances were, but I'm certain this baby wasn't delivered in any hospital."

It made sense, Burgess thought. Given the girl's age, and the evidence that someone had used restraints on her, whoever had had custody of her and delivered this baby would not have wanted her in a hospital, out of his control and in a place where she might tell her story or ask for help.

Dani took her pictures, lowered the camera, and stepped back. "I'm done," she said.

She looked done. She looked as troubled as they all felt, and diminished, wilting like an unwatered flower in her already too-large jumpsuit. She bent and stowed some gear in her bag and he saw her swipe at her face, trying to keep them from seeing her tears.

They gathered around the table as Lee moved in and began

his dictation, noting that they were looking at an undernourished, unnamed male infant appearing to be partly African-American, who looked to be about three weeks old. Younger than Burgess had thought. There appeared to be no external signs of injury but Lee noted a distended abdomen, botched circumcision, and the condition of the navel.

Then he picked up his scalpel and there was a moment's hesitation.

Normally, Lee did autopsies at twice the speed of any other pathologist Burgess had ever seen, always moving like he had somewhere else to be, was on a deadline, or was trying to beat his own personal best. Today, he moved more slowly, and Burgess remembered something Lee had said to him once. A remark that had surprised him at the time because of the ME's unflappable manner. As they were getting in their cars after an autopsy on a child, Lee had said, "I hate doing kids."

It was a sentiment Burgess could completely relate to.

Finally, Lee took a breath and made the first cut.

Burgess checked on his team. Prentiss seemed to be doing okay. Dani less so, but she was holding herself together because she never wanted to be thought less tough than the other guys just because she was small and female.

As Lee moved through the now-familiar steps of the autopsy, his face tightened. He was clearly troubled by what he was seeing. Burgess watched the gloved hands move slowly along the bowel until they came to a stop and Lee nodded. "Just as I expected. This baby has . . . had a bowel obstruction that would have required surgery. If the smoke hadn't killed him, as it did, this would have unless his parents . . . or someone . . . had taken him to a hospital. And this wasn't a sudden thing. The infant had been suffering for some time."

He looked down at his hands, still holding the twisted bowel. "And I do mean suffering. Unable to eat. Which probably accounts for his being malnourished. He couldn't digest his food. What kind of parent could watch that and do nothing?"

The ME raised his eyes from the baby to Burgess. "What do we know about this baby's family? Because someone should be charged—"

"Not much," Burgess said.

He had never seen Lee like this. The man was as cool and clinical as a human could be. "He and his mother—a girl who looks to be, at best, fourteen—were found locked in a closet in a burning building. She was screaming for help. She's still in the hospital, being treated for the smoke she inhaled. She's in rotten shape. Abused. Exhausted. Malnourished herself. Beyond that, we know nothing about her. She had no ID of any kind. So far, no one has come forward to claim her or the baby."

He hesitated, wondering what else might be helpful for Lee to know. "When she was told that her baby had died, she went into some kind of catatonic or fugue state. They're getting a psych consult today. We know she can speak, because she was screaming for help in that closet. Since then, she's never said a single word. About all we know is that she's way too young to be a mother, that she was found in a mosque and was wearing a headscarf, and that someone had been restraining her with handcuffs that were brutally tight."

Lee shook his head. "To keep her from seeking help for her child, maybe?"

"Maybe."

"Every time you think nothing can surprise you," Lee said, and went back to work.

There were no more significant findings, and Lee finished with his usual alacrity, retreating into silence except for his dictation, as though he regretted any display of emotion.

Since Lee's discovery and explanation of its meaning, Sage Prentiss had been growing steadily greener. When the green turned to grayish white, Burgess nodded at Dani. "Take him out."

It was only when Dani took him by the elbow and led him out of the room that Burgess remembered. Prentiss had a newborn son at home. A bad choice as his second for today's autopsy. He should have brought someone from his team after all.

But that was the job. When duty called, you went places you never wanted to go and saw unimaginable things, and you didn't get to wimp out because it was painful or horrifying or ugly beyond belief. You just took what the job dished out.

"I miss your regular team, Joe," Lee said. "Wink Devlin never turns green."

Burgess shrugged. "Guy's got a baby about this age at home. You know how that is."

"I do," Lee said. "So I'm hoping that even with the B team, you're going to arrest some people for this atrocity. Atrocities."

He began to put the baby back together, deft as a card shark. "I'm assuming that the fire was no accident?"

He stepped back from the table and nodded to his silent assistant, who moved in to finish. "Meant to finish off the baby and ensure that the mother caused no further trouble?"

Burgess considered that and shook his head. "I just don't know," he said, "but despite the carelessness and the cruelty, I think someone wanted that baby. The mother didn't matter but the baby did. My gut tells me I may have two unrelated events here that happened to coincide. One involving controlling the mother and baby, a holding place until someone could figure out what to do with them. The other involving a need to destroy the building, or a dispute about the building. A right hand and a left hand not communicating, maybe?"

Lee raised his eyebrows. Normally, neither of them was this talkative. Sometimes, he and the ME weren't on the same page.

But Burgess felt something in the room. Now that Prentiss and Dani were gone, he and Lee could let their professional masks slip a little. Beyond the clinical coldness of the metal surfaces and washable tiles, and the sharp, utilitarian tools, there was heat in the room, an anger that shimmered off both of them at people who used other people like they didn't matter. At the senseless suffering and loss of this tiny child.

Burgess remembered the feeling of his mystery girl's hand in his and imaged that hand trying to sooth this baby.

"It was a Somali mosque, and no one in that community is willing to talk to us. Yet."

"Yet?"

"You know me," Burgess said. "Ever the optimist."

"And if I believe that, you've got a bridge to sell me?"

Burgess didn't deal in bridges. Like Lee, he dealt in lives lost. "I'll find a way in."

They stood side by side as the assistant began to sew up the incisions.

"Seriously. Are you going to get these people, Joe?"

He'd never known Dr. Lee to care like this.

"Just so helpless," Lee said. "All he could do was cry, and pull his little legs up to try and ease the pain. How anyone could watch that and—"

He shook his head. "The poor little guy. An awful life. An awful death. And he doesn't even have a name."

Abruptly, he turned and walked out of the room.

CHAPTER SIXTEEN

On the drive back to Portland, Prentiss kept apologizing. Even after Burgess told him it was okay, he understood, it happened and it was no big deal, Prentiss took a while before he shut up. So much for taciturn.

Burgess wished he was alone in the car. Alone was when he did his best thinking, when he could use the transitions between events to analyze what he knew and decide where to go next. He couldn't do that over Prentiss's defensive apologies and Dani's calming murmur.

His anger hadn't subsided. He wasn't mad at them, but he wanted to stop and tell them to get out. Leave them standing beside the road while he drove on, letting the trails of story simmer in his brain until they began to connect, to make sense, to link up or show him the potential for linkage. Despite the time they'd put in on this case, they had very little that was solid. He hoped by the time he got back to 109 and sat down with Kyle and Perry, their days would have been productive and he'd have something to work with. Maybe Press Devlin would have a line on Butcher Flaherty.

The grass in the median was beginning to green up, and an optimistic woodchuck had come out to see what he could eat. Along the roadsides, the trees were beginning to furze with the first explosion of soft yellow green. He wished he could grab this hopeful promise of renewed life and possibility and wrap it around himself, smothering what felt like deep blackness inside.

He'd jokingly described himself as an optimist. What he really was was a deep pessimist with remnants of a Catholic education crossed with a bulldozer.

He needed to make things happen because people depended on him. His mystery girl and his little lost baby. Kids like Jason that life had kicked to the curb. So if he sometimes had to bulldoze his way through piles of crap, forgetting the curtsey Captain Cote was always urging, and worrying Lieutenant Melia, that was just how it was. Always a challenge. Harder, these days, because of the tail of tin cans his newfound domestic life tied to his bumper. Chris said that being home for family dinner was very important, his presence an important part of integrating their complicated family. A case like this meant dinner might not happen at all, but it added people with a new set of expectations to his already long list.

He sighed and called Kyle, got the usual crisp, "Kyle."

"Burgess," he said. "Getting anything?"

"I remember when that question was kind of a fun one to be asked."

"And today?"

"Squat. My source is nowhere to be found."

"Lotta people playing hard to get today," Burgess said, jerking the wheel to avoid a senior citizen in a Corolla who had drifted into his lane. Stan Perry, who sometimes lacked the milk of human kindness, called them Q-tips, because often all that was visible was a little tuft of white hair behind the steering wheel.

"Maybe young Stanley has had some luck," Kyle said.

"What about our translator?"

"More nothing," Kyle said. "Meet back at 109?" Before Burgess could respond, Kyle said, "Oh fuck!"

"What?"

"Soccer game."

"When you gotta go," Burgess said. "Hope she has a good day."

"Be nice if someone did. See you when?"

"What works for you?"

"I'm new to all this," Kyle said. "How long do these things take?"

"Soccer game? An hour, maybe," Burgess said. "Let's aim for six."

"Family dinner," Kyle said. "How about seven thirty? You learn anything from the autopsy?"

"Kid had a kink in his gut. Needed surgery. Would have been screaming his little head off. We might start asking about whether the Imam's neighbors have been hearing a baby cry."

"Ouch," Kyle said. "Think there will ever be some good news?"

"Wishing and hoping," Burgess said. He disconnected and called Perry.

"Stan Perry." Perry managed to get a paragraph of sullen into those two words.

"Anything?" Burgess said.

"Lotta people done a disappearing act today," Perry said. "The translator. His girlfriend, or whoever the woman is who owns the car that picked him up last night. Her name's Rihanna Daud. Everyone at the Imam's place, unless they've just forgotten that a knock on the door means someone is out there who wants to come in. I'm about ready to start kicking in some doors."

"Some folks back at 109 who might not agree with that approach."

"So maybe we should go sit in their offices, sharpen our pencils and straighten our papers, and they can go out and try to talk to this city full of know-nothings."

"Great idea, Stan. We're getting together at seven thirty to talk about the case, and you should definitely suggest that."

"Can't do seven thirty. I promised my girl I'd—"

Burgess felt a twinge of anger. "I thought we were personal crimes police," he said. "But it sounds like everybody's too busy doing happy domestic thingys to bother with investigation."

"Screw that, Sarge. I'm not feeling happy or domestic."

"She know we're working a dead baby?"

"She only wants to talk about a live baby."

"See what you can do, Stan. I need you there."

"I know that."

"What about that robbery at the mall? Computer stuff?"

"Just grabbed a guy from property. We're heading out there now. Hoping those serial numbers will help."

Perry disconnected.

"Sage," Burgess said, "I need your help."

He filled the young detective in on the problems they were having getting any cooperation from the Imam or his household. "Love it if you could drop by and see if you have any better luck than we've had. If speaking the language helps. And there's a teenager, Ali Ibrahim, probably at the high school. Maybe if you spoke to him away from the house you might get a better response. We get back to 109, I'll give you some names and details."

"Happy to try," Prentiss said. "I'd like to contribute something to this investigation." He started in on another apology, but Burgess cut him off. The best kind of apology was good results.

"You've seen the baby. You know what this is about. We really could use a break somewhere in this thing."

They made the rest of the trip in silence.

Burgess stifled an impulse to drive slowly, knowing what was waiting for him. Melia pacing, Cote snappish because he had no reports. The press breathing down their necks, frustrated by the lack of instant, newsworthy results. A sea of pink message slips, none of which would offer anything in the way of a lead or useful information. He just hoped he wouldn't find any more bodies on his desk. He had a bad feeling about their translator's disappearance.

He sorted through what was in process, looking for a silver lining. Maybe tomorrow, Jason would have something for him, something that would let him put a plan in place about how to have a safe conversation with a Somali girl. Maybe he'd take Sage along as a second pair of eyes and ears.

Maybe Rocky had finished sorting through the corporate maze and they would have a landlord's name and address. Rocky was good, but he was just one person, and they needed a lot of information. It was time to get the AG's office involved, get a warrant for the mosque's records, the Imam's records, see if they could find checks or a lease or other paper trail. With luck, Perry might learn something on his trip to the mall.

He knew the importance of patience. Of nose-to-the-grindstone plodding. No sense in telling his guys to get themselves under control unless he could do the same.

After he'd given the information to Sage, he went to see his lieutenant. The office was peaceful, neat, and quiet, but the impeccable Vince Melia looked like someone had been chewing on him and it had left him frayed. Burgess, being a detective, could figure out who that was. But after he'd dropped into the guest chair and studied his boss more closely, he realized this was different. Melia looked worried and defeated in a way that Cote's persistent nagging didn't usually produce.

"Something wrong with one of the twins?" he said.

Melia looked startled, then nodded. "Lucas. He hasn't been himself. Lethargic. Always getting sick. Like Gina said, kids are always getting sick, but this wasn't normal kid sick. Docs are doing a workup. Best case, mono. Maybe chronic fatigue. Worst case?" He faltered, looked down at his hands, then back at Burgess, his voice almost a whisper. "Leukemia."

The way they worked was to hope for the best and plan for the worst. Burgess didn't think that would be any comfort to his boss. "About this case, Vince. We've got your back. You worry about what you need to worry about."

Melia's mouth stretched in a thin smile. "I'm the lieutenant in charge of CID."

"And a dad. This case is a bitch, but the Crips will solve it. We always come through, don't we?"

"Not before you try my patience. I gonna have some reports from you today?"

"Something to throw to the lions? You bet. I just have to figure out how to bury all the sensitive stuff in a snowdrift of words."

"That's damned poetic, Joe."

"It's the coming of spring, Vince. It gets the sap aflowing, turns a man's thoughts to—"

"There's only one place I want your thoughts going, and it is *not* in the direction of your sap."

"Autopsy got my anger flowing, too, Vince. That was brutal. And Dr. Lee was . . . well, you know how he is. Today he was mad. Really leaning on me about solving this." He filled Melia in on what they'd learned. "It's time we got the AG's office working on the paper side of this. Especially since we're getting zero cooperation from the Imam and his family."

"Good call," Melia said. "Rocky can't do it all."

"No man is an island."

"You can stuff the freakin' platitudes, Sergeant Burgess."

"Yes, sir. Did you know that Sage speaks some Somali?"

Melia's hands were knotted in a tight ball. Burgess watched them uncurl. "That's good news, right?"

"Right."

"You want him on this?"

"I need him on this."

"Okay. Write me some reports. Then get me some results." He stood, and grabbed his jacket, shoving his arms into the sleeves as he headed for the door. "Gina's at the doctor's with Lucas. I've gotta go get Link at school. He's really spooked by all this."

Identical twins—of course Lincoln was spooked about what was happening to his brother. Burgess nodded. "I see the captain, I'll head him off and bury him in paper."

"You do that. Keep me up on any developments."

"Count on it."

Burgess watched Melia's square shoulders disappear from the detective's bay, seeing a reluctance in his boss's walk about leaving a place where maybe he knew what was going on.

Then he went to his desk. Around him, the place swarmed with controlled chaos. He shut it out and settled into his chair, ready for his least favorite part of the job. It looked like a roll of that pink insulation had exploded somewhere in midair and the detritus had drifted down to land willy-nilly on his desktop. Although the department was getting modern and a lot of information now came via e-mail, their sensible obsession with keeping a paper trail meant most messages still came in written form.

He gathered them into a single stack and set them aside as he called up the report form on his computer screen. He might not be much of a typist, but it was far better to work from an on-screen template than to fill this out by hand. He pushed his way through a narrative about the fire scene and one about what had happened at the hospital with his victims. He was about to start on his visit to the Imam when the strain of ignoring all that pink paper overcame him.

He hit print, then snatched them up, turned his back on the screen, and began reading through them. A message from the hospital confirming that a psych consult had been done on his mystery girl, and giving him a name and number to call for details. A message to call Wink Devlin in the lab about prints from the car they'd seized last night at the hospital. Another from Wink asking him to stop in the lab when he had a chance.

There was a message to call Scott Lavigne and one to call Davey Green in the fire marshal's office. Then there was a message from Chris, asking him to "handle it." He hadn't discovered what "it" was yet. He quickly sorted through the pile until he found one from Dylan's school, asking him to call as soon as possible. A second, inviting him to come and pick up his son. A third, saying that Dylan had been suspended and could he please call the principal's office.

Dammit! They had his cell phone number. Why had they called the department? Why hadn't one of the assistants thought to call him? These messages were hours old. They must think him the worst parent on the planet. And this probably meant that Dylan had been cooling his heels outside some administrator's office, waiting for his father to arrive, all that time.

Crap. He snatched up the phone and dialed the number that appeared on all of the messages.

Chapter Seventeen

The woman on the other end of the phone, when he finally reached the person identified on the message slips as Dr. Alyce Jorgensen, assistant principal, sounded way too smug when she said, "Mr. Burgess. We've been waiting for your call for hours."

He admitted to being a ball of knee-jerk prejudices, and one of them was a visceral negative reaction to educators with PhDs who called themselves "Doctor."

"I apologize, Ms. Jorgensen," he said. "I was attending the autopsy of a murdered baby. We can't take calls in there. And you didn't call my cell phone, so that compounded the delay. If you could make a note of that, for your file?" He reeled off the number, then carefully and slowly repeated it, and asked, "Can you read it back to me, please?"

All right. He was misbehaving and he knew it. But even at the fine school his son attended, the administration was all about power and control, and so was he. So he wanted to start this off on the right foot, power-wise, whatever his son was alleged to have done.

He realized that he was acting like almost every parent he'd ever dealt with—the ones who cared about their children, at least, perhaps even the overprotective ones—and had to smile at how easily he'd fallen into this.

When she'd read back the number, he said, "Now, tell me what this is about."

"Well, Mr. Burgess—"

"Detective Sergeant Burgess," he corrected.

"Officer—"

"Detective Sergeant," he said. "Go on."

"Dylan was in a fight," she said, in a tone that suggested the boy had just blown up city hall. "We've given him a one-day suspension. We need you to come and pick him up."

"Tell me about the fight," he said.

"We can discuss the circumstances when you get here, Mr.
. . . uh . . . Detective Sergeant Burgess."

"Fine."

He grabbed his coat and checked for all the usual gear. A lot more stuff than an American Express card that he couldn't leave home without. And this might not be home, but he'd sure spent more time here than anywhere else in the last three decades. He clipped the reports he'd just done together and stopped at the assistant's desk.

"Can you get these up to Captain Cote? He's waiting for them." Then, "The next time one of my kids' schools calls, give 'em my cell number, okay?"

He wanted to do more, but no sensible cop offended the support staff unless a staffer was hopelessly incompetent. They had way too much power over whether life went smoothly. He had enough bumps in his road without creating new ones.

"Kids?" the younger one, Lorna, said, raising an eyebrow.

"Three. Dylan, Nina, and Ned," Burgess said. "I'd show you pictures, but I'm in kind of a rush. Dylan's been suspended."

"I'm sorry," she said. Then, with an impish grin, she added, "You go set 'em straight, Sergeant."

"That's the plan," he said, and headed for the stairs.

Dr. Jorgensen looked too young for her job, though she'd tried to compensate by wearing her hair in a severe bun that made her face look stretched, and glasses with thick, dark rims. After he'd navigated the school security and was admitted to the building, he'd found Dylan slumped in a chair outside her office, and now he entered with his son in tow.

She glanced from him to Dylan and back to him. "I'd hoped we'd get a chance to talk before—"

"It's Dylan's business, too, Dr. Jorgensen," he said, glad she didn't know about interview protocols the way he did. He would never interview two people together if he wanted to get their separate versions of the story, nor if he wanted to be completely in charge of the agenda. He figured she wanted to give him the "official" version before he spoke with his son. He figured that Dylan had a right to hear what the administration had to say. He might be figuring wrong. His son might have done something unacceptably aggressive—he was very inexperienced at this parenting thing—but that was not the Dylan he knew.

He and Dylan sat in the visitor's chairs facing the desk she had retreated behind. He was aware for the first time of how big his son was. How much of a matched set they must seem to her, two hulking men with shoulders too wide for their chairs, one with crisp dark hair, the other graying, both with fierce featured faces set in "show it to me" mode.

Chris would have laughed and softened them both right up. Dr. Jorgensen, on the other hand, seemed intimidated by so much male bulk filling her small office.

He leaned back in his chair, creating the illusion of more distance, and said, "Tell me what happened."

Beside him, he felt Dylan stiffen, preparing to defend himself. He put a light hand on his son's arm. "We're just beginning our conversation here. You'll get a chance to speak."

If she resented him taking over the agenda, he was sorry. But he didn't have time for too many niceties or beating around any bushes.

"As you know, Mr. . . . Detective Sergeant . . . we have a no-fighting rule here at the school."

He nodded.

"And this afternoon, during lunch period, your son engaged in a confrontation with two other students in the cafeteria, during which he yelled at them and then shoved them both with enough force that one knocked over a chair and the other nearly knocked over a table. Several students' lunches were spilled."

Beside him, Dylan drew an angry breath. Burgess held up a hand.

"Were either of them injured?" he asked.

She shook her head.

"Were either of these boys significantly smaller than Dylan?"

She shook her head again.

"Did Dylan tell you why he shoved these boys?"

She nodded. "He said they were picking on a girl in a head-scarf."

"So he just went up to them and shoved them?"

"Well, no. He asked them to leave her alone and stop teasing her."

"And?"

"He says they didn't. Instead, one of them pulled the scarf off and was waving it around, and so he asked the boy to give it back, and when the boy didn't, Dylan grabbed the scarf away from him and sent him sprawling."

It sounded honorable to Burgess. He tried to keep that off his face.

"Is the girl all right?"

"She's fine."

"She got her scarf back?"

"Certainly."

"Have these boys engaged in this type of behavior before?"

"Our concern here, Mr. Burgess, is with *your* son and his behavior."

"Detective Sergeant," he said. "I understand that, Dr. Jorgensen. Just trying to get the whole picture." He gave her an embarrassed smile. "Just the facts, ma'am, you see. I assume you have a policy on bullying? And one on sexual harassment? I would like copies of both of those, please."

She looked like she was ready to explode. Burgess was sorry. He'd gone to this school. It was an excellent school that provided a strong, old-fashioned education in both academic subjects and character. He admired the school. He'd chosen it for Dylan. That didn't mean they never made mistakes. He needed to be sure that coming down this hard on Dylan, when his son was already struggling with so much adjustment, wasn't a mistake.

"They are both in the handbook you were given when Dylan was accepted."

"Of course," he said. "I mean for now, for the purpose of this discussion, if it wouldn't be too inconvenient."

She swung her chair around, grabbed a thin book off the shelf, and shoved it in his general direction.

He'd put his phone on vibrate and now it was doing a demented dance in his pocket. He wanted to check it. Probably needed to check it. But she would take it the wrong way, and things weren't going swimmingly as it was.

He thanked her, took the book, and quickly checked the sections on fighting, on bullying, and on sexual harassment. Satisfied, he looked up at her.

"Let me back up a bit. Were there any teachers or monitors in the room who observed the circumstances which occurred before these boys were pushed?"

"Yes," she said. "There were two."

He had his notebook out, a habit as natural as breathing, and now his automatic response was to take names. "Their names and their titles?"

Reluctantly, she told him. A Mary Stevenson, who was a lunchroom monitor, and Mr. Randall, a teacher.

"And you've spoken with both of them?"

She nodded.

"Do they confirm Dylan's account or are their versions different?"

"They are pretty consistent with his account."

"What about the girl? When you spoke with her, what did she say?"

"She's very shy. Very reticent," Jorgensen said. "She didn't want to talk about it. She doesn't like to make trouble."

She doesn't like to make trouble sounded like this sort of thing had happened before. Beside him, he felt the change in Dylan. His son had stopped waiting for a chance to speak and was watching like this was theater. Which, in a way, it was.

"When you interviewed the two boys, what was their version of the events?"

"They were just teasing her. The girl didn't mind. Your son didn't understand the dynamic and overreacted."

"Were the two boys who were harassing that girl suspended?"

She shook her head.

"Reprimanded? Put on in-school suspension? Given detention? Punished in any way?"

This time, she could barely bring herself to respond that no, nothing had happened with respect to the other boys.

"So my son has missed an afternoon of classes and will miss a day of school tomorrow, but these two boys, who you admit acted in concert and forcibly removed an item of clothing from this girl's body—an intimate item, in fact, given its importance in protecting her modesty—received no punishment? Is that correct?"

When she didn't answer, he opened the handbook for students and parents to the section on sexual harassment, turned it to face her, and slid it across the desk. "As I read your policy, this is a textbook case of sexual harassment. Do you disagree with my interpretation?"

"Just like your son, Mr. Burgess, you are making a mountain out of a molehill."

He thought Captain Cote might agree. Knew how often Cote had been wrong.

"At this point, I'm just locating the mountain and the molehill, ma'am," he said, "so I can understand their relative positions. But just so we're clear. Would the administration's reaction have been the same if these boys had pulled off a different article of this girl's clothing? Like her blouse? What if they had snatched a cross she was wearing around her neck? I think we both understand that that headscarf isn't fashion, it's an aspect of her religion."

He gave her a moment to process that, then said, "Let's hear Dylan's version."

At some point, his son had probably had a pretty clear and coherent version of the events prepared. Dylan was a pretty methodical kid. But what came out was pure emotion.

"Dad, Dr. Jorgensen, those guys pick on Leyla every day. They're always grabbing at her. At her books, at her backpack, at her purse, and especially at her scarf. Keeping her scarf on, that's really important to her. It's part of being modest. They know it upsets her, so they try to pull it down. She's asked them to leave her alone. She's asked the teachers—the ones she can bring herself to speak to—for help. She's very shy, Dad. But they don't pay any attention. They think it's just boys teasing girls. And it's not. It's about her religion. It's about making her feel unsafe and unwanted."

Dylan grabbed a breath and went on. "I've asked them a couple times to stop. They're juniors and I'm just a lowly freshman, so they don't think they have to listen to me. Especially since there are two of them and only one of me. But Dad. But Dr. Jorgensen. What am I supposed to do? Sit by and let this happen, when no one else will do anything? She really . . ."

The size-twelve sneakers shifted on the dull brown carpet and Dylan watched them as he formulated what he wanted to say next. "She really wants to get a good education. No one in her family has ever gone to high school. But she's feeling so helpless she's wondering if she should give it up."

He pulled himself up in his chair and squared his shoulders. Burgess could see himself in the gesture. Nature, clearly, not nurture. The big brother. Burgess figured Dylan would do the same for Nina, despite their endless squabbling. "So I know I shouldn't have shoved them like I did, but they wouldn't leave her alone. I could see that she was terrified. I asked them to stop and they just laughed and Tyler pulled her scarf off. And Mr. Randall was standing not six feet away and he wouldn't do a thing about it. He wouldn't help her."

He shifted his gaze from the shoes to Burgess's face. "What was I supposed to do? Let them pick on someone small and helpless, like Leyla? I couldn't do that."

Unexpectedly, Burgess felt like he might cry. He could imagine his mother meeting this boy. Getting to know her so very decent grandson, and Dylan getting to know her. He felt the pain of that two-way loss like a knife in his gut.

In his pocket, his phone danced and spun.

He put his arm around his son's shoulder, probably a gesture that would leave Dylan not speaking to him for a month, and squeezed. Then he looked over at Dr. Jorgensen.

"This is what you suspended him for? For protecting someone helpless and terrified from a pair of bullies?" He gave that a beat. "As I see it, there are three ways this can go from here. You can retract the suspension based on your further investigation of the incident, punish the other students involved for their infractions, and ensure that this girl, Leyla, is given the adequate protection from sexual and religious harassment she deserves. That would be the best resolution.

"Second, much as I dislike the press, I could share this story with some local reporters. It's just the kind of thing the national news would jump on. Muslim girl harassed at Christian school while male teachers stand idly by and watch. Or I could hire a lawyer and make us all waste unnecessary time and money. I would far prefer that we agree on the first."

She had her hand splayed across her chest like a shocked matron in an old movie.

"None of this has to leave this room," Burgess reminded her. "I'm not going to say anything. Dylan isn't going to say anything. The school's reputation is intact. You get points for treating everyone fairly and for finding an opportunity to remind your students about harassment and respect for religious differences. Seems to me that it's a win-win."

She slapped the handbook shut, turning her back on them as she stuck it back on the shelf. They both watched her back, her shoulders rigid, her head erect, as she stood awhile, her fingers resting lightly on the edge of the shelf.

Finally, she turned back to them. In a slightly strangled voice, she said, "I'll see you in the morning, Dylan."

She took a couple of calming breaths, then held her hand out to Burgess. "Detective Sergeant. I sincerely we hope we do not meet again."

In the moment, he wanted to grant her wish, but he'd be back here again. It was the nature of the job and the nature of schools.

"It's pretty likely that we will, Dr. Jorgensen. Portland police are in and out of the schools all the time. I'm surprised we haven't met before. Have you been here long?"

"Dylan and I started on the same day," she said.

"It's a great school," he said. "I hope you'll be happy here. And don't think, for a moment, that I don't appreciate the difficulty of your job."

Two more breaths, and she thawed.

"Thank you," she said.

"You're welcome."

Burgess and his son left.

CHAPTER EIGHTEEN

Three girls in headscarves were sitting on a bench outside the school, looking like they were waiting for someone to pick them up. Although all three avoided actually looking at him or his son, Burgess sensed an acknowledgment from the smallest one. A gesture so admirably subtle it looked like she'd spent a lifetime keeping everything about herself under wraps.

"Leyla," Dylan whispered. "Don't look at her."

Burgess complied.

As soon as they were in the truck, Dylan wanted to talk, but Burgess held up a hand. "Got to check my phone," he said. "Someone's been awfully anxious to reach me all during that meeting."

Dylan nodded. A quick study in what it meant to be a cop's kid, he stuck his earbuds in his ears and settled back to wait.

Burgess pulled out the dancing phone. Kyle looking for him. Perry looking for him. Melia looking for him. Captain Cote looking for him. The hospital looking for him. When he saw that message, his heart jumped. Please don't let something have happened to his mystery girl.

He decided to call Melia first. "Vince, it's Burgess. What's going on?"

"Officer on patrol found your translator in the trunk of a car. Ambulance has taken him to the hospital, but he's in bad shape, shot twice. Terry says it doesn't look good."

"I'll head on over there. Anything else I should know about?"

"Nothing pressing. The captain would like details about the autopsy, when you have time."

"I'm trying, Vince."

"Keep me in the loop."

Vince always said it. Burgess tried to honor it. He disconnected and called Kyle.

"Fill me in," he said, when Kyle answered.

"About an hour ago, patrol spotted the license number of the car that picked Osman up at the hospital last night in a lot out toward the Westbrook line. Guy stopped to check, saw blood on the seats, and popped the trunk. Found Osman in there. Someone beat him pretty bad, then shot him a couple times and left him in the trunk."

"No sign of the driver?"

"Nope."

"Remind me. Who was that car registered to?"

"Woman named Rihanna Daud. We've got people going by her house. I'm not getting a good feeling about it, though."

"I'll be there soon. Gotta drop Dylan off at home."

"Dylan? Oh crap," Kyle said. "The soccer game."

"Brief me, then head out there. You can still make part of it. Stan can cover things there."

"Stan's gone to the computer store. He was feeling kind of itchy to make something happen."

A feeling they were all experiencing right now.

"Take me with you, Dad," Dylan said. "That'll save you some time."

Amazing what the kid could hear with those earbuds in. Why not take Dylan along? He'd already said he was curious about what his father did. This would be an uncensored glimpse.

"I'm on my way now, Terry," he said, and headed for the hospital.

179

"Where are we going and why are we going there?" Dylan asked.

"Have a translator, name of Hussain Osman, we used for an interview last night. Later, Stan and Terry were looking for him, swung by his house and found someone had attacked him. They brought him to the hospital. We asked him to wait for us after he was treated, so we could interview him about the attack, but he skipped out on us."

Burgess wondered how much of this he should tell. "He didn't show for a meeting today, so Terry and Stan went looking for him. Patrol just found him in the trunk of a car. He's been shot."

"Why?"

"We don't know yet. Hope he lives long enough to tell us."

Was that too blunt? Dylan had been raised by a lawyer and a judge, but how protective had they been? He had no idea. Figured he might as well ask. "Your mom and dad talk to you about their cases?"

"You're my dad."

"Stepdad. The judge. What did you call him, anyway?"

"The other kids called him 'Dad,' so I did, too, but he never seemed to feel like he was my dad."

What an ass the man had been. "So, did they talk about their work much?"

"Mom did. Sometimes she'd take me to court with her, or to the office, if I didn't have school. And in the car, she'd tell me about her cases and ask for my reactions. She represented a lot of kids, see, and she thought my perspective might be helpful."

"At the hospital," Burgess began.

"I know. Stay out of the way and keep my mouth shut, right?"

"Right."

They drove in silence a while, but it was a comfortable silence, not their too-frequent awkward one. "I'd better call

180

Chris and let her know why I'm late," Dylan said. "Or Doro, I mean. She's a cool lady."

Burgess agreed. Doro was a cool lady. A wise lady. She reminded him of his mother. Someone who put love for family first. Unlike his mother, Doro wasn't afraid to speak her mind.

He made a quick call to Sage Prentiss, to see if he'd had any luck getting that floor plan from the Imam. Didn't get an answer, so he moved it back to the to-do list and called Melia again.

"We have someone from the AG's office on this yet? Because I need a bunch of subpoenas for the Imam's records, the mosque's records, and I'm not getting any cooperation there."

"One of your favorite people, as a matter of fact."

Rita Callahan, voice like Brillo on a screen, face like a pounded steak, and the tenacity and charm of a pit bull. Luckily, Burgess didn't need charm and he wanted tenacity. "Great. I'll give her a call."

But she wasn't at her desk, so he left a message, and that became another task that stayed on the ever-growing list.

Kyle was pacing the waiting room, wearing all the controlled potential for a violent explosion a panther might. The other people in the room were watching him warily, like they feared they might be his chosen prey. Burgess knew Kyle had no idea how he struck people. The general population at any rate. Kyle absolutely knew how to turn his cold gaze on someone who needed settling down. Generally, people regarded Burgess, with his bulk and his scarred face, as the scary one, but Burgess knew Kyle was one of his secret weapons. Bring out that cold gray-eyed stare and tightly coiled anger, and people often gave it up pretty quickly.

"Fill me in, Ter, and then get the hell out of here. You're scaring the citizens."

Kyle looked around at the sea of staring faces. "Sorry, Joe. I forget."

"Yes. You do."

"Hey, Dylan," Kyle said. "Pretty soon you're gonna be patting this guy on the head."

"I hope so, sir," Dylan said.

Kyle smiled and patted the boy's shoulder, and the three of them went off into a corner to confer.

Burgess liked his son's innate politeness. Something of a rarity these days. And what he'd learned this afternoon at the school of his son's protective nature. He'd been a big brother, knew something of the job. He liked that his son seemed to be taking it on. Nina and Neddy could use another champion.

Burgess got out his notebook and wrote down Kyle's information. The location of the lot, the name of the car's owner and her address. The same name and same car that had picked him up at the hospital last night.

"We've got Osman's cell phone," Kyle said. "It was in his pocket. I can go over it when I get back to 109, look for calls and texts. You can get his wallet and his clothes. I've arranged to have the car towed. That's how many cars in the last twenty-four? Three?"

"Did we collect Ismail's car or just work it there on the street?" Burgess couldn't remember, and that scared him. Getting to be such an old fart things were slipping his mind.

"At the scene," Kyle said. "Then it got towed to a dealer to get the glass replaced. Captain Cote would have a fit if we'd brought in three cars. He might have to park on the street."

"I wonder why someone is targeting him?" Burgess sad. "Osman, not Cote. That I would understand. There were bad vibes between him and the Imam's crew, but why this?"

"Maybe because of what he said to us as he was leaving. About Hawala?" Kyle suggested. "Maybe we need to talk with our friends the Feds, see if they know anything they're willing to share."

"The Feds" and "willing to share" rarely belonged in the same sentence, but a cop could always hope. "You know anyone over there?"

"We're supposed to have a liaison working with them on just this sort of thing, Joe. Vince was going to check that out, make the call. You know how much our friends over at world's greatest like to deal with rank. Even if they do piss all over it."

Dylan had been trying to keep a straight face. Now he smiled. "You know, Dad—" He put a hand over his mouth, remembering he was supposed to shut up and listen. Then he went on. "I'm pretty good at computer stuff. Searches. Maybe I could help?"

"Maybe," Burgess said. He didn't want to involve his son in this, not even just sitting at a keyboard. Something he'd have to think about. Consider if they kept meeting dead ends. But there was an undercurrent of indifferent violence to this case. A cold savagery that wasn't usual. Something he didn't think they'd seen the end of yet. It made him wonder about motorcycle gangs. Some of the things they did smacked of this. As did some of the drug-fueled violence they saw, both from users so strung out they'd lost touch with their humanity and from dealers who simply cared about nothing but their profits. People who used horrific violence to keep other people in line.

Or was it simply the actions of people coming from a country so riven by war that social structure had crumbled? Two of his kids had already seen unimaginable violence. He wanted to keep the home front a safe place. One of the reasons Akiba Simba Norton's threat had made him so angry. Things at home had to be secure so he could go out and do this job.

"Okay, Ter. I've got this. You go catch the end of that game. We'll meet up later."

Kyle was out the door like he was being chased. He was, of course. Chased by guilt. By the specter of social services and the court watching him, making him prove he was able to be an adequate father to his girls even while working a demanding job. A whole lot of that fell on his girlfriend, Michelle, just like a lot of Burgess's job fell on Chris and Doro. Recent events were giving him a lot more respect for single parents.

He left Dylan in the lobby while he checked in with the ER. Osman was still alive and had been taken to surgery. They would keep him posted. It did not look good. Burgess collected his bloody clothes, his shoes, his phone, and wallet. Left his cell number for updates.

Then, since he was already at the hospital, he went to check on his mystery girl.

Remy was gone and Andrea Dwyer was in his chair by the bedside, reading. She turned quickly as he came in, her hand going automatically to the gun at her side.

"Oh. Joe. It's you. Sorry."

She looked past him at Dylan, lurking in the doorway. "What did you do, Sarge, get yourself cloned?"

"Something like that."

Dwyer unfolded from the chair and went to Dylan, her hand out. "Officer Andrea Dwyer," she said.

Dylan took her hand politely. "I'm Dylan. I'm Joe's son."

"I can see that," she said, rocking all of the boy's adolescent insecurities with her grin and all the rest of her charms. "Just wondering how he did that so fast. Last I heard, Sergeant Burgess was a grouchy old bachelor."

"Oh, he's still all of that, ma'am," Dylan said. "But I believe that grouchy, unmarried men can still father children."

Dwyer laughed aloud. "Got all his father's tact and charm, I see."

Dylan blushed, and Burgess turned away from them to look

at the girl in the bed. She was still curled on her side. That seemed to be her favored position. But now her eyes were open. She was watching them, those dark eyes flitting from him to Dylan and back to him. Beyond the bed, on the rolling table, was an untouched lunch tray.

"Joe Burgess," he reminded her. "And that's my son, Dylan. Which I guess you can tell. Can you excuse us for a minute?"

He herded Dwyer and his son outside the door. "I need to talk to Officer Dwyer for a minute. Do you think you could find your way to the cafeteria and bring back some ice cream? Chocolate, I think. Get one for yourself, if you want. Andrea, you want anything?"

"Coffee would be good. Black. One sugar."

Burgess took ten dollars from his wallet and gave it to Dylan. He and Dwyer stood shoulder to shoulder, watching the boy's retreating back.

"It must be spooky," she said.

"What?"

"Seeing your young self like that. He looks exactly like you."

"It is," he admitted. "Today we were sitting beside each other, and we each folded our arms and shifted our weight in just the same way at just the same moment. He seems pretty genial today, maybe because I just got him unsuspended from school. Usually we're fighting tooth and nail."

"Unsuspended? I'll bet that was something to see."

He sighed. "I don't think I behaved very well, actually."

"Most parents don't under those circumstances."

"So catch me up on our girl."

"I don't think she's screwing with us, Joe. I think she really can't speak, because there were a couple times today when it looked like she really wanted to. Like when Remy left. He's probably left you some notes on this, but the woman from psych says extreme trauma can do this. That we just have to be patient

185

and let it happen on our girl's own terms. She'll talk to us when she's ready. And we're not supposed to push her."

He nodded. "Just wondering what we do with her when she doesn't need the hospital anymore."

Dwyer looked down at the floor, shifted uncomfortably, then said, "She'll have to be here a little longer. She's going to need some surgery. I guess she got pretty torn up, delivering that baby, and no one took care of it. Stitched her up, I mean. I mean, dammit, Joe. Who in hell lets this happen to a child like that? Even a hundred years ago, a midwife knew enough to stitch a woman up. But whoever had her just didn't bother."

Whoever had her. That was just what it looked like. The girl had been someone's prisoner. Had "belonged" to someone who hadn't bothered to take care of her. Maybe someone who wanted a child but the woman, the mother, didn't matter. It was consistent with everything they'd seen.

He saw that her hands had curled into fists. Dwyer spent her life working with the city's kids. She saw no end of awful things. But this was really getting to her. He knew just how that was. The rule was to maintain objective distance and generic caring, don't get involved with victims. Otherwise, the job would bleed you dry. But sometimes, you couldn't help it.

"You getting anywhere with this?" she asked.

From Cote, that would have been a criticism. From Melia, an anxious nudge. From Dwyer, it was just a question.

He shook his head. "Got a couple of helpful witnesses, I think, like Jason Stetson, but we're running into a stonewall from the Somali community."

"So many years of fighting in their own country," she said, "they're pretty careful about who they trust. You can trust your family, your clan, and you can't trust the police. Makes our job a whole lot harder. It's going to change with the next generation. The ones who don't become thugs and gangstas are going to become more American. It's just a frustratingly slow process, from our perspective. I've got some sources who might be helpful. I'll see what I can do."

Impatience washed over him like a fever. This whole case was about waiting.

"I know," she said, as though she had read his mind. "It's very frustrating. But we're going to win in the end. We are, Joe. You have to trust that."

Was this how the torch was passed? When the next generation of cops started stepping up and helping the old farts to limp through their last days?

"I think I need a good, swift kick," he said.

She gave him one of her quick, surprising smiles. "You're our role model, Joe. What is it you're always saying to me? Shoulder to the wheel? Patience and determination? I'm just reminding you."

"Thanks, Andrea."

They watched Dylan returning with a tray. Two cups of ice cream and a coffee. He seemed unusually content, the sullen look gone from his face. Burgess wondered if he should bring his son along more often.

He took a spoon and one of the cups of ice cream, and sat down beside the bed. The dark eyes watched him as he spooned some up. "You like ice cream?" he asked.

He moved the spoon toward her mouth. She shifted, never taking her eyes off the spoon, and let him feed her a bite of ice cream. Then another. And another. Opening her mouth like a hungry little bird.

There was nothing more he could do at the hospital, so Burgess and Dylan headed home. They would call him when Osman was out of surgery and let him know how things looked. Before he started the truck, he checked his messages. There had been no word yet from Perry about the Apple theft and Perry wasn't answering his phone. Rocky had left some pictures on his desk, blowups of the watch and ring and the man who had gotten away.

Shoulder to the grindstone and patience and persistence were all very well, but the stuff on his desk, and the report on the autopsy, could wait until he'd gone home and participated in family dinner. They were all meeting again at seven thirty.

CHAPTER NINETEEN

"Lexi runs like a gazelle," Kyle said. "I barely got there in time, but I got to watch the end and she was just amazing."

"They win?" Perry asked.

"Toughest team they play, and she's youngest kid on her team? You bet they did. She says she saw me watching and it felt like she had wings on her feet."

They all took a moment—even cynical Stan Perry—to savor the good before plunging into their work.

Then, like the silent prayer was over, Burgess handed out Rocky's pictures of the watch and the ring. "Rocky says that's a seriously expensive watch," he said. "Probably in the range of fifteen to twenty thousand dollars. And that's a Maine Maritime Academy ring. Can't read the date, but it has some wear, and our guy looks to be in his early forties. We might get something if we looked at old yearbooks."

"What's someone with an expensive watch doing driving around in a stolen car with a sleazy guy like Akiba Norton?" Perry said.

"That," Burgess said, "is one of the sixty-four-thousand-dollar questions. I expect that he needed an assistant without many scruples. Questions, we've got plenty of. What I'd like is some answers."

He turned to Perry, who was shuffling through some papers. "Stan, you learn anything at the mall?"

Perry nodded. "A whole van load of computers were stolen

before they ever arrived at the store." He handed over some stapled papers. "Here's the report from South Portland PD. Two box trucks pulled in next to the van as it arrived at the loading dock, blocking the van from view. Masked men got out of the truck, held the van driver at gunpoint, and unloaded the merchandise into one of the two trucks. They tied up the driver and left him in his van. In broad daylight."

Perry glanced down at his notes. "It was well planned. Security cameras didn't get anything except shots of two white trucks. And the truck that took the goods was backed in and that part of it was blocked from camera view. The store manager and the police suspect an inside job but they couldn't come up with anything. Turns out our friend Ismail Ibrahim had an alibi. He took a poly anyway. Came up clean."

Perry shrugged. "Maybe they didn't ask the right questions. Like did he know anyone who might have been involved? Like maybe his father, his brothers, or some of his uncles?"

"Is the Imam his father?" Kyle asked.

"Grandfather, actually, but they regard him as their father. He raised them when their father was killed. All the Imam's sons were killed back in Somalia. He has a couple daughters and their husbands living with him, and three adult, or nearly adult, grandsons. It's all right here."

Perry spread out a chart made from taped-together sheets of paper. "This is what Rocky put together. People who are living in the house, and what we know about their relationships. Now, our uncooperative friend Ismail is the middle son. He has an older brother, Muhamud, who doesn't live there, and a younger brother, Ali. Ali is the one who was hiding in the bushes when we were talking to Osman. Muhamud runs a shipping business, allegedly halal meat. I'd be very interested to know what he really ships. Rocky is trying to track down a home address for him. Ismail, as we know, works at the computer store at the mall. Ali is at Portland High."

Burgess thought about what Jason had said. A bunch of black Hondas, white vans, and some trucks—those square white ones that looked like boxes—that came and went at the mosque. It sounded like the mosque building was pretty central to the Imam and his family's operations. So why weren't they more concerned about the loss? Why hadn't they hurried over there? Why was the place strangely vacant, like they were expecting something to happen? Was there some reason it was better to destroy the property, and any evidence that might have been there? How likely was it that any vital records had been removed before the fire?

He needed a clearer picture of the mosque operation and how the family conducted their business. Who had access. Who had had keys to that closet. The hours it was open. All the questions they would normally ask that in this case they were getting no answers to.

They needed someone who would talk to them. They needed to poke more sticks into the neighborhood. Neighborhoods— the one around the mosque and the one around the Imam's house. See if Kyle's informant really knew anything. He needed to talk to Jason's foster mom.

Slow and steady, he reminded himself. Slow and steady.

Tonight, Sage Prentiss was with them. Now Burgess looked at him. "You have any luck getting that plan of the building from the Imam?"

Prentiss shook his head. "Couldn't get my foot in the door. The kid who answered said the Imam wasn't there. I asked had he left anything for the Portland police like he was supposed to and got stony silence."

"You get the kid's name?"

"Ali Ibrahim."

"Anything else?"

Prentiss shook his head. He looked so discouraged. Hard to be bucking for a place on Burgess's crew and striking out on his first assignment. Especially after having to leave the autopsy because he'd turned green.

Stan Perry didn't look much better and Kyle wasn't his usual unflappable self. It was time to rally his troop's spirits.

He told them what he'd learned from Jason. About the fleet of trucks and vans coming and going from the place. About the man on a motorcycle with an eye patch—presumably Butcher Flaherty—harassing the Somalis and quarreling with the Imam. Then he filled them in on the autopsy, Lee's opinion that it was probably a home birth, and the baby's medical condition.

"That baby would have been crying a lot. Someone has to have noticed. I'll go out there tomorrow. Talk to the Imam's neighbors, see if anyone noticed anything."

He watched Kyle's hands opening and closing, like they wanted to be around someone's throat. "Unless you want this one, Ter?"

"I want it, Joe."

"You got it." So he'd take the neighborhood around the mosque, and Jason's foster mother.

He looked at his troops. "We're going to have to pick this apart bit by bit," he said. "Keep looking until we find a way in. Terry, that means getting together with your informant and seeing if she really has anything for us. Stan, see if South Portland PD will let you look at the video of that robbery, and if anything jumps out at you. See if there's anything at all distinctive about those trucks."

He remembered something. "Did you take those serial numbers with you? Ask if the store had a record of what was in that delivery? Or could get it? Or maybe South Portland has that information. If we can tie stolen goods to the mosque, that makes a stronger case for a warrant. Not just to search the

Imam's records, but maybe the house, and maybe his son's business?"

Get in touch with the AG's office and get those warrants went on his own list.

"Damn!" Perry said. "They're still on my desk. I'll follow up in the morning."

The Crips certainly were acting crippled.

"Speaking of records—" He looked at Prentiss. "See if you can find any records of a business operated by Muhamud Ibrahim. Anything that will give us a handle on those trucks. Stan, do you have Rocky's records on vehicles registered to the Imam?"

Perry pulled a sheaf of papers from his stack.

"Are any of them box trucks?"

Perry thumbed through and shook his head. "Vans, but no trucks."

"So we need another search, for vehicles registered to Muhamud Ibrahim, Ali Ibrahim, or Ismail Ibrahim. And the addresses that go with those registrations."

He looked through his notebook, found the address of the mosque, and read it off. "Maybe some of them are registered to the mosque's address, or to some of the organizations that were based there. Sage—"

Prentiss stopped staring gloomily at his notebook and looked up.

"Tomorrow, you check in with city social service agencies, see if they know what was being operated out of that mosque. Who's getting money from the city. The specific people other agencies are working with. I want names—of the agencies and who was running them. I want to know what those agencies were supposed to do. I want to know if they've moved their base of operations. Where they're working from now, if anyone knows. Whether agencies have been in touch with them since the fire."

If he couldn't get at this directly, he'd have to nibble away around the edges. Eventually, the hole would be big enough for them to crawl through.

"Terry, we know anything about the woman, Rihanna Daud, who picked up Osman last night?"

So far, there had been no word from the hospital about Osman's condition. Burgess fervently hoped they wouldn't have another death on their hands.

"Nothing but her address. It's the same as Osman's. We need a warrant to see what's up there," Kyle said.

Burgess turned to Prentiss. "See if you can catch Ali Ibrahim away from the house. At school. On the street. Somewhere that the family won't see him talking to you. And see if you can get him to talk. He knows stuff. Probably knows plenty. Love to get a piece of it. He's all attitude, but maybe, underneath, there's a desire to be more 'American.' Sometimes, that can work in our favor. Especially with an American who speaks his language."

Prentiss nodded and made another note. He was looking anxious, like his list was too long and he had no idea when Burgess would expect him to get it all done.

"When you can, Sage, okay?"

This was how it went. On TV, the cops got one break after another. People reluctant to talk were leveraged into giving it up. There were smoking guns everywhere. Forensic evidence was processed in an instant and cases were solved in an hour. In the program he and the Crips starred in, real people in the real world acted like real jerks and there were no guns or smoke.

Time to end the meeting and send them all home to get some rest. It wasn't like tomorrow wasn't going to be more of the same. A well-rested detective was more alert. Might pick up on nuances and subtleties a weary one might miss. It took energy to be patient and patience would be the name of the game here.

"Go forth and find me something. Find Lieutenant Melia something."

Perry and Prentiss were out the door before he had his papers shuffled together. Kyle lingered behind.

"You heard about Melia's son?"

"Heard they were doing some tests."

Kyle nodded. "I guess things aren't looking good."

"A bad time to have this one on his plate. Guess we'd better start making things happen, huh?" Burgess said.

"Thought that's what we *were* doing, Joe."

Burgess changed the subject. "Tried to talk to Stan this morning. He blew me off. He's got a cute girlfriend living with him."

Kyle nodded. "You said Dwyer says the girlfriend is pregnant and that's what this is all about. That's what Michelle thought was going on, too."

"You think they've got some kind of radar or something?"

"Sometimes I think they're better at reading us than we are at reading them. Not so good when you're a detective."

"I can read my family, Ter. I see who's upset with whom, and why, and how some adjustments might help with that. I just don't have time to do anything about it. Too busy with other people's screwed-up families."

"Right."

"Ter, I never really appreciated—" He stopped. He didn't have to finish. Kyle knew what he meant.

He shoved some papers into his briefcase, got up to go, then sat back down.

"Thought we were supposed to be going home," Kyle said.

"We are. I just want to call Press, see if he's come up with anything on Butch Flaherty. Make sure we stay on his radar screen."

"By being a pain in the ass, you mean?" Kyle said.

"Something like that."

"You know what Scarlett O'Hara says?" Kyle was grinning now.

"Tomorrow is another day. I wish she'd just get back together with what's his name? Rhett Butler? And leave the rest of us alone."

"My mother, rest her soul, loved that book," Kyle said. "I could never get too excited about some guy whose name was Rhett."

"You like 'em better when they're named Butcher? Like Butcher Cassidy and the Sundance Kid?"

"Go home, Joe. You're getting punchy."

The phone on Burgess's desk rang.

He and Kyle both glared at it, daring it to give them more bad news. Finally, Burgess picked up.

"Sarge? It's Press Devlin. Got a line on someone who might know where Flaherty is living these days. Gotta find a guy who knows a guy, but if it checks out, you wanna meet up with me tomorrow and pay the man a visit?"

"Sure. Should I bring an army?"

"Kyle and Perry should do it."

"Call me on my cell when you know something."

"Roger that, Sarge."

Burgess picked up his bag and he and Kyle walked out together. Kyle headed on to his car, but Burgess lingered, listening to the sounds of his city. Inhaling it. Tonight the air smelled of salt. Then he got in the truck, rolled down the window, and headed home.

The wind had died. The night was warm, and little eels of fog were rising from the pavement and parks, softening the glow of headlights and streetlights. It was pretty. Peaceful. And like one of those teenage slasher movies, at any moment, something scary could come at him. Out of the darkness. Or out of his phone.

CHAPTER TWENTY

Burgess was driving on autopilot as he turned onto his street, ready to shuck his clothes and crawl into bed. But cops can't turn off their instincts. They're hard-wired, honed by years of experience, and necessary for survival. He knew cops who, years after retirement, still carefully choose where they sat in restaurants and still lasered the streets they drove, always alert for trouble. He wasn't looking for trouble, but as he was about to turn onto his street, he thought he saw it in the form of an unfamiliar car, lights and engine off, sitting at the curb across from his house. Illumination from a streetlight vaguely showed him two men inside.

Bad guys made threats all the time. Mostly bluster, but sometimes those threats were genuine. This could be something completely innocent, but it was a strange time of night for anyone to just be sitting in a car in his neighborhood, anyone other than a cop. Someone waiting for a friend or dropping off would have had their lights on and their engine running. Someone who lived there would have gone inside. A couple wouldn't have had so much distance between them.

Instead of turning into his street, he cruised past and parked around the corner, then pulled out his phone and called dispatch. He reported a suspicious vehicle and asked for a patrol car to meet him there. Quietly. No lights or sirens. Then he sat back and waited. Two minutes later, a car pulled quietly to the curb behind him and Kenny Munroe came up to his window.

"Bogeyman under your bed, Joe?" he said.

"Not yet," Burgess said. "That's what you're here for. To keep him out of my house."

Munroe's face went serious. "How do you want to do this?"

"Thought I'd slip up beside the driver's door, inquire about his business. Be good to have someone cover the passenger side."

Munroe nodded. "I've got Staines with me. He can come with you. You want me to bring the car? Light 'em up? Or hold off 'til you know what you've got?"

"Hold off. But be ready."

"You've got it, Sarge." Munroe looked thoughtful. "Mind if I call for more backup? If this is trouble, I'd hate like hell to have 'em get away. We're all still smarting from the car that fired shots last night. The driver at the hospital who got away. Not good to have the bad guys winning."

Munroe's instincts were on the money. "Good idea, Kenny. Set it up how you think best. I'll hold off until you have your people in place."

Munroe nodded and trotted off into the fog.

Burgess sat with his window down, inhaling the salty air. Trying not to get angry. Then he looked down the street at his living room window, illuminated only by the bluish glow of a computer screen. He dialed his number and Dylan answered.

"It's Dad," he said. "I need your help with something."

"Everything okay?"

"It will be. I think. Everyone else asleep?"

"Yeah."

"Good. Now, can you shut down your computer screen so the room is dark, and move over to the window."

He heard clicking, and quiet footsteps, then Dylan said, "Done."

"You see that car down there, almost directly across from the house?"

"Yeah."

"Any idea how long it's been there?"

"Since about nine or a little after. Nina noticed it, asked me what I thought. There are two men inside. Not talking. Not doing anything. Just sitting. She thought it was odd. So do I."

Cop's kids, Burgess thought. *They caught on quickly.* "Good instincts," he said. "We think it's odd, too, so we're going to pay them a little visit, see if everything's on the up and up. That's going to go down in a few minutes. Your job is to make sure that even if we make noise that wakes everyone up, no one goes near those living room windows. Can you do that?"

"I can do it, Dad."

"That means you stay away from the windows, too, Dylan."

"Understood. Dad, did you want the plate number? There's just enough light that I can read it."

"I do."

Dylan gave it to him, and hung up.

Burgess hoped he wasn't making a huge mistake. Chris would probably think he was. She was all about protecting the kids, not involving them. But he thought this would be good for his relationship with his son. And he really, really wanted to be sure that if things went south down in the street, the woman he loved and his kids weren't rushing to the window to see what was happening, making themselves perfect targets for some bad guys who'd staked out his house.

He hoped—but didn't for a moment believe—that this car and its occupants were perfectly innocent. Let that hope go when he ran the plate through his computer and it came back as stolen. Car theft wasn't that big around Portland, but the evidence of the past two days would suggest an epidemic.

Kenny Munroe and Rob Staines appeared at his window, and

Burgess got out. He briefed them on how he wanted to proceed, then he and Staines moved through some quiet yards until they could approach the car. He checked his gun. Staines checked his. Then Burgess moved quickly to the driver's door and rapped on the window.

As he did, patrol cars slipped quietly into place, blocking each end of the street.

"Portland police," he said.

The man in the driver's seat didn't respond.

He moved his gun to low ready and rapped again. "Portland police," he repeated, "roll down your window, then put your hands on the wheel where I can see them."

Suddenly, the driver opened the door and started to get out. That was why officers were trained to stand behind the driver's door when doing a traffic stop. Because these situations were inherently dangerous. Because guys like this always thought they were so smart.

As the man emerged, Burgess grabbed his shoulder, pulled him the rest of the way out, and slammed him to the pavement.

On the other side of the car, he heard Staines's calm voice. "I'm going to open the door now, and you're going to step out of the car. Nice and easy now, and keep both hands where I can see them."

Then he heard, "Hey!" and the sound of a struggle, followed by a body hitting the pavement. He hoped Staines, quick on his feet for such a big guy, was winning.

"On your stomach," he told the driver, "and put your hands on your head."

"Take it easy, buddy. I got a bad shoulder," his man complained.

"Should have thought of that before you decided not to cooperate. You have any ID?"

"Fuck you," the man said.

He was unshaven, his clothes were shabby, and he had the battered hands of someone who did manual labor. He smelled like tobacco and the great unwashed. But he had workman's muscles, and the way he tensed when Burgess put the cuffs on said getting cuffed was not a foreign experience. He didn't look familiar.

Across the car, he heard Staines asking nearly identical questions as they moved through the drill to get cuffs on the men before searching them for weapons and ID.

Kenny Munroe and the officers from the second car had moved their cars up, and were coming to lend a hand. Up and down the street, lights were coming on in the houses. There were no lights in his.

"Check him for weapons and ID, would you, Kenny. I want to take a look in the car."

Over on the sidewalk, he heard Staines say in tones of mock surprise, "Why, if it isn't Kimani Yates? We've been looking for you, Mr. Yates. Something about an assault on a security guard over at the hospital?"

So much for good behavior.

Was this just deliberately "in your face," sending someone known to the police to stake out an officer's house, or were these guys just seriously stupid? He wished the answer were stupid and thought otherwise.

The registration was in the name of the man in Cumberland who had reported the car stolen. Burgess put on gloves and searched under the seats. He felt two guns and left them there for the evidence tech to collect. Then he took the keys and opened the trunk.

The contents rocked him back on his feet. Rope, four sets of plastic handcuffs, duct tape, four extra-large industrial-strength trash bags, a big green plastic tarp, a container of clean-up rags, and a bottle of chloroform. And an everyday tool that taken with everything else shook him right to the bone—a shovel.

"Sweet Jesus, Kenny," he said. "Take a look at this."

Munroe peered into the trunk and then into Burgess's face. "Not much doubt about their intentions, is there?"

Four bags. Four sets of handcuffs. There were four people in Burgess's house. The audacity of it stunned him. Time to get some A-level interrogators in to work on this. A tow truck for the car. Make sure there was an evidence tech available. Time to let his family know everything was okay, to stop in before heading back to 109.

Shaking his head and wrapped in a chill that had nothing to do with weather, Burgess pulled out his phone.

CHAPTER TWENTY-ONE

He sent the two bad guys back to 109 in separate patrol cars, with instructions that they were to be put into separate interview rooms and given no opportunity to talk. Then Burgess went upstairs to reassure his family.

When he came through the door, they piled on him, Chris with an embrace, Nina clinging to his arm, Neddy worming his way between him and Chris and clinging to his waist like he was a human life ring. Only Dylan held back, watching from across the room. His expression said he was fine with it, though. His father had trusted him with a task involving the family's safety, and Dylan had come through.

Over Chris's head, which was burrowing into her favorite place in his neck, he caught his son's eye. "Thanks," he said.

"No problem."

Dylan opened the refrigerator and took out the milk, then got the cookie tin. "Who wants milk and brownies?" Chris's mother, Doro, always made sure the cookie tin was full.

That pulled Neddy, and then Nina, away, giving him a private moment with Chris. He led her into the living room.

"What was that about?" she whispered.

"Patrol spotted a stolen car on the street."

She tipped her head back and gave him an appraising look. "That just happened to be parked across from our house?"

He nodded.

"And if I believe that's just chance, you've got a bridge to sell me?"

"Not chance," he said, "But I'm not going to let anything happen to you or our children."

"Our children," she breathed. "Say that again."

He pulled her closer. "I'm not going to let anything happen to you or our children."

"Should I be worried? What do we need to do to be sure they're safe?"

"I don't think you should worry. It's taken care of. But I'm going to put some precautions in place. Like regular patrols on the street. I wonder how Neddy would feel about riding to school in a patrol car?"

"Neddy would love it. I'd hate it," she said. "It makes things seem too dangerous. But what about Nina? And Dylan? And am I going to be safe?"

"It's not likely they'll try something like this again."

She pushed back so she could look into his face, her hands braced on his arms, her fingers gripping him too tightly. "How not likely?"

"Very not likely."

The lights were still off, and in the illumination from the street light, her long hair down and in her pale blue robe, she looked like a girl, not the brave, sturdy woman who shared his life. He felt such a protective wave sweep over him, for her, and for their children. He'd been spared fifteen years of this. Fifteen years of being pulled in two directions, of anxiety, and love. He wondered how Kyle and Melia did it every day.

"Everyone will be okay," he said. "So how did Dylan handle things? What did he do?"

Her smile was beautiful. "He was like a big sheepdog. He herded us into the kitchen, made us sit at the table with the lights off, and told us about the car, and your call, and that everything would be okay, you were taking care of it. He was . . ."

She considered. "He was like you, Joe. He was strong and certain and in charge. I had such a wave of . . . I don't know . . . nostalgia for the you I've never known. For your mother, and what she's missed, not knowing him. And I felt . . ."

Chris was quiet for so long he thought she couldn't find the words, or was ready for the conversation to end. Then she said, "I felt something shift. Like despite all our frustration and uncertainty, despite all the things we get wrong and that we know will go wrong, we're really becoming a family."

He'd felt it, too.

"I have to go back in," he said. "Interview the two men in that car."

"Can't someone else—?" She checked herself. "I wouldn't want someone else to do it." She put her arms around his neck, pressing her body against him, making it terribly hard to leave. But they both knew he had to, and it was better to go with her blessing.

He meant to pass quickly through the kitchen, hug the kids, and be gone, but it wasn't that easy. He wasn't allowed to leave until he'd joined them at the table. The new balancing act. He had a brownie and milk, Nina watching him anxiously until she was sure he wasn't going to bolt.

Finally, he pushed back his chair. "Gotta go talk to some bad guys," he said. "You guys get to bed. It will be morning before you know it."

A round of hugs and he was finally back on the street. Across the way, the stolen car was being loaded onto a truck. One more vehicle for the collection they were making at 109. Pretty soon, the garage would be full. Never mind Zipcar, if they got to keep these vehicles, Portland PD could start their own company, the far more ominous Black Honda.

Their two suspects were cooling their heels in interview rooms, and Stan Perry was standing by his desk, grinning. "Heard you needed another interviewer," he said.

"Heard how?" Burgess said. "Scanner land?"

"Something like that. Which one do I get?"

Burgess wanted them both, but that was because of the circumstances. Two sets of eyes were always better. "You take the driver, and I'll monitor the interview. He's the weak link. And the longer Mr. Yates has to cool his heels, the better. In fact, I'm going to call down to the lab and see if our tech could do a quick check on those guns, see if Yates's prints come up."

He made the call, then filled Perry in on the arrest and what they'd found. "Don't mention the stuff in the trunk until you've got him worked up and talking to you. I don't know if he was in on that or not. Our friend Mr. Yates might have wanted him too far down the road, with money in his wallet, before he shared the details."

He settled in to watch the interview on a monitor while Perry went into the room. The driver, slumped in his chair, wore the forlorn look of someone realizing he's made a big mistake. He'd claimed to have no ID, but turned out to have a wallet in his pocket and a license in the wallet. Henry James Wallace. A Westbrook address. Burgess figured he probably wasn't named after the famous writer. He'd also had a knife on his belt.

"Detective Stan Perry." Perry kicked back a chair and settled into it. "So. You're driving a stolen car, in the company of a convicted felon, with two guns under the seat. Things are looking pretty bad for you, Mr. Wallace. You want to explain this to me?"

"I'm not saying nothin' to you."

"Fine," Perry said. "No skin off my nose if you want to hook yourself up with someone like Kimani Yates. You oughta know, though, that loyalty to Mr. Yates is a one-way street. He'd sell his own mother if he could get a good price. He's putting it all on you. Stealing the car, getting the guns, the whole deal."

"I didn't steal—" Wallace fell silent. Studied the blank walls. Interview rooms were deliberately plain. Table. Chairs. Blank walls. Nothing for a witness to fix on as a distraction. "I need to make a phone call."

"You'll get your chance, Mr. Wallace. Don't worry. You want to call a lawyer?" Perry moved his chair closer to Wallace and leaned way into his personal space. "You gonna lawyer up on me? Because if you are, why don't you just go ahead and say that, don't waste any more of my time. With your record, what we found in the car, and what Yates is gonna say to save his sorry ass, we really don't need anything from you."

He made a show of shuffling through some papers. "I've got your record here. Looks like aside from that one domestic, you've kept your nose clean for a long time. Pity to go and screw all that up now just 'cuz some lowlife asks you to drive him somewhere. You got a job, Mr. Wallace?"

"Sternman on a lobster boat. Mostly filling in for other guys, ya know? I usta do commercial fishing, but with all them catch limits? The jobs have just about dried up."

"Getting back to Kimani Yates," Perry said. "How did the two of you get hooked up together?"

Wallace shook his head. "I ain't—"

Some quick shuffling and studying of papers, and then, like a magician plucking a quarter out of the air, Perry pulled out a card and started reading Wallace his rights.

Wallace waved a hand like he was signaling Perry to stop. Ignoring that, Perry slid a sheet of paper in front of the man and stabbed at the various paragraphs with a vigorous finger as he went down the list, his voice getting louder as he went along. Finally, he said, "Do you understand?" and slammed a pen down.

By this time, Wallace was leaning as far back in the chair as he could. He stared at the pen like it was an object he didn't recognize.

"Sign it," Perry barked.

Wallace signed.

"Now, do you want to call an attorney?"

Wallace shook his head.

"Are you willing to talk to me without an attorney present?"

"I want to make a—"

Perry dropped his voice and leaned in, "Do you want an attorney?"

"Jesus, man, will you get out of my face?"

Perry shoved his chair back. "Mr. Wallace, you didn't want cops in your face, you shouldn't have been in that car tonight, isn't that right? So now what, you're going to whine because you made a bad call? You think I'm picking on you? You're just a poor misguided little man who was doing a favor for a friend?"

He leaned in again. "Are you saying that Kimani Yates, who has a record as long as you are tall, and for things no decent person would want to be associated with, is your friend?"

"I never met him before today. Look, Officer, I—"

"Detective. Are you telling me that you staked out a Portland detective's house tonight, with his family at home, in a stolen car, with someone you never met who happens to be a convicted felon? Why on earth would you do that?"

"I didn't stake out—"

"So it was perfectly innocent, Mr. Wallace? You just happened to be on that street, across from that house, with those guns, in that car and with that accomplice, for *no reason?*"

"He wasn't my accomplice," Wallace said.

"You mean you were his?"

"I wasn't . . . I didn't know . . . Look, I would like . . ." This time, Wallace stopped before Perry cut him off. There was a discernable shake in his voice. Then, almost in a whisper, he said, "I didn't know it was a cop's house. Yates said—"

But that was beyond the limits of his courage. Perry would have to wind him up some more before the story would come tripping out. But come out it would. Wallace had been there as muscle. It was Yates who was ruthless.

Burgess tried to push away images of those two bursting into his house. Of the impact on Nina and Neddy, who had already suffered so much at the hands of conscienceless monsters who had wanted Neddy, and used Nina to get at him. He imagined Chris coming to their defense. And Dylan, trying to protect everyone. His brave little family against bad guys with guns. He wanted to go through the door and rip the man's head off.

He imagined Perry hearing this on the scanner and putting it together. Maybe calling Kyle to consult. Perry wanted a piece of the action because he needed to redeem himself. But he was there for Burgess.

"What did Yates tell you?"

Wallace studied his hands again. They were hard-worn hands, a roadmap of a life as a laborer. Part of a fingertip missing. Knuckles too gnarled for a man barely into middle age. The shiny pink and purple of healed scars. *Give it up,* Burgess thought. Don't tie your fate to a POS like Yates. Like it had been telepathy, Wallace seemed to reach the same conclusion.

"He said the guy who lived there owed his boss money. We were going to scare the family a little. Send a message about what would happen if the guy didn't pay up. That's all he said it was."

That's *all* it was? An increasingly good idea that Burgess wasn't in the room.

"You know the boss's name? Hear him say it?" Wallace shook his head. "Did you meet the boss?" Another shake. "Overhear him talking to his boss on the phone?"

Wallace nodded.

Burgess was already heading out to his desk to look at the inventory of what had been taken from Yates, to see if there was a cell phone. Perry would know he was doing that. Wouldn't want to stop the interview to do it himself, not when he had some momentum going.

Yes. There was a cell phone. A throwaway. It would still show what calls had been made and received. He flipped it open, checked that there was a record of calls made. Good. They could write up a warrant in the morning. He went back to watching the monitor.

"What did you hear him say?"

Wallace studied his hands like the answers were written there. "I really wasn't paying attention. Just wanted to get going, get the thing over with, and get paid."

Perry banged his fist on the table and Wallace jumped. "God-dammit, Mr. Wallace. I am losing patience with you. What did you hear Yates say?"

But Wallace had once again decided not to share, which suggested to Burgess that whatever it was, it wasn't just the "scare" he'd described earlier. That was okay. Perry would settle him down and circle back, and eventually they'd get what they were looking for. Meanwhile, Perry asked Wallace if he'd like a soda or some coffee, and left the room to get coffee.

While he waited for the interview to start again, Burgess started making a list of things to deal with at tomorrow's team meeting. Top of the list went the warrant for that cell phone and its records. For Osman's cell phone records. Osman's apartment. The Imam's house. Warrants, warrants everywhere. Then, because it seemed like Perry was taking forever to find that coffee, he called the hospital to check on Osman's condition. No change. No news.

They were now into what Burgess thought of as the sad time of night. Regular people were sleeping, and cops and robbers, insomniacs, and those who worked the night shift had a mostly quiet and empty world to themselves.

He flipped the monitor and checked on the other interview room, where Kimani Yates was cooling his heels. Perfectly confirming the old saw about the guilty, Yates's head rested on his arms on the table, and he snored softly.

He returned the focus to Wallace as Perry came in, carrying two cups of coffee, and swung right back into questions.

Perry was asking Wallace how he knew Kimani Yates when the door opened and Terry Kyle came in. "Heard I was missing all the fun," he said.

"Stan called you."

"You're a hell of a detective, Joe. We figured, your family targeted and all, maybe we should keep some distance between you and the suspects. But Stan was pretty sure we wouldn't be able to send you home."

"If it were your family?"

Kyle raised an eyebrow. "Dismemberment seems like an option."

"I was thinking torture. But first you and Stan have to get the story."

Kyle glanced at the monitor. "How's he doing so far?"

"He was close. I think Mr. Wallace was less than forthcoming about what the plan was when he used the word 'scare.' But Stan will get there. You might just go sit in the room, though, and cast a cold eye on Henry James Wallace. Let him feel the full weight of our disapproval. It's a good warm-up for Kimani Yates."

"My fate," Kyle sighed, looking heavenward, "to always be

the warm-up act."

"From each according to his ability," Burgess said.

He settled back into the chair to watch the show. Seeing Perry and the suspect drinking coffee made him long for a cup—he was immensely tired and felt older than dirt—but he didn't want to miss anything. He wondered if they should have waited until morning. If they'd get anything from this anyway. When his second wind would arrive.

Kyle walked into the room without a word, stalked past Wallace, and pulled out a chair on the other side of the table, arranging himself so that Wallace could only watch one of them at a time.

"This is Detective Kyle," Perry said. He pretended to consult his papers. "Okay. You were telling me about the conversation you overheard between Kimani Yates and a man he'd described as his boss, right?"

Wallace nodded.

"What did you hear him say?" When Wallace hesitated, Perry added, "We've got his cell phone. We can check the time of those calls and who he called. We've got you at the scene, in a stolen car, with a convicted felon, two guns under the seats. Do you seriously expect us to believe you had no idea what was going on?"

The man looked at Perry. Then he looked at Kyle, who sat eerily still, staring with those cold eyes like a hawk spotting a rodent. He swallowed. Took a gulp of his coffee. Looked down at his hands and back up at Perry. "At first I wasn't listening, ya know how you try not to hear other people's conversations. But then he said, 'All four them? Even the kids?' and I knew I oughta pay attention."

"Yates tell you who was in the house?"

"A woman and three kids."

"Go on."

The scarred hands opened and closed a few times. "He said . . ." Wallace's voice dropped almost to a whisper. "He said, 'What do you expect me to do with them?' " The hands flexed. There was a rasp in the voice when Wallace said, "Honestly, I thought we were supposed to scare them."

"But you understood that to mean that Yates was being instructed to do more than scare the family you were staking out?"

Wallace nodded. Then shook his head vigorously.

"That's not how you interpreted the conversation you overheard between Kimani Yates and the man he described as his boss?" Kyle snarled, and leaned right into Wallace's face.

The man, and his chair, scooted backward until he hit the wall. "That's what I heard, yeah. What was he supposed to do with them. But that's not all they said. Yates listened and then he said, 'Okay. I'll just put 'em in the trunk and bring 'em to you.' Then he said, 'Alive?' And I don't know what his boss said, but then Yates said, 'Alright, whichever way it works out. I've got all the stuff in the trunk. You'll get what you get, depending on how it goes down.' Which I interpreted to mean alive or dead, depending on what happened when we went inside."

He tried to scoot back more, realized he was at the wall, and folded up on his chair like someone was letting the air out of him. "And you've got to believe me, Detective . . . Detectives . . . I wouldn't of gone along with that. I wasn't there to kill kids. You couldn't ever pay me enough to do that. Yeah, I agreed to go in there and scare 'em, like Yates asked me to, but that's all I agreed to. And only 'cuz I really needed the money. I got my rent to pay. I got kids of my own."

Jesus, Burgess thought. *What kind of a man agrees to go terrorize someone else's kids so he can take care of his own?* He knew the answer. The kind they dealt with every day.

He watched Kyle and Perry move their chairs in closer, Wallace's eyes going wide as he realized he had no place to go.

"You were just there to scare a woman and some kids, but you heard that Yates's plan was to abduct them and take them to this boss, dead or alive, and you were okay with that?" Kyle snapped.

"I already told ya. I wasn't there to kill anyone."

"You just happened to have a gun with you, is all?" Perry said.

"He brought them guns. Not me. I don't own one. I haven't had my hands on a gun since . . . since that time with my wife. Since I got arrested."

"But you were planning to use it when you entered the home, weren't you?" Kyle said.

"Yes, but—"

"Yates say anything about where you were supposed to bring the cop's family?" Perry asked.

Wallace's eyes swiveled back to him. "He said 'the warehouse?' like it was a question. But I think he was supposed to take 'em somewhere else, because he laughed, and he said, 'Yeah, that way you can use the backhoe.' "

Burgess started pacing, fighting the urge to go into that room and beat the living crap out of Henry James Wallace.

"What about all that stuff in the trunk?" Perry said. "The abduction kit. Chloroform? Heavy-duty trash bags big enough for body bags. Handcuffs. Rope. Big tarp and shovel? You think all that stuff was just there to 'scare' people?"

Wallace's eyes jumped from one of them to the other. "Body bags?" he whispered. "Shovel? I never seen any of that stuff. I never seen in the trunk. Jesus. God. I never . . . You gotta believe me. I was just there to—"

"You heard the conversation between Yates and his boss, right?" Perry interrupted. "And you were going to take your orders from Yates about how to proceed?"

"Yes, but—"

"And you didn't back out, right? So whatever went down, you were okay with that? Did the two of you have a plan?" Kyle asked.

"I was supposed to knock on the door and say, 'Portland police.' Yates figured they'd open for that, thinking something had happened to the dad and all. And he wanted what he called 'a white voice' to do it. Which, I guess, is why they hired me."

"So you did know it was a cop's family, right?"

Back and forth it went, Kyle and Perry taking turns shooting questions, Wallace's head whipping back and forth as he tried to keep track of who he was supposed to answer.

"How did Yates find you?"

"We've got mutual friends. They heard he was looking for somebody."

"Those friends' names?"

"It was just . . ." Wallace tried to fold his arms in a gesture of defiance. The handcuffs wouldn't let him. He settled for a defiant raise of his chin. "I ain't sayin'."

"How much did Yates pay you?" Perry asked.

"Five hundred before. Five hundred after."

The inventory had listed five crisp hundred-dollar bills from Wallace's wallet, along with a twenty, a ten, and a couple of ones. Nice new bills that might have nice new fingerprints.

"To kidnap or kill four people, three of 'em kids?" Kyle said. "You sure did sell your soul cheap."

When they were done with Wallace, they moved into the second room and woke the slumbering Kimani Yates. As Burgess had expected, Yates was too much of a pro to give them anything. He went from sleep to lawyering up faster than most people could open their eyes, never mind have their wits about them.

Kyle and Perry did their best, but Yates just stared through them and repeated that he wouldn't talk without a lawyer. They knew a lost cause when they saw one, and didn't waste much time on the man.

It didn't matter. The evidence tech had found Yates's prints on both guns, and they were sure they'd also find his prints on the stuff in the trunk. Possession of guns by a convicted felon, plus the stolen car, plus the assault on the security guard was more than enough to hold him, no matter how good his lawyer was. They sent him over to the jail for booking, and went home for a few hours sleep.

CHAPTER TWENTY-TWO

He slept better than he had in ages, and woke, despite the short night, feeling refreshed and ready to go out and kick ass. Ass-kicking was delayed by the rituals of family breakfast—they ate, he watched—and driving Dylan to school, but that felt more like a pleasure than a chore. Maybe it was that shift he and Chris had felt. He gave Dylan some sage advice about keeping his head down for a few days until ruffled feathers settled, then headed over to 109.

By eight forty-five, he and Kyle and Perry were following Press Devlin to the address Devlin had gotten for Butcher Flaherty. Devlin stopped by a row of seedy wooden houses. They parked behind him, and met on a sidewalk caked with winter sand and littered with fast-food discards and cigarette butts. Still, the day was already warm and the sun felt good. It would have been nice to just stand there for a few minutes and enjoy the day. But a policeman's lot is not a happy one. Today, especially, promised to be a constant series of move, assess, adjust, and move on, interspersed with the occasional bit of ass-kicking.

Devlin pointed down an alley. "I cruised by earlier. No sign of his bike—he probably has a garage space around here somewhere—but there's a light on inside, so maybe we're in luck and he's home."

When you go to see the Butcher, you're going to wear your vest, and they were all dressed for action. Flaherty's door was off the alley, on the second floor up a set of wooden stairs. Kyle led the way, thin, nimble, and gun ready. Halfway up, he came to an abrupt halt and held up his hand.

"Oh shit," he said. "Take a look, Joe." He stood sideways so Burgess could pass.

Burgess climbed to the stop of the stairs and stood on the landing, staring at the scummy window beside Butcher Flaherty's door. Buzzing flies swarmed against it, busy little messengers there to tell them that whatever they thought they were going to get from the Butcher, instead they were about to get a nasty crime scene and an enormous headache.

Exigent circumstances. The possibility that life still existed and immediate access was necessary. Burgess had, in fact, seen a few situations where maggots and life had not been incompatible. He stood aside while Press Devlin, younger, fitter, and eager to perform the task, kicked in the door.

The flies had not been lying. The weather hadn't been that hot, but when the door opened, the wave of heat that carried the stench of death toward them suggested that whoever had helped the swollen male body lying in the middle of the floor in a pool of blood to shuffle off his mortal coil had turned up the heat on the way out.

Turned up the heat on their whole case. What was the connection between this death, the fire at the mosque, and the attack on Osman? Were they even related? And how did it all connect to the man with the watch and the ring, and the Imam and his grandsons? Burgess shoved his wonderings away for later. Right now, he had a dead man to deal with.

It was ugly. Maybe not the ugliest thing he'd ever seen, but nasty enough to make him grateful he hadn't eaten breakfast.

They opened what windows they could, then stepped outside to let the place air while Burgess made the necessary phone calls to let Melia know what they had, and summon the medical examiner, evidence techs, and patrol officers to control the scene.

Denizens of the alley in various forms of dress and undress, lumbering like hibernating bears from their caves, began coming out to survey the commotion. These folks were not morning people. He had Stan Perry start organizing some patrol officers to ask immediate neighbors what they might have seen or heard, and pulled Press Devlin aside. "How long before we have his buddies arriving?"

Devlin nodded at a skinny, tattooed man with a graying pigtail and a bandana who was talking on a cell phone. "I'd guess less than fifteen minutes."

"You may want to get a couple of your people over here," he said. "Find out what they know. If this a gang thing. How it might relate to our case."

Devlin rolled his eyes. "Gonna need an army, Sarge."

"Do what you can. And when Rudy gets here, be sure he gets Flaherty's buddies when he does the crowd."

"Brothers in arms," Devlin said. "You'll hear 'em before you see 'em. Roaring right up this canyon and getting in our faces. Speaking of brothers, Wink coming over?"

"I hope so. He's the best."

"He'll bring Dani."

Burgess nodded. He couldn't help his instinctive desire to protect her, but Dani was good at a crime scene, and she didn't want to be protected.

"Yeah. He probably will."

He and Kyle went back upstairs. Once they'd established that there was no one else in the apartment—bad guy, other victim, or someone in need of assistance—they had to wait. They couldn't move around or touch anything until the scene had been videotaped, photographed, and measured. They didn't need to touch the body to establish death. The absence of much of the top of Flaherty's head made that pretty clear. The eye patch was still there, though, a jaunty flag of black across the grotesquely swollen face.

So far, all they knew was that the door had been locked, that the man they assumed was Butcher Flaherty was dead, that they were going to have to bury or burn the clothes they were wearing, and that the death smell would be with them for days no matter how many showers they took or how much Vicks they inhaled.

Whoever had dispatched Flaherty had been looking for something. The entire place was a shambles, drawers pulled out, cupboards emptied, clothes strewn everywhere. What they couldn't know was whether some effort had been made to convince Flaherty to tell them where the sought after item was. The body was too swollen and discolored. Or, of course, whether the item had been found.

"Excuse me, Sarge?" Press Devlin called from the doorway, yelling to be heard over the distinctive roar of Harleys. "I'm putting Remy on the door. Gonna go chat with some of Flaherty's friends, see if they have any idea what this might be about."

Devlin turned to leave. Burgess stopped him. "Press. Hold on," he said. "See if anyone knows where his bike might be."

If the killer hadn't found what he was looking for, it might be with the bike.

Then what Press had just said went home. He was putting Remy on the door. If Remy Aucoin was here, then who was at the hospital, guarding their mystery girl?

"Remy!" He bounded out the door, almost flattening Aucoin, who was responding to his shout.

Their words crossed. "Remy, if you're here, who is at the hospital?"

"Sorry, Sarge, I . . ."

Burgess took a breath. "Remy, who is guarding the girl?"

Aucoin shrugged. "I don't know, sir. My shift commander called and told me I was back on my usual patrol."

Burgess saw red. He pictured her lying there, curled up in the bed, those sad, scared eyes watching, waiting for the next awful thing to happen. Aucoin and Dwyer had made her feel safe. Now, without consulting him or bothering to inform him of a critical decision regarding an ongoing homicide investigation, someone had canceled her security, leaving her vulnerable to whoever had already made two attempts to get at her.

He knew exactly what this was about.

He called Sage Prentiss, told him to get over to the hospital ASAP and call once he'd confirmed that the girl was okay. Then he called Melia. The lieutenant would be on his way here anyway, but Burgess didn't have time to spare.

"I'm two minutes out, Joe," Melia said. "What's up?"

"Someone canceled the security detail on our girl, Vince."

Melia's response was just an angry hiss.

"I've sent Sage over there, but you've got to call him, Vince. This isn't right."

"See you in two," Melia said.

The freaking food chain. Command structure. Melia could go to the chief, but Captain Cote would argue the bottom line, overtime, priorities. Like a victim who had almost died a horrible death in a fire, and who had lost her child, and already been the subject of two kidnapping attempts, was a low priority. But this wasn't about cost. Cote cared more about jerking Burgess's chain than about victims. For a wicked moment, Burgess considered stashing her in Cote's office. But he'd never do that—to her.

If she wasn't okay, Burgess might break his long-standing rule about never talking to the press.

Aucoin's stare told Burgess he wasn't keeping his thoughts off his face. "I just figured they'd sent someone else, Sarge. You

222

mean they—?"

"I don't know, Remy."

Dismissed, Aucoin went back outside to resume his job of keeping track of who came and went at the crime scene.

Kyle was shifting restlessly from one foot to the other. Waiting was a big part of their lives, but he hated to be idle if there was something he could be doing. "Go on, Ter," Burgess said. "Take a look around. Maybe you'll find a motorcycle."

"Maybe I'll find something."

Maybe he would, if the blood maggots hadn't trampled on it. He was a great reader of scenes. Saw things a dozen other detectives would walk right past. Kyle took a step closer to the body, and Burgess realized he was studying Flaherty's boots. Then he left.

Hours later he watched the gurney carrying Butcher Flaherty bump down the stairs and disappear into the medical examiner's van, followed by a trail of disappointed flies. Hospital security was sitting on his mystery girl's room until he could sort that out. Sage Prentiss was back at 109 writing a warrant for the garage that held Flaherty's motorcycle. When that was done, they'd tow it and add it to their growing collection in the department's basement.

He'd had a nice phone chat with their AAG, and she was working with Rocky on warrants for the Imam's house. For Henry James Wallace and Kimani Yates's cell phones and cell records. And he figured he might as well add Butcher Flaherty to the list. Osman's records. The school had called to tell him that Jason Stetson needed to talk. Kyle's informant was eager to get her hands on an iPod, and wanted to arrange a meeting. Osman was still in the ICU, condition unchanged.

Stan Perry had spent hours interviewing Flaherty's neighbors, but none of them had seen or heard anything unusual. Maybe someone being severely beaten wasn't unusual? Press Devlin was working his way through Flaherty's band of brothers, looking for a lead about who might have wanted Flaherty dead. No one was sharing anything of value. The ME thought they were looking at blunt-force trauma and not GSW.

Burgess's head buzzed with questions. None of this seemed to make sense, but history had taught him that if he was patient, the connections would gradually appear. Meanwhile, he reined them in. Sorting out what any of this meant would have to wait until they were finished here.

After another hour, he and Kyle had learned that Butcher Flaherty was no housekeeper and too infrequently did his laundry. He ate canned food and fast food and spent more on drink than nutrition. He had a doting mother in Gray who wrote often and liked to tuck twenties in the letters, perhaps to ensure that he'd open them. The ruse hadn't worked. Unopened letters had been piled up on his kitchen counter, along with unopened bills. The only items of interest were a key wrapped in plastic at the bottom of a coffee tin, and a bank statement buried in the unopened mail that showed periodic deposits of large amounts of cash, all carefully under $10,000.

They had his keys and would get the clothes he'd been wearing at the autopsy. The key from the coffee can, the bank account, and maybe the credit card bills and his wallet were fodder for some able detective. Right now, Burgess felt disabled by anger, impatience, and sinuses and lungs full of the disgusting smell of decomp. There had been no cell phone on the body and they'd found none in the apartment. Did that mean someone had taken it? Did that make his cell phone records that much more valuable? There had been a phone bill in the pile on the counter.

Across the room, Kyle finished going through the pockets and dropped a pair of enormous jeans onto a growing mound of clothes. "We done here, Joe?"

Burgess gave the room one last look. They had found no hidden stashes of cash or drugs. Nothing under the mattress. No reading material except men's magazines, motorcycle magazines, and *Guns & Ammo*.

"We're done. Let's tell Remy to seal this place and go see how Stan is doing."

"Hate to say it, but I'm hungry."

Burgess was, too, but there was no way any of them could eat until they'd gone back to the station and showered and changed. "A good crime scene'll do that to you."

Kyle raised an eyebrow. "This is a good crime scene?"

Burgess just shook his head and gestured toward the door. "After you," he said.

It was like entering a different world, a world with a bright sun high in the sky, making them blink after the dark gloom of the apartment. The air was soft, the sky was a lovely light blue, and the budding trees at the end of the crappy alley were hosting noisy birds.

Predictably, Kyle read his mind. "Which is the real world? This or the one we just left?"

They collected Stan Perry, glowering with frustration over his failure to find a single witness with the integrity to step up, got in their vehicles, and headed back to 109 with all the windows open.

CHAPTER TWENTY-THREE

Forty minutes later, they'd showered and changed and were sitting in a conference room unwrapping sandwiches. The showers helped, but their sinuses were still full, and a miasma of Butcher Flaherty filled the room.

Melia was in his office, on the phone, and the pinched look he'd worn at the crime scene told them he was deeply enmeshed in his son's illness. They all desperately wanted to take concerns over this case off his mind, but the paucity of information gave them small hope of doing that. Up the food chain, they'd care little about the loss of Butch Flaherty, but they'd care about the bad PR value of two violent deaths and an assault that had left another victim in a coma within three days. Crime was bad for tourism, and Portland was courting the cruise ships.

Sage Prentiss had carried his warrant application over to the courthouse, and was headed over to Flaherty's garage to collect the Harley and see what else he might find.

As they munched in collective gloom, Burgess tossed the key they'd found onto the table. "Any thoughts about this?"

"Looks like a padlock key. Storage locker maybe?" Perry said.

It was a good guess. And another task for their endless to-do list. He started putting the incidents up on the white board, drawing arrows to show connections. The dead baby and kidnapped girl with the mosque. The girl with Kimani Yates at the hospital. The girl and the baby with Akiba Norton and the man with the watch and ring. The computer store robbery with the mosque. White box trucks at the mosque and white box trucks at the robbery. Kimani Yates with the stakeout at his house. Osman acting as translator for them with the Imam, then beaten and later nearly killed. Butcher Flaherty harassing people at the mosque. Now Butcher Flaherty dead.

Was there something going on at that mosque valuable enough to make it worthwhile to threaten a police detective? Kill a translator? Kill Flaherty? Why had someone shot at Ismail Ibrahim? What did any of it mean?

He was still hungry, but everything tasted like death. He gave up and threw the rest of his sandwich in the trash. "Cote canceled our security detail at the hospital," he said.

"What's up with that?" Perry said. "You'd almost think he *wanted* her to get killed." Like Burgess, he gave up on his sandwich and tossed it. "So what would you like me to do next, Joe?"

Burgess pushed the key toward him. "See if you can find out what this opens."

"Needle in a haystack," Perry said.

"Maybe not," Kyle said. "Start with the places nearest Flaherty's apartment, work out from there. You might get lucky."

"I used to think getting lucky was a good thing."

Before Perry could fall back into his recent funk, Kyle said, "Getting lucky in a murder investigation is still a good thing, Stan. Maybe one of those places out near Deering Corner. Morrill Street or Warren Ave. Maybe you even get luckier and they'll have surveillance cameras or something."

"I'm going," Perry said, snatching up the key. "Stay tuned for some good news."

"Our prayers go with you," Kyle said. They watched the door close behind him. "Best thing for that lad is to keep him busy. Don't give him time to start feeling sorry for himself."

"Best thing for all of us," Burgess said. "I'm going to see

227

where the AG's office is on those warrants. Then catch up with Jason Stetson."

"And I'm off, iPod in hand, to see a girl about a story."

The morning that they'd missed had been lovely. But as they said about New England weather, you had to get up early to enjoy it. The afternoon sky was gray and a sharp wind had come up, swirling down the streets and lifting the lightest winter sand into clouds that looked like tan smoke. *Sand gets in your eyes,* Burgess thought as he trudged back from the courthouse with a fistful of warrants. A warrant for the Imam's house and outbuildings, his trashcans and his cars. A warrant for Kimani Yates's cell phone. Another for Butcher Flaherty's phone. Yet one more for Hussain Osman's apartment. Warrants for the cars.

That ought to keep them busy for the next several days. He'd turn the cell phones and warrants for cell phone records over to Rocky. He gave the warrants for the Imam's house and Osman's to Melia.

"Vince, can you put someone on the Imam's house? I'd love to do this when he isn't at home. And we're going to need some bodies for this one, for the search and for crowd control."

"Poor choice of words, Joe."

"Right. Today I'd say being a Portland detective is a poor choice of career."

Melia said what he always said, "You've got a bad attitude, Joe."

"And who vetoed my request for that charm course? I was going to learn to curtsey and smile politely. Treat maggots with decorum and respect."

"Not in the budget," Melia said. "Nothing in the damned budget. Pretty soon we're going to have to cut all overtime and recruit a couple volunteer psychics to help us solve cases."

Burgess shook his head. "Nah. We just need better technology. Just insert a chip into the bad guys when they're convicted. Then we'll always be able to find 'em."

"It's too brilliant, Joe. One of those damned amendments, second, fourth, fifth, would say we couldn't do it."

"Yeah. Everybody's got rights but the thin blue line." He studied his boss's face. Melia had aged ten years in a week. "What's up with Lincoln?"

"The bad news or the good news? Bad news is maybe it's leukemia. They're waiting on a test. Good news is it's one they can usually treat. Gina's about out of her mind, though."

"She should talk to Chris. No one's steadier than an experienced nurse at a time like this. Not that she wouldn't be just as bad with our kids—"

He stopped, realizing that Melia was looking at him funny. "I've been on the fence about all this. You know that. Too old a dog to learn new tricks. But after last night, I don't know. Something happened."

"A threat to your family will do that."

"It's not supposed to happen, Vince."

"That was the old world, Joe. In the new world, the world without social structures and imbedded values, without community? All bets are off. Anyway, this one is bad all around. You start with an imprisoned child mother and a dead infant, you know you're dealing with people who have few boundaries on what they'll do to others."

"Speaking of imprisoned child mothers, how are we supposed to keep that girl safe? I've got hospital security covering, but that won't last. They're as sticky about the bottom line as he who will not be named."

Melia sighed. "I'm working on it, Joe. Be a big help if I could toss a suspect on his desk instead of a fresh homicide."

"That was *not* a fresh anything, Vince. That was a half-baked maggot factory."

"I think this case is getting to you."

"Right," Burgess stood. "Take a look at my desk, you'll see all the brochures for exotic places I'm going to visit in my retirement. Just as soon as I toss some suspects on some other desks."

"Speaking of toss—"

"The divine Lorna is typing up some reports even as we speak."

Melia made shooing motions with his hands. "Go away. And call me in a hour and I'll update you on executing those warrants."

Burgess left.

CHAPTER TWENTY-FOUR

In a crazy case like this, crimes tended to pop up like whack-a-mole, sometimes the whole business was like whack-a-mole. When they got lucky, answers might start popping up, too. Burgess hoped that they'd get some of those answers from searching the Imam's house. He had lower expectations about Osman's place, but he'd gotten used to surprises. So maybe there would be something there.

When Melia called, it wasn't to update him on the timing of the warrants, it was to say that the ME had scheduled Butcher Flaherty for tomorrow at 8 a.m. Typical of Dr. Lee. He liked to cut bright and early.

Burgess wrote it in his notebook. Then he sat in the car, waiting for inspiration. He wasn't a spiritual guy. He was a realist. But sometimes his city spoke to him, if he listened carefully to it. With the window partway down, he could feel the rush of the wind. In Maine, it's April, not March, that comes in like a lion. Sometimes the lion likes to hang around. Little windblown bits of sand clattered against the glass like tiny chips of ice and shrouded the windshield in pale, translucent gold.

Sometimes a cold wind can bring clarity. Clarity this time in the form of a phone call from Rocky Jordan. An interesting tidbit. The Imam had found a new temporary location for the mosque. A warehouse down by the waterfront. Owned by a fishing boat captain turned entrepreneur named Addison Westerly. Plans were afoot to turn it into condos. For now, it had become a mosque.

Burgess knew a librarian could be a cop's best friend. As soon as he'd noted Rocky's information, Burgess was on the phone to the reference desk at the Portland Public Library, and confirmed that they did have Maine Maritime Academy yearbooks in their collection. A book that went by the unusual name *Trick's End*. Echoes of a long-ago Masefield poem. That was where the April wind would blow him next.

Or it would have, but Melia called and said he had a team ready, the Imam and his entourage had just left, and did Burgess and the Crips want to execute a search warrant?

Burgess and the Crips absolutely did.

He called Perry and Kyle and headed for the Imam's house.

The expression "it was like herding cats" couldn't have been more appropriate. As he'd imagined the other night when he was there, surveying all the cars, noting how many people gave that address as their residence, and hearing the soft sounds of women and children behind closed doors, the place was a warren. Bedrooms were crowded with beds and the attic was lined with bunks like a dormitory. Only the first floor had a residential character, and there he found what he expected would be the Imam's office. The door was locked and none of the five women who filled the air with their whining, wailing, and complaints admitted to knowing where there might be a key. At any given moment, without any noticeable diminution in the noise level, at least two of them were also talking on cell phones.

All five of them, along with babes in arms and small, clinging children, had been herded into the living room while the search was conducted.

Sage Prentiss was doing his best with his limited Somali, but all it seemed to be earning him was a larger ration of complaints.

"Tell them that if we can't find the key, we'll have to break the lock," Burgess said.

Prentiss translated. The commotion got louder. And no key was produced. Burgess gave up trying to be considerate and instructed two patrol officers to break the lock.

The rest of the house might be shabby and worn, but the Imam had been generous with himself. A large, solid wood desk, an expensive desk chair, three leather visitor's chairs, a banquette under the window piled with cushions, and a row of new, locked file cabinets. There was a lovely rug on the floor. Burgess rummaged in the desk drawer for keys, but couldn't find any. That left him three choices: call a locksmith, break the locks, or simply truck them to 109 to investigate at leisure. In the end, after repeated requests for cooperation that brought no results, Melia made the decision to break the locks.

Anything that looked potentially relevant was loaded into banker's boxes and taken back to the conference room at 109 to be examined. While Kyle searched the drawers and packed boxes for officers to carry out to the waiting van, Burgess went through the Imam's desk drawers. He found some phone bills and insurance bills that might be helpful and added them to their collection. There was no sign of the plan of the mosque that they'd been promised.

A search of the rest of the house yielded little beyond clothing and baskets of children's toys, until Kyle noticed scratch marks on the floor and had a large wardrobe moved. Where it had stood was a locked door. Once again, they asked for a key and once again, they didn't get one. This time, a screwdriver did the trick.

Behind the door was a windowless closet with a blood-stained mattress on the floor, a small basket lined with baby blankets, and some woman's and tiny baby's clothing. A search found nothing personal. No jewelry, hairbrush, toiletries, notes, papers, books, letters, or receipts. Nothing. They couldn't be sure until fingerprints or DNA confirmed it, but it looked like this closet, like the locked closet at the mosque, had been a holding place for their mystery girl and her baby. Maybe even the place where the baby had been delivered.

"The locked closet mystery?" Kyle muttered, as he and Burgess waited for Wink to take photographs and dust the room for prints.

"If they were keeping her here, why move her to the mosque?"

"Maybe that crying baby was driving everyone nuts. The neighbors complained? Or someone here was too sympathetic? Or that was a temporary move on the way to somewhere else," Kyle said, "I wonder if Stan found anything in the garage? Of if there was anything in the trash?"

Searching people's garages, basements, and going through their trash. It was part of their glamorous life. Burgess's reflections were interrupted by a commotion from downstairs, men's voices, raised in anger, and Sage Prentiss, shouting in Somali, words that were recognizable to anyone in any language as "calm down."

"Looks like Daddy's home," Kyle said. "Let's go downstairs and say hello."

The Imam stood in the door of his office with part of his entourage, waving his arms and trying to stop the officers who were carrying out the boxes. The gray beard and hair and wrathful expression looked like the picture of an angry God from a children's bible. An older woman who had come in with him had herded the other women into the corner and was speaking with them quietly.

Burgess threaded his way through the crowd surrounding the Imam. "Mr. Ibrahim? Detective Sergeant Burgess. We met the other night. I'm afraid I'm going to have to ask you to step out of the way and let these men finish."

The Imam turned what could only be called "fiery" eyes on him, and muttered a mixture of Somali and English, the only clearly decipherable word of which was "outrage." The next clear phrase was "city manager." He was starting a third volley, beginning with "discrimination," when Burgess held up a hand, signaling him to stop.

"Sage, you want to give me a hand here."

The Imam sputtered. Burgess kept his hand up. "Be quiet, sir. Please."

When Sage had joined them, Burgess said, "Now, we both know that you understand English. And speak it. But I'm going to ask Detective Prentiss to help with translation."

He gestured for Melia to hand the Imam the warrant that the women had refused to accept. "This is a warrant to search the premises, including the garage and basement, and any vehicles on or about the premises which are registered in your name. We are looking for information relating to the identity of a girl and an infant found imprisoned in your mosque during the fire. Also, as you have refused to cooperate with our investigation or answer our questions, we are looking for any and all documents pertaining to the rental and ownership of the building, as well as to any service agencies operating out of that facility."

He waited until the Imam had finally, reluctantly, taken the document from Melia. "Understand. This is a homicide investigation, Mr. Ibrahim. Do you have any questions?"

"You have violated the sanctity of my home and frightened my family."

Pretty darned good English, Burgess noted.

"Regrettable," Burgess agreed. "And you brought it on them yourself." He gestured toward the boxes. "We will go through these papers. Any that are not relevant to our investigation will be returned to you as promptly as possible."

He changed the subject. "Upstairs we found a locked closet hidden behind an armoire. Items found in that closet suggest that a woman and an infant stayed in there. So tell me, please, sir, whether the girl and the infant found at the mosque were ever present in this house?"

The Imam glared at him, and didn't answer.

"Do you know the name of that girl?" No answer. "Of her child?" No answer. "Is the infant related to anyone in your family?"

Beside him, Sage's calm voice translated. Across the room, the huddled women stared. The Imam ignored the questions.

"We are going to ask the women of your family the same questions," Burgess said. "And you should understand—if we determine that you do know the identity of that girl and her child, and that she was ever present here in your house, you and any members of your household sharing that knowledge will be accessories after the fact to murder and likely subject to prosecution for kidnapping, child abuse, and child sexual abuse."

Across the room, he saw one of the younger women staring at him. She was holding a baby tightly to her chest and there was something in her expression—not the fear and hostility of the others—that suggested she understood what he was saying and that she had something she wanted to tell him. The challenge would be when, and where, and how.

He let Sage finish translating for the Imam, then said, "Do you understand?"

"I understand only that you choose to pick on us because we are vulnerable. Because it isn't enough that we have lost our place of worship and our offices to provide services to our community. When any young girl might have gone into that building, seeking help or advice. I understand that you target us because the baby that died was black. None of that has anything to do with us."

Thank you, Mr. Ibrahim, Burgess thought. The race of the baby had never been reported.

CHAPTER TWENTY-FIVE

Often, investigation was like following a maze. Today it felt like a game of hopscotch. He was at the beginning and his goal at the other end; he kept having to hop on one foot and work around obstacles and distractions, and while he hopped and jumped, the other end never seemed to get any closer.

Whatever he might have thought he'd learn from the woman with the signaling eyes, he didn't. She wouldn't tell him anything in the presence of the others. It had taken more than another hour to get identities from the women, and question them, and it had all been worthless. They all said the girl and her baby had never been in the house.

They had left Wink working the locked closet and Stan Perry and Sage Prentiss to search the cars. He went to see Jason Stetson and his foster mom. Kyle went to see if he could track down his elusive informant. They would meet up when they were done and execute the warrant at Hussain Osman's apartment. Osman's condition remained unchanged.

Burgess was sitting at the kitchen table with Jason Stetson and his foster mother, while a smaller boy in the corner entertained a baby in a playpen. Both Jason and his foster mother looked anxious. There was a sliced, homemade loaf of banana bread on a plate, and the room smelled of baking, and lemon polish, and fresh, strong coffee.

The foster mother's name was Molly. She was late thirties,

Chris's age, and pretty in a wholesome, outdoorsy way, with bright brown eyes and short, efficient hair. He figured she was a runner. He was trying to find a way to help her relax when Jason said, "It's okay, Mrs. Andrews. Detective Burgess may not look it, but he's really nice."

It did the trick. She swatted him affectionately as she said, "Jason, that's not very polite."

Jason grinned and ducked his head, and Burgess grinned, too. Family could make all the difference. A couple years ago, Jason was living with an abusive stepfather and a mother who'd disappeared into a bottle and was definitely heading toward a bad outcome.

"Jason has been really helpful to us in our investigation of that fire at the mosque, Mrs. Andrews. He's very observant. I'm hoping you may have noticed things as well." He led her through the easy stuff first. The rhythms of the day, who came and went, the relationship of the mosque's members with the neighborhood. It pretty much confirmed what he'd already heard from Jason. Then he asked her about the men on motorcycles. Had she seen them? Could she describe them? Had they appeared to be harassing the Muslims?

"Harassing the Muslims?" She shook her head. "I think that's what we're supposed to think, Detective Burgess. Because they're so obvious, riding around on those noisy machines." She smiled a self-deprecating smile. "When you've got a baby in the house, you really notice loud noises. Anyway, as I'm sure Jason has told you, we've seen them roaring through the parking lot and calling out rude things to the women. The behavior you'd expect from a motorcycle gang that's prejudiced against immigrants or outsiders. But I've seen those same men coming at night, not on motorcycles but with those white box trucks, and those times, they seem friendly enough with the Imam and his followers. Well, maybe not friendly. But like they're working together."

Burgess made a note. "What time of night?"

"Late," she said. "After midnight." She gestured toward the baby. "Grace isn't a good sleeper. I never should have put her bedroom at the front of the house. She and Jason have their rooms there. But it was the smallest room, see. And she's the smallest of us." She hesitated. "This used to be a quiet neighborhood."

The "us" warmed his heart, and flashed him back to last night.

A mosque should have been quiet in the middle of the night. And there were those white box trucks again.

"Those trucks," he said. "Did they have anything written on them? The name of a business?"

She shook her head. "Just plain white."

"How many trucks?"

"One or two."

"Did you see them on any kind of regular basis? Did they seem to have a schedule?"

She started to shake her head, but Jason interrupted. "Usually every other week," he said, "and always either on a Sunday or a Monday."

He made another note to figure out what that might correlate to, and pulled out the photo of their mystery girl. "Did you ever see this girl at the mosque?"

Molly Andrews took it and studied it, frowning as she did, then shook her head. "Not that I recognize. She might have been one of those ones who didn't just wear the headscarf but was totally covered. But they're usually the old ones." She passed the photo to Jason. "What about you, Jase? You ever see this girl?"

Jason looked like he didn't want to answer. Then he said, "I think maybe she's married to one of the In Man's sons. Not the one with the scar. The other one. The one the In Man likes better. He . . . the In Man . . . he's always mean, but he's meaner to the scarred one. That is . . . I can't always hear what they say, but I can see their faces, and the In Man is always talking to this son, I think his name is Ishmael, and when that son turns away, his face is always twisted, like he hates his old man or something. And I've seen him looking at the girl like maybe he wanted her for his wife. I don't think he has a wife. That is, I've never seen him with one."

Burgess thought about Ismail's words when they were driving him away from the shooting. Ismail had said he had to contact his family and let them know he was all right. Burgess had just assumed Ismail meant his own family. And he hadn't followed up, had he?

"Jason, have you ever seen this girl with the Imam's grandson? The one named Muhamud?"

Jason looked down at his shoes. "No. I've seen her walking with some of the other women. And I've seen Ishmael looking at her. About her being Muhamud's wife? It's just from something I heard at school. From that girl I told you about? Only she doesn't want to talk to you. You can ask me questions, and I can ask her and bring you the answers, but out of school, she can't be seen talking to you, Detective Burgess. You know how that is."

He knew how that was. He also knew that time kept slipping through their fingers like the sand blowing around out there. Days went by and all they got was more bodies and more work and few answers. He tried to remember whether the younger Muhamud Ibrahim had been among the men surrounding the Imam during their interview. It would be in his notes.

"Okay, Jason. We'll do it your way, but what about—"

"Detective Burgess," Jason interrupted, a confused look on

his face. "You know that stuff that was written on the wall? That hateful stuff? Here's something I don't get. I saw them write that. It was at night, but my window looks out that way, and there's a security light on the building. You know, the kind that comes on when someone moves? And who did that writing? Well, I didn't recognize the man who did it. He's not one of them, but the In Man, he was right there watching. Him and his mean son. The tall one without the scar on his face. This man . . . he wasn't African like them . . . he did the writing and the In Man and one of his sons, the one that isn't Ishmael, he's maybe Muhamud, too, they were watching and telling the man what to write."

As Kyle would say, the plot kept thickening. It was getting to be like a pea-soup-thick fog.

"When was that, Jason?"

"The night before the fire."

Kyle's piss-poor mood matched his own. His informant was playing games with him, setting up meetings and then not showing. She wasn't in any of the places she could usually be found and she wasn't answering her phone or responding to texts.

"I don't know whether she's got some valid information and I should be worried or whether she's just screwing around, Joe," he said.

"Worrying won't help you find her any faster."

They both knew that worrying was part of the business, especially about informants. People could get too cocky or careless and get themselves into a lot of trouble. No amount of cautioning on the part of their handlers made any difference. Most of their informants were cooperating because they were already in trouble with the police. Their lifestyles were not normally cautious and well-regulated.

"Heard some interesting things from Jason Stetson and his

foster mom," Burgess said as he steered through what passed for rush hour in Portland.

"Interesting? Or helpful?"

"Both."

"Do tell," Kyle said. "And can we grab some coffee and something that won't make me think of maggots? Like maybe a blueberry muffin?"

It was almost dinnertime, but dinner, like lunch, was something their morning with the late Butcher Flaherty had put them off. "Blueberries have maggots, Terry."

"Screw you, Joe. Can we just stop. Please?"

Of course he stopped. Burgess believed in feeding Kyle. The man ran at such high revs he burned through his fuel quickly. And Kyle hadn't had the benefit of Molly Andrews's banana bread.

"One of those women at the Imam's house wanted to tell us something," Kyle said, as Burgess beat out a woman in a MINI for the last parking space.

She flipped him the bird. He flipped her his blue lights.

"Yeah. I'm just not sure how we'll ever get a chance to find out what." He swung the door open and got out, feeling old and stiff. "The foster mom says that the same motorcyclists who harassed the Muslims during the day were back there at night, loading and unloading white box trucks."

Kyle stared at him over the roof of the truck. "You're kidding. We've gotta find those damned trucks."

"And Jason says that some white guy wrote that anti-Muslim graffiti at the Imam's direction. Something our oh-so-innocent Imam failed to mention when we interviewed him. Jason also thinks our mystery girl is the Imam's oldest grandson's wife."

Kyle sighed. "I should have come with you. It would have made my day feel productive."

"At least you didn't get the trash, like Stan."

"Low man on the totem pole. Have we met this grandson? This is not our friend Ismail? The one with the scar?"

"No. According to Jason, though we've got to take this with a grain of salt, the oldest grandson, named Muhamud like his grandfather, is the favorite, and the Imam doesn't like Ismail."

"If he's the black sheep, why did Ismail go silent on us the other night?"

"Because someone had just shot at him, Ter? Maybe he'd been showing signs that he was not with the program and that was a kind of 'warning shot.' Or maybe because he knows the Imam's secrets and he's still bucking for his grandpa's love. That happens all the time."

Burgess tried to recreate the incident in his mind. Had that felt like a warning? Had Ismail not really been in any danger? It had felt like an authentic hit to him, and the shooters had been willing to burn a car, instead of just parking it and going back to business as usual. Had that been because he and Perry had been there? He needed to take another look at the scene photos. Wished they had the car back at 109 in their growing collection.

When Kyle had been fed, they drove to Osman's apartment. Burgess had Osman's keys, but when the door was open, they found themselves staring into a nearly empty room. Nothing there but a lamp, a table, and a mattress on the floor. There was no food. No dishes. No clothes. No signs of human occupancy. Either Osman had been in the process of moving in or out or he lived a beyond-monkish existence. Or the place was just an address to hide behind. There were other keys on the ring.

He dropped Kyle at 109 and went to the library to check out his hunch about the yearbooks. As he pulled to the curb, his phone rang. Andrea Dwyer.

"I'm at the hospital," she said. "And before you get anxious, everything is okay. Our girl is fine."

"Thought our surveillance had been canceled."

"It has. I'm off tonight, with time on my hands, so I just figured I'd stop in for a bit and see how things were going."

"You shouldn't have to," he said, again feeling something shift. The small, silent, damaged child in the center of this case was managing to work some kind of positive magic on the people around her.

"I didn't become the kiddie cop because it was going to make me rich."

She had that right. "Thanks. I'll try to swing by later, see how things are going."

"Always a treat to see your smiling face," she said.

His face felt hard and heavy and very far from a smile. But Dwyer could usually coax one out of him.

Burgess grabbed the keys from the ignition and went inside. A helpful librarian helped him locate the books. Twenty minutes later, he was at the copy machine, copying a photo of Addison Westerly.

CHAPTER TWENTY-SIX

Back at 109, he found Melia had people working on the files under Stan Perry's supervision, and wasn't surprised to learn that they'd found an existing relationship between Addison Westerly and the Imam. Rocky's dogged research had established that Westerly was the owner of a company that was the owner of a real estate trust that owned the building that had housed the burned mosque. Westerly's offices were in a building on the waterfront near the warehouse that had become the new mosque site.

Everything they could connect Westerly to—building, vehicles, and boats—was in the company name. Even his driver's license listed the office address. Stan Perry had had patrol go by the office and check out the fishing boat. No sign of Westerly. They'd go by the office again in the morning.

Burgess looked through Rocky's report, hoping for box trucks, and didn't find any.

It felt like they were on the cusp of a breakthrough, in their first death case at least. The feeling that important information was close, coupled with the need to wait, made Burgess restless and cranky. Kyle was cranky. Perry would have been cranky if he wasn't buried in paperwork.

Burgess left a note for Rocky, asking him to locate any businesses operated by the Ibrahims. One way or another, he was going to find those trucks. And Westerly. And the thread that connected everything.

They also needed to track down the links between Butcher Flaherty and the Imam. Or the Imam's grandson. To find the Imam's oldest grandson. He'd checked his notes, and despite a crush of Ibrahims at the Imam's house during their first interview, a younger Muhamud Ibrahim had not been present. Press Devlin was out, still trying to find people with knowledge of Flaherty's activities. The dead biker's friends, he'd reported in a text, were being unusually taciturn.

Leaving Perry to bully those sorting through the Imam's papers, he and Kyle, the family men, shook off the pressure of all the places they needed to be and all the people they needed to see, and went home to dinner.

Hours later, familial duties done, the pressure of unanswered questions had brought both of them back to 109. The office was quiet and they sat at their desks, organizing messages and writing and reading reports, looking for something to break, and prepping for another strategy session in the morning. Despite Burgess's sense that results were close, the whole case felt like swimming against a riptide. He was being pulled along by the force of circumstances and not going where he wanted to go.

"Hey, Joe," Kyle said, tipping back in his chair. "Maybe Stan wants to do maggot patrol in the morning. What do you think? He could take Sage with him, see if the kid turns green again."

It was a good idea if he could just get his inner control freak to go along. Burgess had been dreading the trip to Augusta for Flaherty's autopsy. It felt like there was too much to do here. Perry had been asking for more chances to observe. And Sage Prentiss was ambitious.

"You've gotta let him grow," Kyle said. "He's good. He won't miss things and he'll appreciate the chance. It doesn't always have to be you. You've done your share of maggots."

"You think I'm a control freak, Ter?"

"I know you're a control freak." Kyle changed the subject. "What's up with Osman's place, do you think? I mean seriously, who has an apartment with just a bed, a lamp, and a table?"

"Someone who doesn't really live there?"

"Just what I was thinking. Where does he live, then?"

"What about that woman who picked him up? Rihanna Daud? Maybe he lives with her."

"We haven't talked to her, have we? Maybe she can answer that part of the puzzle. Or maybe she can tell us what was up between Osman and the Imam and his people. And whether that's what got him attacked."

Kyle shook his head. "Always on the list of things we never get to. She hasn't shown up at the hospital to visit him."

"Hiding?" Burgess said. "There's some connection there. She came to the hospital to pick him up and later he was found in the trunk of her car. But we do have an address." He pulled the report template up on his screen. It was the same address as the empty apartment.

"What do fishing boats, mosques, and motorcycle gangs have in common?"

"Beats me, Joe. I'm about ready to start lighting candles to the gods of insight."

"Boats and motorcycles both move things. So do box trucks. But where does the mosque come in?"

"Storage? Distribution point?" Kyle suggested. "Like a warehouse that no one would ever look in?" Kyle popped out of his chair. "Want to take a ride?"

Burgess's desk was piled a foot deep with papers and messages that needed his attention, and he still had more reports to write. But like Kyle, he needed to get out on the street and see if he could make something happen.

He shoved some papers into his briefcase and grabbed his

coat. "Just let me give Stan a call, see if he wants to do the autopsy tomorrow. Then yes, I would love to take a ride."

CHAPTER TWENTY-SEVEN

"Where to?" Burgess asked, as they walked through the garage. But he knew where they were going. They were looking for Rihanna Daud. Back to the empty apartment to look at the mail. To look for clues. And maybe they'd just drive around and look for Osman's gray van.

When they were out of the cement chill and into the darkness of a spring night, they both rolled down their windows and let the cool air blow in.

"Think we're losing our edges?" Kyle said.

"Young guy like you, Ter? I doubt it. It's the distraction factor."

"You mean trying to have a life?"

Burgess didn't need to answer.

They drove through city streets as familiar to them as their own bodies: houses, blocks, alleys, and businesses that had stories to tell. Usually stories of violence. They passed people whose stories they knew. The language of the street. We'll be hearing from this guy before the night is over. There's the woman who's a walking magnet for domestic violence.

They passed a man with a gait like a bowlegged sailor, weaving along the sidewalk in a state of extreme intoxication. A danger to himself and others. Someone else, they might have called patrol and had him taken into protective custody, but not this guy. They knew just where he had gotten his limp. He'd shot at a cop and the cop had returned fire. The rat bastard had

250

sued the department, claiming excessive force, and the spineless city had caved, sending the message: go ahead and shoot at our cops. If you don't die, you might get rich. He didn't look like he was enjoying his ill-gotten gains. He looked like he'd pissed it all away.

That kid there, no more than seven or eight, out on the street by himself this late at night, shivering in a thin sweatshirt? A member of Future Criminals of America. Families, their dysfunction, or the lack of families, doomed so many of these kids. One of the reasons he and Kyle had to fight their desire to wrap their own families in cotton wool, like objects in a precious collection, box them up and keep them safe from the world.

Burgess pointed to a young man on the sidewalk up ahead, an arrogant roll in his walk that spoke of studied indifference. Dylan, who could imitate that walk perfectly, called it the ghetto strut. The boy's hand in his bulging hoodie pocket broadcast "handgun."

"That fellow look familiar to you?"

"Should he?"

Burgess remembered that Kyle hadn't been with them when they called on the Imam after the fire. He'd been out looking for his informant. "He's the Imam's youngest son—or grandson."

"Jesus," Kyle said, as Burgess pulled to the curb and cut the engine. "Not good."

They watched Ali Ibrahim hitch up his precarious FUBU jeans with his free hand and disappear into a convenience store.

Burgess called dispatch, reporting a 1090, a robbery in progress and asked that they approach without sirens. Then he and Kyle slipped out of the truck and headed toward the store, automatically checking their guns and shifting them into low ready as they moved into place on either side of the door; from there they could see inside but were mostly masked by the posters and displays of sodas, beer, and windshield washer piled high against the glass.

Cops could tell the owners a million times, don't obscure the view from the street, but the owners put marketing ahead of safety every time.

Young Ali Ibrahim had a cube of beer on the counter, and was engaged in an argument with the clerk behind the counter, an argument he seemed to be winning because of the gun he held in his hand. The clerk was African-American, a tired, middle-aged man who looked seriously pissed off.

Ideally, they would have observed the robbery, then nabbed Ali as he stepped out the door encumbered by his stolen beer. But the gun, and the look on the clerk's face, told them that the situation could go south very quickly. The look, and the clerk's body language, said he was itching to reach down under the counter and grab whatever weapon he had stashed there.

People who worked in convenience stores had a hard and often dangerous job. Lately, they'd been getting pretty darned sick of being held up by their new African neighbors, even, in some cases, where the clerks were Somali or Sudanese immigrants themselves. The robbers seemed to think the clerks ought to give it up to a fellow countryman. And this was along with all the other folks who considered convenience stores as their own personal banks—those with an itch to scratch, an Oxycontin habit to feed, or an empty wallet and an unquenchable craving for beer. The clerks seemed to think this was something of an imposition.

Ali hadn't seen Kyle the other night, so Burgess signaled for him to go in first, then moved up right behind him, so he could pile in as backup before Ali recognized him and while Ali was distracted.

All these places had back doors, but usually those doors were locked, making this the only likely entrance and exit.

Burgess braced himself to move quickly as Kyle raised his gun to ready position, following suit with his own gun, feeling years of experience taking over as he went into tunnel vision.

Then they went through the door, spreading out to create a funnel on Ali. Burgess flying past Kyle, the two of them moving in unison, putting enough space between them so that Ali couldn't keep an eye on both of them.

"Police," Kyle yelled. "Drop the gun! Drop the goddamned gun!"

Ali turned toward Kyle, his gun turning with him.

God, Burgess thought, as he stared at the boy's baby face. Armed and thuggish as he was, Ali Ibrahim was just a kid. They were about to kill a kid, because kid or no kid, you didn't let someone fire a gun at you. Not if you wanted to go home to your family at the end of the day.

He knew Kyle was thinking the same thing. That this whole case was about kids, and now one of them was just asking them to shoot him. Stupid goddamned gangsta wannabe kid just didn't understand. You draw on a cop and you take the consequences. The consequences were aim at center mass and don't stop shooting until they go down and stay down.

He felt Kyle, eight feet away, thinking the same thing, because no cop in an armed confrontation took his eyes off the shooter, off the gun.

This was going down, and it was going to be a shitstorm.

He watched the boy turn toward them, kept his eyes on the gun.

"Just put it down, dammit, just put it down and nothing bad has to happen," Kyle said.

It was all a matter of judgment. Of trying to keep breathing and hope that while he and Kyle were in that tunnel they would make the right decisions. Hoping no one else came through the door. And all of it going down in seconds.

Seconds that could feel like an eternity. That was tunnel vision. The world faded away. Time slowed down. Watching the kid. The gun. Knowing where the clerk and Kyle were without really looking at either one of them. The edges of his tunnel bright with walls of junk food.

Don't get yourself shot.

Don't get anyone else shot.

Put it down, put it down, lower the gun so we don't have to kill you. Don't make us kill you. The thought was so loud in his head it felt like he'd yelled it.

They moved forward like they were on the same track, their guns coming up together, aiming together, their fingers on the trigger hesitating before squeezing together.

They had every right to fire. To kill this kid before he killed them. Never mind the barrage of publicity that would follow. The family of another freaking armed asshole who draws on the cops shrieking police brutality and their poor innocent boy lost.

He and Kyle had one rule here—go home alive. That was what this moment was all about.

He felt his finger closing on the trigger and the moment, that touch point, before the explosion.

Ali finished turning toward them. Squeezed the trigger. Not an aimed shot. A wild shot.

Kyle ducked, and several bags of chips on a shelf above his head gave up their lives.

There was a moment, when smoke and gunpowder hung in the air. When their fingers were still on the triggers of their own guns, and when any review panel in the whole damned world would have found returning fire justified. When they hesitated, and waited, not dead yet, waiting, against all the rules of survival, to see what that stupid wannabe gangsta child would do. Because he was just a stupid, stupid, dangerously stupid kid.

The boy did the right thing. He dropped his gun on the floor and held out trembling hands in a gesture of submission, tears and terror in his voice. "Don't shoot. Don't shoot. Please. Don't. Don't shoot me. Don't shoot me!"

Burgess and Kyle rushed him, Burgess already reaching for his cuffs, as the clerk brought a baseball bat up from behind the counter and whacked Ali in the arm. His right arm, his gun arm, a good, solid strike that left the boy screaming.

The clerk swung the bat back, readying for another strike, lost in his own tunnel vision.

Burgess got between them. "Okay. Okay. That's enough!" he said. "Enough. We've got this."

Ali Ibrahim, sullen, angry teen and courageous robber of the unarmed, the little prince of fuck-you attitude, the boy who had just risked four lives for some beer, folded up in a blubbering heap on the floor, cradling his injured arm.

Kyle was on the radio to dispatch, knowing the whole city was converging on them, saying, "Slow it down, we've got the suspect in custody," and requesting an evidence tech to the scene, when two patrol cars flew into the lot, sirens off, as instructed, but with their light bars flashing.

Next time, Burgess thought, *he'd be clearer that he'd meant an unannounced approach.*

They could have handed Ali over to patrol, left them to take the clerk's statement, wait for the tech to come and collect the gun and cartridge casing, and continued on their merry way, but driving the poor injured boy over to the hospital themselves seemed like too good an opportunity to miss.

Burgess searched him carefully and cuffed him with tender consideration for his injured arm, then filled the officers in on what had happened. "You'll want to find that cartridge casing. Document those chips he shot up. We'll take the boy over to Emergency," he said, "and then to the jail for booking."

Through it all, the clerk stood by, slapping the baseball bat into the palm of his hand, his breath ragged, coming down from the near-death adrenaline rush they'd all just experienced.

Burgess took him aside and pulled the bat away. "You did a great job just now," he said, "keeping it together. I know how much you wanted to grab your bat and how hard it was not to. If you had, we might be dealing with a homicide right now, instead of a couple bags of dead chips."

The man's face was gray. His eyes jumpy. He swayed a little unsteadily.

"Is there someplace you could sit down?"

He looked over at Kyle. Nodded at Ali, still sitting on the floor. Still blubbering. A stupid, dangerous kid who'd just rubbed a man's nose in his own mortality. He was eager to interview the kid. He needed to take some time for the victim.

"I need a minute, Ter," he said. "Keep an eye on him, okay?"

Kyle nodded and moved closer to Ali.

"In the back there's a . . ." The clerk's words staggered to a stop. He put a hand to his chest. "Oh my God. Oh my God."

Burgess took his arm and led him to the back of the store. Now that he wasn't holding the bat, the man was shaking. "I've got kids at home. Just trying to make a living, and that . . . that piece of crap kid . . . He would have killed me for some beer?"

Burgess didn't think it would be much comfort to the man to share his supposition that the kid had probably never fired a gun in his life. Plenty of kids got their hands on guns for the first time and killed people with them.

He settled the man in a chair and got him a bottle of water. There was a desk, and a phone, and taped to the phone, contact information for the manager.

"This your boss?" he asked.

The man nodded.

"I'm going to call him. Tell him what happened. Say we're

256

sending you home. Is that all right?"

Most of these places didn't pay their help well. Treated them worse. He didn't want the man to stay because he was worried about his paycheck. But the man nodded. He wanted to be out of here. Home with his family. Someplace that felt safer than this.

Burgess nodded toward the front of the store. "You got surveillance cameras?"

"Yeah."

"They work?"

He saw the faintest flicker of a smile. Far too often places had security cameras for show but they didn't work.

"Yeah." A hesitation. "Since the last robbery."

"Good. Then I'll have our tech collect the tape. Our little friend out there, Ali Ibrahim, sure picked the wrong night, the wrong clerk, and the wrong store for his venture into crime. You see him around here before?"

"A few times. Rolling in with a couple of his homies." The man had braced himself with his hands on his knees, like if he didn't, he might topple right off the chair.

Rolling caught it just right. That swaggering attitude, hampered by the crotches of their pants somewhere between their knees, made them move like sailors recently ashore.

"Detective Sergeant Joe Burgess," Burgess said.

"Royce," the man said. "Royce Rawlins."

Rawlins looked down at the floor, and then raised troubled eyes to Burgess. "I'm in the system. That's why I've got the baseball bat and not a gun. Just as stupid when I was young as that kid out there. I did my time. Learned my lesson. Married a good woman and I've got two great kids. But it never leaves me, you know. I doubt I'll ever be able to get me a decent-paying job. I just wish—"

He studied the floor again. Battered. Dirty. A metaphor for

something. "Wish we could tell them kids this. How wanting to be a stupid gangster can ruin your life. I don't know nothin' about that kid out there, but what he's just done . . . not only to me, but to himself. It's just pure stupid."

He pushed himself straighter. "I just keep prayin', Detective, that maybe my own kids can learn from my lesson." He shook his head, a big, graying head with a deeply furrowed forehead. "So damned hard to raise kids these days. Raise 'em right."

It was the truth, the whole truth, and nothing but the truth.

"I'll call your boss," Burgess said, lifting the phone. "Then you go home to your family."

CHAPTER TWENTY-EIGHT

Ali Ibrahim was still snuffling when they took him by the elbows, raised him up, and led him out to the Explorer. Burgess got one of his handkerchiefs from the stash he kept in the console, and passed it back to Ali.

"Wipe your face," he said.

"I got nothin' to say to you."

"We'll see," Burgess said. "Now wipe your face. I don't want your baby snot all over my car. Terry, you want to tell Mr. Ibrahim about his Miranda rights?"

"I do," Kyle said.

He used his formal voice, the one that came on when he wanted to let a bad guy know that the cops had him. He even did it the formal, TV way. He produced the battered card from his wallet and read it to the sulking boy.

Then, before he started the engine, Burgess looked at Kyle and they both got out of the truck, leaving their prisoner behind. "Stay," Burgess commanded. "Try to get out and we'll shoot you."

When they were out of earshot, Kyle braced himself against the side of a building and bent over, like someone who had just run a long, hard race.

"Sweet Jesus," he said. "That was a close one."

Burgess had the same roiling sensation in his gut and his hands were far from steady. "You can say that again. We didn't have that idiot child to deal with, I'd suggest we find ourselves a nice dark bar and knock back a few."

"In the fullness of time," Kyle intoned. "That is an excellent way to settle the nerves."

Or go off the deep end, something Burgess feared and Kyle had done.

Burgess stared at the wall, at the cracking, chipped paint, a yellowing white the color of old eyes. At his hand, spread out like a starfish, and said what they were both thinking. "I hope we haven't just made a terrible mistake. What if the little bastard gets out, turns around, and shoots someone else? Shoots a cop? What if some liberal judge takes a look at that baby face and forgets that three people went through a devastating experience and came within a hair's breadth of losing their lives to that boy's selfish indifference?"

"Not our call," Kyle reminded him. "We just pick the cotton. At least there's video. That always makes it harder to do just a slap on the wrist. And maybe that gun has been used in another crime?"

We just pick the cotton. Too true. The cops did their job, brought in the bad guys and made the best case they could. Then it was up to the injustice system, one that in Maine was sometimes laughably liberal. As were the gun laws. It did not make their job any easier that the bad guys could outgun them with automatic weapons and armor-piercing bullets.

"When you searched him, did he have any ID? Anything on him at all?" Burgess asked.

"Student ID and a library card."

A freakin' library card. It sounded so benign, thugs who carried library cards. "What year is he?"

Kyle rolled his eyes. "Freshman."

"That makes him what? Maybe fifteen?"

Dylan was fifteen. Burgess shivered.

"Or older," Kyle said, "depending on how far behind he was,

or is, and how long he's been in the system. We can check with the school tomorrow. See what the family told them when he registered. Whether there's anything like a birth certificate or what birth date got assigned to him when he came here. But no matter what we learn, no way he's an adult."

"But he just committed a very adult crime. Crimes."

"Like armed robbery and attempted murder of a police officer."

"Officers. Which some bleeding-heart legal aid lawyer will attribute to the violence and lack of social structure in the country he came from. Like any of that mattered to the clerk tonight. Or would matter to his family if he'd resisted and we hadn't come along, or to your family if the kid's aim had been better."

"Sure as hell *would* matter to my family," Kyle said. "The girls would have to go back and live with Wanda."

The content didn't matter, really. They were talking to get their lungs working again. To give their bodies time to bring the adrenaline levels back down. Put space between them and what had just happened.

"Sending him to juvie might be the best thing anyone ever did for that kid. It doesn't look like anyone's setting good examples for him at home," Burgess said. "Actually, based on our experience, they're setting a pretty good example of how not to cooperate. I expect we'll be seeing more of that in the next few minutes. Boy is definitely a graduate of the 'I know my rights' school of bad attitude."

"And the 'everyone owes me 'cuz I've suffered' school as well."

Kyle sighed and pushed off the wall. "Lead on, oh fearless Detective Sergeant. We should be thinking of ourselves. Of warm beds and a good night's sleep."

"Right. We could have been there already, Ter. Next time you suggest going for a drive, I am going to claim I have too much paperwork. Which, in fact, I do."

"You spend too much time at your desk, you'll get soft. Lose your edge. Forget how it is when you mix it up with bad guys."

Burgess started toward the truck. He hoped he still had his edge, had felt like he did tonight, but things could have gone so wrong in so many ways.

"We're heading over to the hospital now," he told Ali as they climbed back in the truck. "How's your arm?"

For an answer, he got a string of obscenities.

"Playing the tough guy won't work with us, son," he said. "Detective Kyle and I both saw you blubbering like a baby instead of standing up like a man. If you're big enough to threaten people with a gun, you need to be man enough to accept the consequences. You should be thanking God . . . my God, your God, someone else's God, that you are still breathing."

Oh what the kid didn't know about how close that call had been. "So let me explain to you how this works. We take you to the hospital, get you checked out, and then we take you over to the jail and you'll be booked on armed robbery and attempted murder of a convenience store clerk and two police officers. Once the booking process is done, you'll get to make a phone call. Clear so far?"

There was no response from the back seat.

"Now, Detective Kyle has read you your rights. You do not have to talk to us unless you want to. But just so we're clear, we don't have any questions for you about what happened tonight. We don't need to ask about that. You've got three witnesses, a surveillance tape, a gun with your prints all over it, a hole in the ceiling and a spent cartridge casing. It's an open and shut, slam-dunk of a case of robbery and attempted murder. Even as a juvenile, you aren't going home any time soon."

He drove a while, let that sink in, then said, "But sometimes your situation can be improved by cooperating with the police. You understand that word? Cooperation?"

"I'm not stupid," Ali said.

They all knew he was.

"We're looking for information about your grandfather. About the mosque. How it operates. What the organizational structure is. We want to know who the girl is who was locked in that closet. Who put her there, and why. What the baby's name was. Whose baby that was and where we find the father."

He watched Ali's impassive face in the rearview. "Sad to think of burying that poor little guy without ever even knowing his name."

Burgess paused to let a tattered man wheel a shopping cart across the street. He'd probably never see one again without expecting to see his friend Reggie. Funny how it surprised him every time to remember that Reggie was gone. But he knew. There was a difference between the victims in the cases they worked, and the victims in their own lives.

But that wasn't always true, either. Every detective had victims they'd never known alive who stayed with them. He had Kristen Marks. He and Kyle shared little Timmy Watts. Getting justice for victims was their life's work and their calling. Getting justice for children made greater demands and took a bigger toll.

Now they had Baby Doe, who had suffered miserably and died miserably.

In the rearview, he watched Ali fumble to undo his seatbelt. Out of consideration for his injured arm, they'd cuffed his hands in front. Now it looked like that might be a mistake. Burgess checked to be sure the rear doors were locked, then said, "Terry?"

Kyle turned suddenly in the seat. "Leave that seatbelt alone and put your hands on your knees where I can see 'em."

Ali jumped like he'd been struck. Opened his mouth.

"And unless you have something worthwhile to say, keep your mouth shut. We've heard enough obscene crap from you already."

The open mouth snapped shut. Evidently Ali *didn't* have anything worthwhile to say.

"So," Burgess said. "That baby . . . your brother . . . he was sick. He needed emergency medical treatment, or he would have died anyway. Did you know that?"

He'd taken a gamble here. What he thought was that the baby was probably a nephew. If Jason was right, the child of one of Ali's brothers. It would have to be someone close to the Imam to have ready access to the mosque, and that closet, without people asking a lot of questions. Maybe the congregation, or whatever they called it, was so submissive they didn't ask any questions. He really didn't know.

"That screaming brat is not my brother."

"Thank you," Burgess said. "So he's your nephew. Which of your brothers is his father?"

Ali Ibrahim could choose the right course here, one that would be hard for him in the short term and beneficial in the long term, or he could cling to his tough-guy pose, put loyalty to family first, and hope that the courts were kind to a poor misguided refugee child.

Tenderhearted judges did not make his job—his and Kyle's— any easier. Juvenile criminals often seemed too well-informed about their prospects for leniency. Burgess could only hope that Ali was not well-informed.

But Ali had lapsed back into silence.

"It's a nice night for a drive," Kyle said. "Seems a pity to rush right over to the hospital, spend more hours inside. Those harsh lights. That chemical atmosphere. Seems like we've done enough of that this week. Be nice to park somewhere by the water, someplace nice and quiet. Watch the moon and the scudding clouds. Remember that poor little baby. That . . . what did our friend Ali just call him? That screaming brat?"

"You're so right," Burgess said. "We've already been over there two nights this week. I'm in no hurry to be there again. And Ali doesn't seem to be in much pain."

He watched Ali shift nervously on the seat as he changed course and headed toward the waterfront.

Burgess swung off the road and into a tank farm, weaving among the tall gasoline storage tanks until they were right by the water. Then he threw the truck into park and they both climbed out.

Portland was an up-and-coming city with great restaurants and interesting shopping and a vibrant music and art scene. It was also an old port with a working waterfront. There was security here, but they wouldn't bother a couple of Portland cops, even ones driving an unmarked. They'd know.

They pulled Ali out of the back seat, led him across the lot, and fastened one hand to a metal railing. A cold, briny wind was blowing off the water. He and Kyle had their leather jackets. The boy, looking miserable and scared, shivered in his thin sweatshirt.

As they were cuffing him to the railing, Ali made one more attempt at bravado. "You mess with me," he said, "and my brothers are going to mess with your families."

"Did you hear the boy, Joe?" Kyle said. "He's threatening our families."

Even in the limited light from a security fixture on one of the tanks, Burgess could read Kyle's anger. There had already been too much threatening in this case. They stood facing the water, backs to their squirming prisoner, voices raised to be heard over the wind.

"He's threatening our families, Terry," Burgess said. "Last two guys who tried that ended up in jail. And there was that one guy, you remember him, ended up in the ICU. They did their best, but he was never the same again. I think he's in some sheltered workshop now."

"And of course, the folks at the hospital have no idea what kind of injuries the lad had when he left the convenience store," Kyle said. "Just that there was a baseball bat involved. And then there's the matter of escape. Ali might have gotten a lot more banged up trying to escape from us. We're just doing our duty, making sure he doesn't escape again, given the danger he poses to the general public."

"True," Burgess agreed, "and a baseball bat can cause some pretty serious injuries. I had a guy once, messed with another man's wife, by the time we got there, the husband had worked him over pretty good. Guy's testicles swelled until they were bigger than softballs. Moving him around so the tech could get a good picture of the damage, I've never heard a man scream like that."

"Guy who did it went to jail, right?" Kyle asked.

"Yeah. But he said it was worth it."

"Had another guy, messed with a girl whose husband was in a motorcycle gang. You don't want to know what was done to him."

"I heard about that one," Kyle said. "Docs over at the ER tried to sew it back on, right?"

"But it never worked right after that," Burgess said.

"You couldn't feel too sorry for the guy, though," Kyle said. "He knew what he was getting into. Just like someone does when they take a handgun, walk into a convenience store, and draw on the clerk. Someone who does that, he knows he's breaking the law. And he ought to know that there are penalties for that if he gets caught."

Burgess kicked at a stray coffee cup that had been blown up against his foot, and watched it roll away. This was a cold, dirty, empty place. It felt like he'd spent half his adult life in places like this, though his path to adulthood, and law enforcement, had begun in a hot, dirty place that only looked empty and was full of unimaginable and unexpected violence. You didn't survive a war like Vietnam without becoming adult. Fear was a powerful crucible.

"I have to wonder sometimes, Terry—how would one of those guys who threaten people at gunpoint feel if someone did it to them? You suppose they wouldn't be afraid if someone pointed a gun at them? You suppose it looks like a fair deal to them? Gimme the beer for free and I won't take your life?"

"Dunno." Kyle looked thoughtful. "One thing I'm sure of— you can't care about how another person feels. And maybe, you wanna be a gunman, you have to be fearless yourself. Let's ask our friend Ali. See what he thinks."

"We know he isn't fearless, Ter. He was blubbering like an infant . . . like a screaming brat."

They were staring through a chain-link fence. Beyond it, the current slapped dark water angrily against the rocks. Burgess was very tired, the aftermath of his earlier adrenaline surge. He wanted to go home and check on his family. Be sure that they were safe. Last night should have taken care of the threats, but this case seemed to have an endless supply of bad guys. Fill up the jail with bad guys, fill up the basement at 109 with bad guys' vehicles, but they just kept coming. It was a thankless task.

Beside him, Kyle was drooping, feeling the same thing. It took patience, and stamina, to play mind games like this.

"He ran away," Kyle said suddenly. "We'd taken off the cuffs because he said they were hurting him, and he jumped out of the truck, and ran. Young and nimble, he climbed this fence.

Then he slipped into the water and we couldn't get there in time. Couldn't get him out."

"It could happen that way," Burgess agreed.

"The freakin' POS threatened my family, Joe. That's two of them in twenty-four hours. I can't do this job if I have to keep worrying about that. I can't."

The thin blue line problem. Cops could only do their job if respect for the job, and fear of the consequences, kept the bad guys in line. When that broke down, the job became impossible.

Burgess turned and walked back to Ali, who had crouched down and folded himself into a ball, trying to get some protection from the wind. He grabbed the boy's bad arm and jerked him to his feet.

"Which brother?" he yelled into the boy's startled face. "Which freaking one of your brothers got that girl pregnant?"

"Muhamud."

"And where did he get her?"

"My grandfather bought her for him. He wanted an American wife."

Behind him, he heard a grunt and then Kyle was right beside him, folding his height down over the boy like a heron about to spear a fish, Kyle's lean frame vibrating with anger.

Kyle's anger made sense. Someone had sold a girl child about the age of his older daughter, and one of this boy's relatives had bought her. Slave trading. In Portland, Maine. In the twenty-first century.

"What's her name?" Kyle barked right into the boy's face.

"K . . . K . . . Kelly," Ali said through chattering teeth.

"And the baby?"

"Muhamud. Like his father. Like my grandfather."

Burgess, playing the good cop, put a hand on Kyle's shoulder. "Easy, Terry," he said, but Kyle wasn't done.

"Where did they get her?"

"Fuck you," the boy spat, trying to squirm away.

Burgess tightened his grip on the boy's arm. Police brutality? Absolutely. Abuse of power? You bet. Better than the normally righteous Kyle, who'd briefly considered tossing the boy in the sea.

They were supposed to let it roll off them. Sometimes they just couldn't. Hold your perfectly justified fire because it was a kid, and then the little POS threatens to turn his thuggish family loose on yours. And it wasn't just about him. Or tonight. The next time they were in that situation, they'd probably shoot. So much harm the kid was sowing and he didn't give a damn. A thug from a whole family of thugs.

"The man asked you a question," he said.

Ali's face was a fixed mask of defiance that went oddly with its sweet, childish roundness. "I'm not telling you shit. Now take me to the hospital, motherfucker. You're hurting my arm."

They both wanted to hurt a whole lot more than his arm.

Burgess released his arm. "I think he needs to consider his choices, Terry. Let's give him a few minutes."

They left the squirming, swearing boy by the fence, got in the truck, and started the engine. As they started to move away, Burgess heard the boy screaming that they couldn't leave him. Obviously, consideration for the welfare of others was a one-way street.

Burgess drove until they were out of sight, then shoved it into park. The heat felt good after the biting wind. Burgess turned on some music and they leaned back in their seats and listened.

"Too bad we don't have coffee," Kyle said.

"Yeah. That would be nice." Burgess checked his phone. Three calls from Chris. And a text message that read only *Tomorrow. 3 p.m. at the library.*

He showed it to Kyle. "Wanna bet it's the woman from the Imam's house?"

Kate Flora

"Might be. Library's a good, neutral place," Kyle said. "Trust, then verify. Before long, Ali is going to finish telling us what we want to know. Then she can confirm it."

Ten minutes. Fifteen. The wind had picked up, a reminder that mid-April was as close to mid-March as it was to the merry month of May. Their sullen little robber would be seriously miserable.

"Think he's ready to talk?" Kyle said.

"Five more minutes and we'll go see."

Ali Ibrahim was huddled into a tiny ball. Burgess grabbed his arm and dragged him to his feet.

"Where does your brother live? At the Imam's house? With you?"

Through chattering teeth, the boy said, "No."

Burgess squeezed. "Where . . . does . . . he . . . live?"

"Cumberland. He's got a house in Cumberland."

"The address?"

Ali spat out a street and a number.

"And why were Kelly and the baby locked in that closet at the mosque?"

"Like I said, that brat wouldn't stop crying. It was just until they could figure out what to do with them. How they could take the baby to the hospital without . . . problems."

"Before that, were they locked in the closet at your grandfather's house?"

Ali repeated a tedious string of threats and curses.

"Take your time," Kyle said. "We've got a nice warm truck."

"My brother wanted her where the women could take care of her when the baby came. And then the baby got sick. It kept crying and Kelly tried to run away to take him to the doctor, so they put her in the closet."

"And everyone was all right with that?"

Ali didn't reply.

270

"Who locked her in the closet at the mosque?" Burgess said.

Again, no reply. However scared he was of them, Ali was more scared of someone else. Well, maybe they had someone else in the house who might give them the answer. Burgess thought they'd gotten all they were going to get, but he had one more question. He gripped the boy's arm as hard as he could, watching the childish face contract as the boy tried not to gasp in pain.

"Where did your grandfather get the girl?" he said.

"Some guy my grandfather does business with. Some big old white guy."

Burgess tried for a name or a description, but Ali knew he'd already said way too much. "That's all I'm saying."

He and Kyle stepped out of earshot. "We are going to find that big old white guy," Burgess said. "Whoever he is. Butcher Flaherty or one of the guys from his gang?"

"Or the guy with the watch and the ring?" Kyle suggested.

"Who might be Addison Westerly," Burgess said. "Or there's the man who was helping the Imam by writing those slurs on the wall. Or someone we don't know about yet."

"Yeah. The player to be named later," Kyle said. "Tomorrow we're gonna kick in some doors and kick some ass."

"I can hardly wait."

Burgess unlocked the cuff from the railing, cuffed the boy's hands together, and led him back to the car.

No one said a word on the drive to the hospital.

CHAPTER TWENTY-NINE

Some white guy my grandfather does business with. Burgess thought about the expensive watch and distinctive ring. So far, other than Butcher Flaherty and his pals, and Henry James Wallace, that was the only "white guy" they'd encountered in this whole stinking mess. But there could be others. The guy with the watch and ring hadn't been old, either, but everyone looked old to a kid Ali's age. Addison Westerly had a connection to the Imam, and to the Academy.

He wanted Westerly in an interview room. He wanted to see the man's reaction when he asked about selling a young girl to the Imam. He wanted search warrants for young Muhamud Ibrahim's house and Westerly's offices. Westerly's house, if they could ever find out where he lived. He and the Crips were looking at another long day. But this time, he felt the excitement that came with a gut feeling they were finally close.

Sick of the sight of Ali and all he represented, they left the boy at the hospital in the custody of a burly patrol officer who would take him on to the jail. Then Kyle went home and Burgess dragged himself back to 109 to write reports.

In the morning, they'd get those warrants. For now, he needed to get it all written down. Westerly. The search of the Imam's house. The armed robbery. What Ali had told them.

Before he settled into any of that, he called Chris.

"I've been worried sick," she said. "I heard there was a shoot-out at a convenience store. I didn't think that would involve

272

you, but when you didn't call . . . I thought the worst."

"I'm sorry," he said. "It's been a very busy night."

"I'm sorry" had become his mantra. From the rising of the sun to the dying of the day and far after, he was sorry.

"You were there. My God. Joe. You were there!"

There was a catch in her voice and an accusation behind her words that he hadn't called to reassure her. As though she was only now discovering that he was a cop. Cops carried guns. And guns got fired. It wasn't as though she was unaware of the risks of his job. They'd met on a case where he'd gotten shot. This was different. Things had changed. They were parents now, and parents had a duty to be more careful for the sake of their kids.

"Terry was with me. It was okay. Nothing happened."

"Nothing happened, Joe? Shots were fired. Someone could have been hurt. Or killed."

"Nobody got killed, Chris, and the bad guy only got hurt because the clerk whacked him with a baseball bat. We had to handle the scene, then take him to the ER—"

"And in all that time, you couldn't find a minute to call me?"

This was not the Chris he knew. The woman who said he didn't need to worry about her wimping out, or becoming needy or clingy. The woman he admired because she was a grown-up and could handle things. The strong, compassionate nurse who wanted to give a loving home to two kids life had kicked around. The woman who'd said she understood what he did and had agreed to let him do it. This was a woman reacting to last night and the threat to their kids.

She said it before he could. "Sorry, Joe. It's . . . I guess . . . I don't know . . . different now that we have the kids. I haven't figured this out yet. I just had this knee-jerk reaction and I thought—"

"I understand," he said. "It is different, and I don't know how to deal with it any better than you do. We need to have a date. Just the two of us. Sit somewhere and talk. But this won't get figured out in a day."

"I know."

He heard what might have been a sniffle. Was she crying? He was usually the king of sounds, able to interpret them on the phone like this, at a distance, all those nuanced sounds of human emotion. Maybe he didn't want to know. "I love you," he said. "We will make this work. I'll try to remember to call and—"

"And I'll try to remember who you are and what you do. I'm not trying to be a ball and chain. I was scared. The kids were scared. It was kind of funny, really. You know how Nina and Dylan are always squabbling. But tonight, after that was on the news, they were suddenly so together. And together in trying to distract and comfort Neddy. And me."

Another sniff. "Dylan is so like you." Then she said, "And this does not mean that you should go and get yourself shot at more often."

Her voice dropped a register, into a husky whisper. "When will I see you?"

"Soon as I finish these damned reports. But the thought of you will give my fingers wings."

"Lunatic."

"Thought I was being romantic."

As he put the phone down, his eyes caught a note from Stan Perry. "Working on those box trucks, and a home address for Addison Westerly."

So Perry had looked through his notes and was already on the case. Sometimes, Perry was like a ferret, slipping quietly around in the dark, finding things out. When the sun came up, he'd be weary but triumphant and still in fine shape to head up to Augusta for an autopsy.

The day felt like it had been about two hundred hours long. He moved like Methuselah's grandfather as he wrote up his interview with Jason Stetson, burying the meat of Jason's information in a wad of stuff about the foster mom, the Muslim's meanness, the annoying crying baby. Then he wrote up the shooting at the convenience store. But when he came to writing up what they had learned from Ali on the way to the hospital, he simply wrote that they had transported the shooter from the scene to the hospital and given the boy, presumed to be a juvenile until further investigation, his Miranda warning.

The information about his grandfather buying the girl as an American wife for his oldest grandson was in his notebook, and in Kyle's. But there was too much risk in putting it in a report that Cote would read. Not until they had more. He simply couldn't risk having the information about sex slaves and purchased wives before someone who would love to blab something that sensational to the media. In the morning, he'd brief Melia and let his lieutenant decide where to go from there.

Before he closed down his computer, he sent a note to Rocky, asking him to look into missing-persons cases involving a thirteen- to fifteen-year-old dark-haired girl named Kelly or Kellie. Another to Dr. Lee, reporting that, if their informant was telling the truth, the baby's name was Muhamud Ibrahim. It wasn't much, but it had bothered the ME in the same way that it had bothered him that the baby had no name. He sent a message to the AAG assigned to the case, asking for a call in the morning, and giving her the basic information needed for more search warrants.

His task list for tomorrow was huge. Finding Addison Westerly. Drafting the affidavits in support of the search warrants, looking for clues about the identity of the "old white man," and finding out where Addison Westerly lived. Serving a warrant on the Imam's oldest grandson. Following up with Rocky about missing girls. Locating Rihanna Daud.

He needed to follow up with Dani and Wink and see if they'd

pulled anything off the car that had had Osman in the trunk. See if they had any prints from the car that had crashed at the hospital. Prints from the closet at the Imam's house. Prints from Flaherty's apartment. Just one damned thing after another. By now, so many prints at so many scenes, they were grumbling in their dens.

Slow and steady won the race. For all of them.

It made his head hurt.

He logged out, grabbed his jacket, and headed home.

CHAPTER THIRTY

Chris was waiting in the kitchen, drooping a little over an untouched cup of tea. She smiled when he came in. "Maybe we should have something stronger?"

It sounded like a good idea. He poured bourbon for both of them.

"Tell me about this case, Joe. Why it matters."

He told her about the girl and the baby and what they'd learned tonight. Things cops weren't supposed to tell their wives and girlfriends. The things that would help her understand why he wasn't home with her and the kids.

When he'd finished, she said, "There's someone out there looking for that girl, Joe. Someone who loves her and will take care of her."

"Nurse's instinct?" he said.

She nodded. "Nurse's. And maybe mom's." He sure hoped she was right.

At 3:30, his phone rang. Stan Perry. "What are you doing right now, Joe?"

"Sleeping."

"Wondered if you'd like to take a drive."

As he slipped quietly from the bed and into his clothes, he hoped this drive wouldn't lead to another gunfight. But he didn't say no.

Perry was slightly manic as they headed out. "Followed a

hunch," he said, "after I saw that yearbook photo of Addison Westerly on your desk. Westerly renting them the mosque? Finding them a new place in his warehouse? I just had to take a look—"

"How much coffee have you had tonight, Stan?"

"I've lost count. But listen, Joe. You know how we couldn't find an address for him, other than his office? Well, every damned thing the man owns is registered to the business, except one." Perry bounced in his seat like a toddler. "Guy forgot about his damned snowmobile. Or maybe he thought he couldn't slip that one past his accountant. Not much need for a snowmobile in a fishing business, right?"

"Right. So you found Westerly's house? And we're going there in the middle of the night?"

"Exactly."

Sometimes you just had to follow that cop gut. "Stanley, you're so good at ferreting things out, tell me this. What is the connection between Westerly, the Imam, and the Iron Angels?"

"Money."

"They're all selling fish?"

"Ya think?" Perry gave him a look. "What else comes in off fishing boats, Joe?"

"Drugs. And guns."

"Right. And how do you move guns and drugs without getting caught?"

This felt a lot like catechism. "Trucks apparently engaged in legitimate business. And motorcycle gangs."

"Right again. One thing that our friend the Imam neglected to tell us is that his long-range plan is to go back to Somalia and become someone important in his town, like the mayor. To do that, he needs money. Money to send back, to earn him friends and respect, and money to take back with him. That's what our friend Osman was hinting at when he mentioned hawala. And face it, Joe, aside from the Catholic Church—before it shot itself in the foot with all the sex scandals, anyway—and televangelists, there's not that much money in pure religion."

"So what are we looking for tonight that we couldn't look for in daylight with a search warrant?"

Perry's grin was manic. "Box trucks. Stuff to put in the warrant. Garages and outbuildings. The lay of the land, so to speak."

"We're scouting," Burgess said.

"And trying not to get our asses shot off. Did I mention guns?"

"I think you did."

The dark roadsides streaked by as he drove, following Perry's directions. North on 295. Off the highway, and onto a maze of side roads. Burgess realized they were in Cumberland. "What's the address?" he asked, as he fumbled out his notebook. Young Stanley wasn't the only one with a cop gut.

Impossible that this could be a coincidence, he thought, as they passed the address Ali Ibrahim had given them and drew up next to Westerly's mailbox. The house itself was out of sight down a long drive. It felt like the gods were finally smiling on them. It also increased the stakes for Perry's little adventure. They were at risk of tipping their hand to not one but two major suspects.

Perry grabbed his door handle, then stopped. "What is it?"

"Some things we learned tonight. You heard about the convenience store robbery?" Perry nodded. "Well the shooter was Ali Ibrahim. He got a little banged up—clerk had a baseball bat and was seriously pissed off—and while Terry and I were taking him to the hospital, we had a little chat."

Perry had taken his hand off the door and settled back in his seat.

"Turns out, according to Ali, that our mystery girl is the wife of the Imam's oldest grandson, also named Muhamud Ibrahim.

Ali said his brother didn't live in Portland, but in Cumberland. And the address Ali gave for his brother Muhamud is right next door to Addison Westerly."

"Holy shit," Perry breathed.

"There's more. Ali Ibrahim says that the Imam bought the girl for his grandson because the boy wanted an American wife, but he wanted one young enough to be trained in traditional ways. And he bought her from 'some old white guy' his grandfather does business with. So much as I would love to slither down that driveway and do some scouting, I would far rather get some broad warrants, come back here tomorrow, and scoop up both gentlemen and whatever their houses have to offer. The risk that we spook them and they move things, or simply disappear, is just too great."

"Still glad we took this ride." Perry reached for his seatbelt. "Hold on. Are those headlights?"

They were. Bouncing yellow lights coming down Westerly's long driveway.

"Looks like a truck," Perry said as Burgess started the Explorer and headed down the road with the lights off. He pulled into a driveway and they waited, watching, as a white box truck came down the driveway and headed away from them toward the highway.

Burgess followed, still without his lights, until they reached the highway, then put on the lights and merged into the sparse predawn traffic. Despite the cold of the morning, he vaguely registered two motorcycles somewhere behind them, but before he could get suspicious, they whizzed past. The truck headed west off the highway, away from the waterfront, and they followed, curious to see where it would take them. The plate was registered to one of Westerly's businesses, WestSea Products, Inc. There was no logo on the truck.

"So if they're in the fish, guns, and drugs business, what was that computer heist all about? Ismail trying to set up in a business of his own? Showing his grandfather that he's no slouch in the moneymaking department?" Burgess said.

"What I think, Joe? You might not believe this, given what a freakin' jerk he was the other night, but I think Ismail is trying to live a regular American life and his family won't let him. I think that he values that job, and his brother and the rest of his family used information they got from him to set up that robbery. You see that long black scrape? It matches the truck in the surveillance video."

"You think that's why they shot at him?" Burgess said. "A little message to stay on the reservation? That would explain him going all belligerent and silent on us."

Perry's grunt sounded like an affirmative.

"But if we wasn't in on it, why would they store the stuff at the mosque? He had to know about that. And then what was the fire—"

Ahead, the truck abruptly turned onto a side street. "Hold on. Now where's he going?"

They watched the truck pull into a small industrial park. As they hung back, driving slowly past a sign advertising self-storage, Perry sighed.

"What is it, Stan? Flaherty's key?"

"Yeah. Haven't gotten to it yet."

"Been a busy day, Stan. You have it with you?"

It seemed the storage warehouse was the truck's destination.

Burgess cruised past, parking down the street where they were partly hidden by a Dumpster. They watched two men get out of the truck, open the back, and take out two oversized wheeled duffle bags. Dark-skinned, round faced, and furtive. You want people to notice you? Act like you're afraid of being noticed.

It might be a purely innocent visit, but that was as likely as pigs starting to fly. He called for backup, no lights, no sirens, dictated what street to take and where to meet. No way he and Stan could cover the warehouse by themselves.

"Their website says twenty-four-hour security, Stan, so why don't you slip along to the office and see if that's the case."

He stayed behind to wait for backup. Minutes later, his phone rang. "We've got good video," Perry said. "They have a key to the building and they're heading for the second floor."

"I'll be there as soon as I've covered the entrances and the truck."

Three patrol cars slid silently in beside him, officers to cover the front and rear entrances and one to guard the truck. He went to join Perry. They stood behind the security guard and watched the two men try their key on a padlock.

"Ain't gonna get 'em nowhere," the guard said. "That key's to the buildin'. Owners gotta provide their own locks for their units. Otherwise, there'd be no security, see."

Burgess figured the key they needed was in Perry's pocket. The two men conferred and then one went back downstairs. Burgess hoped the officer sitting on the truck was well out of sight. Another screen showed the man getting a tool from the truck and heading back to the building.

"This is where I oughta call the police, see," the guard said. "Only I don't gotta 'cuz you're already here. How'd you know to be here?"

"Because we were right behind them," Perry said.

The guard's head bobbed. "Ain't that somethin'?"

"Do you have a record of who rents that space, so you'd know if these two weren't the record owners?"

The guard flipped a hand at a bank of filing cabinets. "I'm just security. My boss does, though. It'll be in there. He's a real stickler about records. He says people are trusting us to keep stuff safe and we'd better earn that trust."

Burgess liked this boss already. He liked this operation—doing what it promised instead of slipshod security and cutting corners. Simple decency and integrity, that was what Maine had always meant to him. During his years on the job, it had become enough of a rarity that it stood out when he found it. He shifted his attention back to the screen.

The man who seemed to be in charge—who looked enough like Ismail Ibrahim that Burgess assumed he was the favored older brother—took the bolt cutters and cut the lock. He tossed it aside and opened the door. The security camera didn't see into the locker—part of giving the owners privacy and security—but it gave them more than enough as Muhamud Ibrahim unzipped one of the duffle bags, disappeared into the locker, and came out with an armful of guns that he put in the bag. His companion was doing the same thing.

"My God!" Perry breathed. "It's a freakin' arsenal."

It would have made such a nice photo and headline for the paper: "Refugee Resettlement Creates New American Entrepreneurs." Everyone loved a success story.

Burgess got on the phone to dispatch, calling for more back-up and the Strategic Response Team, SRT. The he called Vince Melia.

He brought his lieutenant up to speed, then said, "We got a stash here that's gonna make ATF dance like pixies," he said. "And I don't want them in the picture until we've had a chance to do our interviews. And searched Ibrahim's house before they've carried off everything but the foundation and mucked up two death investigations. Which means simultaneously searching Addison Westerly's. Which means we need those warrants ASAP."

"I'll get Press on it right now."

It was five in the morning.

"He's on the SRT, Vince."

"I'll get people on it, Joe. You want me to have Cumberland PD sit on the place?"

"Places. You think they can do that without attracting attention?"

Melia snorted. "I'll see what I can do. See you in a few."

Melia would have to notify the brass. That was SOP. Burgess said a brief prayer that Melia would leave a message or a text and Cote wouldn't get word of what was happening until they'd gotten what they needed here and Ibrahim and his companion were in custody, the truck impounded. Once word was out, there were going to be so many people fighting over a piece of this it would be like wild dogs over a bone. By then, he wanted to be in Cumberland, taking a couple of houses apart.

"Vince? See if Sage can cover the autopsy. We're gonna be busy here for a while."

"Done."

Ibrahim had finished loading one of the bags and was directing his companion to haul it downstairs. The man set off toward the elevator, a bulge in his sweatshirt pocket that said he was armed.

"We meet at the elevator," Burgess said. Perry nodded. He looked at the security guard. "Where?"

The man pointed to a door. "Jus' go through there and down the hall. Is there gonna be shootin'?"

"We don't think so."

"Good. 'Cuz I got me the PTSD, and I don't do so good around guns." Then he answered Burgess's unspoken question. "My job's to watch them screens, and if I see anything hinky, call you guys. The boss wants everything done real legal. He wants a calm head and open eyes. Don't want no cowboy cop wannabe here in the office."

The boss was a prince among men.

He and Perry headed for the elevator.

CHAPTER THIRTY-ONE

In the end, it was a gift. To better haul out the heavy bag, the man backed out of the elevator, right into Stan Perry's waiting arms. Perry jammed his gun into the man's back and barked, "Portland police. Put your hands up."

The man confused "up" with "pocket," and ended up flat on his face on the floor, Perry's foot on the back on his neck while Burgess moved his gun out of reach and cuffed him. Much of what he said was a confused babble, but what was clear was that the man was saying these were *his* guns, and he had every right to take them out *his* locker and put them in *his* truck.

Rights. Property. Mine. They were used to the first—every bad guy knew his rights, or thought he did. Far fewer of them did the cops the favor of claiming ownership in a stash of prohibited, probably stolen, weapons, ownership of a storage locker he'd cut his way into, and a truck they could likely connect with at least one other robbery.

"Thank you," Burgess said as they hauled the man, identified by the papers in his wallet as Hassan Ibrahim, back to the office. Burgess now recognized the man as one of the ones who had been with the Imam during their interview. A phone in their prisoner's pocket chirped. Muhamud was getting impatient. On the screen, Muhamud Ibrahim made another phone call, then finished loading his bag with guns. He stood impatiently in the hall, watching the elevator, presumably looking for the return of his companion.

The cameras monitoring the outside of the building showed Melia arriving along with the SRT vehicle.

"Keep an eye on him," Burgess told Perry. "I'll brief Melia and SRT." He grabbed their prisoner by the upper arm and started to lead him outside.

"Hold on a minute, Sergeant," the guard said. "I think you should look at this."

"This" was an outside camera showing the arrival of a small black Honda. It parked beside the truck and five men got out. This time, their weapons were openly displayed.

"Is there going to be shooting?" the guard asked again.

"There might be," Burgess said, already on the phone alerting Melia. "You got any duct tape around here?"

Puzzled, the guard pointed toward a tall supply cabinet. "Might be some in there."

He continued to look puzzled as Burgess and Perry duct-taped their prisoner to a chair.

"We've got to go upstairs and take care of some business," Burgess said. "Don't want this guy running around, giving you trouble."

An insistent bell was ringing.

"That's them at the door," the guard said.

"Don't let them in."

"As if I would."

"Lock this office door behind us," Perry said. "And don't open it to anyone who doesn't show you a badge."

There was a muffled rumble from outside that became increasingly louder until it was easily identifiable as a group of Harleys. Burgess looked at the guard and saw all the things he'd missed because his head hadn't been in the game, because he'd been moving on instead of being present in the present. The long gray ponytail wrapped in leather. Tattoos. A leather jacket hung on a rack.

"You called them, didn't you?" he said.

The guard nodded. "Man's gotta do," he said.

Burgess looked at Perry. "Looks like Vince and SRT got a war on their hands. Let's go finish *our* business." He turned back to the guard. "Don't hurt this man. Don't open the door to anyone. Not even your buddies. You do and you go to jail. Not a good place if you've got the PTSD. Got it?"

"I got it."

He hoped so. There were stairs at each end of the building. They conferred briefly and headed up the stairs.

Muhamud Ibrahim was in the storage unit, his back to them, packing guns into an oversized plastic bin. He turned as Burgess stepped in, immediately and without hesitation ramming the butt of the rifle he was holding into Burgess's rib cage. *Not a good day to have gone out without a vest,* Burgess thought, as the pain flared. But he'd been going fishing, not hunting.

Just as immediately, and equally without hesitation, Perry grabbed the gun and swung it into the side of Ibrahim's head. Ibrahim was a hardheaded lad. He swayed but didn't fall, and the two of them spilled out into the hall, wrestling over the rifle until Burgess could raise his own gun.

"Portland police. Drop it," he barked.

Ibrahim jerked the gun from Perry's hands, flung it away, and clawed a handgun from his pocket. When a bad guy turns on you with a gun, you don't wait to find out if it's loaded. The Ibrahims had already had one pass, and that was enough.

Burgess fired.

In real time, these things happen in seconds. In the mind, it sometimes happens in slow motion, a progression that can feel like forever. Burgess saw Ibrahim's gun coming up, then his own hand coming up. He saw the bullet emerge from his gun in a blaze of sparks and smoke. Saw the spent casing fly up in an arc, travel through the air, and bounce on the carpet. Saw the bullet traveling toward Ibrahim, something he knew he couldn't see—but he could. Saw it strike Ibrahim. He saw Ibrahim's gun fire a bullet toward the ceiling, then fly out of his hand and travel slowly through the air to land on the carpet behind him.

He saw Ibrahim's look of utter surprise, two dark hands flutter like birds to the chest as Ibrahim fell slowly, slowly, slowly through the air and landed with a small bounce on the carpet. He saw brilliant red blood oozing from between the clutching fingers. Focus came back as Ibrahim started writhing and screaming.

Then Ibrahim quieted, and Burgess bent down to catch the man's whispered words. Regret, fear of death, calls for mother, and prayers—Burgess had heard all of these from injured men. "My brother is going to kill you," Ibrahim said. "You and all your family."

Burgess got on the phone and called dispatch for an ambulance, then called Melia and filled him in.

"He alive or dead?"

"He's making a lot of noise, so I figure alive."

"Well, see if you can keep him that way. We've got ourselves a potential war out here."

"I'll see what I can do."

He shoved the phone back in his pocket. His ribs hurt like hell. He was pretty sure something was broken and that really pissed him off, because he didn't have time for the ER right now. He had places to go and people to see.

"Joe, are you okay?" Perry asked.

"Kinda busted. Look, our guy downstairs. The guard. If he called them, what's the likelihood he'll also let them in, no matter what he said? They're here for the guns."

"And for the Ibrahims," Perry said. "So maybe I'd better hop back downstairs and make sure he doesn't act on that thought."

"If he hasn't already."

Perry sighed. "Right. We'd better both go. And bring Mr. Ibrahim."

Muhamud Ibrahim was not a happy camper. He was bleeding but he was breathing, and his comfort was not one of their chief concerns as they half dragged, half carried him to the elevator. The security of their colleagues, and maintaining custody of the stash of guns was. Luckily, the security guard hadn't been able to open the door for his brethren without also admitting the five men from the black Honda.

It was some time before, between arrests and dispersals, between SRT and the gang officers' negotiations, they were able to send one of their prisoners to jail and the other to the hospital and turn the shooting scene, and the storage locker, over to the evidence techs without any further violence.

Captain Cote, who had rushed to the scene to take command, got some great moments on the news and had departed content. He had not taken the time to ensure that all his people were okay, and for that, the one of his people who was very much not okay was deeply grateful.

Melia wasn't so indifferent, nor so oblivious. "Joe, you're green," he said. "What happened?"

"I need some coffee."

Melia's eyes slid to Perry. "Stan?"

"Rifle butt to the ribs."

Melia rolled his eyes. "We need results, not heroics, Joe."

Burgess cut his eyes toward the building. "You don't call keeping these guns off the street results? And we're gonna get you more results. You got those warrants yet?"

He needed Advil and coffee. Maybe a breakfast sandwich. He needed to sit down for a few minutes and collect his thoughts. He needed to clear the vision of that slow-moving bullet out of his head, push away the pain, and get back to work.

"Kyle has them. But right now, all my evidence techs are

here, and SRT's gonna need a little time—"

"For what, Vince? Cookies and milk? This goddamned standoff tipped our hand. Have we got people sitting on those houses? Because this is all over the news, which means we have to hit Westerly first, before he clears out his house, his office, and his boat. If he hasn't already. Do we even know if he's home?"

"In case you haven't noticed, we've been a little busy here, Joe."

"Sorry, Vince, I—"

But Melia knew.

CHAPTER THIRTY-TWO

He took Kyle and headed out to Addison Westerly's house, sending Perry and some uniforms next door to Ibrahim's house. Sage Prentiss would join them when he was done in Augusta. On the way, he sent a text to the person he was supposed to meet at the library, asking for another day and time. He didn't get a reply.

There were two cars in the garage and a green truck parked in Westerly's yard, but no one answered when they knocked. As Burgess waited, knocking again and identifying himself as a police officer, Kyle slipped around the house to look in the windows.

He was back seconds later, shaking his head. "You've got to see this, Joe."

Burgess followed him around to the back where they could see through a gap in the blinds into a large, pleasant family room. There were two men there, engaged in earnest conversation. One of them was a man they'd never seen before, a broad-shouldered man in his forties with military short hair and a furious face. The other was Westerly, lying on the floor between a blue denim sofa and the fireplace, neatly hogtied.

"Guess we're not the only ones who have business with Westerly," Kyle said. They could see the watch and the ring from the hospital's surveillance pictures.

As a streak of afternoon light fell on the other man's face, Burgess knew immediately who he was. Kelly's father. It was the eyes, so surprisingly dark, and the forehead, that on this man was so fierce, and on Kelly gave her face the heart shape that made it so sweet. Quietly, they went back around to the front and tried the knob. The door was unlocked. They slipped in and made their way to the kitchen, pausing outside the door to listen.

"I've got all the time in the world, Add," the man said. "And you don't. So you can start answering my questions any time. Where is Lori? Where is my wife?"

"I have no idea," Westerly said.

"I think you do. I think you and Lori had a thing going. I think she was living here. So where is she now?"

Westerly's voice was strained, though he tried for easy and conversational. "Untie me, Jeremiah. Untie me and I'll tell you everything."

"Tell me everything now. Then maybe I'll untie you. Where's my wife? Where is my daughter? Where's Kelly?"

"Lori's dead. An overdose. She got into my stash, man, and she didn't know what she was doing."

"Dead as of when?" The man's voice was dangerously calm.

"Almost a year."

"You're lying. We were e-mailing. Until six months ago."

"That was me. I kept it up for a while. But that got old." Stupidly defiant for a man with a rope around his neck. Maybe that had always worked for Westerly. Maybe he'd been the bully in this relationship and thought he still was. Westerly didn't seem to appreciate the danger of his situation.

Burgess and Kyle exchanged a look. In Burgess's the question: should we intervene? In Kyle's: not yet.

"Where is Kelly?" This time, the danger was tangible.

"No idea. After Lori died, the state took her."

"You're a goddamned liar. I've been in touch with the state and they don't know anything about Lori or Kelly. The state has no record of Lori's death, either, Add. I've been looking. Looking for a week now. All our stuff is gone. Our house is empty. There's no record of Lori or Kelly anywhere, and I had a damned hard time finding you. So let's try this again. Where is my wife and where is my daughter?"

There was no response.

"Where?"

Burgess heard rapid feet and then the man must have done something, because Westerly screamed, "Don't!" and then a slightly strangled, "Okay. Okay. I'll tell you!"

He started into the room, but Kyle put a hand on his arm. "Give it a minute."

"I'm waiting," the man Westerly had called Jeremiah said.

"I told you. She's dead. I buried her. Out back behind the barn."

"You buried my wife out behind your barn?"

There was a muffled affirmative from Westerly. It sounded like he was beginning to appreciate his situation. Or to understand that whatever relationship the men had had, it had changed. What could he have been thinking? That a man's wife could die and his daughter disappear and none of it would matter? Maybe Westerly had never expected this man to return. Maybe that last six months was significant.

He looked at Kyle, and Kyle nodded. It was time.

Burgess stepped into the room and held up his badge.

The man said, "He's all yours, Officer, just as soon as I get some answers. I need to find my daughter." So focused on his mission the arrival of the police didn't really register.

Then he sagged suddenly, like a puppet whose strings were cut, and staggered toward a chair. "Do you . . . is she . . . can you tell me where I can find her? This piece of shit says he doesn't know anything about Kelly, and I know he's lying."

Burgess gave the man one of his handkerchiefs. "I know

where she is. Before I send you there, maybe you could answer a few questions?"

"Just tell me she's okay." Voice breaking on the word "okay."

"She's okay. She needs you badly. She needs safety and caring for, but she's okay."

It was part of the truth. The part the man needed to hear right now.

"Goddammit, Officers!" Westerly yelled. "Untie me. This man has invaded my home and tied me up, and you're chitchatting with him instead of helping me."

Kyle waved the warrant before Westerly's furious face. "Addison Westerly?"

"Yes. Dammit. I said—"

"I have a warrant here to search your property: your house, your garage, your outbuildings, and your vehicles." He slapped it down on the coffee table near Westerly's head. "You've been served."

"What the hell is wrong with you people?" Westerly said. "This man is holding me prisoner in my own house and you—"

Burgess looked at Westerly's hands, at the watch and the ring that confirmed their suspicions, and turned to the man in the chair, "Detective Sergeant Joe Burgess, Portland police, and this is Detective Kyle. What's your name, sir?"

"Davis. Lieutenant Colonel Jeremiah Davis. And my daughter is Kelly Davis. She's fourteen."

"Just back from an overseas deployment?" Burgess said.

Davis nodded.

"How long have you—"

Davis hung his head. "Sixteen months. It wasn't supposed to be that long. And I thought . . . Lori said it would be okay . . . Kelly would be okay. She was old enough. And then Lori stopped communicating and I couldn't reach her by phone and then I was . . . ." The strained voice died out as Davis looked for strength to go on. "I was somewhere where I couldn't get back. He—"

Davis gestured toward Westerly, who was sweating with the effort of holding up his feet so he wouldn't strangle. "He says Lori is dead. Says she died of an overdose almost a year ago. He says he answered my messages for a while but that got old, so he stopped doing it. He says the state took Kelly and that's all he knows. And I know he's lying."

"Why Westerly?" Burgess said.

"Because he was our friend. He was the one Lori would turn to if I wasn't here. He's known Lori since high school. Known Kelly since she was born."

Burgess tried to imagine it, and his stomach roiled. Selling a child you've known since infancy into slavery? But a cop's gut wasn't enough. Neither was "some old white guy my grandfather does business with" or Westerly's presence at the hospital. He needed confirmation. He bent so that his face was inches from Westerly's. "What was your relationship to Lori Davis?"

"Untie me," Westerly demanded. "I can't—"

"Answer the question."

If they didn't immediately untie Westerly, they were condoning torture. Torture of a man who had essentially facilitated the rape, imprisonment, and impregnation of a child. Whose associates had forced that child to watch her own child's horrific suffering. He thought he could tolerate a few more minutes of this. He hadn't even noticed he was clutching his ribs until Kyle put a hand on his elbow and steered him toward a chair facing Davis. "Sit down, Joe."

"I need to know—"

"We all need to know."

Kyle stepped closer to Westerly. "You and Lori had a thing going, right, while her husband was away?"

Westerly glared at him.

"We've got all the time in the world," Kyle said. "Do you?"

Terry Kyle. The man who sometimes reminded him that they didn't get to play God. Maybe this was just helping God?

Burgess studied Davis. At first glance, he'd looked okay, but Burgess read bodies for a living. Under the anger, he saw a man out at the limits of endurance. An exhausted man, weary to his bones, who'd borne a world of hurt and fear in the hope of coming home. Davis had been on some assignment that had kept him out of touch, living with the very real possibility that he might never get home. He'd survived it. Gotten back. And come home to this.

"I'm not talking to you until you untie me."

Westerly's legs were trembling. Defiance warred with fear on his sweating face.

"All the time in the world," Kyle repeated.

"You can't do this."

"We're not doing it," Burgess said. "A distraught father, your former friend, just back from many months away in the service of our country, is doing it. Whatever you say to him is between the two of you."

He was lying. He didn't care. No crime to lie to a liar. Was this case turning him into a monster? First Ali. Now this. And in between, he'd shot a man. There was a long, deskbound rest on his horizon. Plenty of time to contemplate his morality. Just as soon as he put this one to bed.

The trembling in Westerly's legs was more pronounced. "Take your time," Kyle said. "Do you mind if we make some coffee?"

"My attorney is going to have a field day with you," Westerly hissed.

"Yeah. Mine is going to have one with you, too," Kyle said. "So listen. We've got a lot of work to do here, executing our warrant, so we'll just get started. You think it over, decide what you want to do, and then you can let us know."

He went into the kitchen and started making coffee.

Westerly shifted his eyes to Burgess. "You *can't* do this to me. You can't let him kill me just because I don't know where his daughter is."

"But you do know where she is," Burgess said, standing up. "And you know who is responsible and you know why. Colonel Davis, Terry is making coffee. Would you like some?"

Davis didn't want to take his eyes off Westerly, but he said, "Sounds good to me." With an effort, he levered himself out of the chair and headed toward the kitchen. He moved like a man in pain.

Burgess lingered. Westerly's whole body was trembling now with the effort of holding his legs up so the rope around his neck wouldn't strangle him. Davis had padded the rope with a towel so it wouldn't leave marks, and the bound arms and ankles were wrapped with Ace bandages. This assault had been carefully planned and executed.

"Where is Lori Davis?" he said.

"Fuck you."

"She buried out in your back field somewhere? How did you keep that from her daughter?"

No response. Westerly's legs swayed and defiance was eclipsed by fear. "Help me," he said.

Burgess smiled. "You know what you have to do."

"I can't. He'll kill me."

"He will certainly want to."

"Look. Detective. Release me and I'll tell you everything."

"And if I believe that, you've got a bridge to sell me, right?" What he said. What he thought was *or maybe some guns? Or someone else's sweet young daughter?* He took out his phone, set it to record a memo, and set it near Westerly, then grabbed the rope and loosened the tension on Westerly's throat. "How did Lori Davis die?"

"Overdose. Cocaine. I was out. She was curious. Got into my stash. She didn't know what she was doing."

Lie number one.

"What was your deal with Muhamud Ibrahim about Kelly?"

Westerly didn't answer.

Burgess released the rope and fear flared in Westerly's face.

"He wanted her. Said he'd take care of her. I had no use for a child, so I gave her to him."

"Gave?"

Westerly didn't answer.

"Gave?" Burgess repeated.

"It was a business deal."

"You gave him Kelly and he gave you something you wanted?"

"Something like that."

Burgess pictured the dark head on the hospital pillow, the scared, sad dark eyes staring at him. The marks from restraints on the still-childish limbs. "You sold a little girl you'd known since infancy to a Somali refugee who wanted an American wife?"

Behind him, Burgess heard Davis start toward Westerly. Heard Kyle restraining him, his voice low, his words caution and reassurance. Don't stop this now. This is what we all came to hear. Davis had withstood war, perhaps captivity and likely torture. Now his sobs were like body blows.

Burgess wished he hadn't had to hear it this way. Wanted to let Westerly strangle. Or leave him alone with Davis. But that wasn't how the system worked.

He didn't want to personalize this too much—everyone had an agenda here—but he had to ask. "The thugs outside my house. Kimani Yates and Henry James Wallace. You sent them, didn't you?"

"So what if I did? Nothing happened, did it?"

Because he'd come home. What if he'd come home half an hour later?

"The fire at the mosque. Was that also a business deal?"

"That freaking Muhamud screwed up. Wanted to stick it to his brother Ismail. Ismail was getting too American, he said. Trying to break away from his family, be his own man. But those computers were too hot. We couldn't move 'em because of the freakin' serial numbers. Cops breathing down our necks. The neighbors getting too curious. That location wasn't working anymore. The building was insured. So the Imam said why not?"

Why not? Because there were two helpless human children locked in that building. Probably Westerly didn't know that. Would he have cared if he did?

"Who set the fire? The Imam?"

"That old fart can't do anything except scare people and use his extended family to push them around. I did it. Christ. Why not. My building, wasn't it?"

Burgess sighed with the relief of it. Thank you, God.

He ended the recording, nodded, and he and Kyle undid the ropes.

"Coercion," Westerly said, stretching his shaky legs and rubbing his wrists. "Not a word of this will be admissible in court."

"We'll see," Burgess said. "Addison Westerly, you are under arrest for the death of the infant Muhamud Ibrahim, the attempted murder of Kelly Davis, and for arson at the premises used as a mosque at 324 Ashton Street. You have the right to remain silent . . ."

He went through the Miranda warning slowly. There was so much more to do, but an arrest felt concrete. A milestone in an incredibly frustrating investigation. He should have waited. Consulted with the fire marshal's office. Lined up his ducks. He needed to do it now.

"Do you understand these rights?"

Westerly fixed his glare on Burgess. "I understand that your fucking career is over, Detective." His furious gaze swept them all. "All of your careers."

Burgess was suddenly very weary. If this was his last case, that would be just fine with him, so long as they got this man convicted.

Afternoon sun streaming in was illuminating the dust motes. They floated like a golden cloud around the filth that was Addison Westerly.

CHAPTER THIRTY-THREE

The hardest days are the ones when an investigator needs to be in three places at once and has to choose. Vince Melia was fond of reminding Burgess that he wasn't the only detective on the force. That other people were competent and could be trusted to handle a search warrant or an interrogation. Burgess knew it was true but he never could shake the urge to be personally involved.

Right now it was four places. Here at Westerly's. Next door at Ibrahim's. Down at the harbor, on Westerly's boat. And what he wanted most—to take Colonel Davis to Maine Med and reunite him with his daughter. He wanted to see their faces when they got together, wanted to hear her voice, which he'd only ever heard screaming. But that was self-indulgent. He was a detective on a case, and despite Davis's poor condition—he moved like someone in serious pain—the man had the stamina to drive himself back to Portland to see his daughter.

So Burgess walked Davis out, filling him in briefly on what had happened.

Davis still wore the poleaxed look of someone trying to process unbelievable information. "I thought he was my friend," he said. "I trusted him." He fumbled with his key, trying to unlock the truck. "He said the fishing business got so bad he had to expand into other operations. Like it was some kind of normal thing."

Burgess shrugged. "Sometimes people hide aspects of

themselves, even from their friends. And sometimes, for the morally weak, it's a slippery slope. Compromise in one area and it gets easier to compromise in others as well."

Davis nodded, like he'd seen some of that himself. "Doesn't let him off the hook, though." He put a strong hand on Burgess's shoulder, squeezing to emphasize how serious he was. "You are going to get him, right?"

Then he remembered who Burgess was. How Burgess was a guy like him. Not someone who got pushed. He dropped his hand. "You think he's telling the truth about Lori?" His voice was raw with pain, laden with the burden of dozens of questions unasked. He leaned against the truck like he lacked the strength to go on. How does anyone process a wife dead and a child a friend has essentially sold into slavery?

"Maybe some version of the truth. Of *his* truth."

"I would have killed him, you know." He finally got the key into the lock. "I still may."

"You shouldn't tell me that." He touched Davis's shoulder. "Go see Kelly. That's all you should be thinking about right now. There's time to catch up on the rest later."

"Do you think she knows about her mother? About what happened?"

"She was around. She has to have known some of it. Your daughter has been through a lot. For now, you need to focus on the present. On reassurance and recovery. After all that's happened to her, she's going to be a long time recovering. She may not want to talk about it right away. Right now, she isn't speaking at all. Some kind of traumatic muteness. You'll just have to take it at her pace."

Burgess thought about Neddy and Nina. All the horror they'd been through. How ready he was to hurt anyone who threatened them. He thought about Dylan, losing his mother and gaining an unexpected father, who was so ready to protect his siblings from danger. "But kids are resilient. Love and stability make a big difference."

"You have kids, Detective?"

"Three."

Joe Burgess. Solitary man. The meanest cop in Portland. Fiercely protective father of three.

"I can suggest a good therapist," he said.

Kelly's dark eyes stared at him from her father's face. Davis put an understanding hand on his shoulder. Another man used to taking care of others. Used to being torn between duty and family. "I'll be back for the rest of the story."

"Tell her I said hello. Tell her I owe her another ice cream."

Davis got into his truck, backed around, and rattled away down the driveway.

Burgess called Chris.

"Hey," she said. "I've been worried. You disappear in the middle of the night, and then I don't hear from you."

"Talk to me," he said.

"About what?"

"Anything. Anything at all. I just want to hear your voice."

"I'm not sure you do. I saw the news, Joe. That was you, wasn't it? In that storage facility? Surrounded by Somali gunmen and Iron Angels."

"You know how I love to be in the middle of the action."

"You know how I don't like you there."

"Then I have some good news for you. Since I discharged my service weapon, I'm probably going to be driving a desk for a while."

"Let heaven and nature sing." He heard the smile in her voice. "Except it means you'll be a beast."

"Are the kids okay?" He realized he had no idea what time it was.

"Glued to the news. Dylan's telling them not to worry. That

you're okay."

"I'm okay. I'm better than okay."

"Why? Because you shot at someone?"

"Because I get to come home to you guys."

"When?"

"After I arrest some more bad guys. But Chris . . . ?" He wanted to give her some good news. "You know how you said you were sure there was someone out there who loved our mystery girl, and was looking for her? Well, we found him."

She was silent for a long time, and when she spoke, there were tears in her voice. "That's such good news, Joe."

He went inside to join the search.

It was going to be a long, hard slog, going through the papers and tying everything together. He thought it was particularly important that the Imam be tied in. That the man not get to sit like a malevolent spider at the center of the web he'd built and let everyone else go down but him. Meanwhile, the task for now was to collect papers, gather bills and records, look for anything that would prove that Lori and Kelly Davis had been in the house. Go through the trucks in the outbuildings. Locate Westerly's stash of drugs. Locate records of real estate Westerly or his many businesses owned that might lead them to Muhamud Ibrahim's place of business. That would lead to other warrants. Keep them busy for days to come.

They had a call in for some cadaver dogs to help them locate Lori Davis's body. If Westerly was telling the truth and he really had buried it behind his own house. If anything the man said could be believed. If such a devious and deliberate businessman—a man who'd likely built a drugs, firearms, and who knew what else distribution network using the Somalis and the Iron Angels—really was dumb enough to bury a body so close to home.

Next door, Stan Perry and Sage Prentiss were going through the same exercise. Cumberland PD had kindly offered someone to drive Westerly to jail. Burgess had sent him to 109, to Melia's kind ministrations, instead. As they moved, examined, and sorted, Burgess's phone kept ringing with updates.

Muhamud Ibrahim was in surgery. Osman conscious but unable to speak. Butcher Flaherty had been tortured before he died, and whoever had killed him had left fingerprints everywhere. And by the way, Dr. Lee had missed Burgess. Since Flaherty's keys had been found in the younger Muhamud Ibrahim's pocket, Ibrahim was their prime suspect. ATF and Homeland Security were circling the storage building and 109 like hungry sharks and had muscled out Portland PD to search Westerly's boat.

Urgency had come from the need to protect their mystery girl. Find the person responsible for a little baby's death. From needing to find the bad guys so their families would be safe. Now they were back to slow and steady wins the race. But in the back of his mind, Burgess heard Muhamud Ibrahim's hateful whisper. "My brother will kill you and all your family." Maybe Stan Perry was right and Ismail Ibrahim wasn't a part of this, but he wanted to haul him in, too, though he had no grounds to do so.

For now, he and Kyle, their evidence techs, and the officers working with them just kept moving through the house. Searching. Sorting. Documenting. Sending stuff back to 109.

Captain Cote had called him for updates. Each time, Burgess had only replied that they were still executing the warrant. Let Melia finish questioning Westerly before they gave that arrest to Cote. Next door, he knew Perry was saying the same thing.

★ ★ ★ ★ ★

Hours later, so tired his eyes were crossed and so hungry he was ready to embrace cannibalism, Burgess and the Crips called it a day. It was more like a day and a half, and they were far from done. But they'd reached their limit.

They headed back to Portland, where Chris and Michelle had promised them a good meal whenever they turned up. They brought Perry with them, and invited Sage Prentiss so he wouldn't feel left out. Prentiss had begged off, heading home to his wife and baby.

It was a dark, dark night with another cold spring wind, and it felt good to be inside where the lights were blazing and the room smelled of pot roast and pie instead of fear scent or death.

Burgess was beyond tired, but even after he had showered and Chris had strapped up his ribs, he lay in bed staring at the ceiling, waiting for his pain pills to kick in. He couldn't shake the feeling that they hadn't yet seen the final act. There were too many loose ends. They still didn't know what had happened to Osman. Or why. Nor had they located Rihanna Daud. The Imam, his followers, and one of his grandsons were still out there, possibly still a threat. The Imam had demonstrated an unwillingness to work with the establishment or to settle differences through dialogue or compromise, and Burgess had just put two of the grandsons out of commission.

There were also the Iron Angels, who had lost one of their own in a particularly nasty way, and lost a stash of guns. They were another group not known for their cooperation or patience with the legal system.

He'd been reading the pulse of this city for a long time. Even as he plodded along, dotting the i's and crossing the t's, a cop learned to trust his instincts. Right now, his instincts told him that the next few days could be explosive.

CHAPTER THIRTY-FOUR

PPL@9. The text came in at four in the morning, waiting for him when he finally dragged himself out of a drugged sleep.

That was cutting it close. It was already eight and he had to drive Dylan to school. His ribs, feeling like he'd been kicked by a very big horse, argued for a day of rest. He got his eyes fully open, struggled to his feet, and gulped the pills Chris had left beside the bed. He felt sour and at odds with the universe. But duty called, and he was a slave of duty.

There were nine messages in his voice mail. Ignoring them, he called Kyle. "Got someone wants to meet at the library at nine," he said.

"And I've got your back. How do you feel?"

"Like crap."

"Only consolation is Ibrahim feels worse."

"Small consolation."

"Check your messages yet?"

"I'm deep into avoidance."

"Stay that way. Cote wants us in his office at nine."

"No can do. Working on a case," Burgess said.

"Funny. So am I."

"The captain will not be pleased with us."

Burgess sighed. "My life's work, pleasing Paul Cote. Gotta get the kids off to school. See you at nine."

"I love hearing you say that," Kyle said.

"Say what?"

"Kids," Kyle said and disconnected.

That nagging feeling that something was about to go very wrong still dogged him, so much so that he did something he never thought he'd do—called the patrol commander and asked for someone to be sure Doro got Nina and Ned to school safely.

He got a brisk "Not a problem, Sarge," and after a quick bit of chatter about yesterday's standoff, it was done. He'd worry about the other end of the day if he got that far.

Dylan was waiting for him, leaning against the counter as usual, book bag over his shoulder, and foot tapping impatiently, but his expression was mellow instead of sullen. Looking at his son, he heard Chris's words: he's like you. A big brother, like Burgess had been, looking after his sibs. A bit of sunshine in the wallow of this case.

Dylan watched with concern as Burgess carefully levered himself into the truck, but didn't say anything. He just tuned the radio to his favorite station, not too loud, and sat, listening. Halfway there, he stirred in his seat, pulled up his backpack, and started rummaging. "Almost forgot," he said, "I've got something for you."

"Nasty note from Dr. Jorgensen?"

"Nothing like that. Actually, I think she likes you. Respects you, at least." He rummaged. "That was something, you know."

"I don't think I behaved very well."

Dylan grinned. "I think you behaved like a parent."

"Tough learning curve," Burgess said.

His son fished out a folded sheet of paper. "This is from my friend Leyla. Something she thought you might want to know."

"Know what it says?"

Dylan shook his head, handing him the note as they pulled up in front of the school. Burgess debated, then said, "Keep an eye out, today after school, and when you get home. Things are still feeling kind of unsettled."

"I'll be careful, Dad. We don't want Chris to be worried."

Burgess rolled his eyes. "Go learn something useful, so you don't grow up to be a flatfoot like your old man."

Dylan grinned. "I hope I do," he said. Then, in a flash, he'd gone up the steps and disappeared into the building.

Burgess unfolded the note. It said only *Rihanna Daud* and an address.

His phone rang. Captain Cote. He let it go to voice mail. The possibility that his boss had anything useful to contribute to this investigation was slight. It was far more likely that Cote wanted to turn the whole thing over to the Feds, who would jerk it around for a decade and, in their never-ending quest to catch the biggest fish, let everyone really involved in torture, murder, gun and drug trafficking, and sexual slavery off the hook in return for some promised cooperation that would never amount to squat.

Or Cote wanted to remind them that the city fathers and mothers required sensitivity in dealing with their new neighbors. Burgess couldn't find it in himself to be sensitive to the feelings of criminals who'd behaved as these people had, and if he was going to treat people evenhandedly, he'd need to be as deeply considerate of the rights and feelings of Iron Angels. As Melia often remarked, he'd sent them to sensitivity training and it just didn't take. Melia was right. Burgess could know that bad guys and their extended families, gangs, clubs, clans, or groups had feelings, too, and just not give a damn.

Wrestling a vest on was so painful it made his already sour mood black, but he was supposed to set an example of good sense and proper procedure. He couldn't very well take rookies to task if he didn't follow his own advice. But by the time he reached the library lobby, he was ready to spit nails.

Things didn't improve when he got a text: *2nd flr. Pkg. gar.*

Blk Honda. He'd had enough of black Hondas. He forwarded the text to Kyle, got a *Roger that, Stan is with me,* and lumbered off down the street. He had no idea what the Crips were getting into. After yesterday's cluster fuck with Iron Angels and the Imam's people, anything was possible.

He ought to call Melia and give him a heads-up but the probability that Melia was with Cote was too great. Lumbering down the sunlit street, he felt like a geriatric Gary Cooper going to meet modern-day bad guys who didn't play by the rules. Given that he kept having flashbacks to yesterday's slow-motion bullets, it was not a pleasant feeling.

Commuters were still pulling in, a mixed blessing that gave him the security of witnesses, but also the necessity to protect those witnesses if bad things went down. Moving into the building with the sense that dozens of eyes were watching, he took the stairs and eased his way out on the second floor into the damp concrete gloom of the garage, edging into a dark corner. He could see the up ramp, but not around the corner.

This was stupid. If he went looking for a black car, he'd be a sitting duck.

He texted *By the elevator,* and waited. Another text arrived, this time an address. The address looked familiar. He pulled out the crumpled note he'd gotten from Dylan, and it was the same.

He texted *Why should I meet you?*

And got back: *Ismail Ibrahim.*

How could this not be a setup?

Kyle's car pulled up beside them and the window slid down. "Everything okay?" Kyle asked.

He looked at Kyle and Perry. "Meeting place has been changed again. To an address we've got for the elusive Rihanna Daud. It's about Ismail Ibrahim."

"We've come this far," Kyle said. "Might as well see it through."

Burgess gave the address and Kyle said, "I'm really feeling like the Three Musketeers this morning."

"Could be worse. I was feeling like Gary Cooper. What about you, Stan?"

"Feeling like that slacker dude in *Knocked Up*," Perry grunted. "Trying to decide how it would feel to join you old farts as a family man."

"In that case," Kyle said, "we'll try not to get you shot."

"Not funny," Perry said.

They headed for Rihanna Daud's. The address was out toward East Deering, near Dylan's school. Near where Osman's empty apartment was. Not far from where he'd been found in Rihanna Daud's trunk.

Burgess was uneasy. In their world, "When you've gotta go, you've gotta go" often meant bad guys waiting when you got there.

They couldn't do a drive-by. It was the last house on a dead-end street. A small, plain white house. One story. In need of paint and repairs. Shades drawn. No garage. No cars in the driveway. There were no people on the street. No cars parked nearby. No signs of life. Anywhere.

"I don't like the look of this, Joe," Kyle said.

Burgess didn't either. His sense that this was a very bad thing in a series of bad things was seriously amped up. He texted: *Come outside where we can see you* and got no reply. Walking up to the door and knocking felt like an invitation to get shot.

The street ended in a grove of trees. Beyond them, more woods, then a tall fence, and the top of something that looked industrial. "Let's drive around," Burgess said. "Get a feeling for the neighborhood. See if there's another way to approach the house."

Kyle nodded.

"My Spidey senses are saying something is very wrong with

this picture," Perry said, breaking his long silence.

"That makes three of us," Kyle agreed.

"Dylan got this address from a girl he knows at school," Burgess said. "And it's where the texter said to meet."

"We should talk to her, the girl from Dylan's school," Kyle said as Burgess reversed into a driveway and headed back the way they'd come. They cruised the streets as they conferred.

"Not easily. She's Muslim. And very shy," Burgess said.

"Better than going in blind."

Burgess agreed. When three experienced cops all shared the same gut feeling that something was wrong, they had to listen. He called Dr. Jorgenson, made his way through some guarded pleasantries, explained their problem, and asked if she could get Leyla to the phone.

"I can have her in my office within fifteen minutes, Sergeant Burgess," she said.

"I would be forever grateful, Dr. Jorgenson."

"I'll do my best," she said. "But Leyla is a worrier. What do I say this is about?"

"Assure her that she's not in trouble, just that the police need her help."

The minutes crawled by. They'd cruised the neighborhood, found a possible approach from the rear, and then parked. Kyle and Perry were out knocking on doors along Rihanna Daud's street before Burgess's phone finally rang. Dr. Jorgensen said, "Here's Leyla."

Burgess heard some soft words of reassurance, and then a tiny, timid voice said, "This is Leyla."

"Detective Burgess," he said, "Dylan's father. We went out to that address you gave and no one seems to be there. I'm going to need some more information from you. Can you do that for me?"

"I can try. But Rihanna was there this morning. I saw her

when I was on my way to school. She said she wasn't going to work today. She had to stay home and take care of—" She broke off suddenly. "Oh. No. I'm not supposed to say that."

"It's okay to tell us, Leyla," Burgess said. "We're the police. We're trying to keep more people from getting hurt, like your friend Rihanna. But we will need your help." He kept talking, not giving her time to think or let fear or loyalty or secrets keep her from speaking. This would have been so much easier face-to-face. "Who was she taking care of?"

And then he knew. Even before she answered, "Ismail," he knew. Why Osman had been so nervous going in with them to interview the Imam. Why he was beaten. How Rihanna Daud figured in all of this. "How is Rihanna related to Hussain Osman?"

"She is his sister."

"And what is Rihanna's relationship to Ismail Ibrahim?"

There was a silence so tangible he could sense her fear about answering. At last she said, "They wish to marry, but the Imam has forbidden it, because she is Bantu, and he has chosen another wife for Ismail."

"Thank you," he said. "Now I understand things better. So Rihanna was home this morning. And she was staying home to take care of Ismail. Do you know why he needed to be cared for?"

"Only that he was beaten. That he defied his grandfather, and he was beaten. She was very sad, and worried that he should go to the hospital, but he refused."

"Leyla, do you know if the Imam or his followers know where Rihanna lives?"

"I do not. Her brother kept another address, and that was the one they gave to people, and for bills and mail and the car."

The empty apartment explained. People were forced to live such complicated lives. It was hard to imagine, here in Portland in the twenty-first century, that tribes and clans would create such barriers between people from the same country. But was it? He thought about his grandparents. How upset they would have been if his mother had married out of the Catholic faith. Things changed so slowly.

"Have you ever been in Rihanna's house, Leyla? Can you tell me how it is laid out inside?"

She had, and she did. In a slow, painstaking way, with a lot of questions, he pulled out information about the layout of the house. Affirmed that there was a back door. And a basement. That was about all he was going to get from her.

He thanked her, and was about to hang up, when she said, "I thought you were going to ask about the motorcycles."

This was really bad news. "Tell me about the motorcycles."

"There were four of them," she said. "Turning into the street this morning as I was leaving."

"Around eight?"

"Yes."

"Four men?"

"Yes."

Her responses were getting smaller and smaller. Burgess thought he was infecting her with his own anxiety, but he had to keep going. "Could you identify any of them if we showed you pictures?"

"Maybe. I'm not sure. They were scary, Sergeant. I tried not to look."

"Did you notice anything distinctive about any of the motorcycles?"

"One of them had a picture on it," she said. "A raised fist with wings like an angel."

Iron Angels. That bastard Westerly had set this in motion. Using people for his own ends without any thought for what he might stir up. The Iron Angels were a clan just like Imam Ibrahim's, with the same need to stake out territory, get the biggest share for themselves, and protect and avenge their own. And with the same indifference to human suffering and human life.

Ismail Ibrahim was the only one of the Imam's grandsons who wasn't in custody. The only one they could still get at. And by now, word would have gotten about, in the way that bad news traveled even when it hadn't been made public, that Butcher Flaherty had been tortured before he was killed by someone who wanted to get into that locker and get those guns. He hated to think what they were going to find in that house.

"I hope Rihanna is okay," Leyla said. Burgess read voices, and in hers, tears were close.

"I do, too," he said, "and thank you for your help. Too often, people don't want to cooperate with the police. I think they have the idea that we are bad, and dishonest, and help other powerful people do bad acts. We're not like that."

"I know that," she said. "I know because Dylan wants to protect people, and he is your son."

Straight to the heart. How long had he been Dylan's father? Four or five months? But maybe that was okay, too.

"Will you let me know? Let me know she is okay?"

"I'll let you know what happens."

Kyle and Perry finished canvassing the street and joined him at the car. "Iron Angels," Burgess said.

"Yeah. Four of them," Perry said. "Parked in the street, went into that house, stayed maybe an hour, then drove away. The lady across the street who seems to spend a lot of time watching that house says they went in and out a few times with some equipment. She says she never saw Rihanna while they were there, and hasn't seen her since. She says her sister, who lives next door, may have more information. I guess the two of them have some kind of competition going. The sister is out right now."

"I wonder what kind of equipment?" Kyle said. "You learn anything, Joe?"

"Definitely Iron Angels. Leyla saw the logo on one of their motorcycles. She says there were four of them. She also says that Rihanna stayed home from work today to take care of Ismail Ibrahim."

"Why does he need taking care of?" Perry said. "Grampa give him a beating for not being more like his brothers?"

"Exactly. That and the fact that he wants to marry this Rihanna Daud, and the Imam doesn't approve because she's Bantu. Leyla says the Imam has another wife in mind."

"What does the Imam want from him? To be in jail like the others?"

"Maybe, if we find him and he's still alive, we can ask," Burgess said, "but I am not getting a good feeling about this."

"Can you get a worse feeling?" Perry asked. "I was already not feeling good."

Shoulder to shoulder, they stood, leaning against the car, staring down the street at the small white house. Burgess couldn't stop the pictures of other crime scenes. They kept piling in, one nightmarish scenario after another.

"This would be a good moment for X-ray vision," Kyle said.

"Or for SRT," Perry suggested. "Or to remember that we're supposed to be meeting with Captain Cote."

Burgess looked at Kyle, and, like the old married couple that they were, Kyle said, "Yeah. We gotta go look in the windows. Shall we draw straws?"

"I'll go," Burgess said.

"We'll all go," Perry said.

The neighborhood was still as death as they walked down the sunny street toward the house. Burgess was seeing red. The many shades of red of remembered scenes. Rusty red, black red, pinkish red, true red. Flat, splattered, oozing, pooled, glistening. He shook his head to clear it, but the images were stuck.

Into the valley of the shadow of death. This was no valley, but they all felt the shadow.

CHAPTER THIRTY-FIVE

Burgess wanted that house to be empty more than he'd ever wanted anything in his life. Empty. Silent. No bodies. No blood. No signs of violence. He wanted to call this a dead end and go back to 109. He'd even take Cote's duck's-ass pout and raving stupidity over another gruesome crime scene. He was badly in need of attitude readjustment or a long, quiet vacation. Next week, the kids were out of school. Maybe they'd go somewhere like Boston, ride the swan boats, see Paul Revere's house.

But what Perry liked to call his Spidey sense was on red alert. They'd been led here for a reason. He didn't know what that reason was yet, but it felt like danger to them as well as to the woman they were looking for. The Iron Angels never liked the police, and his team had kept them from getting their guns back. He was certain now that the messages luring them here had not come from Rihanna Daud.

As they approached the house, they could see footprints in the tender new grass. He said, "Watch out for trip wires or sensors. Watch your feet. Walk where they've walked. Look, but don't lean. And don't touch anything."

They all knew the Iron Angels liked to blow things up and didn't much care who got in the way but he couldn't help reminding them. Why Stan Perry kept calling him "Dad."

★ ★ ★ ★ ★

There was blood. Plenty of blood, but Ismail Ibrahim, lying in the middle of it, wasn't dead. Not yet. He was moaning and begging for relief, the way people in awful pain did. Seven feet away, on the other side of the wrecked kitchen, a woman was tied to a chair, positioned so she had to watch Ibrahim's agony, and wired with explosives so that she didn't dare move. An innocent victim of a struggle between two sets of remorseless men manipulated into competition and unnecessary violence by their puppet-master, Addison Westerly.

When she saw him looking in the window, her eyes widened. There were the streaks of tears on her face. She startled, then forced herself to be still. In a loud voice, Burgess called, "We're going to get you out of there. You and Ismail. Is the door wired? Don't move, just blink if the answer is yes."

She blinked.

Today was not going to be a day when they got good news.

"We're going to get you some help," he called. She blinked again.

"I'd like to send that fucker Westerly in to defuse that thing," Kyle muttered. "We should have let the bastard choke himself when we had the chance."

"We just bring 'em in, Ter, remember. We don't get to play God."

"I was always so certain," Kyle said. "My certainty is eroding, Joe, seeing stuff like this."

"Two Hail Marys and a nice family vacation," Burgess said.

Perry had pulled out his phone.

"Don't!" Burgess said. "Take it out to the street, Stan. You never know what might set these things off."

As Perry moved off, eyes on his phone, Burgess called, "And watch your feet."

So easy to forget. To get careless in the moment. Perry shuddered and walked carefully to the street.

Burgess stayed at the window, where Rihanna could see him, the small bit of reassurance he could give her, as Kyle circled the house. "It's a bitch, Joe," Kyle said, when he'd finished his tour. "Lotta wires. We hadn't been careful, a couple eager beavers back at 109 would be getting themselves promoted to detective."

"Then let's stay careful."

"Roger that," Kyle said. "Stan calling the bomb squad?"

"And Melia."

"I'm imagining a scenario," Kyle said, "where Melia tells the captain about this, and Cote, always wanting to grab the moment, rushes out here and tries to do a press conference in front of the house, and—"

"Don't go there," Burgess said. "We'd have to pick up the pieces. Literally. Tell Stan to get patrol to seal off this street. Don't want some dumbass blood maggot getting himself blown up either."

He needed his mind in the here and now, but was seeing a friend from long ago, shredded by a landmine, tattered, dripping pieces of him hanging in the trees. He closed his eyes and wrestled the pictures back into his lockbox. He couldn't go there now. The sun was bright and hot, a perfect spring day, and he was very cold.

"There's no way to do this quietly. We've got to evacuate the street," he said. "And the houses behind this one. You get Press Devlin on the phone, see if he can get us any inside information. Types of bombs they use, anything that will help us get those people in there out alive."

Another half hour, and this street was going to be jammed with personnel and equipment. Standing here in the treeless yard, he would be cooked. It would be nice to go back to the car, shed his jacket, get someone to bring some bottled water.

Hollering through the window was a pretty ineffective method of communication, but Rihanna Daud's gaze clung to him. Like it or not he was here for the duration.

Whoever had devised this had a very clear understanding of torture. Torturing the intended victims, like Ismail Ibrahim, whose strong young body, slashed in more than a dozen places, wasn't giving up despite blood loss and pain. Torturing the innocent victims, like Rihanna Daud, whose only crime was loving the wrong man. Torturing the police officers who had to deal with this situation with what they were forced to see and hear, as well as with the very real danger of the situation. The press might call writing on the mosque a hate crime. Burgess thought this was the real hate crime.

So he stood outside the window where Rihanna Daud could see him. Stood when Melia tried to order him to a safer place. Stood while a pissed off bomb tech suited him up. He stood while that same sweating tech, Tom Burns, and another, dressed like a pair of Michelin men, moving with the speed of snails and the care of a mother touching a newborn, painstakingly defused the bombs around the perimeter and got themselves into the house through a window.

When they let him go inside, to continue to comfort Rihanna and survey the crime scene in case it later got blown up, he stood, he and the girl gritting their teeth, as a screaming Ismail was carried out. They let him stay because his presence kept her calm, which made their jobs easer. And once he was inside, he and the terrified young woman began to talk.

Little things, at first. Then she said, "It may be that this is my last day, Detective, so may I tell you my story?"

He stood and listened while she told of how their parents had been killed. How her brother, Hussain, had been a college student and one of his teachers, an American who had gone to Somalia to teach, had helped the two of them out of the country.

She told of how they'd lived in a camp while her brother's American friend tried to get them refugee status so they could come to America. How she'd been raped and nearly killed when she'd ventured outside the camp, and other women she was with had driven off her attackers and dragged her to safety.

Her voice was soft and surprisingly calm as she told her story, as though the two of them were people talking in a normal way, and not one of them a weary, jaded cop on shaky legs, the other wired to explode and surrounded by cautious technicians trying to disarm the bomb.

She had met Ismail one day when her car broke down and he stopped to help. That chance meeting had led to more meetings, until the Imam had learned about them, and forbidden them to see each other. She smiled as she told him that it had worked exactly as it always did when headstrong young lovers were forbidden to meet. The Imam's edict had strengthened the bond between them.

"I hope that Ismail will be okay," she said. "I feel like this is all my fault."

God. It was so far from being her fault.

Inside the bomb suit, it must have been a hundred degrees. His side ached. His head ached. He was hungry and his legs were shaking from the effort of standing so long. He reminded himself that his suffering was nothing compared with hers. Or the techs who labored in these suits with death only a single misstep away.

They had been in this room for a hundred years.

"Tell me about you," she said. "Are you married? Do you have children?"

"Three children," he said. He told her about Nina and Neddy and Dylan, and how he came, so late in his life, to have this sudden family.

"I would like to have a family," she said.

322

He had thought the techs weren't listening, but when she said it, Tom Burns's hands froze. Then Burns took a breath and returned to his task.

She was a tiny woman with great poise and dignity, and despite the circumstances, she smiled, and he thought she was beautiful. He had long ago fallen away from the church, but now it seemed to him that if there were ever a time for prayer, this was it.

Somehow, she knew it. "Are you talking to your God?" she said.

He nodded.

"Then I will also talk to mine."

"You have to go now," Tom Burns told him. "For this last bit, we're clearing everyone out except me."

"I promised her I'd stay."

Burns didn't back down. "And you have stayed as long as you could. Before you risk unnecessary heroics, Sergeant, tell me what I'm supposed to say to your wife and your three kids, who are waiting down there at the end of the road for news that you're okay? And your sisters? I'm supposed to tell them you wouldn't leave even though there was nothing you could do in here? Not even when you know it's a direct order from your lieutenant, because you're just too damned stubborn to listen? Is that supposed to comfort them when we have to scoop up pieces of you to give them something to bury?"

Burns's words came from behind his Darth Vader helmet, making him sound ominous and otherworldly. "You've done what you needed to do. You've kept her calm so we could work, and you've comforted her. Now you need to get out of here and let me work."

Burgess looked at Rihanna Daud, small as a child in her

chair. "Please go," she said. "Please. God willing, I'll see you soon."

"God willing," he said.

Burns had to put a hand under his arm to get him started. His legs were frozen in place. After a few awkward steps, he managed to get himself to the door, and through it. Partway across the scabby lawn, Kyle and Perry appeared out of nowhere, seized his arms, and practically dragged him down the street. When they were safely behind the barrier, they helped him out of the protective gear. He had sweated so profusely his clothes were black. It looked like he'd been swimming.

Kyle handed him a bottle of water and they made him sit in an empty patrol car. The engine was running and it was deliciously cool.

"Chris and the kids are down the street," Kyle said. "And Michelle. And my kids. Soon as you can, we'd better get our asses down there and show them we're still alive."

"Am I still alive?"

He felt spacy and disconnected. Rihanna's story, running in his brain, seemed more real than here and now. Pulling himself together was like gathering straw in a wind. "Let's give it a couple minutes, okay. Until Burns does—or doesn't do—what he's trying to do in there."

He could not go down there and tell Chris and the kids that everything was fine while Tom Burns and Rihanna might be blown to bits. It needed to be over, one way or another.

Melia leaned into the car and studied him. "You look like hell, Joe. I'd send you to the hospital to get checked out, but I know you wouldn't go."

"Just praying for a good result here, Vince."

"As are we all."

★ ★ ★ ★ ★

Time seemed to stand still. There were no voices in the street, not even whispers, only the sounds of running engines, the unattended chatter on police radios. Everyone stood behind the barriers, all eyes on a shabby white house where a single man now worked, risking his life to save another.

It would be slow. Painstaking. Exquisitely careful. The ultimate struggle between life and death. Burgess was holding his breath, and no one around him was breathing, either. It was as though their collective will was directed toward that kitchen, toward the man who toiled, and the woman who waited, her face and her story seared into Burgess's mind.

There was a commotion, the watchers stirred, and then Burns came running around the corner of the house, half dragging Rihanna with him. They had just reached the street when the house exploded.

Burns pushed her to the ground, covering her body with his, as pieces of the house showered down on them.

CHAPTER THIRTY-SIX

When the ambulances carrying Rihanna Daud and Tom Burns had driven away—both in need of patching, both going to survive—he and Kyle headed for their families, Stan Perry trailing along behind them like a little brother. Probably his girl, Lily, was waiting there, too.

They were leaning against the car, Chris in the middle, flanked by Dylan and Nina, Neddy in front of her, her arms clasped around him. It was the most beautiful thing he'd ever seen. As he gathered them all into a hug, he recalled Tom Burns's words. "Your wife and kids are waiting down at the end of the street."

"I'm sorry that I scared you," he said. "I'm sorry you had to go through this." He buried his face in Chris's apple-scented hair, felt Nina's bird-thin shoulder under one arm and Dylan's strong one under the other. In the middle, Neddy squirmed and complained he was being smothered.

He never wanted to let them go.

To his right, Kyle's long arms were wrapped around Michelle and the girls. To his left, Stan Perry was kissing his dark-haired girlfriend with the passion born of coming so close to death. The other bomb tech and the SRT commander were huddled with Tom Burns's family, assuring them that he would be okay. A firm blue line was keeping the press at a distance.

Chris had tears in her eyes as she asked, "You coming home or going back to 109?"

He had no idea what time it was. There was so much paperwork waiting. And Joe Burgess, tight-assed stickler for following the rules about writing it down, really didn't care. He took a deep breath, and the air coming in surprised him. He wasn't sure he'd been breathing over the last few hours. He'd woken from a long bloody nightmare and found himself still in the midst of a lovely April day, in the midst of a family.

He was going home.

"Just got to pick up my car," he said, "and I'll be home."

It took a while to extricate himself. His kids didn't say much, they just weren't letting go. Finally Chris got them pried loose and back in the car. Michelle did the same. The Three Musketeers got in Kyle's car, Perry in front and Burgess sprawled across the back seat, and headed back downtown to get their own cars.

"Puts things in perspective," Kyle said. "All that we put them through. I'm thinking it's time to make Michelle a honest woman."

"She's always been an honest woman," Perry said. "You just haven't been an honest man."

"As honest as I could be."

"It does change things," Perry said. "I've been feeling like this thing with Lily was nothing but a big pain in the ass. Now I'm thinking—"

"Oho!" Kyle punched him in the shoulder. "Portland's biggest swinging dick bites the dust."

"It's just—"

"We understand," Kyle said.

Burgess rested, eyes closed, listening. Crips. Three Musketeers. Whatever they were called, they were a team. Often disgruntled. Sometimes dysfunctional. But together, they caught bad guys.

Tomorrow, the next day, the rest of this week or longer, they would be up to their ears in paperwork. Over at the hospital taking statements. Rounding up the rest of the bad guys. They would get the Imam. They would find out who tortured Ismail and rigged those bombs. Right now, what they needed was to be with the people they loved. All those years of going home to his empty apartment, where his friend Jack Daniel's would be waiting for him, family was what he'd tried to avoid. Family was what he'd gotten anyway. A gift he probably didn't deserve.

He stopped at a market on the way home and bought huge bunches of flowers. The smiling checker said, "Boy, you must have really done something wrong."

"Actually, I think I did something really right."

He gave Chris the flowers, then went to change and shower. He rummaged around in the back of his bottom drawer and found the little blue box. His mother's ring. It was just a small stone, but it had graced the finger of the most wonderful woman he'd ever known.

Chris and the kids were in the kitchen, waiting. The table was set and there were three large vases of flowers around. His mother's vases. It seemed so appropriate. He smelled chicken.

His knees were bad and he was so tired he wasn't sure he could get up again if he got down, so he skipped that part of it. He just took Chris's hand. "Today, in the midst of that situation, Tom Burns, the bomb tech said to me, 'Your wife and kids are down at the end of the road, waiting to see if you're going to be all right.' Those two words—'your wife'—they rocked me. The next time someone says that, I want it to be true. So, Chris Perlin, will you be my wife?"

People probably didn't often propose in front of their kids, and for good reason. He barely heard her reply over their clapping and cheers. She said yes.

ABOUT THE AUTHOR

Kate Flora's fascination with people's criminal tendencies began in the Maine Attorney General's office. Deadbeat dads, people who hurt their kids, and employers' acts of discrimination aroused her curiosity about human behavior. Her books include seven "strong woman" Thea Kozak mysteries and three gritty police procedurals in her star-reviewed Joe Burgess series. Her true crime, *Finding Amy,* has been optioned for a movie.

When she's not writing, or teaching at Grub Street in Boston, she's in her garden, waging a constant battle against critters, pests, and her husband's lawnmower. She's been married thirty-five years to a man who still makes her laugh. She has two wonderful sons—one a movie editor and one a scientist—two lovely daughters-in-law, and four rescue "grand-dogs," Frances, Otis, Harvey, and Daisy.